NEW YORK REVIEW BOOKS
CLASSICS

THE CHILD

JULES VALLÈS (1832–1885), French writer and revolutionary, is most famous for his trilogy of autobiographical novels: *L'Enfant* (*The Child*), *Le Bachelier* (*The Graduate*), and *L'Insurgé* (*The Insurgent*). Through Vallès's alter ego, Jacques Vingtras, the books describe the writer's difficult childhood as the abused son of a schoolteacher, his rejection of his classical education and growing admiration for the peasant class, and finally his bohemian life in Paris as a militant journalist and pamphleteer. Vallès grew up in the provinces and came to Paris to study as a young man. Forced by his family to return home, he soon rebelled against his socially ambitious father and returned to the capital. There Vallès associated with other young radicals and published articles in various left-wing newspapers under a series of pseudonyms, which nevertheless failed to protect him from government persecution. Vallès led protests against the repressive policies of Napoleon III and played a significant role in the Paris Commune of 1871; his newspaper, *Le Cri du Peuple* (*The Cry of the People*), became the mouthpiece of the revolt. After the defeat of the Commune, Vallès was exiled for nine years, which he spent mostly in London, writing articles and composing his autobiographical trilogy. Upon his return to Paris, he resurrected *Le Cri* and spent the last five years of his life working furiously on articles, pamphlets, and the last book of his trilogy.

DOUGLAS PARMÉE has translated works by Flaubert, Fontane, Zola, Maupassant, Baudelaire, and Chamfort, among others, and is a past winner of the Society of Authors Scott-Moncrieff Prize for French translation. A lifetime fellow of Queens College, Cambridge, he now lives in Australia.

THE CHILD

JULES VALLÈS

Translated and with an introduction and notes by
DOUGLAS PARMÉE

NEW YORK REVIEW BOOKS

New York

THIS IS A NEW YORK REVIEW BOOK
PUBLISHED BY THE NEW YORK REVIEW OF BOOKS
IN ASSOCIATION WITH MONASH ROMANCE STUDIES

Library of Congress Cataloging-in-Publication Data
Vallès, Jules, 1832–1885.
 [Enfant. English]
 The child / Jules Vallès ; translated by Douglas Parmée.
     p. cm. — (New York Review Books classics)
 ISBN 1-59017-117-9 (trade paper : alk. paper)
 I. Parmée, Douglas. II. Title. III. Series.
 PQ2458.V7E513 2004
 843'.8—dc22
                                    2004017969

ISBN 1-59017-117-9

Book design by Lizzie Scott
Printed in the United States of America on acid-free paper.
10 9 8 7 6 5 4 3 2 1

Distributed to the trade by Publishers Group West

New York Review Books
1755 Broadway, New York, NY 10019
www.nyrb.com

CONTENTS

INTRODUCTION

LOUIS-JULES Vallès was born in 1832, two years after the last Bourbon king of France had been removed by revolution and replaced by the so-called bourgeois king, Louis-Philippe, who to prove this credential carried an umbrella and under whose regime those who complained of their lot were advised: Get rich.

Jules's parents took this approach to heart, determined to rise into the middle classes and to do their utmost—damnedest is the more accurate word—to ensure that their son stayed there too. Jules's father, Jean-Louis, rejected a traditional path of bettering himself by going into the church—another common way, the army, was arduous and not free from danger. In any case, a peasant-bred youngster would in those days have been unpromising officer material. Jean-Louis's distaste for military glory even led him to avoid compulsory military service by the well-established custom of bribing someone to take his place, a practice his son was also to follow, though this didn't prevent him later from condemning it in a newspaper article, under the title "Cochons vendus" ("Pigs for Sale").

Jean-Louis became a teacher, at first not with great success. He was a primary teacher in a deaf-and-dumb school when he married a woman three years older and of even humbler peasant origin than himself. But he had a dogged determination to rise in his profession and *The Child* relates the various stages of his often grim odyssey: from agricultural Le Puy, with its mountains, extinct volcanoes, and rushing torrents so fondly idealized later by his son, he transferred, when Jules was eight, to the far larger important mining and industrial town of Saint-Étienne and five years later to the even larger and more important Breton port of Nantes. Thus, unintentionally, he provided his son with three contrasting views of provincial life as backgrounds for *The Child*. In Nantes, Jean-Louis's fierce ambition was finally crowned with success: he passed the *agrégation*, the final qualification to become a fully fledged teacher in a state secondary school, a *professeur de lycée*.

A splendid academic achievement of which he was justifiably proud, but a poor consolation for a miserable marriage. Seven pregnancies between 1829 and 1835 left only two survivors into adulthood: Jules and his sister, Marie-Louise, who remains unmentioned in *The Child*, perhaps because, after showing early signs of mental imbalance, she died in a lunatic asylum when she was twenty-four. In 1853, after a scandal involving an affair—the Brignolin episode in *The Child* was an early similar marital transgression—Jean-Louis was transferred to Rouen. He died, estranged from wife and son, at the age of forty-nine.

It was in such a divided, embittered household that Jules grew up, his parents united only in striving by every means—except gentleness?—to turn him into an upwardly mobile bourgeois. Thrashed from a tender age by his mother, bullied and beaten by a father curiously blinkered to his son's stubbornness which more than matched his own, Jules nevertheless seemed a relatively docile instrument, quite a model student, carrying off prizes like his father, specifically in arts subjects where the chief requirement was an ability to memorize. Jules eventually rebelled against this regimen, as we learn in *The Child*, and he was never much good at science or math, although we witness a very amusing geometry lesson in the novel. We are left in no doubt, however, that from early on he was seething inwardly, his spirit unbroken, invincibly determined as soon as possible to liberate himself from the shackles of his family. He despised their literary and political sacred cows, starting naturally with his school-bred hatred of classical epics, Homer or Virgil, and moving at various times in later life to a rejection of other icons, even of such a staunch Republican as Hugo. Nor was he foxed by George Sand's sentimental peasantry, whom he knew from experience to be false. Rousseau, too, was a fraud, a self-righteous hypocrite who led straight to the bloodthirsty authoritarian, high-principled Robespierre. In a word, Jules's parents' treatment had turned him—or warped him—into an uncompromising individualistic rebel, anti-family, anti-academia, anti-establishment, and, above all, anti-bourgeois. He'd been unfairly dominated and abused, and he now demanded freedom and justice for all: a freedom march—but one dictated solely by himself.

In Nantes Jules greeted the fall of the bourgeois monarchy in February 1848 enthusiastically, but a few months later, during his stint at the Lycée Bonaparte, he watched with horror the ragged lines of workers taken prisoner after their uprising, savagely repressed by the bourgeois Second Republic which had failed to improve their lot and, specifically, find them jobs. But for even the most moderate Republicans worse was to come: on December 2, 1851, the legally elected president of this Republic suspended the constitution and after a plebiscite—a handy device of power seekers—the voters overwhelmingly supported him to become the Emperor Napoleon III. One of the first acts of his authoritarian regime was to limit the freedom of the press. It was in this political climate that Jules grew into adulthood.

These events take us beyond the time span of *The Child*, and some which fall within it are not recorded. They would have clashed with the unity of the work and were instead to form the basis for the subsequent volumes of the autobiographical Jacques Vingtras trilogy, *Le Bachelier* (*The Graduate*) and *L'Insurgé* (*The Insurgent*). These strongly politicized books give us a clearer picture of how Vallès came to be the frustrated author of *The Child*—frustration often begets the best books.

The child proved father to the man: obsessively rebellious, for the rest of his life Jules was only able to feel true sympathy for those whom he saw as fellow victims or who actively or passively opposed the society he himself rejected: the poor, the disadvantaged, and the rebellious. It was a stance bound to lead to trouble, for as we see in *The Child*, Jules was not only bloody-minded but also impetuous, clumsy, self-absorbed, and naive; he seems in many ways to have found it difficult to grow up. A quarrelsome boy is easier to bear than a quarrelsome man and most people will find it odd, for example, that Vallès, as a man of twenty-four, fought a duel with one of his closest friends. He only broke his opponent's arm but could easily have killed him—or been killed. An act of bravado? A relic of childish masochism? An urge to prove his mettle, to himself and to society? Perhaps all of these and even a death wish? If so, it would not have been the first time he'd been suspected of contemplating suicide: in one of the deepest humiliations of a life liberally strewn with major and minor disasters, in 1852, on returning to Nantes from Paris where he'd been involved in demonstrations against Louis Bonaparte's plebiscite, he was on his father's initiative diagnosed as showing suicidal tendencies and shut up in an asylum for three months. A grave injustice? Maybe only a salutary warning or even an incentive, for a couple of months later, after repeated failures, he finally passed his baccalaureate (so predominantly important in the later part of *The Child*), the graduation examination which allowed him to go to university—and escape from parental tutelage. It is ironic that to achieve this relatively modest result, the fiercely independent Jules solicited the support of a friend's father who was a teacher in the school where the examination was held.

Subsidized by his father, Jules signed on at the Sorbonne to study law, which quickly turned out to be largely a pretext to get away from home. He attended few lectures, did little academic work, and regularly failed his examinations. He had embarked on the bohemianism that was to characterize the rest of his life.

He spent his days first in avid reading in public libraries and private reading rooms, whose fees he was often remiss in paying. He was fond of fiction; his favorite author was the prolific Eugène Sue, whose sensational novels of low life in Paris were written with the exuberance that was to character ize Vallès's own writing. Sue's novels also included attractive if vague ideas of social reform, always close to Vallès's heart. For more solid fare, Jules was especially drawn to Pierre-Joseph Proudhon. Proudhon became one of his idols, as did the revolutionary historian Jules Michelet, whose chief theme, the hero worship of the People, *le peuple*, was also to be one of Vallès's permanent leitmotifs.

Proudhon was a deeply original revolutionary social, eco nomic, and political thinker. His first work, published in 1840, had asked, "What is property?" and replied, "Property is theft." He was violently anti-religious—another key state-ment of his was, "God is evil"—and attacked all existing institutions. Vallès was particularly influenced by his *Con-fessions*, which dealt with the 1848 Revolution, a permanent obsession of all Vallès's social and political writing. There is a clear element of autodidacticism in Vallès which, though it may lead to woolly thinking, is never a bar to lively talk or vigorous writing.

Apart from libraries, Vallès's main havens were cafés where in the company of like-minded Republican bohemians he could discuss literature and art—police spies made politi-cal discussions more discreet. But it was here, with other future friends, that he first met the realist painter Gustave Courbet, whose violently fanatical political views strongly influenced him: and if Courbet was loudmouthed, Vallès was even louder. (Edmond de Goncourt later said that Vallès never understood dialogue, only monologue.) With his bushy black beard and dark glinting eyes, Vallès became a demonic and dramatic figure, a keen theatergoer, particularly fond of melodrama and plays involving crime, though his own theatrical projects never came to anything. His interest in music was confined to opera or operetta; he enjoyed Offenbach's skits on the divinities of Olympus—and by implication on Napoleon III and his regime.

But Vallès's main other pleasure, already foreshadowed in *The Child*, was wandering around town. Observing and reporting the restless activities of the denizens of the streets of Paris (and later of London) were to form much of the material for his journalism. Here he could best satisfy his obsessive love of the heroic People, so many of whom were prevented from sharing in the brilliant affluence of the Second Empire, equally visible on Parisian boulevards. Yet when Jules left his café and the bright lights of the boulevards, he would still have to face the loneliness of his own personal harsh reality: a sordid hotel or lodging-house room for which, cheap though it was, he often had difficulty in paying the rent. Hence, probably, his constant change of address, the standard "doing a bunk" to avoid your creditors. He was doomed to a rootless, restless, unstable life.

When his long-suffering father finally cut off his allowance Vallès was on his own, and poverty threatened to turn into destitution. For a while, he was literally living from hand to mouth—he was known as a hearty eater and a large part of his debts were with restaurants. He had also become something of a sharp dresser, no doubt in compensation for the odd outfits in which (as one learns in *The Child*) his mother used to rig him out, as well as from the realization that in the society in which he would have to earn his living, no employer would offer a decent job to anyone dressed in rags. But smartness doesn't always pay: as we learn from *The Child*, he'd always had a hankering to become a manual worker, but once when he applied for a job as a bricklayer, he was immediately detected as an educated man and bluntly told to go back to his books. In a similarly humiliating vein, when trying to get a job as a shoemaker, he was told it was a skilled trade to be learned in childhood. The only job related to such manual work he ever got was writing for a cobblers' magazine—for which he was paid in shoes.

Some of Vallès's early stopgap jobs were almost surreal and equally humbling: a firm producing a magazine intended for the clientele of bathing establishments (appropriately called *La Naïade*, some of its issues were printed on waterproof rubber sheets) paid him to patronize various bathhouses, where he would ask for a copy of the magazine and, if it wasn't available, make a fuss so as to convince the proprietor to start buying it. Humiliating indeed, but the subterfuge should surely have appealed to Vallès's impish sense of humor.

Desperation breeds cynicism; if you can't beat them, join them. Jules decided to write a book called *L'Argent* (*Money*), a pepped-up version (lots of adjectives, said Vallès) of a dull but accurate account of the operation of the stock exchange, that essential instrument of the exploitative capitalist society which Vallès so vehemently opposed. While manifestly provocative—and those with any sense of irony could hardly interpret it otherwise—it could still be read as a manual on how to make money by financial speculation. The book caused quite a stir and was to lead to one of Vallès's most successful and longest-lived collaborations—though not, inevitably, without hiccups—with the highly respected *Le Figaro*, for which he wrote many articles over the years. (It also led indirectly to a duel with a stockbroker who felt insulted by one of Vallès's later articles; on this occasion, it was Vallès who was wounded.)

It was now, in the mid- to late-fifties, that Vallès, chronically in debt and desperately needing some permanent source of income, chose to become an official. He set about the task in typical fashion—by failing the entrance examination twice. He had a special gift for this: success in exams requires not only knowledge but commitment, concentration, and the intelligence to organize, and Vallès rarely combined all three.

In the end, he found himself established in a menial post as copy clerk in the municipal offices of the fifteenth arrondissement, with pay far too low to meet his tastes. Heavily in debt, he sought refuge in the provinces to escape his creditors, where an even greater humiliation awaited him. As we read in *The Child*, he despised teachers. He also hated religion so much that he refused to describe himself as an atheist, since that implied having a religious attitude toward disbelief. Now, in Caen, he found himself forced by circumstances to fill the most lowly of positions as an ancillary assistant, a *pion* in a school run by ecclesiastics. He lasted just four months but managed to stay on in the city long enough to fail the last examination he ever took, the *licence* (bachelor of arts), before returning to his clerkship in Paris—and to his debts.

But not for long: Vallès was a perpetual optimist, and spurred on by his successes at *Le Figaro*, he arranged to take part in a course of public readings and lectures. He lectured on Balzac, but the authorities who had granted permission for his lecture found it contained subversive material and made sure his employer was so informed. Vallès was told either to resign or be dismissed. He resigned.

The steady job had gone; henceforth, it was sink or swim. He assumed the precarious profession of journalist. Fortunately he had a lively and vigorous pen, was well read, had an observant eye, and had already achieved a certain notoriety. While he would have to tread warily, after eight years of the imperial regime many journals had begun to spring up in the provinces as well as in Paris. There was plenty of demand for copy of all sorts, always with the proviso that, despite the gradual liberalization of the regime, politics were still taboo. Vallès could fill that demand and began a golden period of collaboration with many magazines and newspapers. Basically, all he had to do was to transfer into words his humorous, ironic, and witty café chat on books, art exhibitions, theater shows, social gossip (true or invented), the general colorful life of Paris and its inhabitants.

Here is a sample of artistic and social gossip published in 1857, very early in his journalistic career, which well illustrates his verve, his chatty, gently mocking style (though later his mockery was not always so gentle). In this example, he is playing off the contrast between the sober academic painting of the bourgeois Ingres against the violent rhythms and color of his bohemian Romantic rival Delacroix, including a sideswipe at his less gifted imitators:

> Oh, I was forgetting! It's something a painter told me and the hero of the story is a painter too. Now, what was the name of the man who told me? Oh, I'm sure that doesn't interest you in the slightest... And the name of the hero? Monsieur Ingres in the flesh.
>
> It was at the Exhibition of 185..., oh, some time ago anyway. There weren't many people about, a religious silence prevailed... But there were a lot of people trailing behind this illustrious descendant of the great Raphael, who was eyeing the paintings with a stern gaze, occasionally shading his eyes when passing in front of the purple horses, dirty green skies and blue grass of the Colorists.
>
> All of a sudden he comes to a halt, strikes his forehead, and goes as pale as a ghost. "Heavens above!" he exclaimed. "I forgot to cut off the head!"
>
> Has he taken leave of his senses? Is this some terrible

secret, a foul mystery, some tale of Edgar Poe's which has turned into a horror story? "Heavens above! I forgot to cut off the head!"

The visitors, the officials, the colorists, everybody, are growing uneasy. "Delacroix's dead!" mutter the people around him. The wretched man has struck by night with murderous brushstrokes! He wants to hide all traces of the crime, cut up the corpse into little pieces, paint his head gray and bury it in a cellar.

Meanwhile the murderer had regained his calm, his gaze was serene, his step proud and assured. At that very moment Delacroix came in through another door. "It's not him," breathed the colorists with a sigh of relief. Then who was it? Who was the corpse? Whose head was it?

It was the head of Monsieur Ingres's wife herself. The good woman was so terrified of being buried alive that she had begged her husband to cut her throat before putting her in her coffin: the poor man had forgotten to do it!

The tone is typical Vallès: fashionably flippant (*blagueur*), ironic, with the regulation surprise ending and the touch of black comedy. Yet even in this apparently innocuous anecdote, he couldn't resist a sly dig at the regime: the exhibition of which he pretends to forget the date was the Universal Exhibition of 1855, planned to glorify the brilliance of the imperial regime.

Vallès could never leave well enough alone: his collaboration with this particular journal soon came to an end when he made an oblique but disrespectful reference to the general who had been responsible for crushing the uprising of June 1848. But there was no shortage of other journals ready to use his undoubted gifts. Between 1857 and 1870, Vallès wrote well over two hundred articles for various Parisian magazines and newspapers as well as a couple of dozen, mainly book reviews, for the very reputable daily *Le Progrès de Lyon*. He also wrote large numbers of articles for journals he himself ran. It was in these and *Le Figaro* that he was able to create the truest image of his views and, indirectly, of himself: he became a specialist in depicting a particular kind of Parisian, the people whom he called *les irréguliers*, unorthodox misfits living on the fringes of society, and their more active undisciplined counterparts *les réfractaires*, recalcitrant idealists who rejected society, refusing to follow normal careers, to exercise any traditional trade or profession, join any social institution, become priests, tax collectors, solicitors, who, in a word, wanted to live absolutely free and purely selfish lives. And how free can one be when starving and penniless?

Vallès had to admit that these misfits, crazy eccentrics who wanted to achieve what would seem to the ordinary run of people the impossible, in his words, "to discover perpetual motion, navigate the skies, breed a blue dahlia or a white blackbird"—however stoutheartedly and triumphantly they might set out "in their seven-league boots, would end up, halfway up the hill in worn-out old slippers." Like the street entertainers whom he described so vividly—the tumblers, jugglers, musicians (Vallès himself played the guitar), boxers (Vallès was proud of his own prowess at foot boxing: *la savate*), as well as the Bearded Woman, the Strong Man, the Fat Woman whom he also greatly enjoyed observing and describing—these bohemian outcasts, however picturesque and excellent subjects for feature articles, were nonetheless doomed. Vallès had too much personal experience of squalid bohemianism and even, in spite of verbal revolt, too much native shrewdness, to make it into a cult. He bitterly attacked Henry Murger's *Vie de Bohème* for trying to do so. Yet he admired their courage and took courage himself in the belief, borrowed from his beloved Proudhon, that next to the persecutors themselves (whom Vallès always equated with the bourgeoisie), it is those who think of themselves as martyrs who are most to be hated.

As the sixties wore on, in spite of rebuffs and chronic indebtedness, Vallès's journalistic presence had become considerable. In 1865 he was honored by being elected to the Société des Gens de Lettres, a highly respected literary group actively concerned with ensuring authors' rights. In 1867 he felt confident enough to found a journal which he called *La Rue* (*The Street*) and was able to attract such collaborators as Émile Zola—not yet famous—as well as the already notorious Auguste Blanqui, the most fanatically single-minded revolutionary of the century, who spent forty-eight of his seventy-six years in prison. This name alone foreshadows the fate of *La Rue*. While the right of freer social comment was being enlarged, to stray from social comment to political pamphleteering was still fatal. Even in its first year, one article of *La Rue* was banned; the following year, a whole issue devoted to Proudhon was confiscated. Exit *La Rue*. In any case, Vallès had gained an unsavory reputation with the police through articles he had published in other journals and had suffered two short spells in Sainte-Pélagie prison, which was reserved for press offenders. (It had a lenient regime—visitors were allowed and meals could be sent in. During his second spell, with typical cheekiness, Vallès edited a magazine entitled *Journal de Sainte-Pélagie*.) In this same year, 1869, he became a Freemason—odd conduct for a man generally opposed to institutions; and also campaigned for election to the legislative assembly. The successful candidate got 30,000 votes; Vallès was classed among the also-rans who received less than seven hundred votes in all.

But Napoleon III's luck was running out. In 1870 he hubristically declared war on Prussia, a declaration greeted enthusiastically by the people of Paris, an acclaim which appalled Vallès who was basically a pacifist and certainly no militarist. The French army suffered a rapid humiliating defeat, Napoleon abdicated, a provisional government was hastily elected, and the war ended—except for the left-wing revolutionaries of Paris, who first of all wanted to fight on against the Prussians and then, when that position proved untenable, rose against the newly elected government and set up an independent Paris Commune. Vallès felt the time had come for a final victory by the People over the hated middle classes, joined the Commune, and founded yet another daily, *Le Cri du Peuple*, to support it—the best-selling paper he was ever to edit. Its message was simple: Paris must become an independent, self-governing community and in this community, it was the most important elements, the workers and lower middle classes, who were to inherit their rightful place.

The tone of Vallès's political writings, in contrast to his social commentaries, which were acidly or humorously ironic, had largely tended toward the pompous, rhetorical, and exclamatory. Under the stress of armed conflict they now verged on the hysterical and inflammatory, and in the excitement, his verbal violence spilled over into action, for which he was manifestly unsuited. For a—luckily very short—time, he became the leader of a revolutionary battalion which, under his command, would have been far more likely to harm itself than any enemy. And yet on the whole Vallès attempted to play a moderating influence, opposing, for example, the setting up of a Committee of Public Safety (on the lines of Robespierre's infamous committee during the Terror). Ironically, one of this committee's first acts was to ban all papers, including *Le Cri du Peuple*.

The government troops, which had proved incompetent against the Prussians, easily defeated an amateur rabble, itself hardly united. A brutal massacre took place, followed by a relentless policy of transportation. It was almost an exact repetition of the uprising of June 1848.

Despite his heroic rhetoric, Vallès had no taste for martyrdom. Sentenced to death, he escaped via Brussels to England where, however harshly the native poor suffered under a selfish capitalistic industrial middle-class regime that Vallès was bound to deplore—and was later, in the footsteps of Dickens, whom he greatly admired, vigorously to condemn—was still liberally hospitable to political refugees. He was accompanied by Joséphine Lapointe, a married woman with whom he had had a relationship since the early sixties; she had been with him on the barricades and was devoted to him.

What subsequently happened to the relationship is unclear, but it is established that later, in London, Vallès had an affair with a young woman, said to be a Belgian elementary-school teacher, who bore him a daughter on whom he doted but who died when only a few months old, leaving him devastated. The mother left him. She had indeed little incentive to stay in view of Vallès's comment that he felt attached to her only because of her love for their daughter, an admission smacking of the self-absorption of a monomaniac. Perhaps he shared Balzac's view that love is a social luxury and thus reserved for the leisured middle classes and aristocracy. Proudhon held this strictly utilitarian view of sexual relations as well, but we can also suspect that Vallès's own home life as a child had probably greatly inhibited his emotional development.

There is a suggestion that Vallès had been helped in his London sojourn by a substantial monetary gift from an admirer, but he was soon to be writing begging letters to friends in France. While he felt an admiration for the peasantry and sympathy for the petty bourgeoisie, he didn't share their traditional habits of thrift: when he had money to burn, he burned it.

Exile quickly reduced him to utter misery: he had few friends; his fellow refugees were perpetually squabbling among themselves; he found London dull and the climate appalling. As for the English, he did not mince his words: "treacherous and formidable as a nation, as individuals they are false, coarse, rude, tactless, tasteless, heartless, lacking consideration, wit, or sensitivity: repulsive . . ." But the agony of having to stay among these appalling people was to last for some nine years, with one or two brief excursions to the Continent, including Switzerland—and he didn't think much of the Swiss either. Though he no longer had any civil status in France, through the agency of friends he was able to place large numbers of articles pseudonymously, mainly on aspects of London life but also on authors—Zola, Dickens, and Sue—as well as on Courbet, in a small number of newspapers and magazines; he also published a collection of his old articles under the title of *Les Enfants du Peuple* in 1879. In 1876, *The Child* was serialized under a pseudonym in *Le Siècle*, provoking a considerable scandal. Two years later, as *Le Bachelier*, the second volume of the autobiographical Jacques Vingtras trilogy, was being serialized, Vallès arranged for *The Child* to be published in book form. He was handsomely paid. He immediately celebrated by going off on a holiday to Jersey, but he still longed for the lively boulevards of Paris.

Finally, in 1880, a general amnesty for all former members of the Commune was granted and Vallès made a triumphant return to Paris. By 1883 he had already founded a new journal with an old title, *Le Cri du Peuple*. While the general battle cry remained the same—justice for the poor and the workers, mistrust of the rich middle classes and their supporters, notably the Church—Vallès wrote fewer directly political articles. He really had nothing much new to say and he hardly needed to write about politics when he had as chief political collaborator Jules Guesde, the leading Marxist revolutionary thinker of the day. Vallès could confine himself as in the past to more general feature articles on the life and institutions of the capital or on writers and artists. He was also much sought after socially and published a large number of articles in several other reviews. Not only was he earning a lot of money, he had become a fashionable celebrity, a welcome guest in many places: these were probably the happiest years of his life. The man who had long styled himself as a plebeian was now a prosperous bourgeois. He must have felt saddened that the *peuple souffrant* could not share his pleasures.

Le Cri du Peuple owed its birth largely to the generosity of a Doctor Guebhard, who was the lover and husband-to-be of a young married woman, later to become generally known as Séverine. Vallès had met her in Brussels on his way back from exile. She had fallen under his charismatic spell and was henceforth to be his devoted amanuensis, assistant, secretary, adviser, and, in his last days, nurse. Vallès became completely dependent on her, and it was she who, after his death, was to finish *L'Insurgé*, the last volume of his Vingtras trilogy.

Vallès was now in his early fifties, living on a grand scale to which he was unaccustomed. In 1884 he began to feel unwell; diagnosed as diabetic, early in 1885 he had to take to his bed, in the Guebhards' hospitable flat. He had never lived peacefully and was not to die in peace. Two policemen, feeling insulted by an article in *Le Cri du Peuple*, broke into its offices and in a brawl one of them, who was armed, was shot. In the ensuing investigations the police burst into the Guebhards' flat to search the premises, including prying under Vallès's mattress as he lay in bed. He died a few days later, at the age of fifty-three. Admirers of *The Child* will surely hope that despite his illness he retained enough of his indomitable spirit to appreciate the irony of this final intrusion of the police into the room of a dying man who had so persistently despised them and their role in serving the bourgeoisie whom he equally distrusted, a distrust for which *The Child* offers pervasive justification.

Vallès's whole career was spent in journalism: his two principal published works before the Vingtras books were collections of social and political articles: *Les Réfractaires* in 1865 and in the following year *La Rue*. By its very nature, however, journalism, particularly political journalism, has no claim to longevity; its purpose is to be pungent, not long-lived. The second and third volumes of the Vingtras trilogy are also strongly political: *Le Bachelier* recounts the avatars of a politicized student under the Second Empire, while *L'Insurgé*, as its title suggests, deals largely with political and revolutionary activities immediately before and during the Paris Commune. However lively and dramatic, these books are bound to appeal more to the historically and politically minded than the general reader. Not so *The Child*.

Autobiography was admirably suited to Vallès's special gifts. Unlike his younger contemporary Zola, he lacked the ability to invent a plot or structure a narrative. In an autobiographical work, though, the plot is automatically supplied by the chronology of the protagonist's life, while its substance— a selection, with a few appropriate omissions and changes —lends itself perfectly to the journalistic skills which Vallès had honed over a long period: terseness, drama, an ability to keep a story moving, suspense followed by surprising climax or anticlimax, spiced with wit as well as occasional pathos (the Louisette episode in *The Child*, for example, where we are reminded of Dickens)—these are the daily tools of a good reporter. And Vallès had always had a sharp eye for detail as well as a gift of vivid imagery to render a sensation.

We are fortunate in possessing firsthand evidence of the genesis and progress of *The Child* from a letter Vallès wrote to his friend Hector Malot in France. While not neglecting the social significance of the work, Vallès recognized that it must not be too overtly political. He wanted to produce a novel that could be read by everyone, including, he says, his enemies, an "intimate book of naive emotion and childish passion"—in short, a work of general human interest.

From Vallès's first letter to Malot we also learn the appalling conditions in which he started writing: it was a freezing cold, snowy and windy March day in a cheerless London garret—and a Sunday in Victorian England could only add to the misery of his exile. We are also informed that during the composition of the work, he could hear from the house next door (it seems somehow almost too appropriate) the screams of a little boy being beaten by his drunken mother. He admits that all these circumstances may, in his words, have "blackened his ink." Should we be surprised that this man, such an enemy of injustice, didn't go to the rescue of this young victim? Probably not: Vallès was essentially a man of words, not of action, and since he was, as usual, covered in debt, he was writing at high speed, knowing that he would certainly not be paid until he handed over the manuscript. The incident clearly warns us to take some of the brutality in his work with a grain of salt, though, in any case, we know that it is inevitable that autobiography, consciously or not, contains elements of fiction. Memory is fickle and selective.

In his letter, Vallès mentions only his father's brutality, while in the book itself more space is devoted to his mother's treatment of him. His relationship with his mother is certainly more complex and ambiguous: it is clear that she loves her son, yet her love and her desire to do her best for him, according to her rather limited lights, seem at times to be a disguise, hinted at but never openly stated, for her sadism. She feels some pleasure in hurting him, while he, in his turn, is similarly ambivalent in his attitude toward her, sometimes showing respect and admiration for her determination and spirited nature—indeed, he seems to have inherited it—at other times, poking fun at her peasantlike naiveté and her inconsistencies, showing her social aspirations as grotesque. Often, however, he seems, by accepting his guilt, to be justifying her beatings. His constant, albeit often ironic, self-deprecation does suggest a connivance verging on masochism.

Carried over into adulthood, this is a plausible explanation for his tendency in later life to recklessly throw away, in futile and unnecessary gestures, any credit he may have earned by his journalistic achievements: it seems almost as if, in deliberate self-sabotage, he would set out not to succeed, since by failing, he retained the right to continue to revolt.

Even if exaggerated, the tale *The Child* tells—of constant physical and psychological child abuse, of recurrent mishaps —is appalling. How does Vallès save it from becoming nightmarishly horrifying? The author was himself aware of the danger and tells us his solution which is that adopted by Voltaire, whom Vallès, like his favorite Proudhon, greatly admired: it is the constant use of overt and underlying irony, sometimes descending even to farce and caricature.

As a result, despite Jacques Vingtras's moments of depression, Vallès depicts him not as a passive victim but as arrogant even: resilient, courageous, always ready to treat his disasters with humor, he refuses to be cowed, just as in later life, Vallès himself always refused to accept defeat. And the advantage of distance from the events he is describing strengthens his ironic stance—gentle toward his mother, more pitiless toward his father, and at times vicious toward the teaching profession.

Whatever our interpretation of these complex relationships may be, the fundamentals remain in no doubt and cogent for all of us: we have all had parents; we have known the stresses of growing up, going to school, and the more banal pressure of having to pass examinations—a central issue in *The Child*; we have known the commonly bewildering stirrings of sexuality, so charmingly, delicately, and amusingly treated in *The Child*. More nastily, we have come to face the constant menace, if not prevalence, of child abuse. In a word, we are broadly enmeshed in the issues raised by this novel, as urgent and moving as ever.

Zola once upbraided Vallès for adopting a stance of pure

negation, alleging that his gaze was too strictly limited to exploiting "a small corner of the world." This criticism of Vallès's political journalism contains more than a grain of truth, but it cannot apply to *The Child*: for a girl or a boy, childhood is not just a small corner of the world, it is the whole of existence. However spirited the ironic effort Vallès makes, with the detached hindsight of maturity, to cover up his childhood wounds, and however much he entices the reader to savor his humorous asides and to admire Jacques's refusal to surrender, he also shows him as wounded to the depths of his heart. We can but hope that Jacques's "terrors, pains, and early miseries" do not prove irreversible; that, once damaged, the potential paradise of childhood is not lost beyond recall; that the title of the last chapter, "Deliverance," is psychologically as well as aesthetically convincing.

Moving from near-tragedy to farce, *The Child* has long been recognized in France as a classic. It would be inappropriate to put *The Child* beside the more socially and politically resonant *Confessions* of Rousseau: Vallès has his own specific relevance, eschews dullness or self-pity, and his breakneck style and comically rueful irony make him far more exciting to read. English readers acquainted with Louis-Ferdinand's Céline's *Death on the Installment Plan*, an equally original tragicomic semiautobiography, should not be surprised, however, to detect similarities of style and treatment between that work and Vallès's. Céline admitted to having discovered his own voice through reading Vallès, even as he pushed Vallès's exclamatory colloquialisms into an outrageously explosive slangy coarseness. Both books are masterpieces, discordant works for discordant centuries.

—Douglas Parmée

THE CHILD

I dedicate this book

TO ALL THOSE
WHO WERE BORED STIFF AT SCHOOL
OR
REDUCED TO TEARS AT HOME,
WHO IN CHILDHOOD
WERE BULLIED BY THEIR TEACHERS
OR
THRASHED BY THEIR PARENTS

JULES VALLÈS
Paris

I. MY MOTHER

WAS I BREAST-FED by my mother? Did I get my milk from some peasant wet nurse? I just don't know. But whatever breast I may have gnawed at, I don't remember, when I was tiny, ever being cuddled, made a fuss of, pampered, indulged, given little kisses . . . I was given lots of beatings.

My mother says: spare the rod and spoil the child. And every morning she gives me a beating; if she doesn't have time in the morning, she'll save it until the afternoon, hardly ever later than four o'clock.

Mademoiselle Balandreau rubs me with tallow fat.

She's a kindly old spinster of fifty. She lives downstairs. In the beginning, she was quite pleased: not having a clock, she used me to tell the time. "Slap! bang! wham! whack! whack! It's that youngun upstairs getting his walloping, time to make my coffee."

But one day when I was out in the passage recovering, and holding the tail of my shirt up to cool my bottom which was red and raw, she saw it and took pity on it.

First of all she thought of showing it to the neighbors to get their support for a protest, but realizing that wasn't the best way, she worked out another plan.

Now, when she hears my mother say, "I'm going to beat you, Jacques—"

"Oh, do let me save you the trouble, Madame Vingtras, I can do it for you."

"That's very kind of you, Mademoiselle!"

So Mademoiselle Balandreau takes me away, but instead of beating me, she claps her hands and I start to yell. In the evening my mother thanks her for her help.

"Not at all, anything to oblige," the kind old lady replies, quietly slipping me some candy.

So my earliest memory starts with a beating; my second is full of surprise and tears.

I'm squatting beside a log fire under the mantel of an old fireplace; my mother's sitting in the corner knitting; one of my cousins who acts as our maid, since we're too poor to afford a proper one, is stacking away some crude faience plates on some rather worm-eaten shelves. The plates have a decoration of roosters with blue tails and red combs.

My father has a knife in his hand and is whittling a block of fir wood; as the silky shavings flutter down they look like snippets of yellow ribbon. He's making a cart out of little tongues of new wood. The wheels are already cut out: round slices of potato, their brown skins represent the iron rims. It's nearly finished and I'm waiting all agog and excited, when my father cries out and holds up his hand covered with blood. He's dug the knife into his finger. I went pale and was going over to help when I was stopped by a tremendous thump. It came from my mother—her fists were clenched; she was foaming at the mouth.

"It's all your fault your father's hurt himself!"

She bundled me out into the dark staircase, banging my forehead against the door for good measure.

I start screaming, I beg to be forgiven. I call out to my father. In my childish panic, I can see his hand dangling down, hacked to pieces! And it's all because of me! Why won't they let me in to find out what's happening? They can beat me later if they want to. I continue to scream, but no one replies. I can hear carafes being fetched and carried, a drawer being opened; they're applying a compress.

"There's no great harm done," my cousin comes out to tell me, folding a bloodstained strip of linen.

I'm sobbing, I can't breathe. My mother reappears and shoves me into the little closet where I sleep . . . where every night I lie awake, scared.

I'm maybe five years old, and I think I'm a patricide!

And yet it's not my fault!

Was I forcing my father to make that cart? Wouldn't I much rather have made myself bleed than see him hurt?

Yes, and I scratch at my hands so that I can suffer too.

It's because my mother's so fond of my father! That's why my mother lost her temper.

I'm being taught to read out of a book where it says you must obey your father and mother: my mother was right to beat me.

The house where we live is on a dingy street, hard to climb. From the top you can see the whole countryside, but carriages can't get through, only oxcarts loaded with wood. The drivers prick the oxen with goads as they make their way up, necks straining, tongues lolling out; their hooves slither around; they're steaming. I always stop and watch them when they deliver wood and flour to the baker's halfway up. I look at the baker's boys too, all white, and the vast oven, glowing red—the dough goes in on shovels and there's a smell of crusty bread and burning charcoal.

At the top of the street is the jail. Often there are gendarmes escorting prisoners who are handcuffed and have staring eyes, looking neither left nor right. They seem sick.

Women slip them a coin or two, which they clutch tightly in their hands. To thank the women they just nod.

They don't look wicked at all.

One day they took one of them away on a stretcher, completely covered under a white sheet: he'd stolen something
and then stuck his wrist under a saw; he'd bled so much that
they thought he was going to die.

Being a sort of neighbor, the jailer is regarded as a friend of
the house. Occasionally he drops in for supper, and his son
and I have become pals. Sometimes he takes me with him to
the jail because it's more cheerful up there. There are lots of
trees and laughter and games. There's one prisoner, very old,
who builds cathedrals from corks and nutshells.

At home nobody ever laughs; my mother's always grum-
bling. How much more fun it is with that old jailbird! And
there's a tall prisoner nicknamed the Poacher, who killed that
gendarme at the fair in the Vivarais.

The prisoners get bunches of flowers which they clasp to
their chests and hide away. When I went through to the
parlor, I saw that it was women who were giving them.

Other prisoners get oranges and cakes brought by their
mothers, as if they were still little boys. I'm a little boy too,
and I never get cakes or oranges.

I can't remember ever seeing a flower in our home. Ma
says they're a nuisance and after a couple of days they start
smelling nasty. The other night I pricked my finger on a rose
and my mother exclaimed, "That'll teach you!"

When prayers are being said, I always get the giggles. It's hopeless for me to try and stop myself! Before I kneel down, I offer
up a little prayer to God, swearing that I'm not laughing at
Him, but once I'm down on my knees, I just can't help myself.
My uncle's got itchy warts which he scratches; he starts to bite
them, and I explode. Luckily my mother doesn't always notice,
but God can see everything, so what must He think of me?

But I didn't laugh the other day. We'd had my aunt from
Vourzac and my uncles from Farreyrolles to supper and were

busy eating our pie when suddenly it got dark. All during the meal we'd been feeling hot; it was so stifling that we'd taken off our coats. Now the thunder started to growl. The rain was pouring down. Big drops were going *plop* in the dust. It was as cool as a cellar and there was a smell of wet earth. In the street the gutters were frothing like soapy water and then hailstones started to crunch on the windows. My aunt and uncles looked at each other, and one of them stood up and started to pray. Now they were all on their feet, bareheaded, young and old with foreheads full of sadness. They were praying to the Good Lord not to treat their fields too harshly and not to kill the tender blossoms of their crops with His white buckshot.

As they were saying "Amen," a hailstone came in through the window and bounced into a glass.

Our family comes from country stock.

My father's father was a proud peasant who wanted his son to go on to study and become a priest. He sent him to live with an uncle, himself a priest, to learn Latin; then he was sent to a seminary.

My father—the man who was to become my father—didn't stay in the seminary. He wanted to go to college, gain an honorable position in society, and he set himself up in a tiny room tucked away in a gloomy street from which he would emerge during the day to give a few lessons at two sous[1] an hour and before returning in the evening to woo the peasant girl who'd become my mother and who at the time was dutifully performing her role as the devoted niece of an invalid aunt.

The result: you squabble with the priestly uncle, you say good-bye to the Church, you and the country girl fall in love, and come to an understanding, you get married! You also fall out with your father and mother who have to be served an injunction to prevent them from obstructing this match between Indigence and Poverty.

I was the first offspring of this marriage made in Heaven. I came into the world in an old wooden bed, in the company of village bedbugs and seminarists' fleas.

The house belongs to a fifty-year-old lady who has only two teeth—one reddish-brown, the other blue—she's always laughing; she's kindhearted; everybody likes her. Her husband drowned in a vat while he was making wine, a fate which sets me dreaming and makes me very scared of vats and very attracted by wine: it must be extremely good stuff for Monsieur Garnier—that was his name—to drink so much that he died. Every Sunday Madame Garnier drinks some of this wine which smells like the man she loved. The dead man's shoes are also on a shelf, like two empty mugs.

In the house where I live, they drink a lot.

A priest who stays on our landing never gets up from the table without being goggle-eyed, with gleaming cheeks and glowing red ears. His mouth gives off fumes like a wine barrel and his nose looks like a peeled tomato. His breviary is fragrant with wine, onions, and herbs, like a fish stew.

He has a maid, Henriette, and when he's had a few drinks, he ogles her out of the corner of his eye. People sometimes exchange whispers about him and her, behind their backs.

On the second floor there's a Monsieur Grélin. He's an officer in the fire brigade, and on Corpus Christi he's in charge of the town square. Monsieur Grélin's an architect, though people say he doesn't know anything about architecture, and that he's the reason why the Breuil[2] is always flooding. He's cost the town fifty thousand francs and if it wasn't for his wife . . . They mutter something about his wife, I don't quite know what. She's nice, his wife, with big dark eyes, tiny white teeth, and just the trace of a mustache. She always flounces her petticoats and clicks her heels as she walks.

She's got a southern accent,[3] and sometimes we mimic her.

People say that she has "lovers." I don't exactly know what that means but I do know that she's kind to me and gives me a little tap on the cheek as she goes by; I like being kissed by her because she smells nice. The people in our house seem to avoid her without letting her see it.

"You say she's on good terms with the deputy?"

"Yes indeed, the best possible!"

"Oh dear me, poor old Grélin!"

That's what I hear, and my mother says a few words more which I don't understand.

"And women like that are flooded with offers of jobs for their husbands and given lovely clothes for their birthdays while respectable women like us have a hard time keeping body and soul together!"

Isn't Madame Grélin respectable? What does she do? What's wrong? Poor old Grélin?

Yet poor old Grélin couldn't seem more cheerful! They're always kissing and hugging their children, and all I get is slaps and a lot of talk about hellfire, and I'm always being told off for being so rowdy.

If I were Grélin's son I'd be much happier, but there we are! So the deputy mayor would come and call on us when my father wasn't at home. Why should I care?

Madame Toullier lives on the third floor: now there's a really respectable woman!

Madame Toullier brings her needlework to our place and she and my mother talk about the people upstairs, downstairs, and those from Raphael and Espailly as well. Madame Toullier takes snuff, has big hairs sprouting out of her ears and bunions on her feet. She's more respectable than Madame Grélin! She's more stupid too, and uglier.

———

What other memories do I have about my life when I was a little boy? I can remember that in winter the birds come and peck in the snow; in summer I get my short pants dirty in a nasty, smelly yard; that one of the tenants is fattening up turkeys in the cellar. I'm allowed to knead the little pellets of moist bran that they stuff down their throats, choking them. The real fun is to see them suffocating; they go blue; blue seems to be my favorite color!

My mother often comes down to pinch my ears and give me a clout. It's for my own good, so the more she slaps me, the more I'm convinced that she's a good mother and I'm an ungrateful brat.

Yes, ungrateful because at night, while I'm rubbing my bruises, it sometimes happens that I don't start off by saying "God bless Mommy," and it's only at the end of my prayers that I ask God to keep her safe and well, so that she can go on looking after me and taking such good care of me.

I'm a big boy now, I'm starting school!

And what a lovely little school it is! What a lovely street! And how lively it is on market day!

The horses are neighing, the pigs are lunging and grunting, with a rope tied around their legs; the chickens are cackling away in their cages; the country women are wearing green aprons and scarlet petticoats; blue cheeses, fresh farmer's cheeses, baskets of fruit; pink radishes, green cabbages!

There was an inn quite close to the school and they often unloaded hay there.

Hay that you buried yourself in up to your eyes, that you came out of all sweaty and bristly with wisps of it caught in your neck, all down your back, on your legs, pricking like needles!

In the hay you'd lose your books, your little basket of food, your belt, one of your clogs. All the fun of the fair and the thrill of danger. What times they were!

Whenever a hay cart goes by now, I take my hat off and walk behind it.

II. MY FAMILY

On my mother's side, two aunts: Aunt Rosalie and Auntie Mariou—I don't know why they call her "auntie," perhaps because she's more affectionate. I can still see her big, gentle, white laugh on her brown face; she's thin and rather graceful: she's womanly.

Aunt Rosalie is older and enormous, a bit bent. She could be a cantor in the church: she looks like old Jauchard, the baker who leads the singing of the Psalms at Vespers on Sundays and starts off the hymns when they do the Stations of the Cross. She's the man of the house. Her husband, my uncle Jean, doesn't count; he's quite happy scratching away at a little wart, a sort of beauty spot on his crumpled, drawn, wrinkled face. I've noticed since then how many peasants have faces like that—wily, wizened, and weaselly. There's a touch of the theater or the court in their blood, which went astray some night during a celebration or a comedy performance in a barn or an inn. They still have a whiff of the strolling player, the dispossessed aristocrat, old nobility, with a further whiff of pigsty or dunghill: shriveled by their origins, in the bright sunlight they still look puny.

As for Auntie Mariou's husband, he's definitely a herdsman! A good-looking fair-headed worker of the land, five foot seven, beardless but with glossy hair on his round, fleshy, golden-brown neck; his skin's straw-colored, his eyes cornflower blue, his lips poppy-red, his shirt permanently unbuttoned, with a striped yellow vest and a furry velvet-cord tricolor hat that he never takes off. You can see men like him in paintings depicting country gods in landscapes.

On my father's side, two aunts.

My aunt Mélie is a deaf mute—and yet she chatters and chatters away!

Her eyes, her forehead, her lips, her hands, her feet, her sinews, her muscles, her flesh, her skin, nothing's ever at rest; she gabbles, inquires, replies; she harasses you with questions, requires answers; her eyeballs dilate and close down; she puffs out her cheeks and draws them in; her nose leaps around! She touches you here, she touches you there, abruptly, thoughtfully, wildly; there's no way you can bring the conversation to an end. You have to go along, meet every sign with one of your own, a gesture for every gesture, a ready riposte, a flash of wit, keeping your eye sometimes on the sky, at others on the cellar, grasping her thoughts as well as you can, by the head or the tail, in a word, give your all—whereas with your normal gossips who've got just a tongue, you need only listen with half an ear. There's no bigger chatterbox than a deaf mute.

Poor girl! She never found a husband. It was inevitable, and what she earns from her manual work is barely enough to make ends meet; not that she's short of anything, in fact, but she's so fond of pretty clothes, our Aunt Amélie!

You have to listen to her little grunts and watch her gestures, follow her eyes when she's trying on a hat or a fichu; she's tasteful, she knows how to stick a rose beside her dead ear and find the right color of ribbon to go best with her bodice—next to her heart, which is trying to speak.

Great-aunt Agnes.

She's called "blessed."[1]

There's a whole crowd of old spinsters called that.

"What does 'blessed' mean, Ma?"

My mother tries to find a definition but can't: she talks about being consecrated to the Virgin Mary, vows of "innocence."

Innocence. My great-aunt Agnes represents innocence. So that's what innocence is like. She's a good seventy years old and her hair must be white; I can't be sure, nobody can, as she always wears a black scarf tied tightly around her skull, like a headband of taffeta; she has, I may add, a gray beard, a wisp of hair here, a little bunch of curls there, and warts everywhere that look like black currants bubbling on her face.

In other words, with her black headgear, the top of her face reminds me of a burned potato and the bottom, of a potato that's sprouting; the other morning I found a potato—purple and puffy, under the stove which was as like great-aunt Agnes as two peas.

"Vows of innocence."

My mother is so good at talking and so bad at explaining that I'm beginning to imagine that being "blessed" is something unsavory, that they've either got too much or not enough of something.

Blessed?

There are four "blessed" women living together—not all with fiery-colored warts or ash-gray skin like Great-aunt Agnes, who likes pretty clothes, but all of them with a trace of a mustache or a bit of whisker or muttonchop and the inevitable headband, the black piece of plaster!

Now and again I'm sent to see them.

They live at the end of a deserted grassy street.

Great-aunt Agnes is my godmother and she adores her godson.

She wants to put me in her will, to leave me what she has—not her headband, I hope . . .

It seems that she keeps a few old coins in a stocking, and when they talk about a neighbor in whose house they found a bag of old coins at the bottom of a jar of butter, she laughs in her beard.

I don't have much fun at her place, waiting for someone to discover her butter jar!

It's dark in that room, a sort of large attic held up by beams which are so rotten and worm-eaten that they look as if they're made out of old corks!

The window looks out onto a yard which gives off a smell of baked mud.

The only thing I do like are the curtains, which are enough to keep me thoroughly amused; they're purple, and you can see on them little figures of men, dogs, trees, a pig—the same images repeated again and again. But I enjoy looking at them from every angle and what's best is I can see all sorts of things on my great-aunt's curtains when I look at them with my head stuck between my legs.

I can see the hunt—that's the subject—in all sorts of colors. Yes, that's it! The blood runs down into my head, my brain's like the bottom of a barrel: apoplexy! I'm forced to pull my head out by my hair in order to stand up and put it back on straight, like a bottle being emptied.

They never stop praying—Amen! Amen!—before the turnip and after the egg.

The turnips are the basis of the supper I'm offered when I go to visit the Blesseds; they let me have one raw and one cooked.

When I scrape the raw one with my knife, it goes all frothy and on my tongue it has the taste of hazelnut and the coldness of snow.

I don't enjoy gnawing away at the cooked one so much—they do it on the foot warmer, which my aunt always has between her legs and which is an indispensable part of the Blesseds' furniture. Eight blessed legs, four warmers that are used as sewing boxes during the summer; in the winter they turn the bits of charcoal over with their keys.

Occasionally, there's an egg.

They pull the egg out of a bag, like a lottery ticket, and they boil it, the poor thing! It's a real crime, a cockicide, because there's always a tiny chick inside.

I eat this fetus gratefully since they've told me that not everybody gets one to eat and I'm one of the lucky few; however, I'm not very enthusiastic because I don't like to soak my bread with chicken abortions by the teaspoonful.

In winter, the Blesseds work with a *globe light*—one candle set between four globes full of water casting a short harsh gleam of white light with golden reflections.

In summer they set their chairs outside on the street, by their doorway, and you should see them working away on their lace pillows.

With its green bands, pink ribbons, pearl-headed pins, with its threads that look like trails of silvery slime on a bunch of flowers, its clattering bobbins, the lace pillow is a whole little world of life and gaiety.

You must listen to it chattering away on the lace-makers' laps on warm days at the doorways of silent houses in the street of the Blesseds. You only need five or six of them working and the din is like a beehive or a brook, and when the clock strikes twelve—silence.

The fingers stop, the lips move: the short prayer of the Angelus. When the Blessed who is saying it has finished, the others all respond *Amen* in a melancholy voice, and once again the lace pillows resume their chatter.

My uncle Joseph, the one I call Nunky, is a peasant who's turned himself into a tradesman. He's twenty-five years old and as strong as an ox. He looks like an organ-grinder: tanned, with big eyes, a wide mouth and fine teeth, a very black beard, bushy hair, a neck like a sailor's, and enormous hands covered in warts—those famous warts that he scratches during prayers!

He's a member of a trade guild, he's got a big stick with long ribbons, and he sometimes takes me along to the house of the carpenters' guild mother. There's drinking and singing and all sorts of stunts. He takes hold of me around the waist and throws me up into the air, catches me, and then throws me up again. It's fun and it's scary! Then I clamber over the laps of the guild members, I finger their measures and their calipers, I take a sip of their wine which makes me feel rather ill. I bump into their "masterworks,"[2] I knock against planks, my eyes are poked by their tall collars, and I'm scratched by their earrings. Yes, they wear earrings.

"Do you have more fun with the 'scholards,' Jacques, than you do with us?"

"Oh no!"

Scholard is the word he uses to describe elementary- or secondary-school teachers, teachers of Latin or drawing who sometimes come to the house and talk all the time about school. On such days I'm solemnly ordered to keep quiet and forbidden to put my elbows on the table; I have to keep my legs still and eat the fat off the plates of people who don't like it! I'm bored stiff by the scholards and so happy with the carpenters.

My bed is beside Nunky Joseph's and he never goes to sleep without telling me some stories—and he knows a lot. Then he drums a tattoo on his tummy with his hands. In the morning he teaches me boxing. He crouches down so that I can punch his big broad chest. I try kickboxing too, and almost always lose my balance.

When I hurt myself, I don't cry—my mother would come.

He goes off in the morning and comes back in the evening.

How eagerly I wait for him to return! I count the hours till he's due home.

After supper he takes me off and keeps me until bedtime in his little workshop downstairs. In the evenings he works for himself, singing songs that I like and throwing wood chips in my face. It's me who puts out the candle and he lets me stick a finger into his varnish.

Sometimes his pals come around to see him and have a

chat; they stand leaning against the wall with their hands in their pockets. They're very friendly to me and my uncle's very proud. "He knows a lot already, that boy! Just tell us that fable of yours, Jacques!"

One day, Uncle Joseph left.

It was a sad story.

Madame Garnier, the widow of the drunkard who drowned in his own vat, had a niece in Bordeaux who she'd sent for at the time of the disaster.

Tall and dark-haired with enormous eyes as black as black could be and so fiery! She uses them in the same way I use a bit of broken mirror to send flashes of light around the classroom, swirling in the corners or shooting up to the sky, carrying you with them.

It seems that I must have fallen passionately in love with her. I say "it seems" because I can only remember one passionate scene of frightful jealousy.

Who do you think it was directed at?

At Uncle Joseph! He'd started courting Mademoiselle Celina Garnier. I've no idea how he set about it but in the end he'd asked to marry her and she'd accepted.

Did she love him?

Today I find I can't answer that question. Today, now that I've recovered my reason, that time has spread its cover of snow over those deep feelings. But at the time when Mademoiselle Garnier got married, I was blinded by passion.

She was going to be someone else's wife! She was turning me down, me, such a pure young boy! I didn't know the difference between a man and a woman; I thought that babies were born under cabbage plants.

When I was in a vegetable garden, I sometimes looked around, walking among the vegetables thinking that I could become a father too.

All the same, I'd give a start when my aunt Celina used to give me a little tap on my cheek and say something to me in her Bordeaux accent. Whenever she looked at me in a certain way, my heart would go pit-a-pat, just as it had when I was on a swing at a fair on the Breuil.

I was already a big boy: ten years old! This is what I said to her: "Don't marry my uncle Joseph! In a while I'll be a man. Wait for me, promise you'll wait for me! It's just a joke, isn't it, today's wedding?"

It wasn't just a joke at all: they really were married and went off together.

I saw them go.

My jealousy was on the alert: I heard the key turn.

That key tore at my heart. I listened, I kept a lookout. Nothing! Nothing! I felt I was done for. I went back to the wedding feast and *drowned my sorrows in drink.*

Since that day I've never dared to look Uncle Joseph in the eye. However, when he came to see us the day before he left for Bordeaux, he didn't mention our rivalry and said good-bye to me like an affectionate uncle and not like a resentful husband!

And then there's my cousin Apollonie: they call her Polonie.

Yes, that's how those peasants baptized their daughter!

Dear cousin! Tall, leisurely, with blue eyes, periwinkle-blue; long chestnut-brown hair, snow-white shoulders, a smooth white neck slashed by a shiny black velvet ribbon from which hung a golden cross; a tender smile and a languid voice; as soon as she starts to laugh, she turns pink, and then red when people begin staring at her. While she's getting dressed I devour her with my eyes—I don't know why—and I feel all funny as I watch her holding her shift between her teeth and pulling it backward over her plump shoulders when it starts slipping down—this is on the days when she sleeps in our small bedroom so as to be the first to get to the market with her slabs of butter as firm and white as the shapely pats of flesh she has on her chest. People jostle to buy Polonie's butter.

Sometimes her long fingers tickle my neck and make threatening gestures at my ribs; she laughs, strokes me, hugs me. I hold her tight as I defend myself. Once I bit her—I didn't mean to bite her but I couldn't help gritting my teeth—and her flesh had such a scent of raspberries. She cried out, "Naughty boy!" and gave me a slap on my cheek, quite a hard one. I thought I was going to faint, and as I answered her with a sigh, I felt my chest going tight and my eyes soft.

She went and flung herself down on her bed complaining that she'd caught cold. From the back she looked like the white pony ridden by the young son of the prefect.[3]

I thought of her all the time I was doing my prose compositions.

Sometimes I go for a long time without seeing her—she stays in her house in the village—and then, all of a sudden, along she comes like a breath of fresh air.

"Here I am," she announces. "I've come to pick you up to take you down to our village! Would you like to come?"

She gives me a hug! I rub my snout against her rosy cheeks and bury it in her white neck and let it slide down over the blue veins of her breast!

Still that scent of raspberries!

She sends me off and I scurry away to pick up my clothes and change my shirt.

I put on a green tie and steal a spot of my mother's pomade, so as to smell nice too, and so that she'll put her head on my hair!

I've packed my things, I've put on my cream and my tie, but when I peer into the mirror, I think I look quite ugly and so I ruffle my hair again! I cram my tie into my pocket and with my cap half falling off, I run, open-necked, to get another hug. It tickled me but I didn't tell.

The stableboy slapped the horse's crupper—it's a light chestnut brown with tufts of hair above its hooves; it's my Auntie Mariou's, which people ride when there's too much butter to carry or too much blue cheese to sell. The animal ambles along, clip clop clip clop, very stiffly, as if its neck was about to break, with its moss-colored mane flopping over its big eyes that look like sheep hearts.

My aunt or my cousin straddle it like men—my aunt's calves are as thin as charcoal sticks; my cousin's look soft and fleshy in her white woolen stockings.

"Gee-up! Gee-up! Get along!"

That's Jean tugging at the horse and turning it around. It's had its oats and it neighs as it draws back its lips and bares its yellow teeth.

It's been saddled.

"Pass Jacquinou up to me," says Polonie who's managed to pull her dark twill skirt down over her knees and has settled her solid flesh on the shiny leather of the saddle. She helps me up onto the crupper.

"I'm on!"

We now realize that we've left my clothes rolled up in a bundle on the inn table, lying in the puddles of wine surrounded by flies.

They hand them to us.

"Tie them on, Jean. And now, Jacquinou, put your arms around my waist and cling tight."

The poor horse has a jerky gait and is very bony, but I suddenly realize that the words I've had to recite are true: "God's work is good."

My mother's beatings have literally tanned my hide and made it tough.

"Tight, I said! Tighter!"

And as I hold on to her below her fichu dotted with small painted flowers looking like golden beetles, I can feel the warmth of her skin. I'm pressing her soft flesh. And this flesh seems to be growing firmer under my fingers as they cling tightly to it. A moment ago—when she glanced back at me over her shoulder with her lips parted and her breasts swelling—as she turned her neck the blood surged up into my skull and made my hair sizzle!

In the Rue Saint-Jean I relaxed my grip a little. It's the track followed by the sheep and cattle, and we rode more slowly. I felt very proud. I was imagining that people were watching and I behaved as if I knew how to ride: I turned around, resting the palm of my hand on the horse's crupper and digging my heels into its sides, saying "Gee-up!," just like a horse dealer.

Now we've left the outskirts of the town and passed the last saddler.

We've reached Espailly!

No more houses! Just a few in the fields; flowers clambering up walls, like rosebuds over a white dress; a slope covered in vines and the river down below, stretching out under the trees like a snake confined by a band of yellow sand softer than cream and speckled with pebbles gleaming like diamonds.

In the background, mountains, their black spines green with pines, cut into the blue of the sky where the clouds stretch out like flaky scraps of silk. A bird—an eagle, I expect—had flapped its giant wings and was hanging in the air like a cannonball suspended at the end of a thread.

I'll always remember those somber woods, the shimmering river, that great eagle . . .

I'd forgotten that I was a pounding heart pressed against Polonie's back. My cousin didn't seem to be thinking of anything at all, and I recall hearing only the sound of horse's hooves and a cow mooing.

III. SCHOOL

SCHOOL.[1] Like all schools—and all prisons—this one looked out on a nondescript street which, however, wasn't far from Martouret, the Martouret which formed our main square with its town hall, fruit market, and flower market, a meeting place for the local scamps, the cheerful center of the town. And at the end, the street was full of bustle. There were taverns—we called them pubs—displaying a tree stump and a bundle of branches outside as a sign. From these pubs came sounds of quarrels, a whiff of wine that surged up into the brain, sharpening the senses, making me feel stronger, more joyful.

That scent of wine! It still makes my nostrils twitch and my chest swell!

The drinkers used to make a tremendous racket; with their ribbon-bedecked whips and colorfully decorated tunics, they seemed carefree, enjoying life—shouting, swearing, shaking hands as they clinched a deal over a pig or a cow.

Yet another cork pops. A laugh explodes and the bellies of bottles clink in the pub-keeper's hand! The sun casts a golden glow on the glasses or lights up a button on this jacket here and grills a swarm of flies in that corner over there. The inn is full of cries and delicious smells—strong ones too—smoke and buzzing sounds.

———

Two minutes away lies the moldering old school, exuding boredom, reeking of ink; the people who go in and out lower their eyes and voices, muffle their steps in order not to offend against discipline, disturb the silence, unsettle the work of the school.

What a pack of old men!

I'm taken there by Mademoiselle Balandreau. My mother's not feeling very well. Before I leave, they get my basket ready and off I go to shut myself away until eight o'clock, at which time Mademoiselle Balandreau returns to take me home. Sometimes I feel very downcast and I cry as I pour out my woes to her.

My father[2] is in charge of the first senior prep class, the one for math, rhetoric, and philosophy. The boys don't like him, they say he's a *bastard*.

He's got permission from the headmaster for me to stay in his classroom, and I sit beside his chair slaving away at my homework while he studies for his *agrégation*.[3]

Getting me to sit beside him was a mistake. The big boys aren't too unpleasant to me—they can see I'm shy, scared, and a hard worker—they don't say anything to hurt me, but I can hear all the things they say about my father, the way they refer to him; they make fun of his big nose, of his old overcoat. They make him seem ridiculous in my childish eyes, and I suffer without realizing it.

At such times he occasionally speaks to me roughly: "What on earth's the matter with you?" "What an idiot the boy looks!"

I've just heard a nasty remark about him. I'd been trying to stifle a big sigh and hold back a miserable tear.

During the evening prep class he often sends me to fetch a

book or take a message to one of the other supervisors who's tucked away on the far side of the courtyard, miles away. It's dark and windy, sometimes it means going through a long hall, up a gloomy staircase—it's quite a trip. Bats are hidden in corners to frighten me. I pretend not to be scared, but I don't feel really comfortable until I'm back in my father's classroom, where it's stifling.

Sometimes, when Mademoiselle Balandreau's late, I'm left all alone. My father has taken the other boys off to supper.

How slowly time seems to pass! Nothing but empty silence all around me, and if anyone does come, it's only the lamplighter who doesn't like my father either—I don't know why. An old man with a growth on his face, a cap made from the skin of an animal of some sort or other, and a gray jacket, the kind they wear in prisons: he smells of oil, never stops mumbling through his teeth, gives me an unfriendly look, roughly tugs my chair from under me without warning, plumps his lamp down on my exercise book, tosses my little overcoat onto the floor, shoves me aside like a dog, and goes off without a word. I don't say anything either, nor do I say anything to my father when he comes back. I've been taught never to "tell tales" and I never do and never shall during my whole time at school, which will lead to endless persecution at the hands of the masters.

In any case, I don't want my father to suffer just because I do and I conceal any ill treatment I receive so that he doesn't get into quarrels on my account. Although I'm still very young, I've got a sense of duty. I have the feeling of being the son of a convict—no, something even worse, the son of a prison warder in charge of convicts! And so I put up with the boorish conduct of the lamplighter.

I listen to the derisive remarks about my father and pretend not to hear them—not so easy for a boy just ten years old.

27

Some nights when they were late picking me up I got terribly hungry. The dining hall was sending out the delicious smell of grilled meat and from across the courtyard I could hear the clink of knives and forks.

How I cursed Mademoiselle Balandreau for not coming!

Later I discovered that she was being delayed on purpose: my mother insisted to my father that unless he was completely spineless, he could feed me his leftovers or else supply me with supper by asking for a little extra for his own.

If it was her, she'd have done it long ago. All he'd need to do would be to wrap it up in a bit of paper. If he liked, she'd provide him with a container.

My father had always resisted, poor man! The fear of being seen! How ridiculous he'd look if he was caught! How ashamed he'd be! Sometimes my mother tries to force his hand by leaving me starving at suppertime in the prep room. He refused to capitulate, he preferred to let me suffer a little—and he was right.

However, I do recall that one evening he slipped away from the dining hall and brought me a little breaded chop which he pulled out of an exercise book of prose translations where he'd hidden it: he looked so flustered and, when he left, so pleased and excited! I can still see the place where I was sitting and recall the color of the exercise book, and I've forgiven many wrongs my father committed against me later on in memory of that chop he sneaked for his son one evening in that school in Le Puy.

The headmaster is called Hennequin—sent to this godforsaken hole in disgrace.

He'd written a book called *Oscar's Holiday*.

It's given out as a prize and according to what I've heard and read about authors, I'm filled with immense respect and speechless with admiration for the author of *Oscar's*

Holiday, who has condescended to be a headmaster in our small town—my father's headmaster—and who raises his hat to my mother whenever he meets her in the street.

I devoured *Oscar's Holiday*.

I can still see the green paperboard binding, a mottled green which turned white when thumbed and which made your hands sticky. It had a white leather back, was printed on waxed paper, and was hard to open. Well, the pages of this inauspicious volume awaken in my memory an impression of crispness and freshness.

There's a fishing story that I've never forgotten.

There's a net glistening in the sun, drops of water trickling like pearls, the fish are wriggling in its meshes, two fishermen are up to their waists in the water, the river is shimmering...

Hennequin, this fired headmaster, who wrote in celebration of young Oscar, had succeeded in trawling his wide net for the length of a page and catching that river in one corner of a chapter.

The philosophy teacher—Monsieur Beliben: short, slight, with a pint-sized head, three wispy hairs, and a thready, vinegary voice.

He was very fond of proving the existence of God, but if anyone tried to interject a comment, even in support, he'd indicate that he objected to being interrupted; he needed the whole table, just like a game of patience.

He proved the existence of God with little bits of wood and a few beans.

"Here we place a bean, so! And there a match. Do you have a match, Madame Vingtras? And now I've set out man's vices here and his virtues there, I come to the PROPERTIES OF THE SOUL!"

Often at this stage people who weren't in the know looked

toward the door to see if someone was coming in. Or they looked at his pocket to see if he was going to pull something out. The properties of the soul! This was the upper crust, real high-quality stuff! My mother was flattered.

"Here they come!"

In spite of ourselves we still keep turning our heads to welcome these distinguished people, but Beliben took you by your overcoat button and rapped impatiently on the table. Hang it all! Did they or didn't they want to prove the existence of God?

"It's all the same to me, what about you?" my uncle would say to the man sitting beside him, who replied "Shush!" and craned his neck for a better view.

My uncle nonchalantly put his hands in his pockets and gazed into space.

But the teacher with his God was keen to have my uncle on his side and brought him down to earth by playing on his vanity and appealing to his professional pride.

"You're a joiner, Chadenas, and you know how, with the help of your calipers . . ."

We had to sit it out to the bitter end until finally the little man pushed back his chair, stretched out his hand, and pointed to one corner of the table: "That's God THERE."

We were all still watching, with everyone crowding around to see the beans together in one corner, with the matches, the bits of cork, and various other bits and pieces of rubbish that he'd used for his demonstration of the SUPREME BEING.

Apparently all the virtues and vices and *properties of the soul* had finished up, in-ev-i-ta-bly, in the last heap. Every bean was present and correct. Therefore GOD EXISTS. QED.

IV. THE SMALL TOWN

THE PANNESAC GATE.

It's a stone gate, and my father even claims that when you look at it you can get some idea of the appearance of a Roman monument.

At first that inspires me with a feeling of awe, then it bores me. I'm beginning to have had just about enough of Roman monuments.

But the street itself! It smells of seed and grain.

All along the walls the bundles of wheat have toppled over and collapsed like sleepy men. The air is full of fine flour dust and the cheerful din of markets. This is where bakers and the millers who bake bread come to pick up their supplies.

I have a great respect for bread.

One day when I'd thrown away a crust of bread, my father went and picked it up. He didn't speak to me roughly as he always does.

"You must never throw bread away, son," he said. "It's hard to earn. We haven't got all that much ourselves, but if we did have more than we need, we'd give it to the poor. One day you may not have enough yourself and you'll realize how much it's worth. Don't forget what I've just told you, son."

I've never forgotten.

This remark, which perhaps for the first time in my short life wasn't made in anger, but with dignity, sank into my consciousness, and ever since I've felt great respect for bread.

For me, harvests are something holy. I've never trampled on a sheaf of wheat to pick a poppy or a cornflower. I've never killed the bread sprouting on its stalk!

What he said about the poor impressed me too, and perhaps it's his simple words that have made me always respect the hungry and come to their defense.

"You'll realize how much it's worth!"

I've realized.

In the doorways of the side streets there are bakers' boys dressed in skirts like women, barelegged, wearing short blue tunics over their shoulders.

They have cheeks as white as flour and beards as golden as bread crusts.

They slip across the street for a quick drink and leave a white patch on the hand of any friend they happen to meet or on the shoulder of some man as they brush by.

The owners are standing behind the counter weighing the round loaves and they too are wearing coats that are whitish or the color of rye. In addition to the round loaves, there are cakes in the windows: brioches looking like plump noses or tarts like crumpled bits of tissue paper.

Beside the beans or seeds looking like fleshy green fruit or gleaming like pebbles in a river, the shopkeepers have wooden bowls containing lead pellets.

So that's what they put in a gun? Which kills hares and pierces birds to the heart? It was even said that the shot sometimes had the force of a bullet and could break a man's arm or jaw.

I dug my fingers into the shot just as earlier I'd dug my fist into the bags of seed, and I could feel it rolling and slipping around my joints like drops of water. I collected what had fallen out of the bowls and sacks, like holy relics.

In Pannesac they also sold fishing tackle.

Any garish or brightly tinted object, even if only the size of a pea or an orange, anything that made a strong cheerful patch of color, whatever it was, stamped itself on my eye—the eye of a sad little boy—and I can still see the shiny red floats and the lovely fishing lines shining like threads of yellow satin.

To have a line to cast into the cool rivers, to haul in a fish gleaming like a sheet of zinc foil in the sun and which would turn into gold in the butter!

A gudgeon, caught by me!

My whole imagination was carried away on its fins!

So I'd live on the produce of my fishing, just like the islanders I'd been reading about in the voyages of Captain Cook.

I'd also read that they made panes for the windows of their huts out of fish paste, and I could see the day when I'd be fitting out all the windows for my family. I was planning in my mind to scrape my every "bite," storing the residue of scales and crud in my big pocket.

I did in fact do this later on, but the fermentation at the bottom of my pocket produced unexpected results, and I became an object of disgust for my neighbors.

This shook my trust in travelers' tales. I was assailed by doubt.

At the end of Pannesac there was a grocer's that added to the gentle smells of the market a hot, smothered, pungent odor of salt cod, tallow, blue cheese, fat, and pepper.

The cod predominated, reminding me more than ever of the islanders, their huts, glue, and smoked seal.

Then I'd cast a final glance back at Pannesac. I was regularly almost run over near the stone gate.

I'd have to fling myself out of the way to let the big carts pass as they brought in all these supplies from the country, these gardens in baskets, these harvests in sacks. The carts looked like the festive carriages of an Italian masquerade, complete with their cast of white-faced, powdered performers, and Pierrots built like Hercules!

Right up at the top there's the Teachers Training College.[1]

The son of the principal sometimes comes to pick me up to play.

Behind the college there's a garden with a swing and a trapeze.

I look longingly at this trapeze and the swing; however, I'm forbidden to go on them.

My mother has asked the boy's parents to make sure I don't get on the swing or climb on the trapeze.

The principal's wife, Madame Haussard, isn't keen on having to keep an eye on me all the time and has made me promise to do as my mother has told me. I obey.

Madame Haussard is very fond of her son, as fond as my mother is of me; yet she lets him do what my mother has forbidden me to do!

And I see other boys, no older than me, using the swing too.

So they're going to break their backs?

No doubt they will; and I wonder to myself if parents who let their children play games like these just want them to get killed. Cowards and murderers! Monsters! Not daring to drown their little ones, they send them off to the swing and the trapeze!

Why should my mother have condemned me not to do what other children do?

Why deny me a pleasure?

Because I'm more fragile and breakable than my friends?

Have I really been glued back together like a salad bowl?
Is there some sort of mystery in my makeup?
Or perhaps my bottom's heavier than my top?
I can't weigh it separately to find out, that's for sure!

Meanwhile I nose around under this little piece of gymnastic equipment, looking at it and touching it as I jump up and down like a dog trying to reach a lump of sugar perched out of reach.

Yes, I'm longing to hang upside down!
Oh dear, my mother! My mother!
Why won't you let me hang upside down?
Just once!
And you can beat me afterward if you want to!

But it's this melancholy mood which itself helps to make the evenings I spend on the main square in front of the college all the lovelier when I go out there full of sadness at the sight of the trapeze and the swing in the garden vainly offering to take me into their arms!

The breeze ruffles the hair over my forehead and carries away my sulkiness and sorrows.

I don't say a word, sometimes sitting on a bench like a very old man, scratching the soil in front of me with a bit of branch or suddenly looking up to watch the fire dying away in the sky.

"You're not saying much," remarks the boy from the college. "What's on your mind?"

I'm not thinking of my mother nor of God nor of school . . . And then without warning I start leaping like an animal who's been tethered in a field and has suddenly broken free. I start to growl and I frisk about like a goat—to the amazement of my friend who watches me capering around, half expecting me to begin grazing on the grass.

I'm tempted to do it too.

V. MY CLOTHES

ONE DAY a man who was passing through on horseback caught sight of me in the distance and took me for one of the local attractions. He galloped up closer and was quite surprised to find that I was a human being. He dismounted and politely asked my mother if she'd be good enough to tell him the name and address of the tailor who'd made my clothes.

"I did," she said, blushing with pride.

The man got on his horse and was never seen again.

My mother often told me about this apparition, this man who'd gone out of his way to inquire who made my clothes.

I'm often dressed in black because "black is always in fashion," and when I'm wearing a coat—a tailcoat—and a top hat, I look like a stove.

However, as I wear out my clothes very quickly, they bought for me, in some country place, a fluffy yellow material to wrap me in. I look like the ambassador of Lapland. Foreigners raise their hats to me; academics eye me closely.

But the cloth my pants are made out of gets very stiff and dry, making me sore and even drawing blood.

What rotten luck! From now on I won't be able to live a normal life, I'll just have to shuffle around.

I'll be barred from all the usual children's pursuits—playing prisoner's base, running, jumping, getting into fights. I shamble around on my own, sneered at or pitied, just useless! And at the age of twelve, in the center of my hometown, segregated in these trousers, I'm doomed to suffer the secret anguish of an exile.

Madame Vingtras sometimes shows a touch of mischief.

During carnival, I'd been invited to a fancy party. My mother had dressed me up as a charcoal burner. Just as she was delivering me there, she was called away somewhere else but she took me as far as the door of Monsieur Puissegat's house where the dance was being held.

I didn't know my way, got lost in the garden, and gave a shout.

A maid came up and asked, "Are you the Choufloux boy who's come to help in the kitchen?"

I didn't dare say no and they put me to doing the dishes the whole night.

The next morning when my mother came to pick me up, I was just rinsing the last glasses. She was told that nobody had seen me: they'd searched everywhere.

I came into the room all ready to throw myself into my mother's arms, but at the sight of me the little girls started screaming, women fainted; the sudden appearance of this dwarf in the midst of all these pretty dresses seemed really weird to everybody.

My mother had great difficulty in recognizing me herself: I was beginning to think I was an orphan.

Yet I'd have only needed to take her into a corner and show a certain scarred and purple part of my anatomy for her to exclaim on the spot, "That's my son!" A lingering vestige of modesty held me back and I confined myself to pointing with my finger, and so made myself understood.

I was taken off—the way they bring down the curtain on some freak.

———

In three days, it's time for the presentation of the prizes.

My father, who shares the secrets of the gods, knows that I'll be getting some prizes, that his son will be called up on the platform and have a crown—much too large—placed on his head, that he won't be able to remove it without getting scratched, that he'll be kissed on both cheeks by some bigwig.

Madame Vingtras has been let in on the secret and she's meditating.

How will she dress this fruit of her womb, her child, her Jacques? He must shine, he must stand out—we may be poor but we don't lack taste.

"The first thing I must do is to make sure my son's well dressed."

She rummages around in the large wardrobe that contains her wedding dress, some umbrella covers, remnants of skirts, odd scraps of silk.

Finally she scratches herself on a garish piece of material, so filelike in quality that it scrapes your fingers when you touch it. When exposed to the light of day, it glints like a saucepan! A really lovely material inherited from my grandmother and which cost "a mint of money."

"Yes, my boy, a mint of money in the old days! I'm going to make you an overcoat out of that, Jacques, and do without myself, all for your sake!" And my mother looks at me delightedly out of the corner of her eye, nodding her head and smiling the smile of a victim relishing her sacrifice.

"I think I know someone who's spoiling you, young man." And she keeps on smiling and wagging her head, her eyes overflowing with affection.

"I'm mad! Never mind, we'll make a frock coat for Jacques out of that!"

Yesterday evening they tried the coat on me; my cars are

bleeding, my nails are ragged. The cloth is overpoweringly gaudy and excruciatingly prickly!

Good Lord deliver me from this garment!

The heavens turn a deaf ear to my prayers. The coat's ready . . .

No, Jacques, not quite ready yet. Your mother's proud of you, Jacques, she loves you and is determined to prove it to you.

Do you imagine that she's going to let you wear that coat before adding a decorative touch or two, a beauty spot, a pompom, a little something on the lapels, down the back, around the cuffs? You don't know your mother, Jacques!

And can't you see her playing, proudly yet discreetly, with some green fruit pits?

She even gives him a little tickle on the neck.

He doesn't laugh—he's scared of those fruit pits.

The fruit pits are buttons—bright green, a cheerful green, and shaped like olives—and they're going to be stitched in a long row, Polish style, yes, Polish style, Jacques!

So if, in later life, he said harsh things about the Poles, why be surprised . . . You see, the name of that nation was sewn, in his mind, to a terrible memory . . . the frock coat of the presentation of the prizes, the frock coat of the fruit pits, with the buttons as oval as olives—and pickle green.

Added to which they'd rigged me out in a top hat which I'd brushed the wrong way so that it towered threateningly over my head.

Some people took it for my hair and wondered what fury had seized me to make my hair stand up on end like that. "He must have seen the Devil," murmured the Blesseds, making the sign of the cross.

I had white trousers. My mother had bled herself white.

White trousers with stirrup straps!

White trousers which looked like a device for a clubfoot and which stretched my pants leg to the splitting point.

It had been raining and as we had to hurry, I had mud splashes up to my calves. My white trousers, wet through, were sticking to my thighs.

"MY SON," announced my mother triumphantly, pushing me forward when we arrived at the entrance.

The man checking the invitations nearly fell over, peered at me for a while under my hat, investigated my frock coat, and threw his hands in the air.

I went into the hall.

I'd taken off my hat by catching hold of the nap; I was now recognizable—it really was me. No further mistake was possible. I could never subsequently claim an alibi.

But while I was climbing over a bench to join my class, one of my stirrup straps snapped and my trouser leg shot up like a catapult, exposing my shin. I now looked as if I was in my long johns. Outraged at my shamelessness, the ladies took refuge behind their fans.

From the heights of the dais, they've observed a certain unrest at the back of the hall.

The bigwigs are exchanging whispers, the general stands up to look: they want to discover the cause of the mystery.

Just at that moment, "Pull your trousers down, Jacques!" my mother exclaims in a voice that explodes like a gunshot in the silence, drilling me through and through.

From the platform all eyes focus on me.

An end must be made to this scandal! One of the officers, more decisive than the rest, barks an order: "Remove that boy with the pickles!"[1]

———

The order is executed discreetly. They lug me out from under the bench where I'd taken refuge in desperation, and the headmaster's wife, who happens to be there, leads me from the hall with my mother and into the linen room where they undress me.

My mother contemplates me more in sorrow than in anger.

"You're not made to wear nice clothes, my poor boy!"

She says this as if I've got something wrong with me, like a doctor giving up a patient as a hopeless case.

I let them do all they want to me. They rig me out in the castoffs of a small boy, and this small boy is still not small enough because his clothes hang around me like a tent in which I'm dancing. I'm taken back to the hall; people are beginning to think that it's all a practical joke.

A moment ago I looked like a leopard; now I look like an old man. They smell a rat.

In some parts of the hall, the rumor is spreading that I'm the son of the magician who has just arrived in town—that he wants to attract publicity with some new stunt. This version gains ground, but fortunately there are people who know me, and know my mother. They have to accept the facts and the rumors die down of their own accord. Finally, I'm forgotten.

I listen to the speeches in silence; I'm busy picking my nose, which is not easy when your sleeves are so long.

As a result of this rumpus, the presentation of the prizes has been moved into a dormitory. They've taken out the beds, heaping them up, along with all the other accessories, in an adjacent room. You can see into this room through a glass door that should have had a curtain but didn't. You could make out piles of chamber pots, which had been in use during the term but which had been removed from under the beds for the holidays: they rose up in a white pyramid.

This was one of the most cheerful corners: a mischievous ray of sun had chosen the belly of one of the chamber pots to have a little fun playing with its own reflection, flirting with it, dancing around, having the time of its life, the cheeky thing!

In front of this room was the podium where the staff of this dreadful dump—I mean the school—had lined up. Monsignor in the middle, the prefect on his left, the general on his right, silver-braided, purple-hued, white-crested, with a golden breastplate like the riders in the Bouthor Circus. What a pity there wasn't a camel.

I did think I saw an elephant, but it was a high official who had head, chest, belly, and feet the color of an elephant—a customs officer by profession or else a captain in the police, I can't quite recall which. He was as round as a barrel and puffing and blowing like a dolphin: he had many characteristics of a performing seal.

It was he who placed on my head the crown for my prize—for Bible History! He grunted, "Well done, lad!" I half expected him to bark "Papa" and dive back into his tub.

VI. HOLIDAYS

During the holidays I loved spending time with the Soubeyrous and at Farreyrolles.

Monsieur Soubeyrou is a local market gardener.

My father gives private lessons three times a week to his son, and as the boy's rather sickly and doesn't go out much, I am occasionally invited over to keep him company. I take the most roundabout way.

Free at last!

I haven't been given any errands, with orders to come straight back—and without breaking anything. Nobody's come along to keep an eye on me, telling me not to linger as I go down the street or slide down the guardrail.

No, for one afternoon my time is all my own. ONE WHOLE AFTERNOON!

"Would you like to go to Monsieur Soubeyrou's?" asks my mother.

"Yes, Ma."

But I don't seem too keen and pull a bit of a face.

That's how it is. If I answer too quickly, showing that I enjoy going there, my mother is capable of stopping me from going.

If anything's really unpleasant, if it makes me want to cry, my mother immediately insists I do it.

"Children must be taught not to be willful and to accept everything. Ah, all those spoiled children! It's very bad of parents to let them satisfy their every little whim."

I say, "Yes, Mother," in a way that makes her think I mean "No," and don't show any sign of pleasure as they dress me up and lecture me on all the things I am not supposed to do.

I walk down into the town.

I don't stop at the Martouret because my mother can still see me from the windows of our apartment, perched right on the top floor of the tallest house in town.

In the market square I pretend to be hurrying along like a good boy, but in the Rue Porte-Aiguière I take cover behind the first fat man who passes and slip into the courtyard of the White Horse.

From this courtyard I can see sideways up the street and feast my eyes on the front window of the saddler where there are lots of tassels and little bells, blue pompoms, long whips the color of cigars, and harnesses gleaming like gold.

I lie low long enough to discover whether my mother is still on the lookout at the window; then, as soon as I feel safe, I come out of the courtyard of the White Horse and start looking into the shop windows at my leisure.

There's a tinsmith busily beating some lovely red copper on which his hammer leaves a mark like the rump of a dappled gray mare, making the windowpanes go *zing-zang* at every stroke. The sound makes me blink and my skin crawl.

Then there's Arnaud the cobbler, with his sign, a large green boot, arched and spurred, with a gold tassel. In the window there's a display of ankleboots in blue satin and pink silk or plum-colored with bows looking like bunches of live flowers.

Beside them there are slippers looking like Christmas clogs.[1]

But the gardener's son is expecting me.

I tear myself away from the smell of boot polish and the sheen of patent leather.

I go into the Breuil . . .

Here there's a bootblack, always busy, nicknamed Moustache.

My dream is that, one day, I'll get my shoes cleaned by Moustache. That I'll go up to him, just like a grown-up, put my foot out—without trembling, if I can— and appear accustomed to such a luxury, nonchalantly pull some money out of my pocket and, like the gentlemen who toss him a couple of sous, say, *Have a drink on me, Moustache!*

I'm never going to succeed, but I'm practicing.

Have a drink on me, Moustache!

I've tried every tone of voice; I've listened to myself very carefully—worked at it in front of the mirror, made the gesture.

Have a drink!

No, I can't manage it!

But every time I go past Moustache, I stop and look at him. I prepare for the ordeal, circle around his box of brushes and polish. Once he even called out to me, "Shine your boots, boss?"

I nearly passed out.

I didn't have two sous—I never managed to have two at the same time until later on, in another town—so I had to shake my head and make a sign, with a pale smile like a woman who's trying to tell you: "I'm forbidden to love!"

———

45

At the end of the Breuil there's the tannery with its blocks of peat, its skins that are drying, its sharp smell.

I adore the smell that it gives off, mustardy and green—if you can say green– like the pieces of leather with their gamy odor when they're wet or sweating in the sun as they dry out.

Later, whenever I came back to Le Puy, I could detect and smell the Breuil tannery miles away. And each time I came anywhere within four miles of one of these factories, I'd sniff and turn my nose gratefully toward it.

I can't remember which way I went or how I got there, how the town came to an end.

I recall only that I found myself going along a ditch that had a nasty smell and then walking through a lot of grass and plants that didn't smell very nice either.

I was arriving in market-garden country. How ugly market gardens are!

I loved green meadows, sparkling water, verdant hedgerows as much as I disliked that countryside of gardens with its stunted trees and colorless plants growing, like an old man's beard, in sandy or muddy land around the fringes of towns.

A few dirty-yellow, dried-up, mangy leaves drooping, the color of the ears of someone suffering from consumption.

Everything, everywhere, had been degraded, and all the time you kept disturbing swarms of insects feasting on the carcass of a dead dog.

Not a trace of shade!

Melons looking like white-hot cannonballs, red and purple cabbages—you'd think they were suffering from apoplexy—the smell of leeks and onions!

I've arrived at Monsieur Soubeyrou's.

I'm with the sick little boy in the greenhouse.

He's very pale, with a big smile and long teeth; the whites of his eyes are spotted yellow. He shows me lots of books which they've bought for him so that he doesn't become too bored.

Aesop's Fables with color prints. I can still remember one of those prints which represented Boreas, the north wind, the Sun, and a traveler.

The traveler has chocolate-colored sweat pouring down his forehead and an enormous overcoat the color of wine dregs.

"Would you like to amuse yourself helping me water the cabbages?" asked his father. He's holding a watering can in each hand and he's been going around barefooted and bare-legged, with his trouser legs turned up ever since he's been awake.

His calves are hairy and suntanned, and look like grilled pig's feet; his shirt is soaked through and drops of water are trickling down his hairy chest.

No, I don't want to amuse myself helping him water his cabbages!

I'd hate to deprive Monsieur Soubeyrou of any pleasure and I answer his question with a fib.

"I fell over and hurt my back yesterday."

I'm fond of cabbage—when it's cooked!

I haven't escaped from my mother's washtub and my father's dirty dishes to come and draw water in other people's houses!

I draw quite enough water during the week, and I smell of onions quite enough for my taste.

No, Monsieur Soubeyrou, I'm not going to follow you over to the well; I won't pump the water from the well; I won't undertake the honest toil of the gardener.

I'm a beastly, vicious little boy! So what?

But I refuse to draw water!

IN FRONT OF THE STAGECOACH TERMINUS

On the way back, I go the long way around and pass by the Stagecoach Café.

It has a sign with each letter in the shape of a person: an old woman, a peasant, a soldier, a priest, a monkey.

They're painted the color of tobacco juice, on a gray background, and they tell a story, starting with the S of Stagecoach and ending with the É of Café.

I've never had time to work it out.

Time to go home.

In addition, while I was looking at the sign and exercising my curiosity on the old woman's petticoat, the peasant's large collar, the soldier's knapsack, the priest's neck bands, the monkey's tail, all around me horses were being hitched, carriages were being cleaned, the grooms, the postilions, and the drivers were going about their business, wielding their brushes, their whips, their horns.

Travelers were arriving to find their seats, to try to get one in a corner.

Sometimes when I was there, a coach arrived: it drove across the Breuil creating a terrible din, raising clouds of dust, splashing up stars of mud.

It was besieged by a gang of porters squabbling over the baggage, and its yellow sides disgorged benumbed passengers stretching their legs in the cobblestone street.

They would fall into the welcoming arms of a member of their family or a friend, they shook hands, exchanged hugs: an endless stream of "Good-bye" and "See you soon!"

Some had become acquainted in the course of the journey; men were saying a reluctant farewell to ladies who replied, "Where shall I have the pleasure of meeting you again?"

"Perhaps we'll see each other again. Ah, here comes my mother."

"Here's my husband."

"I can see my brother with his wife."

There were Englishmen who weren't uttering a word and traveling salesmen talking nineteen to the dozen.

They were all milling around, slipping away like the insects I uncovered when I lifted a rock at the edge of a field.

I saw some, however, who stayed where they were, scanning the Breuil and the boulevard, waiting for someone who didn't come.

Some of them were swearing, others were crying.

I remember one young woman who had a long, rather sensitive face.

She waited quite a long time.

When I left, she was still waiting. It wasn't for her husband because she was standing beside a small trunk on which you could read the word: MADEMOISELLE.

A few days later I met her in front of the post office; the flowers on her hat were faded, her black dress of merino wool had shiny reddish spots, the tips of her gloves had been rubbed white. She was inquiring if a letter had come for her addressed to general delivery.

"I've already told you there weren't any."

"That's the last post?"

"Yes."

She thanked them, in spite of their brusqueness, then gave a sigh and went and sat down on a bench in front of the Horseshoe. She stayed there until she was forced to leave by the gazes and smiles of some passing officers.

A few days later, we were told that the body of a drowned woman had been found at the edge of the water. I went to see and recognized the young woman with the pale face.

———

I'm going to pay a visit to my aunts in Farreyrolles.

I often arrive as they're sitting down to eat.

It's a large table with a drawer at each end and big benches along the sides.

In these drawers there's a jumble of knives, old onions, bits of bread. Around the edges of the crusts there are blue spots, like verdigris on old one-sou coins.

The family and the servants plump down on the benches.

Eating proceeds between prayers.

Uncle Jean says grace.

They all stand up, bareheaded, and say "Amen!" as they sit down again.

As a boy, the word I heard most often was *Amen!*

Amen! And the wooden spoons start clattering; it's a dull, stupid sound.

Now come great slicings of bread, like sweeps of a reaping hook. The knives have horn handles, with little circular yellow rivets; they look like the golden eyes of frogs.

They slobber as they eat, opening their mouths from side to side. They blow their noses with their fingers and wipe them on their sleeves.

They dig each other in the ribs with their elbows—it's their way of tickling.

They laugh like big babies. When they guffaw, they bray like donkeys or bellow like bulls.

Now they've finished—they put the frog-eyed knives back in their large pockets that reach down to their knees, wipe their mouths with the backs of their hands, brush off their lips, and drag their large legs from under the table.

If the sun's shining, they'll go off to stroll around the yard; if it's wet, they have a chat under the stable porch, barely lifting their clogs, which resemble tree stumps into which they've inserted their feet.

How fond I am of them, with their big, wide-brimmed hats and long leather aprons! They've got soil on their hands, in their beards, and even in the hair on their chests; their skin's like the bark of a tree and their veins are like tree roots.

Sometimes when their leather aprons have slipped down, the wind blows their shirts open and below the triangle of tanned skin that ends in a point on their solar plexus you can see white flesh as soft as the back of a shorn ewe or a piglet.

I go up to them and touch them, just as you feel a farm animal. They look on me as an exotic luxury creature—I come from a town!—some of them compare me to a squirrel, but most of them compare me to a monkey.

That doesn't put me off, and I go out with them into the fields and borrow their goad to prick the cattle.

I walk knee-deep in the furrows; I roll in the grass when they're harvesting the hay; I cheep like the quails do as they fly away; I turn somersaults like the chicks falling out of their nests when the plow comes along.

Oh, what wonderful times I've had in the meadows on the banks of a brook fringed with yellow flowers trailing down into the water, with white pebbles lying on its bed, and which swirled away the bunches of leaves and the golden branches of elder that I threw into the current.

My mother doesn't like me standing there openmouthed, not saying a word, staring at the water flowing by.

She's quite right; I'm wasting my time.

"Instead of taking your Latin grammar along with you to prepare your lessons!"

Then pretending to be unhappy and concerned: "How can you possibly stand there with green stains all over and covered in mud . . . And to think we've bought you a new pair of shoes for them to be treated like that! Come on, back to the house with you and you're not to go out this evening!"

I know that my shoes are being ruined in the fields and that I ought to be wearing clogs, but my mother doesn't want that! My mother is having me educated and doesn't want me to be country-bred like her!

She wants her Jacques to be a *gentleman*.

Has she made him a frock coat adorned with olives, bought him a stovepipe hat, given him trousers with stirrup straps for him to go back to the dunghill, return to the cowshed, wear clogs?

Yes, I'd sooner have clogs. What's more, I like the smell of Florimond the plowman better than that of my teacher, Monsieur Sother. I'd sooner make shocks of hay than read my grammar, and lurk around the cowshed than hang out in the classroom.

All I want is to bind sheaves of corn, pick up stones, tie bundles of firewood, carry faggots.

Perhaps I was intended to be a servant!

How dreadful! Yes, I was born to be a servant! I can see it! I can feel it!

Heavens above! At least my mother must never learn about that!

I'd happily be Pierrouni the little cowherd and go off munching a green apple and holding a branch in my hand, to take the cattle off to pasture next to the brambleberries close to the orchard.

Among the bushes there are wild red roses and, high up, a small tuft like a beard which is a nest. There are ladybirds like tiny flying green beans and green flies among the flowers looking as if they're drunk.

They let Pierrouni go around with his shirt wide open, bare-chested, when he's hot. He lets his hair blow whenever he feels like it.

They don't keep saying to him all the time, "Stop fidgeting! What on earth have you done to your tie? Sit up straight—are you a hunchback?" Yes, he's a hunchback! "Button up your waistcoat! Pull your trousers up! What have you done to the olive? That olive on the left, the greenest one! Oh dear, that child will be the death of me!"

But the grown-up farmhands are also happier than my father!

They don't have to wear waistcoats buttoned right up to hide a shirt they've been wearing three days in a row! They're not afraid of Uncle Jean in the way my father is afraid of the headmaster; they don't need to hide in order to have a laugh or a glass of wine; when they've got the money, they sing for all they're worth, out loud in the fields where they're working; on Sundays they can be as rowdy as they like in the local pub.

On the seat of their breeches they wear a patch which looks like a plaster: it's green and yellow—but that's the color of earth, of leaves, of branches, the color of cabbages.

My father, who isn't a servant, trembles with anxiety that is painful to watch as he ekes out his black twill trousers which have already eaten up ten skeins of black darning thread and been the death of a dozen darning needles—but his pants remain pockmarked, flimsy, and limp!

If he fails to bow to this one or that one (there are hats to be raised to all and sundry, to the headmaster, the deputy headmaster etc., etc.), if he doesn't raise his hat and bob and bow to them (something which the seat of his trousers can do only reluctantly), then he'll be invited to call on the headmaster!

And he'll be required to offer an explanation, not like a farmhand—oh no!—but like a schoolteacher. He'll be forced to apologize.

People talk about him, laugh at him, the boys make fun of him and so do his colleagues. He's given his wages (my

53

mother calls them "his emoluments"), and he's sent off in disgrace to get his trousers better mended, with his wife, who's still got a horror of peasants, and his son, who still likes them.

I once had a fight with young Viltare, the son of the third-form teacher.

What a to-do that was!

They summoned my father and my mother to appear; the headmaster's wife stuck her oar in; Madame Viltare had had to be placated; she was shouting, "If mere supervisors' sons can now go about murdering the sons of senior teachers!"

Young Viltare had thrown ink on my pants and stuffed some asphalt down my neck. I didn't murder him, but I did punch him and trip him up . . . he fell over and bumped his head.

They brought the bump along to show the headmaster (who couldn't have cared less and didn't give a damn about either Monsieur Viltare or Monsieur Vingtras but who has to "ensure good order and discipline in the hierarchy"—I hear that phrase all the time). He sent for me and I had to apologize to Monsieur Viltare, Madame Viltare, shake hands with young Viltare, and then go home to get beaten.

My mother told me to be there at a quarter to five.

It's not like that at Farreyrolles.

The other day I got into a scrap with the little swineherd. We rolled over and over in the grass, tore each other's hair out, and kept bashing at each other. He gave me a black eye, and I smacked him on the ear and made it go numb. Then we got up and started going after each other all over again!

And then?

And then—we smoothed down our tousled hair, he by

putting on his hat, me by putting on my cap, and we were made to shake hands. All that evening everybody kept laughing about it—between first and second grace, in front of the soup tureen—and instead of hiding from my uncle, I showed him that I'd got blood on my hanky.

It's the day of the *Crowning of the Queen*.

That's the name they use for the village festival, when they elect a king and a queen.

They arrive covered in ribbons: ribbons on the king's hat, ribbons on the queen's hat.

They're both on horseback and followed by the good-looking local boys, farmers' sons who've brought some money in their pockets to buy presents for the girls.

They fire off guns, they cheer! They dance around in front of the municipal offices, which look as if they've hung out a green flag: it's the branch of a large tree.

The local gendarmes are in full dress uniform, with their rifles slung crosswise, and my uncle tells me that they've filled their cartridge pouches. They look pale and not one of them is certain that they won't end up that night with a cracked skull or broken ribs.

One of them is the most hated man in the district, and he'd certainly never come back alive if he was on his own on a path and met the son of the poacher Souliot or of old Ma Maichet who was sent to prison for having bitten and clawed the police when they came to arrest her for having picked up scraps of dead wood.

After church, we sit down to eat.

The poorest person has his liter of wine and his bowl of sweetened rice, even Thin Jean who lives in that wretched shanty over there.

There are bits of fat pork—and white bread!

The glasses are filled to the brim and when they run out of glasses, they take a bowl and drink the wine like milk—it's from the Vivarais and it foams as we draw it from its big barrel over there, next door to the cows.

Veins are swelling, buttons bursting!

We're all stuffing ourselves, masters and farmhands, the farmer's wife and her servants, the head farmhand and the young swineherd, Uncle Jean and Florimond the plowman, Pierrouni the cowherd, Jeanneton the milkmaid, and all the female cousins who've arranged their largest hats and put on enormous green belts.

After the meal, there's dancing on the lawn or in the barn.

Look out, girls!

The boys chase them, romp with them in the hay, or forcibly sit down beside them on the trunk of the dead oak in front of the farmhouse which is used as a bench.

The girls always raise their elbows just in time to be kissed full on their cheeks.

I dance the bourrée too, and give as many kisses as I can!

There's a sound of galloping horses! It's the gendarmes riding by . . .

They're on their way to Destougnal's pub at the far end of the village; the Sansac boys have come over and there's been a brawl.

In the pub people are killing each other.

Come on, men! Farreyrolles to the rescue!

You're jumping over ditches, bending down as you go to pick up stones, breaking off knotted branches from the bushes as you leap over them. I can even see someone carrying an old gun! The shouting has stopped, they're pale and out of breath.

There's the sound of breaking bottles, screams of pain— this way! this way!—almost like sobs.

It's hairy Bugnon calling out!

They've launched themselves on that pub like flies on a dunghill, just like the bull I once saw hurling himself on a red apron one evening in a meadow.

Red! There's a lot of it on the windows of that pub and on the mouths of the peasants.

Is it Vivarais wine or Farreyrolles blood!

My brain is on fire because I've got Farreyrolles blood in my childish veins too!

I want to join in the fray with the others.

I feel someone seize my coattails and hold me back, making me spin around and fall into my aunt's arms. She hadn't stopped her sons from going to Destougnal's pub, but she doesn't want her young nephew to take part in this slaughter!

If I can throw a stone at the police from behind a tree, I'm definitely going to! How I love this life of plowing, crowning the queen, and fighting!

VII. THE JOYS OF FAMILY LIFE

M Y FATHER'S colleagues and some of the boys' parents call
on us to bring me a few small New Year's gifts.

"Say thank you, Jacques. Don't stand there like an idiot."

When the visitors have left, I enjoy taking the toy or the
sweets, the jack-in-the-box or the bag of sugared almonds. I
beat the drum, I blow the trumpet, I play an instrument
which you hold between your teeth and which sets them on
edge—it's enough to drive you mad!

However my mother doesn't want me to go mad! She
takes the trumpet and the drum away from me. I fall back
on the sweets and start licking them. However my mother
doesn't want me to show such sycophantic behavior. "You
start by licking those round sweets and you end up licking
someone's—" She breaks off and looks at my father to see if
he thinks the same and whether he knows what she's talking
about—and he does indeed lean forward to indicate that he
understands.

So I've been left with nothing to whistle into, to drum on,
or to set my teeth on edge, and they've only let me have the
tiniest little lick of the delicious sweets, and then just with
the tip of my tongue! Eugénie and Louise Rayau were there

and were laughing and blushing a little at the same time. Why was that?

So no more thick blue paint that sticks to your fingers and makes them smell nice, no more taste of white wood from the trumpet!

They've snatched it all away from me and locked up every one of my New Year's gifts!

"Ma, please let me play with them just for today! I'll go outside in the yard, you won't hear a sound! Just today, Ma, till this evening and I'll be such a good boy tomorrow!"

"I hope you will be, Jacques, because if you're not, you'll get a beating. Imagine giving such pretty things to this horrible boy for him to ruin!"

Those bright little spots, those cheerful patches of color, those sounds of toys, those penny trumpets, those sweets wrapped in lace corsets, those sugared almonds looking like drunkards' noses, those crude hues and delicate flavors, that soldier who oozes, that sugar which melts, those delights for greedy eyes, those tasty tidbits for the tongue, those smells of glue, those scents of vanilla, that debauchery of the nose, that bold brassy blare striking the eardrum, that whiff of madness, that little surge of hot blood—how wonderful it all is, once a year! What a pity my mother's not deaf!

What hurts me most is that the others are enjoying themselves so much. A glimpse through the window shows me that our neighbors in the house opposite have got drums that have split, horses that have lost a leg, broken Punchinellos, and all of them are licking their fingers. They've been allowed to break their toys and devour their sweets.

And what a dreadful noise they're making!

I start to cry.

That's because just looking at toys doesn't mean a thing to

me if I haven't got the right to do what I like with them, to unstitch them, break them, blow into them, and stamp on them if the urge takes me.

I like them only if they belong to me and I don't like them if they belong to my mother. I'm attracted to them because they make loud noises and grate on the ear; if they're put on the table like a death's head, I don't want them. I've got no interest in sweets if I'm allowed to have just one, like getting a good grade for being a good boy. I like them when I've got too many of them.

"You've got a screw loose, boy," said my mother when I told her this, but all the same, she did give me a sugared almond.

"Here you are, eat it with a bit of bread."

At school, we've been told about philosophers who can sum up a moral in a word. My mother has been blessed with this gift, and in a flash of inspiration, with just a passing remark, she can remind me of a law to govern a well-conducted life and a well-ordered mind.

"Eat it with a bit of bread!"

Which means: Silly little boy, you were going to be stupid enough to crunch and gobble down that sugared almond just like that! Have you forgotten that you're poor? Tell me what good that would have done you! Instead, you're turning it into wholesome nourishment, making it part of a proper meal! You'll be eating it with *bread*!

I'd sooner have bread by itself.

SAINT ANTHONY'S DAY

Next Sunday is my father's name day.

My mother's been drumming this into my head sixty times over for the last two weeks.

It's your father's saint's day!

She's repeating it in a slightly irritated voice.

Apparently I don't seem to be sufficiently moved.

"Your father's called Antoine."

I know that, and I don't feel particularly thrilled by the thought. It's not a mysterious and gripping revelation: His name is Antoine, so what?

I'm a bad son, no doubt.

If I was good-hearted and really liked my father, what she's telling me would make a greater impression. I rack my brains, I beat my breast, I take stock of myself, I scratch my head, but I don't feel any difference in myself at all. I can recognize myself in the mirror, I'm still as ugly and as grubby as before. Yet on Sunday, it's his name day.

"Have you learned how to offer him your best wishes?"

I figure I'm a little too old to have to learn how to offer my best wishes to anybody. I don't know how I'll dare to go into his room, what I'll say, whether I have to laugh or to cry, whether I'm supposed to fling myself on my father's beard and stick my nose—properly wiped, of course!—into it and rub it; whether it will be the act of a dutiful son to prolong the gesture and leave it there for a couple of seconds or to remove it immediately and exit backward, with signs of emotion, mumbling, "What a special day!" And at that point, I'll start again.

"Yes, dear Father."

I'm trembling at the prospect! I'm afraid of looking stupid.

No, I'm afraid they'll guess that I wished it wasn't his name day.

My father's name day!

———

I get even more worried when my mother announces that I ought to present him with a pot of flowers.

That'll be so difficult!

But my mother knows how to express my emotion and joy at having to congratulate my father on being Antoine!

We begin rehearsing.

As a start, I mess up three sheets of special greeting paper; I stick out my tongue, wiggle it around, and curl it as I write in capital letters—it's hopeless: I block up my O's, I clog up the tails of my G's with ink, and make a smudge every time on the word "gladness." My reward is a series of clips around the ear. Oh dear, my father's name day is proving very painful!

In the end I manage to produce a few sentences framed between borderlines, golden, purple—and borne by doves. Thanks to the pauses I've made after each syllable in order to add flourishes, the words are lurching around like drunks!

My mother gives up and decides that there's no point ruining yourself by buying reams of paper. I sign at the bottom—another blot, another clip around the ear. It's finished.

It remains to work out the ceremony.

"The letter like this, the flowerpot like that, you go forward . . ."

I walk forward and break the two vases representing the flowerpot—that's four more slaps, two per vase.

At last the wonderful day arrives: my nights are spent dreaming that I'm walking barefoot on bits of broken pottery and being impaled on rolls of ornamental "greeting paper"— this is extremely painful!

Buying the pot of flowers creates tremendous confusion in the market.

My mother picks them up and sniffs them, as if they're game; she does this to a good hundred before making up her mind and the florists begin to get angry—she's disturbing their displays, upsetting their classifications, jumbling up the different "families"; a botanist would have no idea where to look!

People are complaining, calling her rude names—and even her son as well, whom they're not afraid of calling "runt," "little squirt" . . . It's time to make ourselves scarce.

At the end of the marketplace, my mother stops and says, "Jacques, go back and ask the fat man—you know, the one at the end—if he's willing to let you have that geranium for eleven sous."

So I'm obliged to return to the fray and tackle the fat man, who is, in fact, the very man who called me a little squirt.

I've got goose bumps, but I still go, looking as if I'm trying to find a pin on the ground, walking with my head down, my thighs pressed tightly together, like a rusty spring that doesn't open up freely. I hold my eleven sous.

The fat man takes pity on me and lets me have the geranium without making too much fun of me. The others aren't too unkind either, and I make my way back to my mother with the pot of flowers which is the emblem of our delight . . .

> *This flower please accept*
> *For from my heart it leapt!*

FRIDAY NIGHT

Friday evening, full dress rehearsal, wrapped in shadow and mystery.

My father—Antoine—is not supposed to know anything about what's happening. He knows everything: last night he even knocked over the geranium, which had been badly hidden, and I saw him surreptitiously pick it up and furtively spruce up its leaves.

He nearly stepped on the stiff sealed letter of felicitations and made a crease that is still there. Yet I'd hidden it in the bedside table.

He knows everything, but with childlike naïveté and patriarchal kindness, he's pretending to know absolutely nothing. It has to come as a surprise.

On the morning of the solemn day, in I go: he's in bed.

"What? It's really my name day?"

With a smile, he turns a conjugal eye toward my mother.

"So old already! Come here and let me give you a kiss!"

He kisses my mother, who's holding my hand, like Cornelia leading the Gracchi,[1] like Marie-Antoinette trailing along with her son. She lets go of me to fall into her husband's arms.

Now it's my turn. I was expecting to offer my best wishes first and not be kissed until after handing over the flowerpot. Apparently, kisses come first.

I step forward.

I'm holding both the eleven sous' worth of geranium and the rolled-up greeting letter, and this makes it awkward climbing onto the bed.

My father helps me up, he finds me rather heavy; I've got one leg on the bed—and I slip. My father catches me, he's obliged to grip me by the seat of my trousers and I twist slightly.

It's not my face that he can see nor can I see his. What a situation!

I can feel the geranium escaping my grip; it does escape and the potting soil spills all over the bed. The blanket had been partly lifted.

They kick me out—literally—and I'm not given the chance to savor the pure joy of kissing my father on his name day and being kissed by him in return; but I don't have to read out my greetings. It's been heard, bungled, and now it's all over. There's a little manure in the bed.

———

My mother's name day doesn't arouse the same emotions in me: it's more straightforward.

Many years ago she declared emphatically that she didn't want any expense to be incurred on her account. Twenty sous are twenty sous and that's one whole franc. For the price of a pot of flowers you can buy a sausage. And don't forget the price of a sheet of *greeting* paper! Why have such unnecessary expense! You'll say that it's nothing? It's all right for people who aren't in charge to say that but she, who is in charge, who does all the cooking and runs the whole show, she knows that it definitely is something. Add four sous to a franc and there's no way of making that come to less than twenty-four sous!

Not that I ever dreamed of contradicting her—in fact, I have other things on my mind (I have a pain in my stomach)—and she's looking at me while she's speaking, and she's speaking energetically, extremely energetically.

And when you don't take care of plants, they die.

She seems to be saying: It's no good beating plants!

The great treat being offered by my mother is Midnight Mass, because it's free.

Midnight Mass!

Snow on the roofs and along the tops of the walls.

It's melted where people have walked on it, and we're squelching along in the mud.

It's sad up there and dirty down below!

The pork butchers are packed with people.

People are ordering black pudding to eat tonight; and the other evening our grocer killed a pig especially for the occasion.

My memories of Christmas are dominated by the robust, coarse smell of cured meats.

Everywhere I can see a devilish little pig's tail, even in church.

The waxed cord at the end of the lamplighter's pole, the pink ribbon used as bookmark, and even the solitary, colorless lock of hair corkscrewing down beside a curate's purple ear. Even the flames of the candles, the smoke twirling up through the holes of the censers, seem to be just so many pig's tails which I'm longing to pull, pinch, or undo; which in my imagination I screw on to the backside of a fat, grunting pink piglet, and which makes me forget Christ's Resurrection, the Good Lord, Father, Son, Virgin and Company.

I can sniff a salty smell, a seaside smell, and in my mind I scratch the yellow wax to turn it into bread crumbs or mustard!

I leave my mother to go off with the neighbors to the grocer's, which is next door to us.

Our grocer's customers are a godless bunch.

They're standing at the counter digging into sausage and drinking a bottle of white wine.

I've had a drop, and the prickle of the wine and the saltiness of the meat have lifted my spirits.

Their conversation is as spicy as everything else.

I don't understand one word of it but I can see that they're saying rude things about Heaven and the Church, and that in spite of this they're full of good cheer and enjoy healthy appetites.

"One more slice, a piece of garlic *host*! And don't stop pouring, Madame Patin! We'll all be meeting again in hell, won't we? All pretty women end up there . . . Don't you think Saint Joseph was a cuckold?"

VIII. THE HORSESHOE

THE HORSESHOE...

I'm going there with my cousin Henriette.

She's going there to meet the local saddler Pierre André. Like her, he comes from Farreyrolles, and she has news for him from his family, private news that I'm not supposed to hear. They go off by themselves to exchange it, and she whispers into his ear.

I can see him over there, leaning forward; their cheeks are touching.

When Henriette comes back, she's pensive and doesn't say anything.

There's also the Aiguille Promenade, bordered with tall poplars. From a distance they make a sound like a fountain.

It's autumn; they're dropping their golden leaves; their stems are still alive and their skin is as tender as a pear's.

I enjoy kicking through these piles of leaves.

Farther on, lofty chestnut trees with their chestnuts lying on the ground.

I fill my pockets with them to take home and thread them on a string like a rosary, though I wasn't thinking of the Good Lord while I was doing it!

I'm imagining that I'm making holes in kidneys, those lovely fresh, purple kidneys that I glimpse in the butcher shops.

———

What I like is the sun filtering through the branches and casting bright patches of light that spread out like yellow spots on a carpet, and birds who have legs like wire springs and heads that are never still—and above all, I love this cool air and this silence!

The only sound to be heard is the bell of Saint Mary's convent and the tinkling of harness bells, down there on the white road.

"Listen, Mademoiselle Balandreau, you can't hear anything but me . . ."

And I let out a yell or throw a stone high in the air, so that it fills the whole horizon before it falls back down to earth.

It's like getting a punch in the chest!

Sometimes a lady and gentleman sit down on a bench in the distance and whisper to each other.

Mademoiselle Balandreau takes me away, but I look back.

How they're kissing each other!

THE MARKETPLACE

My aunts go there on Saturdays to sell cheese, chickens, and butter.

I go and visit them there, and each time it's a real celebration.

That's because there's a lot of shouts, noise, and laughter!

Hugs and squabbles.

Swearing matches that cause red eyes and blue cheeks, lead to clenched fists and tearing of hair, broken eggs, overturned stalls, matronly blouses wrenched open. I find it pure joy.

I'm swimming in family life, juicy, exuberant, and healthy.

My nostrils are filled with natural smells: fresh fish, cowsheds, orchards, woods.

There are sharp scents and sweet ones, coming from baskets of fish and baskets of fruit, rising from piles of potatoes and heaped up flowers, from slabs of butter and from pots of honey.

And how countrified the clothes are!

The men's jackets stick out like birds' tails, and the women's petticoats hang in the air as if held up by a mushroom.

Shirt collars like horses' blinkers, trousers with cow-colored front flaps, with moon-sized buttons, fluffy yellow shirts like pigskins, shoes like tree trunks.

Enormous umbrellas made of ox-red cotton, long sticks with knobs shaped like onions, little black hens knocking against the walls of their cages, and proud roosters strutting around, cock-a-hoop.

It's an open-air Noah's ark, unpacked on a bed of straw, leaves, and dung.

Through their lion's mouths, fountains are spewing out sheets of cool, clear water.

A sad-faced man with a head like a weasel, who seems neither a peasant nor a worker but a beggar dressed in his Sunday best or a prisoner just released yesterday, is showing little live wolves in a basket.

Jailbird! Beggar!

He certainly belongs to some such breed of person.

The farmers don't want anything to do with him because there's been trouble in his life.

He's the son of someone who either died on the guillotine or as a convict.

He prowls around the edges of woods, on the banks of the river, or in the mountains.

When he can manage to catch a fox or a wolf—sometimes he wounds an eagle—he'll put the animal or the nestling on show in towns for a couple of sous; in villages, for a scrap of fat pork.

I was scared of him until one day my uncle Joseph spoke to him and gave him ten sous.

"How're things going, Slippery Sam?"

As he went away, Uncle Joseph says, "Poor little bugger! He doesn't get a square meal every day."

ON THE BREUIL

I've had lots of exciting times on the Breuil.

They've set up a canvas tent, looking like a big top, upside down, and when I was on an errand, I saw a big black man near it.

It's the Bouthor Circus, which has come to town.

They've got an elephant and a camel, a band whose members wear shakos and red tunics with gold facings and epaulettes that look like pies.

They paraded around the town beating big drums; the equestrienne's wearing a riding habit and the men are dressed like generals.

The countryfolk watch them openmouthed; the street urchins skip along after them.

One of the horsewomen drops her riding switch.

Ten of us fling ourselves on it to pick it up. After that, we fight over who'd give it back to her. She was laughing; her eye caught mine and I had the same feeling as when my aunt from Bordeaux used to kiss me.

I've got to see *that woman* again!

And I'll be able to see the elephant and the camel again too.

On the poster they're shown kneeling down, dancing on their hind feet, uncorking bottles—with a clown dressed in motley leaping over them.

I did see them again, all of them, and the clown even threw himself, as a joke, into the front seats and butted me in the tummy.

"He fell on me!"

"That's a lie, it was on me!"

"I can prove it, I've got white on my jacket!"

"You didn't get your skin scratched—my cheek's all red, it was him who did that!"

And then we had a fight about who'd been knocked over, got a white patch or blood on his cheek because of the clown!

And now it's time for the lady equestrian!

Here she comes! I can't see anything! She seems to be looking at me . . .

She jumps through hoops, shouting, "Jump! Jump!" as she bursts through the paper.

She wraps a pink scarf around her head, she waggles her hips, she sticks her bottom out, she strikes a pose. Her breasts are jumping up and down in her bodice and under my waistcoat my heart is keeping time with them.

"What on earth's the matter with you, Jacques? You've turned as white as the clown!"

I'm in love with Paola! That's her name.

I want to see her again, I have to! But I haven't got the ten sous—that's the price of the cheap seats.

I'm going to go, all the same.

I get dressed up—secretly taking my Sunday waistcoat out of the wardrobe—and I set off for the Breuil, saying that I'm going to play with my pal Grélin.

It's nighttime. I cross the pitch-black square until I glimpse the Chinese lanterns glowing red in the mist. The band has left to go back inside; the show has begun. Behind the canvas walls I hear the crack of the long whip.

She is in there!

And I haven't got ten sous—I don't have anything, anything at all . . . only my love!

I walk around the marquee, I stick my eye to any gap, I stand on tiptoe, at the risk of breaking my toenails; not a single opening for my burning eyes to peer through!

This way . . .

Here the canvas is not so long and it's torn near the post, if I can tear it just a little bit more . . .

I've enlarged the hole, in goes my foot—I mean my head—in the direction of the stables.

I'm flat on my stomach, in the mud, and I'm crawling along like a thief, like a murderer in the night, into a circus full of people!

Here I am! I crawl under some planks, scrape myself on the pole, scratch my hands; my nose, which got flattened against a beam, has given up the ghost; I can't feel it anymore; I'm afraid I've lost it on the way; what I've got left doesn't look much like one; but one more effort, one last injury, and I'll be able to see *her* by moving up behind that fat housemaid.

I'm going to climb up . . . I'm climbing—I miss a handhold . . . I grab on to something . . .

A yell! Utter confusion! . . .

There's a woman grasping her skirts and shouting for help!

People are imagining that the marquee's collapsing!

I'd grabbed a handful of some fleshy part of the maid, I don't know quite where; she thought it was the monkey or the elephant's trunk which had lost its way.

They take hold of me by any part available; they shove me like horse dung into the stables; they question me; I won't answer!

People gather around me. She's there, close to me. *SHE* in person! I can hear but I can't see her because of my swollen nose.

———

I get back home in time to explain to Madame Grélin, which will save me from a beating (oh, Paola!), and I tell her everything—everything except my secret love! Compromise a woman? Never! I blamed it all on the camel, which has a broad back, and on the elephant whose trunk had aroused those suspicions . . .

And when I sometimes try to think back on the Breuil, my memory always seizes on Paola and that fat bit of the maid. For me, the Breuil is that circus, under those tights and under that skirt.

IX. SAINT-ÉTIENNE

THROUGH the influence of a friend, my father's been promoted to the teacher in charge of a senior class in a primary school in Saint-Étienne.[1] He's had to leave *on the double*. My mother and I remain behind to settle various matters, get packed, etc.

We're off at last. Good-bye, Le Puy!

We're in the stagecoach. It's December and it's very cold. Our fellow passengers are a traveling salesman, a fat woman, and a little old man.

The fat woman has breasts like balloons and a cleavage that shows off some V-shaped white flesh, sweet to look at and as tasty as a slice from a leg of lamb. Her eyes have very long lashes, rather like my aunt's.

A joke from the traveling salesman—its meaning completely escapes me—causes her to open her lips and emit a loud guffaw. From then on they do nothing but exchange pleasantries and even nudges and pokes, utterly scandalizing my mother who draws away, nearly squashing me into the corner, to the great delight of the little old man who rubs his hands together while wagging his head and winking.

When we arrive at the staging post, they get out together and I can see them through the window of the inn giving each other radishes—still laughing and nudging each other with their elbows.

The traveling salesman offers the fat woman a bunch of flowers, which he buys from a beggar, and asks her to stuff it into her bodice; she ends up agreeing to put it where he wants.

She's so much more cheerful than my mother!

What's that I've just said? My mother's a saint who doesn't laugh, doesn't like flowers, who has her position to maintain—her honor, Jacques!

The other woman is a woman of the people, a shopkeeper (as she's just said as she climbed back into the coach); she's on her way to Beaucaire to sell cloth and run a shop at the fair. And you're comparing that woman to your mother, young Vingtras!

We arrive in Saint-Étienne.

It's night; my father's not there to meet us.

We stand waiting, surrounded by our luggage. The streets are deep in snow and I look at the stark shadows of the streetlamps against this sheer whiteness. With flashing eyes my mother scans the square as she strides up and down, biting her lips and wringing her hands, endlessly pestering the people in the office with questions.

They ask her if she wants to come in or stay outside, how long she intends to continue to block the entrance with her luggage.

"I'm waiting for my husband; he's a teacher at the school."

They don't seem in the least impressed!

I'd be very happy to stay in the office, my feet are frozen, my fingers are numb, my nose smarts. I tell my mother.

"Jacques!"

That "Jacques!" was a sinister omen for our entry into this city—and she mutters between her chattering teeth, "Just listen to that, now! He'd let his mother freeze to death while he'd sit toasting his thighs!"

But she can sit toasting her thighs too! There's nothing to stop her; they asked her if she wanted to sit down by the fire.

My father arrives quite out of breath.

"I'm late . . ." (He wipes his forehead.) "Did you have a good trip?" (He reaches out toward my mother and misses her.)

He turns toward me.

"Ah, here's Jacques!"

"Did you imagine I was bringing someone else with me?" my mother inquired.

"No, of course not," my father said, "that is to say . . ." He doesn't quite know how to go on.

He tries to give me a hug too, and fails, just as he didn't succeed in hugging my mother. He's not having much luck with his hugs and it's the same with his kisses.

"I was caught up with the bursar, Monsieur Laurier, you know . . . I thought the coach . . ."

Nobody's saying a word to him, not one single word!

We take a cab to get to our house.

During the journey, complete silence—silence and snow. My father looks out of the window, my mother is crouching in the corner, I'm sitting in between, not daring to move for fear they'll hear my bones shifting, my head turning. I'm flicking a tassel of the umbrella with my fingertip. At that moment, the umbrella slips out of my grasp. I lean forward to catch it, my father turns his head—smack!—our heads collide. We sit up like a couple of Punches. Another bad move—wham, bam!—we're keeping strict time.

The sickly smile reappears on my father's face; mine is changing visibly. It was a contest between a hard-boiled and a soft-boiled egg. My father was able to withstand the shock: he's smiling. Nice guy! But I've got a bump that is swelling—it's as big as a house. My father reaches out in the dark to feel it and also because my forehead seems to be coming nearer and will shortly get in his way. He sticks his hand out and catches hold of my nose. He thinks it's his duty, more fatherly, more gracious, more befitting his dignity or better for my health, to dwell for a moment on this nose, which he seems at this moment to be either blessing or consulting.

Of my mother there's nothing to be seen or heard, except for the sound of silk being scratched—her nails are taking it out on her belt.

In this silence, the rasping sound is rather terrifying. For soothsayers, it would portend disaster and, indeed, one disaster at least was to befall us in this sad and snow-covered city through which our cab was silently winding its way.

The house in front of which our cab discharged us stands on a street corner.

It has a miserable-looking entrance: the stones in front of the doorway are all loose, the staircase is worm-eaten, and the wood of the handrail—which has lost some of its banisters—is rotten. Under our feet, the stones wobble; the rail shudders in our hands—we're all embarrassed. It seemed to us as if we were doomed to silence for all eternity. My father is fussing around.

"Go ahead," he said. "Be careful, there's a step. And there's a hole there, too. Hold on to the rail."

He's playing with the key hanging from his little finger; it's a lonely, futile gesture, like a baby's.

I was dragging the umbrella along the floor.

Normally when I let this umbrella stick into my mother's dress or hit her in the side, I get yelled at for being a clumsy idiot and she clouts me.

I'd give a great deal to get a clout—it makes my mother happy; it cheers her up; it's like the flip of a wagtail or the dive of a duck. She reaches out and there's her son's cheek. What a joy for my mother to feel that he's within reach and to be able to say to herself, that's him, that's my boy, the fruit of my womb; that cheek belongs to me: smack!

But not at all.

Her arms are folded and she's keeping them hidden under her shawl . . . So there we are: she's in no mood to feel well disposed.

My father is getting through large quantities of matches; they keep breaking off with a little crack, which is the only sound to be heard in front of this locked door, in this passageway, icy cold from the wind, with my mother and me close against the wall, like clothes in a morgue.

Never have seconds seemed so long . . .

Finally the chemistry of the match works and my father is able to put the key into the lock.

We're in an enormous room into which the flickering light of a streetlamp penetrates through two immense windows.

It falls straight onto my mother, who is standing silent and motionless, as stiff as a corpse, as impassive as a tailor's dummy, and as solemn as a ghost.

. . . .

But I can always rescue the situation with my head or my behind, my ears which are tweaked, my hair which is pulled, by sliding, squatting, or tumbling over, like the clown in a pantomime or a magician's stooge.

All of a sudden I feel myself stumbling . . . I fall over!

There was a piece of orange peel under my heel, as they can see when they bend over me, as if over a problem. I can disconcert mathematicians by the unexpected nature of my operations. Suddenly reminded of her love for her son by this pratfall that looks like a practical joke, my mother is the first to notice the orange peel.

She folds her arms and walks up to my father.

"So people are eating oranges here! Oranges!"

She stamps her foot . . . and stamps it again . . . I don't understand the meaning of all this.

I'm flat on the ground and have to lift my head to see what's happening; from my point of view as historiographer of all this, I'm in the situation of a legless cripple, brought along only to be dumped like a sack that's too heavy.

However, I don't have any wish to die where I've fallen! And I mustn't listen to my mother who's standing there while I'm still in this indifferent posture, cutting myself off from her and seemingly disdaining her. You've kept her waiting too long already, Jacques!

Get up and place yourself between your mother's words and your father's dismay. On your feet, ungrateful boy!

But I can't!

I've tried to move . . . and it's impossible!

I've fallen on an engraving and broken the glass.

They're forced to recognize these distressing injuries and the few drops of blood sprinkled over the floor offer my father— as well as my mother—a pretext for fresh action. I feel a thrill of pleasure—as much as I dare without inflicting too much pain on myself, obviously. But I'm still very happy to have put a stop to that silence—*broken the ice*, as well as the glass— and my father and mother are extracting the shards.

They wash me off like a gold nugget; they weed me like a field.

It's a conscientious and meticulous operation.

In the course of cleaning me up, hands accidentally touch,

words have to be used over my wounds, a sly reconciliation is in progress; and I think my father even lingers over the weeding process to give time for his wife's anger to cool down completely. True, I'm bleeding a little; sometimes I'm on all fours, at other times flat on my stomach following their instructions—depending on where the sharp pieces of glass come out. But I feel that I've done my family a good turn, and that's some consolation, isn't it?

Instead of pushing so many beans into corners, why shouldn't Monsieur Beliben say, "See how subtle and kind God is! What did He use to patch up a quarrel between husband and wife? He took a child's bottom, young Vingtras's, and made it play a . . . *fundamental* part in their reconciliation."

It made me ill and gave me a fever. But the storm had blown over; the question of the orange peel was settled quietly; a reason was given for arriving late at the station; dressings were applied to anger and to me, in various other places.

The question of the orange peel was settled, but it seems to me that some mystery still surrounded it all the same.

When he'd said that he'd been held up by Monsieur Laurier, my father had lied; this I learned by hearing a conversation between him and a colleague who called on him when my mother, worn out by the journey, the long wait, the storm, and above all by cleaning me up, was taking a nap.

"You say that and I'll say this. We'll warn old So-and-So. And as long as the women don't take it into their heads to greet us on the street . . . Anyway, there's no danger, is there?"

I heard all this lying in bed, flat on my stomach, sometimes slightly sideways, and I asked myself who the women might be.

X. GOOD PEOPLE

I'D FIND it hard to describe the apartment which we went into, as I've said, breaking in, with a flickering streetlamp, and a posthumous reconciliation—if posthumous is the right word . . .

We had no sooner moved in than a great event occurred.

My mother had to go off to see about an inheritance—possibly Aunt Agatha's—and I was left alone with my father.

It's a new life—he's never at home, I'm free, and I live on the ground floor, with the children of the cobbler and the grocer.

I adore cobbler's wax, glue, pricker-thread; I love the sound made by the paring knife as it slices into the thick of the leather, and the clang of the hammer on new calfskin and the blue stone.

We have a nice time among all these clogs and the oldest son sort of looks like my uncle Joseph. He's a member of a trade guild, too, an official, and I sometimes tie the ribbons onto his stick and brush his ceremonial frock coat. On ordinary days, he lets me drive in nails and have odd pieces of red Moroccan leather.

I'm almost one of the family. My father has boarded me there; I don't know where he has supper, presumably at the school, with the teachers from the lower school. I swallow immense quantities of soup served in chipped bowls and when there's goat stew, I get my drop of wine in a big glass.

It's a really happy family—friendly, chatty, kindhearted: they all work but they chatter while they do it; they squabble between themselves but they like each other.

They're called the Fabres.

The other family on the ground floor, the Vincents, are grocers.

The grocer is Madame Vincent; she's always laughing. I find them all cheerful, these people I meet and my mother looks down on merely because they're peasants, make shoes, or weigh out sugar.

Madame Vincent's husband isn't there. He's been seen just once and he was dressed like an Arab in a white burnoose, but he only stayed a couple of hours before going off again.

It seems that they're *legally* separated—I don't understand what that means—and he lives in Africa, in *Algeria*, Fabre says.

He'd come to fetch one of his sons. Madame Vincent, who's always laughing, wasn't laughing that day! There was really nothing to laugh about; I could hear her through the door saying sharply, "No! No! No!," and the boy was in tears: "I want to stay with Mum!"

"I'll give you a horse, with a pistol, like this one!"

A pistol! A horse!

If my father had promised me that and in addition to taking me far away from my mother! If he'd taken me away with him, without the frock coat with olives and the stovepipe hat, what a sigh of delight I'd've breathed—but only after I was outside the door, because I would have been afraid my mother would hear and want to have me back! Oh yes, I'd've gone all right!

The Vincent boy on the contrary was in tears and clutching his mother's skirts.

There was more noise . . . The father was becoming angry, the mother was raising her voice, and the son was sobbing . . .

Then the door opened, the white burnoose went out. It never appeared again.

All the same, I felt sorry for him. I saw him skulking on the corner of the street; he was watching the house he'd just left, where his wife and child were. He stayed there for quite a while, and I thought I noticed that he was in tears.

I'm meeting fathers in tears, mothers crying. In our family I've never seen anyone laugh or cry—they whine and they shout. The fact is that my father's a teacher, a man of the world, and that my mother is a firm, courageous mother who wants to bring me up properly.

The Vincents, the Fabres, and the young Vingtras form a rowdy, joyful, and impossible bunch.

"Jacques, Ernest, you're unbearable!"

It's Madame Vincent trying to be angry and not succeeding... it's Monsieur Fabre saying it meekly, with the gentle smile of an old man.

"Unbearable! If I ever catch you at it again...!"

They catch us at it again and again, and still manage to bear with us!

Good people... They cursed and swore, they used strong language, but people said that they had "hearts of gold," that they were "as straight as an arrow." In that blend of pepper and cobbler's wax, I could breathe an atmosphere of joy, of health; their hands were grubby but the heart had the upper hand; they waggled their hips and held their fingers spread out; they spoke incorrectly—even "commonly"—it goes with the job, the older Fabre boy used to say. They made me want to have a trade too, and to live the good life where you're not afraid of your mother or of the rich: all you needed was to get up early in the morning, sing, and bang away all day.

And then there were the beautifully painted awls. You could see a shine being given to the long snout of an ankleboot, the arched heel of a boot, and you could fiddle about with shoe polish which smelled a bit vinegary and prickled the nose.

Good people!

They didn't beat their children and they gave money to charity. It wasn't like us.

During my whole childhood, I would hear my mother say that you mustn't give money to the poor, that they'd go off and spend any money they got on drink, that it'd be better just to throw a sou in the river, at least it wouldn't end up in a pub. All the same, I've never been able to see a man asking for a sou to buy bread without feeling sad, a sort of weight on my heart!

Yet how can that be?

Madame Vincent liked to see her son take a sou out of his pocket to put into the hand of some poor wretch. She'd give Ernest a kiss and say, "His heart's in the right place!"

So did Madame Vincent want her son to do something wrong? Yet she loved him, otherwise she'd have let him go away with the man in the white burnoose.

Oh dear, they made me feel uncomfortable, those two nice mothers, Madame Vincent and Madame Fabre. Luckily that feeling didn't last long and didn't trouble me for one minute once I started thinking about it.

They didn't beat their children because they would have been sad to see them crying! And Ernest was allowed to give money to the poor because, being softies, it made them feel good.

My mother was made of sterner stuff. She sacrificed herself, she stifled her weaknesses, she strangled her first impulse so as to adopt her second one. Instead of kissing me, she pinched me—do you think that didn't hurt her? Sometimes she even broke her nails doing it. She was beating me for my own good, you see. More than once her hand let her down and she was forced to rely on her foot.

More than once, she was reluctant to bruise her own flesh as well as mine: she'd pick up a stick, a broom, anything that would prevent her from making contact with the skin of her child, her beloved child.

I could well understand these excellent reasons and these heroic sentiments urging my mother on, so well that I used to accuse myself, in God's eyes, of disobedience and say two or three quick prayers to absolve myself. Unfortunately I had very little time to myself and my mea culpas were left in the air because Ernest, Charles, or Barnaby, one of the Vincents or the Fabres would call up to me to come sledding or walking or scuffling for no reason at all—or else for a taste of jam: there was always some barrel, some tub, some jar to be finished off or some squabble to settle; to lend a hand in the grocery or the workshop, to do a job . . . or just for fun.

We used to go up to the second floor to torment the plasterer's wife.

The plasterer's wife was a tall blonde, very gentle, extremely neat and tidy—a trifle listless; sometimes, in the course of our games, she'd let us crowd into her bedroom when her husband wasn't there, but as soon as she heard him coming, she packed us off downstairs; she'd close the door and come back looking even more tired in the face and listless around her hips. She was always talking to Madame Vincent about having a baby, saying that she was afraid it wouldn't be this time, that her husband was desperate . . .

If one of the Fabres, the one who was eighteen or the one who was twenty-three, happened to be going by at that moment, she would stop talking; but as a sort of joke, he would make a passing comment that made her blush to the roots of her blond hair; she'd still try to smile nevertheless but she seemed gently embarrassed.

"You've got a spot of plaster here" (pointing to a white

speck) "and some eiderdown there" (brushing a bit of fluff from her shoulder), and he'd wag his head jokingly.

"Oh, that Monsieur Fabre . . ."

"For goodness sake!" he exclaimed one day. "They don't grow under rosebushes, do they?"

I was in the room when he made this comment: "They don't grow under rosebushes, do they?"

This remark went into my ear like bradawl and stuck there like cobbler's wax.

Had they been misleading me?

My mother's back. The inheritance has been settled, I'm not at all clear in what way. And once again I'm under the whip, free only when she's away for some reason or other.

But on Shrove Tuesday a colleague's wife came to fetch her unexpectedly to consult her about some clothes—she's got such good taste!—and at the same time to spend the day with her. My mother didn't have time to shut me in—I'm my own master and it's Shrove Tuesday!

On that day, it's the custom to heap up a pyramid of charcoal in every street, a pile shaped like a haystack, like a big black cotton bonnet, with a fuse which is lit in the morning.

We'd heard that they'd be coming over from the next street to demolish our structure; there had been no love lost between the two streets for a long time. The son of the landlord of The Golden Lion, a young scamp, suggests posting a lookout, with a slingshot and some stones in his pocket; we're instructed to open fire with the slingshot if the enemy is seen in the distance making a massive advance and, if caught unawares and captured, to hit back with a stone in your hand.

I'm one of the first to be put on guard duty.

And now I reckon I can see young Somonat, one of the Rue Marescaut gang, poking his nose out from behind the door of the church.

I think I can see him signaling: they'll launch a mass attack; I'll be overrun, cut off . . . What will the innkeeper's son say? The whole street? Will I ever dare go through there again if I don't put up a heroic defense?

My decision's made: I've got my pile of stones, I load my slingshot and let fly, firing at random in the direction of the Marescauts, sending a hail of stones whistling through the air. I can hear them thudding against the wooden doors and on the closed shutters! I'm raking the area haphazardly, just as you do with a cannon—I'm imagining that I'm at the siege of Arbela or at Mazagram.[1] We translated Quintus Curtius's account of the battle yesterday. The story of Mazagram is quite recent. People are talking of nothing else but that and Captain Lelièvre.

And people will be talking about my feat too, damn it!

I'm bombarding a whole district with stones, putting people's lives at risk, bringing the normal life of a whole town to a halt.

People are coming out of their houses to watch—not for long, because I'm still wielding my slingshot, though I'm beginning to wonder how the siege will end.

I've heard windowpanes shatter, I saw one stone fly into a room, I may have killed someone. The Marescauts are not answering! So I was wrong, they weren't attacking. So I'll be captured, sentenced, my father will lose his job.

What am I going to do?

I've heard that to arrange a cease-fire, you put out a white flag; I've got my handkerchief—it's a blue one. Retreat? Perhaps I can, the street's deserted, suppose I get away quickly, to my left . . .

Off I go, at full speed.

What's happened? I've fallen over. People are gathering around. I've got a broken arm.

Monsieur Dropal happens to be passing—he's the doctor and they stop him. What will he say?

If it turns out to be nothing much, what will happen to me?

How would I ever go back and face my mother? And what will the people that I've been pelting with stones do?

The doctor's shaking his head and saying "aha" in a sad voice. I pretend to be unconscious so that I can hear better.

"It's serious, serious!"

Thank God! Can someone please go along quickly to tell my mother that it's serious so that she doesn't start telling me off and giving me a beating?!

It was serious. I couldn't speak at all, not one word. Better luck than I deserved: they're saying that I've lost my voice! Isn't that convenient! No explanations required; I'll probably be sick for a long time, and when I'm cured, everyone will have calmed down.

I couldn't speak for a long time; but I didn't talk as soon as I got my voice back.

I could plainly see that while I was getting better, my mother was adding something up.

"That's two francs worth of diachylum[2] already!"

A good woman! She insisted on thrift and never forgot the importance, in a family, of law and order as the only guarantee of salvation, for without it you'll end up in hospital or on the scaffold.

As for me, I was terribly worried at the thought of getting well again.

I was full of apprehension for the time when I'd be fit enough to be punished, even if I didn't need a beating to make me want never to do it again—I didn't feel the slightest inclination to experience another siege, suffer another fall, such a terrible surge of emotion. I'd've liked my mother to know that, my father to understand it, and then perhaps they wouldn't need to hit me.

They didn't hit me, they did worse.

They knew that I enjoyed spending time with the Fabre family. That's how they punished me.

In addition, my mother had long been jealous and ashamed; it pained her to see me hanging around in the company of cobblers and for some weeks now she'd been planning how to get me away from them.

But Ma Vingtras liked a chinwag and the Fabres used to listen to her. In their simple, guileless way they may even have thought that this lady who wore a hat was their superior. In any case, they listened with a friendly ear to what she had to say and politely pushed the cobbler's wax and glue to one side whenever she came to fetch me.

She wanted her Jacques to stop mixing with cobblers, but she didn't want to lose her audience.

My Shrove Tuesday exploit gave her the opportunity to turn the situation around and get the best of both worlds.

She punished me by refusing to allow me to visit them; however she didn't quarrel with them.

"Jacques must be punished, mustn't he? He must be punished but the poor boy has already suffered enough."

"Oh yes," agreed Madame Fabre, thinking that her approval —even from a cobbler's wife—would weigh the scales in favor of forgiveness for me.

"And so I'm not going to give him a thrashing."

I could hear this conversation, not because I was cavesdropping but because I was behind the door. My mother knew that and maybe she wanted me to hear.

It was the first time I'd been out: I was still in poor shape and weak, having been fed for the last two weeks on pretty thin gruel; my mother knew that too rich a diet does more harm than good and that the veins can be poisoned as much by cow juice as by grape juice; my gruel came from cows. "Cows are more delicate," she'd say. "Cows for children, beef for adults."

So I was receiving my sustenance only from a bit of diluted cow. I still felt a bit of a wreck from my fall, and my head seemed like an empty globe. I'd lost a lot of blood but the little that remained leaped into my mouth and surged into my hollow cheeks—I could feel them glowing.

"They didn't want to beat me!"

They wanted to do something more than that.

"I don't want to give him a beating," my mother repeated, "but as you know, he's fond of spending time with your sons and I shall stop him from seeing them. It'll be a good lesson for him."

The Fabres said nothing—poor people, they didn't think they had any right to question decisions reached by the wife of a teacher in middle school, and on the contrary were quite bewildered by the honor granted to their young ragamuffins by the implication that they were the favorite playmates of Jacques, who was learning Latin.

I could understand their silence and I also understood that my mother had guessed where to strike, what would really hurt my spirit. Sometimes as a boy, I cried—there are and there will be tears on more than one of these pages—but for some unknown reason, my memory of my desperate distress on that day is particularly bitter. My mother seemed to me to be committing an act of cruelty that was really vicious.

I was still very poorly, almost disabled, and after being confined to my bedroom for weeks on end, I had the need to talk with children like myself, get news from them, and tell them all that was happening to me.

They'd looked so kind and good as they'd come up to me on the staircase and had said so affectionately, "You're so pale!" Their voices contained real feeling, almost friendliness. Nice young boys, a fine brood of cobblers, kindhearted kids! I was very fond of them. It would have been better for my mother to have given me a thrashing and let me go on seeing them once my arm was well.

XI. THE SCHOOL

So NOW my father was in charge of the top form in the elementary school.

I was in his class.

I've never smelled such a stink. The classroom was next door to the toilets and those toilets were the ones used by the little boys!

For one year I drank in that poisonous air. They'd put me next to the door because it was the worst place and being the teacher's son, I had to be the sacrificial offering in the vanguard, at the forefront of danger . . .

Sitting beside me was a little kid who later became a VIP, an important prefect, but who at that time was a dreadful young rascal, extremely funny, incidentally, and not a bad type at all.

Indeed, he must have been really nice for me not to have borne him a grudge for the two or three beatings my father handed out to me because he'd heard a funny noise coming from our direction or when a jet of ink spurted from between our shoes. It was my neighbor having fun.

Every time I saw him plotting some practical joke, I trembled, because unless he gave himself away through recklessness or was blatantly guilty, it was I who took the rap, that's to say, my father would get down from the podium and come and pull my ears or give me a kick or two—sometimes three.

He had to prove that he didn't favor his son, that he had no preferences. The only favor he did me was knocking the stuffing out of me; his only preference was for kicking my rear end.

Did it make him unhappy to have to knock his offspring about like that?

He might have been unhappy, but the practical joker sitting beside me was the son of a local bigwig—swamping him with punishments or twisting his ears would have led to strife with the mama, a tall flirtatious lady who used to come into the parlor in a long swishy silk dress and gloves with three buttons, as fresh as butter.

To avoid trouble, my father used to pretend that I was the culprit when he knew quite well that it was the other boy.

I didn't hold this against my father, certainly not! I thought—I felt—that my hide was useful for my father's business, his form of exercise, his job, and I offered my hide. Go ahead, Dad!

I more or less maintained my (rotten) place among this group of mischievous brats keen on giving hell to the teacher's son by reason of the hatred they naturally felt for my father.

I was helped by his public thrashings: nobody saw me as an enemy, they would have been more likely to pity me—if children were capable of feeling pity.

In any case, my apparent lack of reaction wasn't conducive to arousing pity; for the sake of appearance, I dodged the blows as well as I could, but when it was all over, I didn't show the least sign of fear or pain. In this way I was neither a butt nor a pariah; boys didn't try to avoid me, they treated me as one of them, not as lucky as some and better than many, because I never said, "Please, sir, it wasn't me." And then again, I was strong, my fights with Pierrouni had toughened me up,

I was brawny, as they used to say when you tightened your arm and flexed whatever biceps you had. I'd gotten into scrapes— I'd *had it out* with Rosée, who was the strongest boy in the lower-school mob. That was what it was called: *having it out.* "Are we going to have it out after school?"

That meant that at five past ten or five past four, you intended to bash away at each other in the backyard of the Red Cockerel, an inn where there was a corner where you could fight without being seen.

I'd landed a few punches on Rosée that hadn't passed unnoticed—by his nose, or at school. Just think! I had my father's permission.

He'd gotten wind of our quarrel—over stealing a pen—and of what had provoked it.

Rosée had no connection with any of the bigwigs. What's more, his uncle, a local councillor, had had a bone to pick with the school board. I could *have it out.*

And with every punch I aimed at him, poor kid, I thought that I was planting a seed, a seed of hope in the field of paternal promotion.

Thanks to this lucky venture, I managed to escape the most appalling of dangers—that of being, as the son of the teacher, persecuted, cast out, beaten up. I've seen others made desperately unhappy.

But what if my father had forbidden me to fight, what if Rosée had been the mayor's son . . . supposing on the contrary, I'd had to take a beating?

You must do what your parents tell you, for it's their daily bread that is at stake. You must let yourself be laughed at and hit, suffer and cry, poor boy, the son of a schoolteacher . . .

And then there are principles to be upheld!

"What would happen to society," Monsieur Beliben used to say, "a society in which . . . in which . . . You must have principles . . . I need one more bean . . ."

I'd had the good luck to come across Rosée.

Wherever he may be in the world, if he's still alive, I hope he'll accept my profoundest gratitude . . .

> *Chalice with nostrils, blood of my savior,*
> *Salutaris nasus, yet one more kiss!*[1]

One day I was punished: it was, I seem to remember, because I was pushed by a big boy and tumbled under the legs of a young prep supervisor who was passing by and who himself proceeded to fall backward, head over heels! He got a terrible bump and broke a little flask in his side pocket; it contained the nips of brandy he drank—furtively, in tiny swigs, rolling his eyes. He'd been observed: he seemed to be offering up a prayer and he was rubbing his belly. And I'd caused his little flask to be broken—and the lump which was swelling up. The little supervisor had a tantrum.

He put me in solitary—he personally shut me up in an empty classroom, locked the door, and left me alone behind the dingy walls, facing a map that was suffering from jaundice and a blackboard with white circles . . . and a sketch of the deputy headmaster's mug.

I walk around inspecting all the desks. They're empty—each one needs to be cleaned—the pupils have moved elsewhere.

Nothing, a ruler, rusty nibs, a length of string, a small checkerboard, the corpse of a lizard, a lost glass marble.

In a slot, there's a book—I can see its back. I split my nails trying to extract it. Finally, with the help of the ruler and by forcing open the desk, I succeed in getting it out: I've got it in my hand and I'm looking at its title: *ROBINSON CRUSOE*.

It's grown dark.

I suddenly realize that night has fallen. How long have I spent in this book? What's the time?

I've no idea but let's see if I can still read! I rub my eyes, I *stretch* my vision . . . the letters are growing dim, the lines are all tangled up. I can just manage to pick out the scrap of a word and that's all.

My neck's aching all over, and I've a pain at the back of it, my chest feels empty; I've stayed with my head bent over each chapter, without lifting it, without hearing a thing . . . overcome by curiosity, glued to *Robinson*, in the grip of a tremendous emotion, stirred to the innermost depths of my brain and my heart. And at this moment, as the moon is showing a glimpse of its curve over there, I'm seeing all the birds of Crusoe's island flying past in the sky while the top of a tall poplar rears up like the mast of his ship! I'm populating empty space with my thoughts the way he filled his horizon with his fears. As I stand at this window, I'm dreaming of being alone for all eternity and wondering where I can *grow* some bread . . .

Hunger takes over: I'm absolutely ravenous.

Am I going to be reduced to eating the rats I can hear in the *hold* of the classroom? How can I make a fire? I'm thirsty too. No bananas! Ah, he had fresh limes! And to think how I adore lemonade!

Click! Clack! Someone's fiddling at the keyhole.

Is it Man Friday? Or the savages?

It's the little prep supervisor who remembered, as he was getting up, that he'd *forgotten* me and who's come to see if I'd been eaten up by the rats or whether I'd eaten them.

He looks a bit embarrassed, poor man! He finds me freezing, bruised, hair all dried up, my hands burning; he apologizes as best he can and hauls me off to his room where he tells me to light a nice fire and get warm.

He has some tuna fish marinating in a pan and "perhaps even a nip of I'm not quite sure what, over there in the corner, left behind by a friend a couple of months ago . . ."

It's a tiny flask of spirits, his pet vice, his liquid relaxation—his yellow hobby.

He can't stay, he's got to get back to his class. He leaves me on my own—on my own with some tuna (an Atlantic fish), a drop of spirits (that blessing for sailors), and a fire (the beacon of shipwrecked mariners).

I dive back into the book, which I'd slipped under my shirt next to my skin, and I devour it—along with a bit of tuna, a bite or two—in front of the glow in the hearth.

I felt as though I was in a cabin or a hut and had left school ten years ago. Perhaps my hair has gone gray, or at least I've acquired a tan. What's become of my old parents? Did they die without knowing the joy of embracing their long-lost son? (It would've been a golden opportunity for them because they'd never embraced him much before.) Oh, my mother! My mother!

I say, "Oh, my mother," without paying particular attention—it was so I'd be doing what they do in books.

And I add, "When shall I see you again? See you, and die!"

I'll see her if it's *God's will*.

But when I appear again before her eyes, how will I be recognized? Will she recognize me?

Not to be recognized by the woman who'd surrounded you with such tender care ever since the cradle, wrapped you in affection, in a word, a mother?

What can ever replace a mother!

God knows mine could be replaced perfectly well by a thick stick!

Not recognize me! But she knows very well that behind my ear there's a lock of hair missing, since she pulled it out one day. Not recognize me? But I've still got the scar of the injury I sustained when I fell down—which made her forbid me to see the Fabres. The marks of her care, of her solicitude, can all be read in white stripes, little blue polka dots. She'll recognize me; once again, I'll be able to be loved, beaten, thrashed, not spoiled . . .

Spare the rod and . . .

And, thank God, she did recognize me! She recognized me and she screamed, "So there you are! When you make your mother stay up till two in the morning, keeping a candle burning and the door open, I'll make sure to teach you a lesson! And now he's yawning as well, in his mother's face!"

"I'm sleepy."

"You've done more than enough to be sleepy!"

"I'm cold."

"So we'll light a fire especially for him, using up a whole bundle of firewood!"

"But it was Monsieur Doizy who . . ."

"It was Monsieur Doizy who forgot you, wasn't it? If you hadn't made him fall over, he wouldn't have needed to punish you and he wouldn't have forgotten you. Just listen to him! Still trying to make excuses. Well, here's all that's left of a candle I started on only yesterday. And all that to stay up wondering what had happened to his lordship! Go along, let's not start pretending we're cold, let's not look as if we're feverish. Will you stop making your teeth chatter like that! I wish you'd get really sick for a change, perhaps that might cure you once and for all!"

I didn't think I was so much to blame. In fact, it *is* my fault; but I can't help it if my teeth are chattering, my hands are hot, and I've got shivers down my back. I caught cold last night on those benches with my head resting on the desk; reading that book also upset me.

Oh, how I'd love to get some sleep! I'll take a nap on this chair . . .

"Get off there," my mother said. "No sleeping in the middle of the day! What sort of habits do you think you're getting into now?"

"It's not a habit. I feel tired because I didn't get a proper rest in my bed."

"Your bed'll be there tonight, unless you take it into your head to go off *hanging around* again."

"I wasn't hanging around."

"What do you call staying away from home? Now it's his mother who's to blame, is it? Go get your books. Have you done your homework tonight?"

Oh, the desert island, the wild beasts, the constant rain, earthquakes, animal's skins, the sunshade, the footprint of the savage, all those shipwrecks, those storms, those cannibals—but not tonight's homework!

I had the shivers all that day. But I wasn't alone anymore! From that time on, there was a corner of my imagination that—in the prose of my life, full of beatings—was blue and a dream of poetry, and my heart would sail away to lands where you suffer and you work but where you're free.

The number of times I've read and reread *Robinson*!

I set about finding out who it belonged to; he was a third-form boy who'd got lots of other books hidden away in his desk: he had *Swiss Family Robinson*, the *Tales* by Canon Schmidt,[2] the *Life of Cartouche*,[3] with illustrations.

Now comes an episode in my life that I could hide. No, I won't. Today for the first time I'll divulge my secret, like a dying man who sends for the public prosecutor to come and hear about a crime. It's a painful confession to make but I owe it to the honor of my family, to respect for the truth, to the Bank of France, to myself.

I WAS A FORGER! Fear of penal servitude, of driving to despair my parents who manifestly adored me, covered my *forging* face with an impenetrable mask that no hand hitherto has succeeded in tearing away.

I'm denouncing myself and intend to tell in what circumstances I committed this forgery, how I strayed into this shameful way of life, and the cynicism that I displayed while pursuing this infamous course of conduct . . .

Engravings! *The Life of Cartouche*, the *Tales* of Canon Schmidt, and the adventures of the Swiss Family Robinson belonged to one of my schoolmates—a red-haired thirteen-year-old.

He agreed to part with them . . . on odious conditions, which I accepted. I can even recall that I had no hesitation.

Here's the background to this abominable bargain.

At Saint-Étienne, as in every other state school, credits are given for good work. My father has the right to issue credit slips to classes other than his own because every two weeks he had prep supervision duties in one class or another; he took them all in turn, and he could hand out either rewards or punishments. The boy who had the books with the engravings agreed to lend them to me if I was willing to provide him with credit slips.

My hair didn't stand on end.

"Can you copy your father's signature?"

My hand didn't tremble like a leaf, my mouth didn't dry up.

"Let me have a credit for two hundred lines and I'll lend you *The Life of Cartouche*."

My heart was pounding wildly.

"I won't just *lend* it to you, I'll *give* it to you!"

The blow struck home, the pit was dug, I threw my honor to the winds, I took leave of decent society, I became a party to *forgery* . . .

And so, for a period of time which I dare not calculate, I churned out credit notes, stuffed that boy with counterfeit signatures. True, he was the one who'd first thought up this criminal scheme, but it was I who, to my undying shame, became his nefarious accomplice.

For this price I received books—all those he possessed himself. He received a lot of money from his family and would even keep frogs hidden behind his dictionaries. I could have had some frogs too—he offered me some—but though I was capable of disgracing my father's name in order to get books, because I was passionately interested in travel and adventure and couldn't resist that temptation, I'd made a vow to myself to resist all others, and I never even touched the tail of a frog, so help me God! I'm not going to make anything but a complete confession.

And isn't it enough to have betrayed the public trust, forged an honored and honorable signature, for two years? Yes, it went on for two long years. We eventually stopped, either because we were tired or else because there was no longer any point in it, I can't remember exactly; and nobody ever found out that we were forgers. But I was one . . . and it did me no harm whatsoever. You might think that I would be troubled by a sense of guilt, turn pale with remorse . . . Unfortunately there are criminals who are impervious to shame, whose vicious behavior doesn't stop them from playing with spinning tops and sticking paper tails on june bugs without a care in the world.

I was that kind of criminal: lots of paper tails, lots of

tops. Perhaps that's the cure; I've never looked so hale and hearty, appeared so frank, so open, as during the time I was a forger.

It's only now that shame has overtaken me and that I blush as I confess. You begin by forging credit slips and you end up counterfeiting banknotes...I never thought of banknotes—perhaps because I had other things on my mind, or I'm lazy, or I didn't have any ink at home: but if counterfeiting credit slips for good work leads to a convict prison, then I ought to be in one.

And who's to say that one day I won't?

XII. POLISHING—GUZZLING— CLEANLINESS

I'M TOLD to do housework.

"A man must be able to do anything!"

It's not too bad: washing a few plates, some feather-dusting. But I'm pretty ham-fisted, and now and again I break a bowl or a glass.

My mother scolds me: "He's doing it on purpose and if that butterfingers doesn't stop behaving like a bull in a china shop, we'll end up in the poorhouse soon."

Once I cut my finger to the bone.

"And now he goes and cuts himself!" my mother shouts in a fury.

The trouble is that she always has a method . . . like Descartes, whom Monsieur Beliben used to mention occasionally: I'm supposed to make bouquets out of the vegetable peels!

"He hasn't got the faintest idea!"

And seizing the watering can and a broom, she draws patterns on the floor with the water or dust, smirking to herself as she sways gently back and forth.

Oh, I know I'm not graceful like that, that's for sure.

Sometimes she puts on her energetic act: she takes a leather cloth with pumice on it, grabs a stiff brush, and launches an attack on some gleaming copper or the corner of a piece of furniture.

She goes *Uh, uh!*, grunting like a baker's boy kneading

dough: it's enough to make loaves start sprouting all over the floor! It even makes my back pour with sweat . . .

But I'm energetic and brawny, I take the cloth out of her hand and continue the fight. I fling myself on the piece of furniture or hurl myself against the banister. I eat up the wood, devour the paintwork.

"Jacques, Jacques! Have you gone mad?"

Yes, my enthusiasm has gone to my head. I've become a polishing monomaniac.

"Jacques, will you stop now? That young ruffian would demolish the whole house if we let him have his way!"

I'm at a total loss: either I'm accused of being lazy because I don't rub hard enough or else I'm called a young ruffian if I rub too hard . . .

I haven't got the faintest idea. Yes, that's true. Not even capable of washing the dishes *gracefully*! What's going to become of me later on? I'll have to eat nothing but cold meat— a slice of bread and bacon and ham in its paper wrapping. I'll go and have supper in the country, so that I can drop any leftovers on the grass.

(Perhaps I'm a poet? I like having my supper in a meadow!)

If I do that, there won't be any dishes to wash and God won't make me clear up the little birds droppings.

The most dreadful thing about this business of washing dishes is that I'm forced to wear an apron, like a maid. Sometimes my father is visited by parents, the mothers of pupils, and they catch sight of me through an open door, rubbing, wiping, and washing dishes in my Cinderella outfit. They recognize me and they don't quite understand what's happening; they don't know whether I'm a boy or a girl.

Onions are an abomination . . .

Every Tuesday and Friday, we eat onions and ground meat

and for seven years I've never been able to eat onions and ground meat without being sick.

This vegetable disgusts me.

Yes, just like a rich man! Heavens above! Arrogant, miserable little boy that I am, I allowed myself the luxury of not liking this, that, and the other, and looked unwilling when I was given something I didn't like . . . I *mollycoddled* myself. Above all I attached too much importance to my own feelings, let the smell of onions turn my stomach—what I called my stomach, let's be quite clear, because I don't know if poor people have a right to have stomachs.

"You must *force yourself*," my mother would shout. "You're doing it on purpose," she'd add, "like you always do."

That was her endless refrain: "You're doing it on purpose."

But luckily she had grit and determination, and five years later, when I went into the fourth form, I was able to eat onions and ground meat. She'd shown me that you can succeed in doing anything, that it's all a matter of willpower.

As soon as I'd managed to eat onions and ground meat, she stopped cooking it. What was the point? It cost as much as anything else and it smelled dreadful. Her method had carried the day; that was all she wanted—and later on, whenever I faced a problem, she'd say, "Now remember onions and ground meat, Jacques. For five years you couldn't keep them down and at the end of that time, you could. Just remember, Jacques!"

I remembered, all too well.

I *did* like leeks.

What can you do? I hated onions, I loved leeks. They were snatched away from my open mouth, as a pistol is from a criminal, or like a cup of poison from some poor wretch bent on committing suicide.

"Why shouldn't I have them?" I asked tearfully.

"Because you like them," the woman replied; full of good sense, she didn't want her son to have any passionate desires.

You'll eat onions because they make you sick, you will not eat leeks because you love them.

"Do you like lentils?"

"I don't know."

It was dangerous to commit yourself. I'd say something definite only after due consideration, after carefully weighing every aspect of the case.

You're lying, Jacques!

You're saying that your mother is forcing you not to eat the things you like.

You like leg of lamb, Jacques.

Does your mother stop you from eating that?

Your mother roasts a leg of lamb on Sunday; you get some.

She serves it cold on Monday—does anyone refuse to let you have any?

She fries it up with onions on Tuesday—the day of the onions is sacred—you're served two portions instead of one.

And how about Wednesday, Jacques? Who sacrifices herself on Wednesday for her son? And on Thursday, who leaves the whole of the lamb for her child? Who? Tell me, Jacques!

It's your mother—like the pelican![1]

Finish off the leg of lamb—you have the first choice, Jacques!

"Pick the bone! I'm not going to stand in your way, Jacques, never fear!"

Just listen, it's your mother urging you not to feel any qualms, eat as much as you like, she doesn't want you to hold back. Feel free, go ahead, there's still some left, no need to be shy!

But on the seventh day, the Lord rested! That's the eighth

time there's been lamb, I can hear a sheep bleating in my stomach . . . Mercy, for pity's sake!

No, no mercy, no pity! You like roast lamb . . . and you're going to get it!

"Didn't you say you liked lamb?"

"Yes, on Monday . . ."

"And on Saturday, you say the opposite! Put vinegar on it! Come on, finish up that last mouthful! I hope you enjoyed it?"

Yes, it's really quite true! They used to buy a leg of lamb at the beginning of the month when my father was paid. They had two meals from it; then I had to finish off the rest—with salad, in a sauce, ground, mixed with rice. They did everything to disguise this dismally monotonous diet, but in the end, I could feel myself turning into a ewe . . . I was bleating and at any mention of the Good Shepherd, I'd let off a volley of farts.

Bath time! My mother had turned it into a form of torture.

Fortunately, she took me off for a thorough scouring only once every three months.

She'd scrub me until she could scrub no longer, making me soak up through every pore the soda and tallow fat exuding from a bar of household soap (only two sous a bar!) which stank like a candle factory. She forced it into every orifice of my body. It made me slobber at the mouth and my eyes smart for a week after.

Thanks to that household soap, I came to loathe cleanliness!

I had a weekly clean-up at home.

Every Sunday morning I looked like a calf. On Saturday I'd been scoured and buffed; on Sunday I was washed down . . .

My mother would dowse me with bucketfuls of water, pursuing me like Galatea,[2] and like Galatea I had to run away so as to be caught, you lovely boy! I can still see myself in the wardrobe mirror, modest in my immodesty, running over the tiled floor that was being washed down at the same time, as naked as Cupid, a rococo tailpiece, an angel scraped thoroughly clean.

All I needed to look like a calf's head was the lemon between my teeth and parsley up my nose—I already had the same insipid, bluish, flabby sheen—but my God, wasn't I clean!

Ears! Oh God! Ears! They twisted up the end of a towel and drove it all the way in, like a drill or a corkscrew.

This little twist was pushed in so vigorously that it made my tonsils swell up; my eardrums were bleeding, I was deaf for a good ten minutes, I could easily have worn a placard . . .

Cleanliness is next to godliness, my boy!

Being clean and sitting up straight, that's all you need, my boy!

I'm as clean as a whistle but I don't sit up straight.

The fact is that while doing my homework, I often fall asleep and lean forward, resting my head on my arms.

My mother wants me to sit up straight.

"We've never had any hunchbacks in our family till now."

She says it in a threatening voice, and if I ever did have any inclination to become a hunchback, she dispels that desire on the spot . . .

XIII. MONEY

"I've GOT a pain, Ma."

"It's worms, my boy!"

"I really don't feel very well."

"Get along with you, softy! Well, if you had a private income of ten thousand francs ... ! When you've got a stomachache, just do what my father used to do: turn a somersault!"

Money! Private income!

Like all youngsters, I get promised rewards, a couple of sous for being good, and every time I'm first in my class it's a silver ten-sou piece. But do I actually get them? No I don't: my mother loves me too much for that.

All the same, my mother doesn't deprive me of the reward to take the money herself.

The three sous didn't go toward the housekeeping, they ended up safe in a piggy bank whose gaping slot laughs in my face ...

"That's for you," my mother used to say, showing me the coin before slipping it into the hole!

And I'd never see it again!

"It's to buy you a man,"[1] she added.

Hidden in that little money box is my replacement who's taking in all those ten-sou pieces and the many sous that other boys, my schoolmates, spend on Sundays and market days to get into amusement stalls, to buy cheroots or brass cannons.

In this way—always sensible, teaching what's right and what's wrong without pedantry—my mother, who kept in touch with the modern world, inspired me to hate *standing armies* and forced me to think about *the blood tax*. Occasionally I'd rebel, quoting my classmates who got to spend their money instead of hoarding it up "to buy a man."

"Ah, you see, they'll probably be unfit for military service!"

She even sounded sad. She spoke with compassion of these poor children who rightly sought consolation by spending money, since Heaven had deformed their limbs and made hunchbacks of them—with no apparent outward sign of it.

"And how can that be?" she would ask, talking to herself and verging on blasphemy.

"It's a crime perpetrated by Nature—almost a divine injustice. He has spared you," she went on, patting me on the back to show me that there was no hump and that she could, indeed must continue—it was her duty as a mother —to provide for my substitute from the depths of the money box.

And suspicious, ungrateful, and longing for a ride on the merry-go-round, I often used to feel sorry that I wasn't a hunchback, and I'd pray to God to commit an injustice on me—one I could hide away under my shirt, which would save me from the draft and give me the right to take my money so I would never again have to put anything into that devilish money box.

The school inspectors will be coming shortly.

My father is working his pupils to death and arranging for the good ones to prepare for the inspection. He distributes their various assignments. He'll be asking this particular boy about this passage and another passage from someone else.

"Tribouillard, you'll take the *omission of the relative*. Caillotin, you've got *Bible history*—bone up on the *prophets* . . .

"Please sir," asked Caillotin, "how do you pronounce Ezekiel?"

My mother raps her forehead, like André Chénier.[2]

"Jacques, if you're in the first three before the inspector's visit, I'll give you . . . Look, this is going to be for you, just for yourself . . . to do just what you like with."

She showed me a gold coin—one whole franc. Oh, why make me lust for filthy lucre? Is that the proper thing for a mother to do?

In my mind a struggle raged—but not for long.

"Just for me? I can spend it any way I like? If I want to, I can give it to a beggar?"

"Give it to a beggar!" My mother wavers; she's appalled by my mad idea, but she replies, before God.

"Yes, it'll be for you. I do hope that you won't give it to a beggar!"

But this is a real revolution! Till now, I've never had anything to call my own—not even my skin . . .

I get her to say it again.

MIDNIGHT

To be first means boning up on history—I'm cramming like mad!

Saturday arrives.

The headmaster comes in. The boys all stand up. He starts reading:

"Greek Composition: First, Jacques Vingtras."

———

"Well?" my mother asks as she comes in.

"I'm first."

"Ah, that's good. You see you can do well enough when you get down to it! Tomorrow I'll make you a lovely *pachade*."

The *pachade* is a kind of dough mixed with potatoes, a yellow concrete slab, without any butter. This is what my mother is presenting as a rare delicacy. But the *pachade* is irrelevant—I want my twenty-sou piece . . . It's not mentioned. It's such a serious matter that I don't dare bring it up myself. My mother's making a huge fuss preparing the *pachade* and shows me an egg—caked in muck—and says, "That looks like a big one to me!"

What a joke! Have I won my twenty sous or not? Wasn't I promised them? Perhaps I'm going to have to ask for them. Why do I have to? Has she forgotten?

I can certainly detect some embarrassment in this coy reference to the "big egg," in her forced smile. I can see that she does remember . . . Perhaps she's standing on her dignity—it's up to her son to remind his mother of her promise . . .

"What about my twenty sous, Ma?"

She doesn't reply right away; but then, suddenly coming over to me, in a very different voice from the one she'd used to make her charming, skittish remark when she'd shown me the large mud-covered egg, she says, "Jacques, will you let your mother have that money, on trust?"

In the tone of her voice you can hear all the dignity of a defeated woman who accepts her fate in advance but asks a favor of her conqueror. She's not defending her purse, you can have it! The coin is lying on the table. But she's begging for time.

Yes, Mother, you can have it on trust. Oh, keep those twenty sous, please keep them, whether you'd like to have them to plug a gap in your housekeeping or you want to use them on my behalf in some deal—and without saying a word, looking rather as if you were begging for forgiveness, you're adding my capital to yours, you're letting me buy an interest in your business, you're making me an associate in your family firm! Thank you!

My mother's a good businesswoman; she knows how to make money work for her. She's told me, very often, how, by the time she was four, she already knew how to earn her living.

She began by buying a pigeon for seven sous that she'd earned looking after the geese. She fattened up the pigeon, sold it, and bought a newborn lamb, fresh from its mother's womb.

She sold the lamb and bought a calf of the same age.

As soon as there was an animal in labor, my mother would rush up and watch this natural phenomenon with curiosity and wait, cash in hand, ready to slap it down as soon as the animal dropped out—cash on the barrelhead, or under the belly!

I'm not so strong-minded! If I had three sous, I'd spend them and would never think of buying a suckling rabbit and using the proceeds to acquire a freshly launched calf!

On one occasion I did think that I was going to have forty sous that I'd be able to keep from the conscript replacement and give to the wooden horses of the merry-go-round. Once again it was a question of being first in my class twice or three times before the headmaster's ball.

And once again, I managed it.

On this occasion I'd set my terms carefully. I'd asked, "*It would be mine? I'll get to keep it?*" I'd indicated that I didn't want to add this sum of money to the amount I'd already invested in the family business. You can put five francs into a firm, you don't put seven!

"*I'll keep them?*"

"*You'll keep them.*"

My mother didn't go back on her word. She handed over the two francs. I put them into my pocket but when I mentioned going on the carousel, my mother reminded me of the contract.

"You said you'd *keep them.*"

And she added that if I meant to get change for the coins, she'd have a bone to pick with me. When I protested, she said, "Now you're making me out to be a liar! That's the last straw, my lad!"

I couldn't deny it. I'd turned myself in. I'd condemned myself to death out of my own mouth.

I was reduced to lugging these two francs around with me like a blind man with his placard.

Every night my mother asked to see them.

One day, I failed to produce them!

I'd gone into the Thirteen Sous Bazaar in Marengo Square: *Nothing over thirteen sous!*

I bought some suspenders with leather tabs. They were a delicate pink!

As soon as I'd done this, I realized the magnitude of my fault. I'd broken into that coin: I'd gotten thirteen sous worth of braces. There were only twenty-seven sous left! What would Mother say? Might as well be hanged for a sheep as for a lamb: I said to myself that I had to press on to the bitter end.

Enjoy yourself—*après moi le déluge!*

I began by diving into a side street to undress and put on my suspenders. After a few vain attempts, being continually interrupted and looked at askance by people amazed to see me standing half naked in their doorways, I thought it wiser, if less *noble*, to go into a more private place, the first I could find.

I only had twenty-seven sous left—twenty-seven coins. Never before had I had such riches at my disposal! My pockets were bulging—they even overflowed. *Ting-a-ling!* The coins are spilling out on the ground—and even elsewhere!

It's horrible; I salvage only twenty-two sous. I'm getting desperate!

I go over to one of the games set up in Marengo Square.

"Three shots a sou! Your chance to win a rabbit!"

I pick up the gun, take aim, and fire . . . keeping my eyes shut, like a banker blowing out his brains.

"He's won a rabbit!"

The crowd picks up the cry, the crowd is eyeing me, they reckon I must be Swiss. Someone says that in Switzerland, children learn to shoot when they're three years old and by the age of ten, they can split a nut from twenty yards away.

"You must give him his rabbit!"

In fact, the stall holder doesn't seem in any great hurry to do so, but the crowd gathers around and takes him on: if he doesn't hand over the rabbit—which is there, nibbling away—they'll turn *him* into rabbit stew.

I've got it, I've got it! I pick it up by the ears and walk away.

You should see all the people! The rabbit's struggling frantically. He'll be slipping out of my grasp any minute!

As in every contest, people take sides. Some back the rabbit, others back the Swiss boy—that's me. I can feel the weight of responsibility on my shoulders. The rabbit gives an occasional jerk, which terrifies my supporters. I'd like to change hands and hold him by his tail for a while, but I don't dare do it in front of the crowd.

I don't have the courage to turn around, but I can sense that their ranks have swollen.

We're marching along in step.

I'm a few yards ahead of the column, all on my own, like a prophet or a gang leader . . .

Along the way, people are wondering what we're doing. Am I driven by some kind religious belief? Is it some kind of social protest?

Well maybe, but right now I'm afraid I'm going to have to

let the rabbit go! Is he a banner I'm carrying along? Then I need to let people know.

My fingers are tightly clenched. Soon I'll be holding nothing but the ears. The rabbit makes one final effort . . .

He's gotten away . . . right into the seat of my pants! Hand-me-downs from my father that have been badly taken in—baggy up top, tight around the legs. The rabbit stays there.

People are getting worried, they're asking questions.

Crowds don't like being messed with. You don't make off with someone's banner just like that!

THE RAB-BIT! THE RAB-BIT! They're chanting, just like an audience that's been waiting too long.

People are peering out of their windows; curious bystanders are joining in.

The rabbit is still caught between me and my pants. I can feel him.

If only I could get away myself! I'll try. There's a passageway handy—I slip into it . . .

They're looking for me, but I know every nook and cranny.

Where to go? I meet Monsieur Laurier, the school bursar. I've run errands for him in the past, I've delivered letters to a lady, I know his secrets. I'm ready to blackmail him—he has to rescue me! I tell him everything.

"Well then, here's your two francs. I'll come home with you and say that I've been looking after you—and just hand that animal over to me!"

My mother believes our lies.

"That's quite all right, Monsieur Laurier—as long as he was with you. Do you know if anything's been happening in town this afternoon? They're saying that the miners are trying to start a riot and have set fire to a convent . . ."

Next day.

"Eat up, Jacques, do eat up! Don't you like rabbit anymore?"

This morning she'd bought a rabbit, going very cheap because it's a little bit squashed and bits of shirt had been found in its teeth.

Where's the skin?

I go into the kitchen.

It's *him* . . .

XIV. BACK HOME

JACQUES is going to spend his vacation back home where he was born.

I get this news from my mother.

"We're going to forgive you all the tricks you've been up to this year, you see, and we're sending you to stay with your uncle; you'll go horseback riding, trout fishing and you'll be eating country sausage. Here's three francs for your traveling expenses."

The truth is that my uncle the priest, who's *going on seventy*, has mentioned putting me in his will and has asked for me to keep him company over the vacation.

The old priest, who has some savings put aside, has a friendly solicitor who's tipped my father off. The letter was lying on the table, so I know all about it. I'd be left a sum of ... to be paid to me when I came of age: that's the idea behind the will.

I've got my overcoat over my arm, a flat cap, and a water bottle.

"He looks like an Englishman."

This remark fills me with pride.

My father (he's spoiling me!) takes me off to the café to have a quick one for the road.

"Go on, drink it up, it'll do you good."

I drink the brandy down in one gulp; it makes me sneeze for the next five minutes and my eyes water as if I'd been crying all night. My tongue is burning so much that I'd like to dip it in the gutter.

"Be nice to your uncle."

That was my father's last piece of advice.

"And be very careful when you're wearing your new jacket!"

That was my mother's final shout as I left.

Off we go, crack the whip, driver!

The farewells had been brief and to the point . . . I was to get to my great-uncle's as quickly as possible.

No great show of feeling.

And for my part I couldn't wait for the horses to get going—fast . . .

I spent the night savoring my bliss. I had a drink, slept, dreamed, drank some cordial at the buffet, pushed up windows, got down *going up hills*.[1]

At six o'clock in the morning, I'm standing in the center of Le Puy, in front of the Coach and Horses.

I leave my luggage at the office and walk up the street to our old house, where Mademoiselle Balandreau will be expecting me. We'd written to tell her I'd be coming, without specifying the day.

I knock.

I certainly don't have to wait long! The dear old spinster comes toward me, all disheveled, overjoyed to see me. She can't stop hugging me . . . as my mother never has.

She sets about making me comfortable: she's concerned that I may be tired and have been cold . . .

"You must be tired out. Now off with that overcoat. It's not possible, it can't be you. How you've shot up! All night in the coach, poor boy—you must be sleepy. Did you get any sleep?"

"Not a wink."

I'm lying like a soldier, but it'll please her to think that her little darling didn't get a wink of sleep and still looks so strong and as fresh as a daisy. What a big boy, who can manage without sleep!

"Would you like to lie down? Look, go and lie down—you don't want to? But you will have a cup of coffee, won't you? You know, like I used to give you without letting your mother know, you remember, with milk—you always took the cream off the top—you used to say: Can I have the skin . . ."

How she loves me!

We make the coffee together. She looks like a witch and I look like a demon, she with loops of ribbon sticking up out of her hair, grinding the coffee, me, among the ashes blowing on the flames . . .

Like all old maids, who like their food and drink, she absolutely adores her coffee—and it's good by God! It's made my lips all greasy. My cheeks are glowing. It's the same bowl where I used to steep my muzzle in the old days, taking extra-large gulps because my mother might come along and she didn't like anyone else to spoil me, apart from herself, and anyway, white coffee's bad for children—"It gives them *phlegm* . . ."

"Come in and see him!"

She's gone off to get the neighbors and returns with all her cronies. In the corner, there's a young girl.

"Don't you remember Mademoiselle Perrinet?"

What, is that the little girl who always wore long velvet knickers, had ruffled hair, with whom I used to have fights, who used to scratch me—I can still show you the marks—who was in fact a really nasty piece of work, and there she is now with a lovely braid of hair held up by a tortoiseshell comb, with a blue bow on her bodice, a little white tulle ruff around her golden brown neck, and a touch of fluff on her cheeks and lip?

"Aren't you going to give each other a kiss?"

I don't dare, she's waiting...Someone gives me a push, she comes forward. Not too much!

I'm red in the face, so is she, a little. In the old days, we've played "husbands and wives", we've had dolls' dinner parties together and that big scratch that I've still got—it looks like a small white thread—came from her, I think as a result of a fit of jealousy.

I can remember that and maybe she hasn't forgotten either.

My trunk is down at the stagecoach office.

I say this as my feeling of vanity revives; it's agreed that I'll go down and pick it up with the help of a neighbor's young son.

"It's very heavy for you," says Mademoiselle Balandreau.

It contains my whole wardrobe—a few shirts, my new jacket, a parcel for Aunt Rosalie, a package for my old uncle, and a stone for another gentleman.

This gentleman is someone important who collects stones and has been looking everywhere for a "kidney stone."

For the last six months I've been hearing about this kidney stone, always with the same feeling of amazement; in the end, they found an iron-colored object that my father carefully wrapped up and that I'm to deliver to the collector—he's related to someone or other in the senior ranks of the academic hierarchy. Monsieur Vingtras's professional prospects may be affected by this kidney stone.

However, the word kidney still makes me feel embarrassed, and when a lady who happens to be there while I'm unpacking asks what the blue pebble is, I say that I don't know.

I go off at once with the nameless stone to deliver it to the recipient who turns it over and over, examining it the way you test an egg. As he shows me out, he puts five francs into my hand.

"That's to help you to enjoy your holiday."

I've just been for a walk around the town. I've been along the river, trying to find a deserted spot. I needed to be alone.

I'm sitting on a fortune! So young, at my age, with no need to render any accounts to my parents, with the right to dispose of it as I please, to spend it recklessly or to save it up, to put it in a jar or to throw it to the winds!

Perhaps there's some hidden crime involved?

No, the recipient of the stone, Monsieur Buzon, is an honest man, he has a nice face—he even looks a bit stupid—and people say that criminals never look stupid. His situation is above reproach.

And yet ... I'm still not clear in my own mind whether I should keep this gentleman's money!

Oh, I was wrong to take it! I'm nothing but a beggar boy!

"Mademoiselle Balandreau, will you please take these five francs back to him—please. Please tell him I took it without thinking!"

And I gave her no peace until I'd tugged her by her dress up to the door of the "kidney stone" man.

I'm hiding in a corner to see if she goes in.

When she comes out, she says, "It's been done," and she gives me a kiss, rubbing her nose several times.

"You're crying!"

"Oh, you dear little boy," she says, no longer trying to hide her tears. "He's such a nice man, he didn't want to take the money. I told him he had to. I'm crying. Am I crying? It's seeing you do that, such a young boy like you! So proud at your age."

She wipes her nose and eyes.

As for me, I feel like throwing stones at the windows; a little more, and I'd have broken five francs worth of windowpanes!

Into the saddle!

My uncle's expecting me tomorrow. A group of his parishioners who've been here for the fair is due to leave; they're going to take me along with them. One of them has in fact just bought a horse. I'll be on it and we'll be riding together to Chaudeyrolles.

We're meeting at Marcelin's.

He's the landlord of an inn in the suburbs. His white wine and pork chops are famous for miles around.

When you go in, you're met by the warm scent of a dunghill and animal sweat from the stables; it breaks over you like a wave. In the bar you can smell the pungent odor of hot vinegar poured over the chops and biting into the parsley.

There are also powerful whiffs of blue cheese.

It's a vigorous odor, tangy, noisy, full of life.

People are cracking jokes in the local patois and filling their glasses to the brim.

I'm playing with a pair of old spurs that are lurking around the table and I'm weighing in my hand various thick sticks with leather loops; some have a story attached to them which people tell. There's the skin of some bailiff on the tip . . .

Hi-ho! Time to go . . .

I can still hear the sound of clinking stirrups, the flip-flop of leather, the champing of bits, along with the name of the stableboy, Baptiste.

I'm too short! They dump me into the saddle and shorten the leathers.

A bit more! Still a bit more! My legs are so short. Now I've got them! They pass me the reins.

"This is what you must do and then this . . . Have you ever ridden before?"

"No."

"Never mind. *Don't git scared!*"

We're all mounted. There are five of us, including me. No-body's paying much attention to me. They think I'm old enough and have enough sense to look after myself. I feel so proud!

CHAUDEYROLLES

When I arrive, I'm aching all over and very sore, but I act as if I wasn't tired.

My first impressions were depressing.

The cemetery is next to the church and there aren't any children to play with; a bitter wind whips low over the ground, angry because it can't find shelter in the leaves of the tall trees. I can only see scrawny fir trees, tall as masts, and over there the mountain looms, stripped bare like the skinny spine of an elephant.

It's empty everywhere, all empty, with only cattle lying on the ground or horses standing motionless in the meadows!

There are paths covered with gray stones like pilgrims' scallop shells and rivers with reddish banks, as if blood had been shed; the grass looks somber.

Then gradually that raw mountain air sets my blood racing and my skin tingling.

I open my mouth wide to gulp it down, I unbutton my shirt so that it can beat against my chest.

Isn't it odd? When it has washed over me, I feel that my vision is so pure, my head so clear!

The fact is that I've come from coal country and its factories with grubby feet, its furnaces with sad backs, its billowing smoke, the filth of its mines, a skyline you could cut with a knife or sweep up with a broom . . .

Here the sky is clear and if a few wisps of smoke drift up, it's a cheerful note in space—they're rising, like incense, from a fire of dead wood lit somewhere over there by a shepherd or from a fire of fresh vine shoots that a cowherd is blowing on in that hut, close to the clump of fir trees . . .

There's the fishpond into which all the water coming off the mountain is frothing down, so cold that it burns your fingers. In it a few fish are darting about. A small grill has been put there to stop them from getting away. And I spend hours watching this water bubbling and listening to it coming and seeing it going away as it swirls like a white skirt over the stones!

The river teems with trout. Once I walked into it up to my thighs; I felt as though my legs had been cut off by a saw of ice. Now I enjoy feeling this sudden icy thrill. Then I thrust my hands into every hole and explore them. The trout slip out between my fingers; but old Régis is there and he is able to catch them and throw them onto the grass where they look like silver blades pricked with gold and tiny patches of blood.

In his stable my uncle keeps a cow; I'm the one who mows the grass. How the scythe hisses through the lush meadow grass when I've sharpened its edge on the blue stone dipped in the cool water!

Now and again I hack into a bird's nest or a nest of vipers.

I carry the fodder to the cow myself and when she hears me coming she greets me by lifting her head. I've been given the job of taking her up to the pasture and bringing her back myself. The friendly local folk address me as if I'm someone of importance and the young shepherds treat me like one of their pals.

I'm so happy.

What if I were to stay and become a peasant?

I mention this thought one night to my uncle when he'd had dinner served by the fireside and drunk some of his favorite dark rosé.

"Later on, when I'm dead. You'll be able to buy a property. But you wouldn't like to be a farmworker, would you?"

I'm not so sure about that . . .

When it rains and there's no chance of going fishing or in search of wild currants at the foot of the mountains, among the scabby rocks—or else when the sun's shining like a steel sheet turned blue by heat and grilling the bare shadeless countryside—on these days I shut myself away in my uncle's library and read and read . . . There's the biography of famous men by Abbé de Feller.[2] I pounce on any passage about Napoleon and have daydreams full of Sainte-Hélène. I look out the window at the deserted landscape, the empty horizon, searching for Hudson Lowe.[3] If I could only get my hands on him.

My uncle is expecting the local parish priest for the *conference*.

They're here. I can hear them sitting around the table saying nasty things about the curate of Saint-Parlier and the curate of Solignac; they don't seem to be in the least interested in the Good Lord!

My uncle hardly ever joins in the conversation. He can do this because of his age; he even makes himself out to be older than he is, pretending to be deaf and almost blind but the wine has loosened the other priests' tongues. A fat one who looks like a drunkard is bursting the buttons of his filthy wine-stained cassock and rumpling up his clerical bands, yellow with coffee stains. There's a thin one with a face like a snake who's drinking only water, but his way of swiveling his eyes to and fro scares me. I once saw a villain, who put poison in other people's glasses in the theater in Saint-Étienne, and he looks just like him.

The rest are guzzling like pigs, and when they have a prayer to say they do it with their mouths full.

Beneath their dirty cassocks you can see their underwear.

The fat, grubby one turns to me.

"Is this your nephew, your reverence? Well, he's certainly got a healthy appetite, anyway, that boy. What a sturdy boy!"

He runs his hand down my spine. I feel disgusted and embarrassed.

"And what are you doing about the Protestant Maclou?" a voice inquires.

"He's now at the Lake of Saint-Front."

"With the other bunch! They've set up a nest there."

"A vipers' nest," hissed Snake Face.

So there are some Protestants! I've read what they say about them in the Chaudeyrolles library—and the Protestants who were burned at the stake, who are condemned to Hell, seem to me a breed of souls in torment.

One day I go off on my own to Saint-Front. It's a long trip and all the way I'm thinking of Saint Bartholomew's Day and I can see red crosses[4] against the blue sky.

Here's the lake with a couple of boats moored in the reeds and some huts lost in the surrounding fields.

I'm told to go over to the one on the left, the hut of Jean Robanès; all I need to say is that I'm the priest's nephew and they'll offer me a drink of milk and show me the Protestants.

They make me welcome. "And as for the Protestants," a man tells me, "there's one just over there, standing in that furrow."

He has a harsh, sad look—thin, sallow, with a pointed chin—and is stiff as a ramrod.

Aren't the police keeping an eye on him? Do people talk to him? Is he chained to a cannonball? In the Bible, I remember, all the ungodly are punished, and the books in the library call them scoundrels! I mention this to my uncle that evening; he makes a poor reply and I begin to think that the infamous Protestants are rather like those animals in La Fontaine's *Fables* who have the power of speech. It's all a big joke!

Time to leave.

My uncle has to make his rounds and in any case, I have to go back to school in Saint-Étienne.

We're following the route that I came by, but this time I've got a quieter horse. I've been given some underpants, and they've padded me and rubbed tallow in beforehand. In any case, I've been riding now for a month, I'm toughened up, and as I turned around in my saddle to bid a final farewell to the countryside, I feel full of joy. I kick my horse with my heels to make him gallop and I pat him like an old friend . . .

My uncle leaves me at the Mission Cross.

"Work hard!" he says.

"You'll write to Dad to let me come back next year?"

"To your father! It's not your father who'll try to stop you coming though maybe your mother will—you see, I'm not in her good books."

I know that.

During the first few days of my visit, I heard the maid talking in the bedroom.

"He's Madame Vingtras's son?"

"Yes."

"Is she the one who said such nasty things about you?"

"That's all over and done with now, I've forgiven her—and I'm fond of the boy . . ."

My uncle wasn't good-looking: he had tiny eyes, a large nose, and was hairy in all sorts of places, but he was kind.

I knew he sensed that I was unhappy at home—that when I said good-bye I was leaving my happiness and my freedom behind. He was as sad as I was.

"Good-bye," he said, giving me a hug and a handshake, which pleased me even more than the hug.

"Good-bye," he said. "You'll find something in the bottom of your bag. Don't say anything about it to your mother."

He held out his old gray fingers again, nodded his head and left.

If only that kind old uncle had been my father!

But it seems that priests can't be anybody's father: I wonder why?

I'd sent Mademoiselle Balandreau a letter warning her of my arrival, a letter which she'd shown around to everybody.

"Hasn't he got lovely handwriting? Just look at those capital letters!"

She's gotten a bed ready for me in a tiny closet next to her own bedroom. It's pint-sized but I have the right to shut the door, fling my cap down on my bed, and dump my overcoat with a sigh of relief. I'm behaving like a bachelor, I'm tidying up some papers, I'm humming to myself . . .

What's this something that my uncle said was at the bottom of my bag?

Ten francs!

Since they come from him, I can accept them . . .

I'm rich all of a sudden!

It's lovely weather and already by nine o'clock I'm down in the town, a free man and exulting in my freedom; I'm feeling lighthearted and strong. I'm striding along, my heels slamming into the pavement, soaking up everything that comes into sight as I go: the cloud in the sky, the soldier on the street. I prowl around the market, skirting the town hall. I go strolling down the Breuil with my hands behind my back, kicking odd stones with the tips of my shoes, like the tax collector walking in front of me, whom I'm mimicking a bit.

I haven't got any homework, no punishments, no father, no mother, nothing.

There's the town crier who stops on the corner of the square and gathers people around him by beating his drum; there are officers with gold epaulettes I pass close by; I've got the right to join any group of people in the street I want to!

Every morning I get my shoes cleaned by Moustache. Just think of that!

And it's taken only one month of vacation, looking after the cow, making excursions into the countryside, taking lonely walks, to open up my mind and my heart!

In the evening, we go to the café; there are four or five of us, old school pals. We throw a coin to see who pays for our coffee, our glass of spirits, and we light up our brandy! All this smoke, this whiff of spirits, the click of billiard balls, the popping of corks, the whole thing sharpens my senses: I feel as if I've grown a mustache and could lift the billiard table!

When we leave the Horseshoe we go for a stroll—like gentlemen of leisure. When anything interesting turns up, we stop in a group. Sometimes I walk backward in front of our gang.

Then our youth takes over.

"You're *it*! Can you jump over that bench? Can you hold this stone out at arm's length?"

"Bet I can knock Michelon down!"

I don't know if I'm stronger but they think I am because I'm so determined! I'd burst a blood vessel before I'd drop that stone or beg Michelon for mercy!

I'm *my own master* and I can do what I like. I'm even a sort of leader, the boy they listen to and who the other day said "Stay out of this!" when an idiot threw a stone at us. I caught up with him, yanked him back by his belt, and gave him a swollen ear in front of our gang. "Say you're sorry!" He was bigger than me.

We went on a boat trip. Nobody knew how to row and we almost drowned a dozen times. Oh, what fun we had!

They wanted to make me skipper.

"You must be joking! Choose Michelon! I'm going to take forty winks."

And I stretched out in the boat, staring up at the sun, which made me blink, trailing my hand in the blue water . . .

One of my uncles, I don't know on what side of the family, comes running after me in the Martouret, barely leaving himself time to go warn Mademoiselle Balandreau that he's carrying me off in his buggy to meet his family; he'll send me home the day after tomorrow.

"Off we go, Jacquot! Gee-up, Gray!"

As we drive out through the suburbs, he lets me take the reins. I crack my whip now and again just for the fun of it and wave it about. I seem to be swearing: "Gee-up, you old nag!"

We stop at the White Horse for Gray's feed of oats. I jump down from the buggy like a clown and crack the whip like a horse dealer.

The uncle from I'm-not-sure-which-side is as pleased as punch.

"This is my nephew," he announces proudly to everyone in the inn.

We eat our dinner with our elbows on the table and, while eating eggs in wine, then eggs and bacon, before finishing with a hard-boiled egg, he tells me the history of his branch of the family: he married so-and-so, he's descended from first cousin, etc., etc.

"You'll be meeting your cousins, they're pretty girls!"

They are pretty. And how wide-awake and mischievous they seem.

Now it's my turn to be like a girl. I become awkward and feel stupid. They speak excellent French for country girls. They went to school in the neighboring market town.

"Have a glass of wine!" they say to me.

"Yes, a glass of wine."

In pubs or inns I only accept wine to drink someone's health, and the clinking glasses make a cheerful sound. It's the same way with the brandy! I order it to set it on fire: the blue flames are pretty. But now, suddenly, I feel overshadowed by these cousins with their bold looks and ringing voices and I'm going to drink—red wine for Dutch courage.

"Cheers!" they say after pouring a drop—a very small drop—of wine in the bottom of their glasses.

They've filled mine to the brim.

I think I'm a bit tipsy—look out, you two!

And the truth is that I really do have one hell of a nerve, I'm as bold as brass!

They wanted to show me the orchard. Good deal! Off we go to the orchard—I get into it by jumping over the gate.

That's the sort of person I am!

My cousins watch in amazement and I laugh as I come back to help them over: one, two, up we go!

They give little squeals and fall into my arms as they land; they hang on to me for support and we're all going to fall over! And that's exactly what does happen, we all lose our balance and topple over on the grass. They're wearing blue garters.

What beautiful weather! A golden sun! Big drops of sweat are pouring down my temples and they've also got beads of perspiration trickling down their cheeks. The air's full of the monotonous drone of bees buzzing around their hives behind the currant bushes . . .

"What on earth are you up to down there?" shouts a voice from the farmhouse door.

What are we up to? We're being happy in a way I've never been happy before and am never going to be happy again. I'm ankle-deep in flowers . . . and I've just kissed cheeks smelling of strawberries.

We'll have to go back, they're calling us! We come sedately like sensible people and each of my cousins has caught hold of me with one arm; they're leaning against me slightly, crossing hands, and tugging my elbow each time they want to tell me or ask me about something.

On top of which they've already started telling me off! They claim that I'm not answering their questions or else I'm giving them the wrong answers. "If you keep making fun of us like that, we're not going to talk to you anymore . . . Do you mind!"

They're giving me tiny slaps, they're complaining about me!

The fact is that to avoid trouble, I've adopted a system: each time they ask me a question that seems to me too difficult to answer, I give them a kiss.

Oh, how right I was to drink that wine!

133

They're trying to *catch me out*.

"Do you know any geography?"

"Not much."

"You must know what the chief town of . . . is?"

I don't have the faintest idea and to get out of answering, I give them kiss after kiss, as a result of which I lose my poise, in spite of my glass of red wine, and if they weren't giggling and trying to dodge my kisses, they'd see that I was as red as a beet.

We're sitting down to eat. It's noon. In the yard the farmhands' clogs are beating time for dinner and everybody comes indoors, even the chickens, who are expecting their grain, are crowding around the doorway. A lame chick hurries up, dragging its claw; the area around the farmhouse is deserted; in the fields I can see the plows coming to a halt and the plowmen sitting down to eat the soup that the green-aproned maid has just brought to them.

The great calm and silence of midday has descended.

On our table (there's a separate dinner being served for the nephew) there's a white cloth, fruit displayed in shallow bowls, and a sprig of wild rose that quivers in water, as fresh as a plume of green feathers with tiny red bells.

A vague fragrance of elderberry wafts in—oh, how my heart leaps at the sweetness of that scent!

After dinner.

"How about taking our cousin for a drive in the buggy?"

"Gray's too tired," the father said.

"Yes, of course. So where are we going to go then?"

Down to see the elders, I suggest, and a moment later

we're busily cleaning out the pith of elder branches to make whistles that shine like brass. Cousin Marguerite cuts her finger and big drops of blood fall on the white leaves.

We pull up tufts of grass to stanch the wound then leave those nasty trees that have made her cut herself far behind.

We move off toward the pond in which ducks are splashing about; we go into the barn where the threshers stop when the young ladies and their cousin come in! Then they start up again, swinging in a big circle and beating in time, the sheaves on the echoing floor. I get hold of one to have a go: I can feel the arm swing as it shoots off like a catapult and then comes back like a hammer, making a breeze as it catches the air . . . If it came into contact with a head, it would crush it like an eggshell.

At the bottom of the field there's a hole full of water and dead branches, with little green frogs gleaming in the sunlight. I make a fishing line using a bit of wood I found lying on the ground, a piece of string that I dig out of my pocket, and a pin provided by Marguerite. Her sister offers a length of bright red ribbon and fishing begins.

What a Babel as the first frog bites! But it's got to be pulled off the hook and nobody dares do it, the frog gets away and the girls run off.

I follow them! We spend a wonderful day roaming through the fields, wading into the river up to our knees! I chase them, jumping from stone to stone rubbed smooth by the current.

All at once my foot slips and I fall into the water.

I emerge streaming, with my trousers soaked and sticking to me: I go off to lie in the sun. I'm steaming like a pot of soup.

"Shall we wring him out?" says one of my cousins, twisting her hands like a washerwoman.

They go off by themselves to remove their stockings behind

a rock that barely hides them; whatever they may say, their legs are soaking wet . . . and so white!

At last we're dry and off we go again in high spirits.

Our eyes are sparkling, our skin glowing. We go along paths edged by blackberry bushes and full of purple plums as sour as vinegar, which we eat by handfuls—I swallow the stones, to show that I'm a man.

We get mad, we get lost. But we always make up and meet again, arm in arm, inquisitive: I tell them what I do in Saint-Étienne, the pranks we get up to at school; they talk about boarding-school larks, this and that, and finally they exclaim, "Which of us do you like best?"

"Yes, which one, Jacquot dear?" said Marguerite, confronting me point-blank and throwing polite formulas to the wind.

Not knowing how to answer, I kiss them both.

They work over my face with a flower and stand back to bombard me with purple plums.

In the evening, feeling pretty weary, we all sit chatting on the warm stone in front of the house like little old people outside the door of an inn.

Oh, Marguerite's definitely my favorite! Every time she finishes a sentence, she catches hold of my hand and ruffling my hair with her fingers, says, "Push your hair out of your eyes, you don't look nice like that!"

They take me up to my bedroom which is next to the hayloft—the hayloft where last winter they hung the grapes and piled the apples with bunches of fennel and tufts of dried lavender. Their scent lingers behind and I keep the door open so that it comes into *my place*—yet one more place that's *mine* . . . for just one night.

I walk to the window and watch the hamlet's lights go out in the distance. A nightingale rustles in a pile of firewood and starts to sing. A cuckoo goes *cu-ckoo* in the trees of the big wood and the frogs are croaking in the marsh reeds.

I listen and finish by not hearing anything.

The rooster startles me awake. I'd gone to sleep with my forehead resting in my hands, and I shiver as I undress and fall into a dreamless sleep, stupefied by scents, glutted with happiness . . .

Two days spent like that—quarreling, making up, in the bushes and the flowers and the hay: the broad sweep of the thresher, the gentle song of the rivers, and the scent of elderberry!

Time to leave!

"You'll be writing to me," sighs Marguerite as she says good-bye. "Look, here's a little bunch of flowers to remind you. Good night!"

She holds her forehead up for a kiss—only her forehead. Over these two days, she's been letting me kiss her on the lips; she looks very serious and I can see her standing there and waving her handkerchief in the distance like ladies of the manor in books when their husbands-to-be ride off: I feel for the bunch of flowers that she stuffed into my shirt and prick my finger on the thorns. I suck the finger.

We'll meet this bouquet again, with tears in its withered flowers . . .

XV. PLANS TO ESCAPE

I'M GOING into the third form.[1] Teacher: Professor Turfin.

He came second in the *agrégation*; he's the nephew of a departmental head in a ministry; he wears stiff collars and a long frock coat; he's got a fleshy, wet lower lip, china-blue eyes, and long lank hair.

He despises assistant tutors and despises the poor, bullies scholarship boys, and pokes fun at anyone who's badly dressed.

He makes other boys laugh at my expense. I think he's trying to make my mother look ridiculous too.

I hate him.

As the son of one of the teachers, I'm granted privileges.

Although I'm a day student, I'm punished like a boarder. I'm always in detention and hardly ever able to get home. They bring me a bit of stale bread from the school dining room.

"By doing this, I'm getting him a free lunch and saving old Ma Vingtras a bit of her *hash* as well."

This is Turfin talking to one of his colleagues, who smiles; he's talking in an undertone, at a distance, but I suspect he wants me to hear.

I merely shove my hands deep into my pockets and pretend to be laughing! I'm crying. How many sobs I've stifled when nobody was watching!

I'm turning into nothing but a "detention freak!"

Lines and more lines! Made to stay behind, given detention, solitary confinement . . .

I prefer solitary confinement to being kept in.

Inside my four walls I'm free. I can whistle, make small paper balls, draw funny figures, and play marbles against myself.

With pieces of wood and bits of string I can build a gallows to hang Turfin on. When evening comes, I can get down to work and finish my punishments.

At nine I'm sent back home.

Solitary doesn't scare me; I get a little feeling of pride going home at night through the deserted courtyards, meeting a few boys as I pass who look on me as a rebel!

We often come across Malatesta on his way from some other place of solitary confinement. He's the leading troublemaker in the senior prep classes.

He's just starting his final year here.

Next year he's going to be admitted to Saint-Cyr.[2] He's the star student at the school; they wouldn't dare expel him for all the tea in China.

He wears a gold-braided kepi and *he's taking fencing lessons*!

As he goes past, Malatesta gives me a nod and says, "Hail, Vingtras!" Hail as in Latin, and Vingtras as though I were already a grown-up.

It's being kept in that annoys me most.

When I'm in detention, I just accumulate more punishments. I'm so clumsy! First it's an inkwell which I knock over, then my pen dropping on the floor, my papers which fly all over the place, my desk lid which I manage to pull off . . .

"A hundred lines, Vingtras!"

Bang! My pile of books falls on the floor with an infernal crash!

"Another hundred lines!"

"Please sir!"

"Answering back! Five pages of Greek grammar!"

More and more! All the time!

They're trying to bury me under punishments, that lot!

I hardly ever get a glimpse of the sun!

On Sundays, as on every other day, I turn up for the long detention from three until six in a classroom which on this day is really dismal because of the oppressive silence, the melancholy sound of a passing footstep, of a door slamming, of a lone hornet, the cry of a hawker in the distance . . .

There are about a score of us.

A scratching pen, a cough, the supervisor walks around the room a couple of times looking at the sky through the window.

"Please sir . . . leave the room?"

He gives a nod, and on the pretext of going to the lavatory, I loiter for a while in the long hallways. I poke my nose into empty classrooms, I throw a marble out of a window, I flip a tiny ball of bread to a sparrow, I eye the matron and try and steal some fruit from the dining room, then, on one foot, I hop back to the classroom.

Once again I bury my head in whatever paper's left on my desk and scribble away with any remaining ink. The last thing I'm thinking about is what I'm writing, which is why sometimes in my lines you'll find "Turfin the lout, Turfin the moron . . ."

TUESDAY MORNING

There's a Latin passage to translate.

I was looking up a word in a very small dictionary that my father had given me instead of a Quicherat.[3]

Turfin thinks it's a crib.

He comes over and asks to see the book that I was hiding a moment ago.

I show him the little dictionary.

"That's not the book."

"Yes it is, sir!"

"You were copying your translation."

"That's not true—"

Before I finish speaking, he slaps me across the face.

I get beaten by my father and mother, but they're the only people in the world who have the right to strike me. That man is hitting me because he loathes the poor.

He's hitting me to demonstrate that he's a friend of the deputy prefect, that he came second in the *agrégation*.

If only my parents were like other parents, like Destrême's, who came to complain that one of the teachers had given their son a gentle slap!

But instead of being annoyed at Turfin's behavior, my father turned on me because Turfin is a colleague, because Turfin has influence, and because my father thinks—rightly—that a few slaps more or less won't have much effect on my noggin. True, but they do leave a mark in my heart.

I feel a dull surge of anger against my father.

I can't stand it any longer; I must get away from home and from school.

Where am I going to go? I'll go to Toulon.

I'll sign on as a cabin boy on a ship and sail around the world.

If I'm given kicks or lashes, I'll be getting them from a stranger. If they flog me too much, I'll jump overboard and swim to some desert island where there aren't any lessons to be learned or Greek to translate . . .

And there's one consolation: even if you're tied to the

mainmast or in chains down in the hold, there's the hope, in due course, of becoming an officer and earning the right to punch the captain's nose.

Turfin is able to torment me as much as he likes without giving me a chance to get my own back.

As long as I'm still a boy, my father can make me cry and bleed; I've got to obey and respect him.

The family code gives him the power of life and death over me.

After all, I am a thoroughly bad boy!

When, instead of learning Greek verbs, you watch passing clouds or flies buzzing around, you deserve to have your head bashed and to be beaten black-and-blue.

You're a good-for-nothing: instead of dreaming of wearing a mortarboard and an academic gown with an ermine-lined hood like a schoolteacher, you want to become a cobbler, spend your life with glue and wax, stitching with thread and wielding a paring knife!

You think that in an academic gown you'll be poor and in a leather apron you'll be free—it's an insult to your father!

It's wrong of me and he's right to beat me.

With my vulgar tastes, my longing to become an apprentice, and my working-class obsessions, I'm a disgrace to my father!

My parents are providing me with a good education and I don't want it!

I'm happier with farmhands and cobblers than with people who've passed the *agrégation*; and I've always felt that my uncle Joseph was less stupid than Monsieur Beliben!

"Such a gifted boy and such a slacker!" they keep on saying. But it's because I'm so physically gifted that I'm bored by all these classrooms and prep rooms where I'm shut up all day. My legs have got the fidgets and my head's aching.

I'm cheerful by nature, I enjoy having a good laugh, I sometimes feel I'll burst if I can't have one! Whenever I can escape from punishments and solitary confinement, get away from any sort of teacher, I leap around like a big dog, I'm as lively and exuberant as a black man.

A black man!

Ah, I've been dreaming of being a black man for ages!

In the first place, black women love their children, so I'd have had a mother who loved me.

And at the end of the day, they like to spend their time weaving baskets, they braid lianas, they carve coconut shells and dance around!

Chirpy chirpy, bamboula! Shake a leg, Canada![4]

How I'd loved to have been born black! But I wasn't: just my luck!

Well, if I can't be black, I'll join the navy.

It'll be better for all concerned.

I'll be the death of them—they've been telling me that all the time, haven't they?

So they'll be reborn, revived!

I'll be leaving them my share of beans, my slice of bread—but it'll be their job to polish off the leg of lamb!

Polish off the leg of lamb?

I really am a nasty piece of work! I'm not just looking forward to the pleasure of getting away from that leg of lamb, I'm consumed by a desire for vengeance, and like some young Jesuit, I'm saying to myself that they're the ones who're going to have to eat that leg of lamb—roasted, heated up, cold, in a vinaigrette, in a black sauce, ground up, as meatballs—just as I had to do!

And what a hypocrite I am—and I don't stop at that!

I tell myself I have to practice, get myself into training, toughen myself up, so I'm trying my hardest to find every possible way to get myself *thrashed*.

On board it'll be a rough life, I'll have to break myself in

in advance or, rather, they'll have to break me in for the job;
so for weeks now, I've been telling them I've broken bowls,
lost bottles of ink, used up all my paper! I have to say that I'm
always devouring paper and swallowing ink, I just can't help
doing it!

My father has no suspicions at all and falls for everything,
poor old chap!

In the space of two weeks, I've worn out three of his rulers
and a pair of his boots—he breaks the rulers over my knuckles and sinks his boots into my backside . . .

I'm costing him a small fortune, I'm ruining the man!

I think he'll forgive me later, once he realizes the purpose behind it all; and anyway, he doesn't seem to find it too
boring.

Just a bit tiring, perhaps, when he's spent too much time
beating me—it makes him hot! Then I drag myself over to
the window to close it, so that he doesn't catch cold from
the draft . . .

At night, I'm sleeping in a trunk—wearing my shirt.

> *In my shirt I sleep!*
> *Almighty God, please keep*
> *This holy deed*
> *Safe to succeed!*

Shall I go by myself?

What a bore! When there are a number of you, you can
capture a ship, become a buccaneer, lead a mutiny if neces-
sary, and, when you're tired, found a colony.

It so happens that Malatesta left only yesterday.

His mother has suddenly fallen ill and he's gone to visit her.

He adores her—even though she's a bad mother!

She's always sending him watermelons, dates, and oranges;
and unknown to the headmaster, she arranges for him to receive money.

"I suppose your mother's got lots of money?" I asked him one day.

"No, but she is really nice!"

"So you're very fond of her?"

"Yes, I'm fond of her."

As he says that, there's the trace of a tear in his eyes.

And he's going to be a soldier!

To have such a bad mother and be so fond of her! A mother who comforts him when he's punished, who perhaps cuts down on the amount of bread she eats so as to send more oranges to her son!

"What does your mother do?"

"She runs a cooked-meat shop in Modena."

And he doesn't seem to feel ashamed!

Cooked-meat shop! That explains everything... She's *as common as dirt*!

My mother would never run a cooked-meat shop. Never!

Oh yes, my mother is proud, I'll grant her that.

Even if it hadn't been for her own sake, she would have refused to sell ham, for the sake of her son...

She preferred to live in poverty or to advise my father to be a coward!

She preferred to live a stupid, stunted, squalid life but she was the wife of a civil servant, a lady, and one day her child would say, "My father was a teacher!"

A fat lot of good that'll do me. My parents seem to have a funny idea of how much an *academic gentleman* is worth.

If she could hear not only what the pupils are muttering—that's not important—but what their parents are saying, she'd realize what people think of schoolteachers! If she knew how they're despised even by their superiors—the headmaster, the inspector, the deputy headmaster—who, when a rich mother complains, reply, "Don't worry, Madame, I'll give him a rap on the knuckles he won't forget in a hurry!"

In the little closet where they usually shut me up before taking me off to solitary confinement, I can eavesdrop on what's being said in the headmaster's study, and whenever I can, I put my ear to the wall to listen.

One day a teacher came to complain that one of the servants had been insolent to him. The headmaster didn't hesitate: he sends for the assistant whom he uses as his secretary. "Monsieur Souillard, Monsieur Pichon has complained to me that Jean was insolent to him in front of the boys—one of them has got to go. I think highly of Jean: he keeps the toilets very clean. Monsieur Pichon is an idiot who has no particular recommendations from anyone; he'll spend a hundred francs on books for an etymology he's writing; he dresses slovenly in a way likely to bring our school into disrepute.

"Add this note in the margin of his report file.

"*Pichon*: quarrelsome with servants, has dirty habits, knows his classics. Would be a valuable addition to the staff of another establishment."

Ah, long live cooked-meat shops, say I!

And cobblers too! Long live grocers and cowherds!

Long live the blacks!

I'll do anything, absolutely anything, rather than become a schoolteacher . . .

So I can't count on Malatesta who's at his mother's shop in Modena and has even left a whole box of candied fruit untouched in his desk, which we're sharing among ourselves during detention.

I look around to find some other accomplice; I'm casting the deep-set gaze of a sea captain over my troop of schoolmates. I sound out a few of them: they hesitate. Some of them say that they're not bored at home, quite the opposite, they have a lot of fun. Their fathers laugh and joke with them and their mothers have the same defects as Malatesta's . . .

"So you don't get beaten?"

"Yes, now and again, but whenever that happens I'm happy because I'm sure that in the evening I'll be taken to a show or else given ten sous. My father gets pretty embarrassed and they—he and my mother—try to work out how it happened. 'You're to blame—no, it's you— At least you didn't really hurt him? Well, I did hit him pretty hard, what a brute I am!' "

"You really did hurt him, at least?" my mother asks my father, unlike those other stupid parents. "I hope that this time he really felt it!"

And it must be admitted that my mother's being logical. If children get beaten, it's for their own good, so they can remember that every time they do something wrong, they'll get their hair pulled or find themselves with bleeding ears, in fact, that they're going to suffer for what they've done . . . She has her system and she applies it.

She has a greater sense of responsibility than the parents of that boy who's given ten sous every time he has his face slapped, whose parents hit him without knowing why and are then sorry they've hurt him . . .

I can't understand why my pal is so fond of his stupid parents who are so lacking in energy.

I've landed on a mother who's sensible and methodical.

So I'm not going to be able to find anyone to come with me?

How about Ricard?

He's one of nine children.

They all get mercilessly beaten—what a blessing!

I put out a feeler. When I say a feeler, I'm speaking figuratively: he forbids me to touch him (his ribs are too sore)—he's a filthy dirty boy—he explains that it's because they're dirty that their mother beats them; but she's extremely dirty herself!

She also beats them because they use bad language; they swear like troopers; the five-year-old is always shouting, "Shit!"

There's only one member of the family who's a good boy and never swears—my classmate.

He still gets beaten. Now why on earth is that?

It's because in families there mustn't be any favorites—that always has a bad effect. The others might complain.

And also: *he just stands there like an idiot.*

He stands there like an idiot—that's why they beat him.

The others get beaten because they're noisy and rude and foulmouthed; he's beaten because he's quiet and doesn't say anything.

He just stands there like an idiot.

He has one further weakness (who hasn't?): he's a bed wetter.

That's the secret of his misery, that's why he's sad, that's why his mother keeps on shouting that she's going to tan his hide—and then start all over again!

And his parents seem to think that he does it for fun, that he enjoys doing it, that he's trying to be a smart aleck or to provoke them, as a game or a threat or an aristocratic whim, just because he's got nothing better to do. Yet the poor boy does everything he can—and whatever he does is no good. He wakes up surrounded by the evidence of his crime and they have to hang his bedclothes out of the window to dry every morning.

They flaunt his shame. Everyone knows what he's done wrong, just as when the flag is flying over the palace, everyone knows that the King is in residence in the Tuileries.

He sheds tears of distress, the poor little bugger, and at night he goes without everything at supper, he drinks through a straw . . .

He prays to God and the Holy Mother—all in vain—and he's trying to find a saint who specializes in this sort of sin; he relapses, hopelessly, and faces his mother's reprisals. She has an odd phrase to announce that the fun is beginning. As she raises her cane, she proclaims in her loud, rolling voice, "And now we're going to *make the rabbit shed a tear!*"

Doubtless it's a cruel and ironic allusion to her son's complaint and to the operation carried out by rabbiters on the rabbit[5] who's been hit by their deadly buckshot . . .

I convince him. He'll be allowed to hang his hammock separately on board ship and no one will know that the rabbit has shed a tear!

Supposing I had a word with Vidaljan as well?

He's the son of a tax assessor; like me, he gets thrashed to within an inch of his life.

He's another boy who'd like to be something his father wouldn't like him to be: he wants to be a magician.

We had a magician who visited the school. The boys paid one franc each. Vidaljan was unlucky enough to be chosen to go up on stage and hold the pack of cards; he saw the doves having their throats cut, the handkerchief being burned; he rubbed shoulders with Domingo, the stooge.

"Excuse me, young man, what's that you've got in your pocket?"

And out of his pocket a wig was extracted.

"So you keep your savings in your hair?"

And a five-franc piece is grabbed out of his hair.

"And now thank you, young man."

He went back to his seat in front of the whole school; he was mobbed, questioned, envied, his classmates are consumed by jealousy.

Why was he the one they chose? Why'd they pick him?

"He's lucky," says Ricard, thinking that next night . . .

———

Ever since that evening when he was given that role in the light of all the magician's candles, the attention of the crowd, under the rapt gaze of the *big boys* and the *middle school*, Vidaljan has made up his mind, he's decided what his vocation is; he's going to start on his career at once. He has always had a knack for magic tricks!

He's the biggest sneak thief in the school; he had already enjoyed dipping into other people's desks and he could extract a pencil resting on a schoolmate's ear without the owner ever suspecting; he could cut an orange into eight pieces and hide one of them in a handkerchief.

He'd already conjured away the whipping top, the glass marble, and the pen with the death's head. He had a collection of little drawings he'd gotten out of his friends' boxes by means of some special keys.

Not that he was an art lover, but he enjoyed picking locks and slipping his fingers into cracks. He'd steal demerit books and the lists of grades from teachers' pockets. He once stole a teacher's wallet and for a week Monsieur Boquin's secrets had been at his mercy.

As a result, poor Boquin had missed a chance of getting married and nearly lost his job.

Vidaljan produced an improved version of the pen used for writing lines: he'd succeeded in fastening four nibs together, something never seen before, as even Gravier admitted—and he had spent three months in a boarding school in Paris; Vidaljan could now write four lines of Virgil at once!

He was drawn toward magic; he then became infatuated by white magic.

He bought *The Secrets of Young Albert*.[6] We saw him with goblets and thimbles, vanishing peas, dried toads, and empty eggshells.

He was making gunpowder.

That's what made me decide to approach him, in spite of the vague distrust that his habits aroused in me.

Two days earlier he'd been knocked almost unconscious by his revered progenitor when he'd discovered that instead of doing his homework, his son was making machines; and while making his bed, his mother had found snakeskins and brass tacks nestling with the familiar bedbugs.

I offered to appoint him my lieutenant.

He accepted—so did Ricard.

On the appointed day, however, the flag is flying at Ricard's window and he throws a piece of paper—slightly damp—down to me; it's full of painful details. He's been abnormally criminal and been given more than his usual beating; he's quite incapable of moving...

And Vidaljan? He doesn't turn up either. The boys are arriving one after the other, the bell rings, they all go in, he's not there. What's happened?

I make my way furtively in the direction of his house. I meet some gossiping women who are saying that the area has been almost blown up and the Vidaljan boy with it. "He dropped a match into a bowl that he was making gunpowder in; he'd got the idea from that young layabout, the son of that woman who always haggles over everything, the one who goes about with her shawl tugged tightly around her back, you know, she's as flat as a pancake: Vingtron, Vingtras? They'll be looking for him now, I hope they shut him up in jail."

"But look, there he is, I recognize him," shouted one of the gossiping women, suddenly spying me where I was crouching in a corner and on the point of making myself scarce.

They grab me—take me back to my house.

What a walloping I got from my mother!

She stopped beating me only after I swore, by all that was holy, never to run away again.

And Vidaljan? He recovered and stopped making gun-powder.

And Ricard? The shock of Vidaljan's accident brought about an emotional upheaval and he stopped wetting his bed.

Well, that was something, anyway.

XVI. DRAMA

A NEIGHBOR, Madame Brignolin, has become a friend of the family.

She's a plump, jolly little creature, with glowing eyes, as lively as a cricket; it's a pleasure to watch her tripping along, joking and flirting, leaning backward as she laughs, meanwhile smoothing her hair with a rather expansive gesture that looks like a caress! And she has a way of jigging up and down which even my father seems to find odd because it makes him blush, go pale, fall silent . . . and knock over chairs.

Funny little woman! She's got three children.

Bringing this lot up and keeping them out of mischief involves frenzied activity: she's never still, dressing one, soaping the other, sticking a cap on this little noggin, a bonnet on that little pate, mending trousers, ironing dresses, blowing this boy's nose, wiping that girl's face. Forever on the move!

At night she brings out a smart housecoat and plays a little music on an old grand piano; at the end of each piece she produces a deep *boom* down among the low notes and a high-pitched *ting-a-ling* among the high ones: *Boom boom, ting-a-ling, ting-a-ling* . . .

"Monsieur Vingtras, you're as dull as dull, that's because you haven't had a shave, you see! Come back tomorrow, after going to the barber, and I'll give you a kiss—you can give me the first taste of your shave!"

At the same time she whisks past him and places her hand on his, brushing against him with her skirt. She even takes his arm and offers her waist for him to hold.

"Let's have a waltz," she says.

And she dances gaily up to him on her saucy little feet, leaning backward from the waist, with her hair flowing, and swings her partner away; after a couple of turns around the room—which is too small—she gives a laugh and collapses on a chair—which creaks—in front of my father who doesn't say a word.

Then off she dashes in the direction of the kitchen from which sounds have been emerging.

It's the little girl who's fallen over, the little boy who's broken a jug; she rushes away in a swirl of muslin, is swallowed up and disappears, only to come rushing madly back, doubled up and hooting with laughter, with both hands squeezed between her knees and shaking her pretty head as she tells some unseemly misadventure that has just befallen one of her offspring.

As she passes, once again she manages to brush against Monsieur Vingtras and gently nudge him.

Monsieur Brignolin is rarely present; he's a scientist, associated with a factory producing chemicals; he has already invented lots of things that keep his furnaces—and his own pot—boiling. He's an expert on anti-adulterants; I've even noticed people laughing when that word was mentioned.

There's a cousin of hers in the house: Mademoiselle Miolan.

She's twenty years old: gentle, obliging, and pale, waxen pale, and I hear people saying that she hasn't long to live.

Madame Brignolin is very kind to her, and we all like her; she makes rosettes for us out of bits of ribbon—her thin fingers are so clever! In her pocket she has a wallet with corners of mother-of-pearl, the only object that she won't let us touch: "I keep my heart in there," she said one day and people say she's dying of a broken heart.

On the day Madame Brignolin was telling us all this, my father was standing close to her. My mother wasn't in the room. I turned my head and saw that Madame Brignolin's hand was resting on my father's and her eyes were looking into his! He himself was looking embarrassed. She gave a gentle smile and said, "You big silly!"

I guessed that I was making them feel uncomfortable, and simultaneously, they gave me a look meaning: "Not in front of the boy," or else, "What's he doing here?" I've never forgotten that "You big silly," so full of tenderness and that gesture, so gentle.

For Mademoiselle Miolan they've rented a little place in the country where we go and spend two or three hours an evening, after school; when the weather's fine, we spend the whole of Sunday there.

What lovely times they were for the Brignolin kids and me!

This house in the country is set far from pretty surroundings —it's at the end of a deserted track, coal black, sandy yellow, and dusty green, with an odor of burning and cinders; shoes make a rasping noise when you walk on it and carriages a crunching sound. There's a mine there and two brickworks whose flat roofs stand out in the middle of empty fields; the grass is sparse and coarse, and in places it seems to be hanging like tufts of hair left on a camel's back; there's coal and brick rubble, reddish and dull in color, like clots of curdled blood; but we build it all up into shapes of doorways and huts, make holes in the ground and light fires in them, blowing on the flames until they glow and smoke swirls up into the wind. That gives us the feeling of having done some work and reminds us of Robinson Crusoe. We're all alone on this immense plain—as if we ought to be living without relying on towns; we talk like grown-ups and feel the emotions always aroused by silence.

When we are tired of this emptiness and stillness, when the chill of night falls and one by one the sounds drop into an abyss, we make our way back to the cottage with its red hat and green shoes.

There's a tiny garden, two trees, beds of pansies, and a sunflower.

I can still see those pansies with their golden eyes and blue lids, I can feel the velvet of their leaves, and I can recall that there was one tuft that I tended; there are still a few of its petals in an old book that I'd put them into.

When it's time to light up the house, we can see the lamp shining in the distance, like a star.

The ladies and my father improvise a supper of fruit, milk, and dark bread. We've gone to fetch the meal from the far end of the village. How calm it all is! It brings tears of happiness to my eyes.

On Sundays, what a commotion there was! We carry the provisions, Madame Brignolin puts on a white apron, my mother tucks up her dress, and my father helps to prepare the vegetables. We ourselves are thrown a few raw carrots to nibble on and we lend a hand in the cooking, turning the chicken in front of the charcoal fire (catching the tears of juice as they fall); we spread general confusion and disorder—and things get broken—but nobody complains.

There's a rattling of saucepans and a clattering of plates and then the sound of chomping jaws accompanied by the popping of corks—with our dessert, we're given a sip or two of sparkling white wine.

We drink to each other's health—and then keep repeating the dose . . .

Our first toast is always for Madame Vingtras.

She goes all red as she replies: her peasant blood flows more freely in this bucolic atmosphere, with its little country pub smells and the sight of those farmhouses in the distance!

She gives barely a thought to my trousers which I have to roll up, my new shoes which are caked with lumps of mud. In any case, Madame Brignolin is there to prevent her from doing it.

"Everybody must have fun!" she proclaims, putting her hand over my mother's mouth and tugging at her arm to drag her off for a walk or a trip around the garden.

My father looks really happy!

He's playing like a little boy; when we play puss in the corner, it's he who's the puss, he who pushes the swing, and when we're tired of playing, he sings (he's got a thin, weak voice). After him, Madame Brignolin launches into songs from the south of France.

My mother—peasantlike—says that those are tunes for namby-pambies and breaks into a song from the Auvergne:

> *Digue d'Janette*
> *Te vole marigua*
> > *Laya!*
> *Vole prendre un homme!*
> *Que sabe brabailla*
> > *Laya!*[1]

"*Laya!*" repeats Madame Brignolin, adopting a vague dancing pose herself, flinging her head back, and sticking out her bust, then suddenly gathering up her skirts and thrusting out her hips!

She taps her foot, clicks her fingers, and ends by seeming

to fall into a swoon, pushing her chest out as she gives a great gasp through half-closed lips. She stayed like that for a full second without laughing, before bursting into a lively song blending a cachucha and a bourrée, Spanish and Auvergne dialect:

> *La Madona et la fouchtra,*[2]
> *Laya!*

"What does that mean?" asks Monsieur Brignolin, always down-to-earth. He occasionally joins us, with disastrous results to our sauces.

He tries out concentrated juices based on chemicals that have a "scientific" flavor and ruin our supper.

If we're playing some game, he muddles everything—he can never guess right!

He's always *it*.

"You're *it*!" These words are said by Madame Brignolin in a peculiar way and almost always when looking at my father; then, giving her husband a shake, she adds, "Come on, you're no use except to offer your arm to someone—take Madame Vingtras's—will you let me have yours, Monsieur Vingtras? Jacques, you can dance with Mademoiselle Miolan."

Poor girl! While we're playing and making lots of noise, she often gets a spasm in her chest or a fit of coughing, which turns her pale face all red and makes her fall back onto the pillow that provides a cushion for her reclining chair—but she still goes on smiling and gets annoyed if we offer to make less noise because of her.

"No, certainly not, please have fun. It makes me happy and that does me good, please go on!"

Her voice peters out but she goes on waving her hands to tell us, "Please have fun!"

UNEMPLOYED

All of a sudden, life is changing.

Up till now, I've provided the drum for my mother to beat on: *Ratatata, ratataee!* She's been trying out all types of whackings and various sorts of clothing materials on me, she's worked me over in all directions, pinching me, giving me welts, knocking me about, pummeling me, boxing my ears, drubbing me, scratching me up and scratching me down—and tanning my hide—all without succeeding in turning me into an idiot or making me deformed, hunchback, or bandy, without making onions sprout in my stomach or fleece grow on my back, in spite of all those legs of lamb!

For the moment her affection has shifted elsewhere. Her eagle eye is no longer concentrated on me.

Formerly you could hear only *slam-bang, whack-whack,* and off we go! I was called a layabout, a "cursed"—cursed for Goddamned, of course—good-for-nothing. She also always said "booger" for bugger.

For the last thirteen years I hadn't been able to be in her presence for five minutes—no, less than five minutes—without annoying her, without exacerbating her love . . .

What's happened to all this activity, this clamor, these clips around the ear?

I didn't really mind being called a scoundrel or a ruffian, I'd gotten used to that. I even felt vaguely flattered.

Scoundrel! Like in the novel with the illustrations. And then I could easily sense that it gave my mother pleasure to hurt me; that she needed the exercise and could indulge in these gymnastics without going to the gymnasium where she'd have to put on shorts and a little cotton top—that was some job imagining her in shorts and a shirt . . .

With me there was no danger of missing: I was a sitting duck all ready for plucking, a lamb to the slaughter. I was going to be fleeced.

So for a while now I've had nothing to freshen me—or warm me—up, like the sheaf of wheat moldering in the corner instead of quivering under the thresher, like the goose, pinned down under its feet, swelling in front of the fire.

I'm no longer required to stand up and go—a submissive target to my mother: I can remain sitting indefinitely!

This state of unemployment is making me nervous.

It's nice to be able to go on sitting down, but when we resume our past practices, when there's a return to being thrashed, how will I cope? I'll have been ruined by such Capuan luxury[3]: I'll have lost the armor plating I've acquired, my well-drilled underpants, the tanned texture of my hide!

What on earth is taking place?

I can't quite understand, but it seems to me that Madame Brignolin is somehow involved in the miserable gloom reigning at home, in my mother's icy-cold anger.

She spends whole evenings tight-lipped, with a set look, never uttering a word. She hides behind the window, lifting up the curtain, as if she's tracking some prey.

"So you've stopped seeing Madame Brignolin?" a neighbor inquires of her one day.

"Oh no, not at all!"

"But not quite such close friends?"

"Oh yes, we are! In fact we're going on an excursion together to the country next Sunday."

I'd heard about this trip, a sort of reconciliation after some weeks of chill between us.

I've even picked up a few words that my mother has been muttering to herself, "Pay no attention, leave them by themselves, then steal up on them . . ."

They've made up: they meet on Thursday and make arrangements for Sunday.

And on that very day I'd been given a detention!

I'd dropped a piece of coal right in the middle of a lesson—a piece that I'd picked up near our cottage. I'd heard Monsieur Brignolin say that splinters from the mines contained diamonds and ever since I'd been picking up any fragment with a shiny vein or a speck of yellow.

The teacher thought I was making fun of him—I was caught and on that Sunday I had to stay in town and do detention at one, in the boarders' classroom, in the main building.

So good-bye to our cottage!

I watched them go off with their picnic baskets.

The ladies were wearing new dresses for the occasion.

Madame Brignolin looked charming in a dress with a rather low neckline, a blue-striped scarf, dark blue ankleboots, and she smelled wonderful, really wonderful.

My mother was wearing a green shawl for the first time. It clashed disastrously with the pink spots of the muslin dress floating mistily around Madame Brignolin.

I'd been instructed what I had to do: lunch of cold green beans dressed in olive oil; serve my detention, then go on to the bursar, Monsieur Laurier, for dinner.

"That's more than you deserve," my mother said.

The prospect was pleasant enough for me not to feel too sorry at having to miss my excursion into the country. I accepted my fate willingly enough.

I ate my cold beans, went off to play marbles with some young chimney sweeps I knew, arrived late for detention, covered in soot, pretended I needed to pay an urgent visit to the toilet, thereby succeeding in taking a stroll around the gymnasium where I unhooked a trapeze and nearly broke my back, blotted my lines, drank a bit of ink . . . and by that time it was six o'clock.

The detention was over; we were released. I went upstairs to find Monsieur Laurier.

"So there you are, my boy."

"Yes, sir."

"So you're always in detention?"

"No, sir."

"Hungry?"

"Yes, sir!"

"Like to eat?"

"No, sir!"

I thought it was more polite to say *no*, my mother had firmly impressed on me never to accept anything right away, you didn't do that in polite society. "You don't go throwing yourself at an invitation like a greedy glutton, do you understand?" And she practiced what she preached.

We sometimes went out to dinner with pupils' parents.

"Won't you take some soup, Madame Vingtras?"

"No . . . yes . . . like that . . . just a little . . ."

"You don't like soup?"

"Oh yes indeed . . . but I'm not feeling very hungry . . ."

"Goodness me, not yet hungry?"

"You must always leave a little on your plate." That was another thing she'd told me.

"Leave a little on your plate!"

This is what I did with my soup, to the amazement of the bursar, who'd already thought me very stupid when I'd said that I was hungry but didn't want to eat.

But I know that you must always do what your mother tells you . . . my mother's an expert on good manners, so I leave some soup in the bottom of my bowl and have to be persuaded . . .

The bursar offers me some fish.

"Oh, no thank you!"

I'm not going to eat fish just like that, immediately, like some peasant!

"Wouldn't you like some carp?"

"No thank you, sir!"

"Don't you like carp?"

"Oh yes, sir!"

My mother had strongly urged me to like everything in other people's houses: if you didn't like what was being served, you seemed to be snubbing your hosts.

"You do like it? Well, good."

The bursar tosses me a piece of carp as if he thinks I'm a half-wit, who can try it if he likes and leave it if he doesn't.

I eat my carp—laboriously.

My mother had also said, "You mustn't sit too close to the table; you must never behave as if you're in your own house by making yourself too comfortable." I was sitting as awkwardly as I could—my chair was miles away from my plate: a couple of times I almost tipped over.

I've eaten all my bread!

My mother told me never to "ask"; children must wait to be served.

I'm waiting! But Monsieur Laurier has lost interest in me—he's forgotten about me and is eating, absorbed in his newspaper.

I make a slight clatter with my fork and tap my teeth like a windup toy. This frantic clicking finally succeeds in making him squint at me over his paper, but he sees that I still have some carp left on my plate, with lots of sauce.

Having to eat it without bread is making my stomach turn but I'm afraid to ask for any.

Bread! Bread!

My hands are as filthy as a lamplighter's but I don't dare wipe them on my napkin too often. "It'll look as if your fingers are too grubby," my mother had told me, "and seeing a really dirty napkin when they clear the table will leave a bad impression."

I wipe my hands on the seat of my trousers—which disconcerts the bursar as he catches sight of this out of the corner of his eye—he doesn't know what to think.

"Have you got an itch?"

"No, sir."

"Then why are you scratching yourself?"

"I don't know, sir."

It's obvious that these vague replies, my enigmatic fatalism, have finally filled him with an overwhelming feeling of repulsion.

"Have you finished with your fish?"

"Yes, sir!"

Monsieur Laurier removes my plate and pushes a plate of veal sweetbreads in mushroom sauce in front of me.

"So come along now, dig in, don't hold back, eat all you want."

Aha! Now the master of the house himself is inviting me, I fling myself on the sweetbreads.

No bread! No bread!

Veal and carp come together in my stomach in a sea of sauces. They are locked in desperate conflict.

I feel like I'm carrying a ship inside me, a ship made of melting butter. My mouth feels like I've eaten a jar of cheap hair oil.

Dinner's over: about time! Monsieur Laurier dispatches me home, though not before he's put on his glasses to examine the tiger-skin effect I've produced on my blue trousers. The tiger himself slinks away with his tail between his legs.

———

I'm lying fully clothed on my bed. A sliver of moon peers through the windowpane. Not a sound!

My head's burning and one side of my skull seems to have been bashed in.

I can remember everything: the bread I didn't have, the fish swimming around, the calf sucking the udder...

It doesn't matter: at least my manners were impeccable. I've suffered, but I kept my chair a long way from the table. I didn't give the impression that I was begging for bread: I've remained true to my mother's instructions.

9:00 P.M.

Two hours sleep, my headache's gone. If I saw a calf in my room, I'd leap out of the window. But that's not very likely, and while I get undressed, I daydream . . .

10:00 P.M.

I'd lit the candle and was reading, but the candle's burning low, and there's only a tiny bit left for when my parents come home.

I clamber up into the loft, which you get to by going up a small ladder; in summer it's stifling hot, in winter it's freezing cold, but once up there, I'm free, all on my own, and I like this little sort of hanging cupboard where I can cut myself off from the world and whose wooden walls have witnessed all my secret anger and secret pain.

MIDNIGHT

I'd dozed off! Suddenly, I awake.

Confused sounds, piercing cries, one in particular that goes straight to my heart, stabbing it like a knife. It's the voice of my mother...

I spring down the ladder in my shirt. The ladder wasn't attached, and I fall, making a dreadful noise. I nearly crack my knee open on the stone floor.

The drama is taking place between my mother, leaning wide-eyed backward over the banisters, and my father, pale and disheveled, tugging her toward him.

In tears, I fling myself between them. What's happening? I'm trying to shout.

"Stop that!" says my father, placing his hand over my mouth and almost breaking my teeth with his fist. "Don't do that!" His voice sounds both angry and terrified . . .

I'm bending over my mother who has fainted; I cover her face with my tears . . . A child's tears falling onto a mother's face seem to be a good thing! Mine suddenly open her eyes, she recognizes me and says, "Jacques! Jacques!" She seizes my hand in hers and squeezes it. It's the first time she has ever done that.

I've never experienced anything but her horny fingers and steely eyes, her sharp voice: now, at this moment, she gives way to a sudden burst of affection, a weakening of her spirit, and gently surrenders her hand and her heart.

From this moment of kindness forced out of her by fright, I realized that any gesture of kindness I received in life would always win me over.

"Get back to bed," said my father.

I went back to bed chilled to the bone. I caught cold from the stone floor of the staircase and then from the big bedroom with the windows open so the invalid will get lots of air!

What's happened?

My heart's in turmoil too. In my fever I'm incapable of putting two ideas together rationally! One by one, the hours slip past.

I watch night ebbing away and dawn coming in; a kind of white smoke is rising on the horizon.

Like a murderer, I saw the hours of darkness passing, one at a time, in front of me; while other children slept, my eyes remained open; I've followed the round moon across the sky, sightless like the face of a madman; I listened to the pounding of my innocent heart above the silence of my bedroom. A cold draft of old age swept through my life, snow fell on me. I feel that disaster has overwhelmed me.

What's happened? I'd like to know.

I've often faced painful situations but I've never trembled the way I was trembling that day, when I wondered how I was going to be greeted, how my father, who'd looked so pale and had said, "Don't shout!" would look at me.

I was afraid that when my parents saw me, they might be ashamed.

I kept asking myself how their son was supposed to look, what words he ought to say, if it wouldn't be a good idea to go and kiss them— but which one should I kiss first?

I was trembling all over . . . oddly enough, more scared of seeming awkward, of approaching them or crying at the wrong moment, than frightened by this unknown, mysterious drama.

And that's how it is, we're never sure about the feelings of the people closest to us. We're afraid of irritating them by our bursts of affection. We feel instinctively that their sufferings mustn't be treated carelessly, their heart won't be able to forget, that they'd be left with a scar or a bruise, red or black, of sadness or anger . . .

And so we hesitate, we draw back.

Not say anything? But they may accuse you of being unkind, since you seem so indifferent to their suffering!

Say something? But they'll bear you a grudge for drawing

attention to their fault or crime, because that morning, by your tears—you're making a scene—you've revived the memory of ghosts that ought to die away after the last cry, with the first ray of sun!

And so I didn't know what to do!

The sun had long been up. Normally my father would be out of bed by seven, getting ready for his eight o'clock class. I used to get up as well.

I did the same as I always did: I got dressed, but slowly, and didn't put my shoes on; I sat on my bed and waited.

From their bedroom, not a sound: a deathly silence.

Finally, at a quarter to eight, my father called me . . .

He didn't seem surprised to see me up and dressed. Through the door, he asked me to bring some paper and ink; he wrote a letter to the deputy headmaster and a second one to a doctor and told me to deliver them.

"When you've done that, come right back here."

"I'm not going to school today?"

"No, you need to look after your mother who's not feeling very well. If the deputy headmaster asks what's wrong with her, say she's had a very upsetting experience in the country and she's in bed with a fever . . ."

He said this without appearing greatly affected, with a touch of vulgarity in his demeanor—he was slopping around in his slippers on the parquet floor and buttoning up his trousers.

What had happened?

I never knew exactly. From the shouts that had been flying around during their stormy exchanges, from outbursts of squabbling that I overheard, I gathered that my mother had laid an ambush and surprised Madame Brignolin and my father whispering together in a corner of the garden on this ill-starred Sunday excursion.

It seems that a scene of jealousy and hostility had erupted that continued far into the night, until I had witnessed their return.

There was nobody I could ask about it; in any case, just the memory of that occasion weighed on me like an incubus. Rather than discovering any more about it, I was trying to put it out of my mind!

Discover what? What was done was done!

Perhaps I'm the one who suffered most—the young, innocent child!

Ever since that day—was it my fever or her remorse, shame or regret?—my father was different to me. Until then he'd lived away from home, on the grounds—or pretext—of having to take extra classes in school or having to attend lectures given by the senior teachers for teachers who hadn't got the *agrégation.*

Now, four evenings out of six he spends at home—scowling, stony-eyed, tight-lipped, pale, dejected, ready to explode, acting unkindly on the slightest pretext.

He speaks to my mother drearily, sometimes shrilly or with a sigh; you can tell that he's trying to seem kind and that he's suffering; his politeness toward her is painful to watch and his sham affection makes you sorry for him.

I can see that he's an embittered man.

It's really horrible at home! And we all walk around slowly, talking in whispers.

I'm living in a world of silence, breathing an atmosphere of oppressive sadness.

Sometimes this silence is broken by my screams.

My father needs to transfer his suffering onto someone else and he relieves his anger and grief on me. My mother has relaxed her grip on me and my father has seized his opportunity.

He lashes me with a riding crop, batters me with a post,

for anything, for nothing, out of the blue: often I know for sure I haven't deserved it.

For a long time I kept a piece of malacca cane which he broke on my back and to which, without thinking, I fastened a steel blade; I'd said to myself that if I ever committed suicide—and one time I did think of killing myself—I'd use that.

This was how it happened.

My father comes home suddenly, pale in the face. He almost breaks my arm as he grips it.

"You lazy lout!" he screamed, grinding his teeth. "I'm going to teach you!"

I foresaw some really cruel punishment—and in fact I was only just recovering from my last beating which had left me black-and-blue all over.

He claimed that in the course of a discussion on scholarship boys and non-fee-paying pupils in the headmaster's study, when my name came up, the headmaster had gone over to him and said, "Monsieur Vingtras, your son could be doing far better than he's doing at present were he to work harder. We think you ought to devote more time to him . . . Do you take my meaning?"

"And it's you, you miserable oaf, who's made the headmaster give me a talking to!" He flung himself on me in a fury.

The physical pain was bad enough, but the moral blow was much larger.

So I was destroying his career, I was responsible for his disgrace, for his being transferred to another school—perhaps even being dismissed! And I beat my breast as a mea culpa even harder than my father's fists pounded me. In despair, I might even have killed myself if I hadn't thought that I'd repair the damage that my father was accusing me of having caused him.

I settled down to work really hard; I no longer got punished at school, but at home I was still being beaten just the same.

Even if I'd been an angel, I'd have been punished by having the feathers torn from my wings. I'd made a resolution to accept any punishment, however harsh, without flinching, and as I held back my tears and showed no sign of pain, my father's fury knew no bounds.

Two or three times I must have cried out, like people being tortured to death: even he was horrified! But he was so sick in mind, his mood was so black, that he'd always begin again. I think he really was convinced that I was a despicable lout. He saw everything through his repulsion and anger.

Sometimes—and this was even more horrifying—my mother intervened. Even she—who in the past had struck me mercilessly in the face—accused my father of behaving like a barbarian!

"Don't touch that boy!"

From time to time they make up their quarrel—and join forces to beat me! These reconciliations never lasted long.

I'm miserable, but my father's reproach still rankles. I tell myself that I have to expiate my crime, submit to his blows, and put my nose to the grindstone so that his professional situation, already compromised, doesn't suffer from my laziness a second time!

I do everything possible: sometimes I stay up till midnight, and my mother, who in the past used to accuse me of going to bed too early, now accuses me of burning too much midnight oil. "And what's the point? It's all nonsense anyway!"

My father accuses me of reading novels on the sly, nobody gives me any credit for the effort I'm putting in, and they don't even seem particularly happy about the good results I get—I've moved right up to the top of the class.

And to get that far, what hours of boredom I've had to spend!

That *Gradus ad Parnassum*[4] in which I try to find the best adjective or long or short syllables! What a loathsome book that is; it fills me with horror!

My *Alexander*[5] has ragged corners—that's where I've bitten it in rage; I've got some of the leather binding in my stomach . . .

All the Latin and Greek seems to me barbarous, outlandish; I cram it into me and swallow it down like mud . . .

I never talk to anybody, I've stopped chatting with friends. People used to like me better and I can hear them saying, behind my back, "It's the result of his father beating him all the time!"

They also say, "Don't you think he's become sly and turned into something of a goody-goody?"

I came at the top of the class in some subject or other and the boy who's first has to take the essays along to the headmaster. He was having a private conversation with someone and I was told to wait next door, in a little room where you can hear everything that's being said.

They were discussing us.

"We've agreed not to say anything about the Vingtras affair, haven't we?"

"Yes, not a word. It would harm his whole professional career and in any case, having a wife like that, you know, if I were him, I'd . . ."

"Yes indeed! And always going on about how she used to look after the pigs . . . and the local dance hops where she used to do jigs! Whoops-a-daisy! While Madame Brignolin, well . . ."

"Not so loud!" said the headmaster, "suppose my wife heard you . . ."

In my little room, I was feeling scared. I could imagine them going over to the door and peeping out to see if anyone was listening . . .

It was the headmaster talking with the inspector of schools; I'd recognized their voices.

"What's the boy like?"

"A miserable little wretch they dress up like a clown in a circus and beat like a carpet. Not stupid, his heart's in the right place. The last inspector liked him a lot...So I used him as an excuse: 'Devote more time to your son.' Meaning: spend more time with your wife—and the message wasn't loot..."

I spent the whole next day in a daze.

My father became annoyed and jostled me angrily.

"Are you thinking of going back to your daydreaming, you lazy bum? We're due for a school inspection any day now. You're not intending to disgrace me the way you did last year and make us all suffer for your laziness, are you?"

What disgrace? What laziness?

My father had lied to me.

XVII. MEMORIES

THE SCHOOL bursar, Monsieur Laurier, who has transferred to a first-rate school in the west of the country, has heard of a vacancy in Nantes for a grammar teacher,[1] a lower grade but at secondary-school level. Monsieur Laurier went to great lengths to help my father get it.

The news of the appointment has come through!

We're going to leave Saint-Étienne. I've just finished putting my father's *agrégation* notebooks in order: Greek composition here, Latin translations there; there are lots of them.

My parents are making their calls to say their good-byes.

They leave the house and I can see them going down the street, not speaking to each other.

Approaching Kléber Lane, they instinctively turn away and cross over to the other side of the street, avoiding the house where Madame Brignolin lives . . .

I let my eye run down the street that leads on one side to the school and on the other to Marengo Square; this reminds me of my pleasure and sorrows, the long hours of boredom and the short minutes of happiness.

Ah yes, I've grown up! I'm no longer the frightened, very simple child arriving from Le Puy. The only thing I'd ever read was the catechism and I believed in ghosts. I was afraid only of what I couldn't see: God, the Devil. Nowadays, I'm afraid of what I can see: unpleasant teachers, jealous mothers, and desperate fathers. With my ink-stained fingers, I've made contact with life. I've had to shed tears through being unfairly beaten and to laugh at the stupidities and lies uttered by adults.

I've lost my early innocence. I have doubts as to the goodness of Heaven and the commandments of the Church. I know that mothers' promises are not always kept.

Just now, as I was prowling round in the apartment where the furniture is lying about like the dismantled scenery of a play, I saw the smashed money box where my mother used to put the funds to "buy me a man" and which she has just broken open.

Is this the silence, the impression of sadness, that will overcome me all my days whenever I've left a place where I've lived, even if it was a sort of prison?

Is this the smell emanating from this heap of objects? I don't know, but all these memories combine whenever I'm leaving a place.

Here in this corner, there's a bit of blue ribbon. It belonged to my cousin Marianne. They sent for her to come from Farreyrolles on the pretext that she'd been born with ladylike manners and that staying with us for a while couldn't fail to give her the polish and style that was acquired in the company of people of taste and education . . .

Poor cousin Marianne!

They used her as a scullery maid and treated her as badly as they did me—minus the thrashings.

We used to work together in the kitchen—I did the hard labor: "A man must be able to do everything." I'd scour the bottoms of the pots, she'd shine their round bellies. When we came to the plates, I'd scrape off the leftovers, she'd wipe them clean: such were our orders. My mother had pointed out that the dirty part of a pot was the underneath and the dirty part of plates was on top. That was why I was given the hardest jobs.

She was also forced to go on wearing her little country bonnet. At Farreyrolles, she'd been very proud of this bonnet and she knew that the young men thought she looked smart in it. But in Saint-Étienne it used to make people laugh. They'd look the other way or eye her with curiosity.

But my mother quickly stepped in.

"The truth is that I love her as much as I love my son, you see! I don't make any distinction between the two of them." And she used to add, "Jacques could even feel annoyed about it."

Oh yes, I am annoyed. I wish that she would make a distinction between us: it's bad enough for her to push me about without pushing her about too!

Monsieur Laurier himself remarked that the bonnet was inappropriate in a town. My mother retorted, "Do you think I'm ashamed of my upbringing? Do you expect me to feel embarrassed about my sisters and be scared to go out with my niece because she's wearing a country bonnet? Oh no, Monsieur Laurier, you don't know me very well at all!"

One day, however, when she thought that she'd broken her niece's will sufficiently and provided proof enough that she wasn't ashamed of her origins, she disposed of the country bonnet but *imposed* the wearing of a cap and she made a dress for Marianne.

"I'm never going to go out dressed like that," said Marianne when she tried it on.

"So you're suggesting that your aunt lacks taste, your aunt is a stupid woman who doesn't know how people dress, who mucks up everything she does? So I mess everything up, do I?"

"I didn't say that, Aunt."

"And two-faced as well! Oh yes, go around saying that I make a mess of my nieces' dresses! Perhaps you'll be saying that I let them starve next!"

A pause.

Then all at once, turning toward me, in a voice that came from deep in her heart, you could hear the aunt being expunged—and being resurrected as a mother.

"Jacques!" she exclaimed. "Jacques, my son, come, come kiss your mother..."

So much love, such an outburst of affection, this heart which, suddenly, had started to beat above the womb in which she had carried me, the whole thing made me terribly confused and I went toward her as if my feet were glued to the ground.

"So you won't come and kiss your own mother!" she exclaimed, flinging her arms into the air, saddened by my reluctance.

I moved more quickly—she caught hold of my hair and pulled me toward her, giving me such a vigorous kiss that I went flying backward and ended up against the wall where my skull drove in a nail!

Oh, these mothers, when they're seized by a sudden burst of affection! All the same, that nail left a dent...

These mothers who we think are cruel and who suddenly swoop on their son and need to kiss him!

And what a swoop! But it's hurt me and I'm rubbing the back of my head.

"Will you stop scratching yourself like that, Jacques! And by the way, I looked at the bottom of the big pot a moment ago—if you call that cleaning properly, my boy, you've got another thing coming! I bet it's not been touched for two days at least!"

"I did it this morning, Ma!"

"This morning! Are you daring to...?"

"Promise, Ma!"

"So it's me who's wrong? You're calling your mother a liar?"

"No, Ma."

"Come here!"

She slapped my face.

Dear Marianne, from then onward, she was really miserable. She wrote to her mother, who was very fond of her, asking to come home right away.

But when the letter came from Farreyrolles, my mother replied, "Are you trying to take your daughter's word against mine? Are you accusing your sister of being a liar? Do you think, as she said, that I mess things up? Do you? Well, if you do, go ahead!"

I've inserted the punctuation.

They didn't dare take Marianne away immediately. And she stayed for another month.

She suffered a lot during that time, but how happy I was!

She was blond with big blue eyes that were always moist and somewhat cold, they seemed to be swimming in water. Her hair was almost flaxen in color and her cheeks were speckled with freckles; but her neck was white, with skin as delicate and tender as curdled milk . . .

I saw her, years later, through a grill, tucked away in a convent; she'd become a nun.

"If I'd stayed on longer in Saint-Étienne," she murmured, half closing her eyes, "perhaps I'd have never come here."

"Are you sorry you did?"

She moved her pale face, framed in the white coif of the Sisters of Charity, away from the judas hole and made no reply; but I thought I could see two tears fall from her clear blue eyes and I seemed to detect a gesture of regret and tenderness . . .

She vanished into the quiet of the silent hallway adorned with an ivory figure of a bloodstained Christ.

There's the black desk I used to sit at, which was so high that my books had to be put on the chair.

How many sad and gloomy evenings I've spent there and what wretched Sunday mornings when I was required to produce ten lines of verse or learn three pages before I was allowed to put on my white shirt and nice clothes!

My father often used to knock my head against a corner of this desk when I was caught looking out the window at the sky instead of keeping my eye on my books. I was so lost in my dreams that I never heard him coming, and as he rubbed my nose against the wood, he'd call me a lazy good-for-nothing.

It's a very sensitive thing, a nose, I don't think people realize just how sensitive.

One day I cut a nick in the desk. This led to my being left with a permanent scar on my face, the result of a slash with a ruler that he gave me in punishment.

There's a basket, all chewed up, full of odd bits of crockery.

That's where Mirza used to sleep, the puppy bitch that the previous headmaster—the one dismissed in disgrace—had given us to look after. He couldn't afford to take her with him—he didn't know whether, in the miserable place where he was going to be dumped, he'd even have enough bread to feed his wife and child.

Mirza died having puppies, and they called me a stupid, silly fool for bursting into tears when I saw the tiny dead animal and didn't dare touch her cold body and carry the basket downstairs, like a coffin!

I asked to be allowed to wait until the evening to go and bury her. A school friend had promised to let me use a corner of his garden.

I had to take her and carry her away while my mother

watched; she was sneering. My father jostled me on the stairs and I nearly fell down them while carrying her. At the bottom, as I emptied the basket onto a rubbish pile beside the doorway of this ill-fated house, I turned my eyes away. She landed with a dull flop and I ran off, lamenting, "Why do it there when she could have been buried?"

It was a childish idea, to prevent her having her head cut off by the garbageman's shovel or having the guts squeezed out of her by the wheels of a cart! For a long time I had this vision of her body guillotined and dismembered instead of having a nice little place underground where I would have known that there lay a creature who had loved me and licked my hands when they were bruised and swollen and had watched me with eyes in which I thought I could detect tears for her young master as he was wiping away his own . . .

XVIII. THE DEPARTURE

W HAT JOY! We're going away, far, far away!

And Nantes is on the sea! I'm going to see big ships, naval officers, the men keeping watch! I'll be able *to gaze on tempests*!

I can already imagine the lighthouse winking its blood-red eye; the alarm gun booming through its mouth of bronze its desperate groans for shipwrecks!

In *France Maritime*,[1] I've read tales of boardings, of rafts, of whaling... and having been frustrated from becoming a seafarer as a result of the Vidaljan fiasco, I've flung myself on books where birds wheel and swoop over the Atlantic!

I've already made up tales of shipwrecks as if I were one of the heroes, and as I write them down I think that they come from reminiscences of books read, things jotted down, in the silence of my spells of solitary confinement.

Shipwrecks, desperate groans from the mouths of bronze cannon's, swooping birds: I'm pretty sure they come from Fulgence Girard,[2] my favorite *thunder and lightning* expert. I'm repeating these words to myself like a parrot tied to the mainmast; but beneath all this there's the galley slave hoping, this time, to escape.

In Nantes I'll be able to make my getaway whenever I want. With the *deep blue sea* on your doorstep you can slide right into the wide Atlantic!

I'm no longer my father's property, I'm hiding in the powder magazine, I slip into the muzzle of a cannon and by the time they discover that I've disappeared, I'd be well out to sea!

The captain's cursing and swearing—shiver me timbers!—when he sees me come out of my hiding place and offer myself as a cabin boy, but he can't throw me overboard because I'm one of the crew . . . !

While I'm waiting to escape by means of *the briny deep*, my current trip is already full of poetry.

First, we have the stagecoach—on the top deck—and we're going into a railway station!

The locomotives snort like donkeys or bellow like cattle and shoot fire through their nostrils. The whistle blasts are heartrending!

ORLÉANS

We reach Orléans at night.

Our trunks are left at the station.

But there are things which mustn't be left, says my mother, and clings to a lot of them; they all get piled up—on me; I look like a basket-seller's shop and I'm having difficulty walking.

There's always some box or other falling on the ground and being picked up—by the light of the moon.

Nobody can make up his mind: we're being carried away by the lateness of the hour and the immense quiet of the night into a sort of inner meditation—exhausting as far as I'm concerned since I'm humping everything on my back.

Of course, there were plenty of railway and hotel porters at the station, waiting to take us off to the Golden Lion, the White Horse, the Gamecock. "Just round the corner, sir!" "Here's the hotel bus!"

To go to the White Horse, the Golden Lion, the Gamecock! My heart was pounding with excitement . . . but my parents aren't crazy, they're not going to give in like that to the blandishments of the first offer . . . or follow a stranger in a town they don't know . . .

My mother's good at summing people up, she wanted to find a face that appealed to her and now she prowls around, dragging my father along like a blind man, searching haphazardly and shooting questions which get lost in the dark and the general hubbub.

She did this to such good effect that we eventually found ourselves all alone, like a bunch of orphans . . .

The lights are being extinguished; the street's left with one solitary oil lamp in front of the main entrance, a sort of nightlight; and here we are wandering about in silent despair in a square where we've finally landed. My mother says to my father, "It's all your fault," to which my father replies, "What do you mean? I'd say it's yours!"

"Well, you say . . . !"

We called out to the few passersby who were still around. We even thought we saw a sedan chair but our cries were swallowed up in space.

There's a full moon—every memorable night in my life has been witnessed by a full moon . . .

It's flooding the square with its radiance and our shadows are leaving dark blotches; they look pretty strange too.

With my biblical scaffolding I look huge, and when my father or mother goes running after something which has fallen on the ground, the shadows become elongated and collide on the paving stones—you should see my father's nose!

I can't laugh—if I laugh, I'll drop something. And anyway, I don't feel very much like laughing . . .

———

"There's someone over there!"

I swing around like a peasant with her bucket, like a juggler waiting to catch a ball; my head's being forced down into my chest, my arms are being tugged out of my shoulders; I'm being telescoped . . .

"There's someone!"

"It's a woman! I tell you it's a woman!"

"What's she standing on?"

"On?"

"Yes, what's she standing on?" (My mother is shrill, really shrill.)

"Hello there, ma'am!"

The only things moving are my bags and packages which are now well on their way to spilling on the ground.

. . . .

"We've all been wrong . . ."

It's my father speaking in a deeper, more reverent voice; his vocal cords seem to have been moistened by a tear.

"All wrong," he repeats, in a tone of sincere repentance.

"What we have in front of us isn't a man or a woman: it's the MAID OF ORLÉANS."

He pauses for a second.

"The Maid, the Virgin, Jacques!"

I've heard about her at school: the virgin of Domrémy, the shepherdess of Vaucouleurs!

"It's the Maid, Jacques!"

I know that I'm supposed to be impressed. I'm not impressed. And I've got too many baskets!

My mother has assumed the unrewarding role in the family:

she wants to be the materfamilias as depicted in the Bible, and she's hardly had time to do anything more than beat her son and make him dance to her tune; she knows about Joan of Arc by reputation but she doesn't know the chaste name that history has granted her . . .

"When you've finished using your filthy language to our son . . ."

She is dumbfounded to hear my father using words to her son which ought not to be uttered, while I'm carrying around luggage at two o'clock in the morning in a provincial town which we don't know . . .

"It's Joan of Arc," repeats this father accused of using obscene language, "the girl who saved France!"

"Oh yes," replies my mother vaguely, adding in a pleased voice: "Let's sit down beside her."

And there we spent the night—a bit hard but it did support our backs.

We were noticed by a policeman who came over to speak to us.

The officer took us for a family of devoted pilgrims who had come there and dropped exhausted—with a lot of luggage, mind you—at the feet of the saint; he was quite civil but he told us that we had to move on. He volunteered to take us to an inn kept by his brother-in-law at the end of the street, next to the market.

"You're not hungry?" my father inquired on the way.

"Why should I be hungry?" my mother retorted.

I have to tell you that in the course of the previous evening, my father had suggested eating at the buffet in Vierzon, in case we weren't able to find anywhere to eat later on. My mother had turned down this suggestion and she had no intention of letting her decision be questioned by being asked if she was hungry now.

My father said nothing. The policeman cast a frightened glance at my mother.

We've reached the inn.

It was just waking up: a stableboy was prowling around with a lamp, a farmer's wagon was being hitched up. The policeman attracted his brother-in-law's attention by tapping on a partition.

A grunt.

"Coming, coming . . . !"

Through the cracks, there's a glimmer of light, and we can hear the man getting dressed, yawning, slopping about in his shoes with his suspenders flapping.

"These people would like a bed and a snack."

As he mentioned the word *snack*, he looks at my father. He's remembering my mother's "Why should I be hungry?"

She interrupts him. "Just a bed. We'll eat when we wake up."

"Suit yourself," says the innkeeper; he doesn't mind in the least whether he serves his warmed-up leftovers in the morning or the evening, and he'd even prefer, once the travelers have gone to bed, to go back to bed himself.

I can hear my father's stomach growling like thunder under an archway; mine is also squealing—it's an exchange of tummy rumbles. My mother can't restrain her own gurgles or her yawns either, but at the station she'd said that there was no need to have dinner and that we won't be eating until tomorrow. *We are not going to eat!*

At the same time she called out to my father, "*You* can eat if you want!"

My father just shook his head; he opened his mouth like a fish and mumbled, "No, I'll wait till tomorrow."

He knows what that means.

It means: I don't want you to have a crumb of bread, a

slice of radish, get anywhere near a sausage, or sniff a piece of cheese!

My father takes himself off to bed; my mother follows. They've put down a straw mattress in a corner for me.

I'm dropping with fatigue; I go to sleep, my parents do the same.

But all three of us wake up now and again, roused by our rumbling stomachs.

My mother joins in the chorus like the rest—but she's not about to surrender. She's a capable woman, my mother! I really admire her! I do! What willpower! And what a difference from me! If I was hungry, I'd say so—and I'd even have a bite . . . if there was anything!

I'm coarse-grained, a sissy, a little squirt!

Just look at my mother who, to remain true to herself, to stick to her guns, spends the night tightening her belt and waits until morning to break her fast. You'll see, she'll pretend to be the sort of woman who eats reluctantly, purely as a matter of routine. Your mother is a Roman matron, Jacques! A Roman, not like you. First of all, look at that nose of yours! It doesn't just turn up, it's bulbous!

We've had lunch—my mother picked at her food, but I saw her in a corner gobbling up some calves liver which she'd asked for in the kitchen and which had been hidden in a piece of bread for her. She wolfed it down!

My father ate until he was fit to burst—his ears turned blue . . .

He didn't argue last night, because his hands were tied; when we left, he acted most unwisely: he handed over all our money to his wife.

My mother had said, in an innocent voice, "I've got bigger pockets than you, they'll hold the money better. I can pay for everything on the journey."

Initially my father didn't appreciate the full extent of his misfortune or the seriousness of his error; but at the first change of horses, the blow struck home: he had no money at all, not a single franc, not even a couple of sous. He'd given away all his small change in tips to railway porters and such. Now he didn't even have enough to buy a glass of currant brandy.

He was parched.

"Let me have some money."

"You need money?"

"Yes, Jacques's thirsty."

My mother turns toward me:

"You're thirsty?"

I'm happy to support my father when I can, but why, when *he's* thirsty, say that it's me?

I don't reply to my mother's question; her eyes are looking at her son and then back to her husband, cold and ironical.

"I'm sure he can wait," she says, retreating into her corner, apparently no more concerned with her husband than if he didn't exist.

Things went on like this for three days: requests for money, refusals to hand it over!

My father lost his temper. There was even an argument, first outside the door of an inn, then in the room; my mother carried the day—and my father apologized to her.

The truth is, my mother's tough and completely outspoken. She often claims, "I'm as straight as an arrow!"

And since she's outspoken, she accuses her husband, loudly, in front of innkeepers and travelers, of being a heartless, loose-living man.

She tells her story noisily. She names names.

"You're still brooding over having to give up that Brignolin woman. Oh yes you are! You want to guzzle and try and forget.

No doubt the gentleman wants money so that he can abandon his wife and son and go back to his lady love."

My father had asked for the large sum of ... five francs! You could hardly, with that amount ... !

He's like a cat on hot bricks, trying to stem the flow, break up the words, destroy the impression; but my mother is so frank!

"I hope you're not trying to shut me up, are you? There's no need to tug at my elbow: what I'm saying is the plain unvarnished truth and you know it! Fortunately there are people about; you're not thinking of hitting me in public, I imagine?"

ON THE BOAT

The boat[3] offers some relief—fortunately my mother doesn't feel very well.

She went too long without food and she ate the calves liver too quickly—and she didn't sleep a wink. Finally her headache sends her off to bed.

My father did the decent thing and stayed until he was sure she was resting properly, fast asleep and without any energy left to pounce on him ...

He goes up on deck ...

AN OLD ACQUAINTANCE

"Chanlaire!"

"Vingtras!"

Chanlaire is a former prep supervisor from Le Puy with an uncle in Nantes; while he was a teacher he was on bad terms with his uncle but they've made up now, and Chanlaire is on his way back to his house after a business trip to Paris on behalf of his firm.

He's happy and earning money.

"What a coincidence!"

"We must have a big celebration! Aren't you with your wife?"

There's a hopeful note in this question and he seems disappointed when my father replies sadly, "She's down below," and then, more cheerfully, "sick."

"Nothing serious?"

"Oh no, nothing serious at all."

"So that needn't prevent us from removing the foil from the cork of a bottle of burgundy, indeed, quite the opposite . . ."

He turns to look at me.

"You know, your boy has shot up. And what a mop of hair. And those eyes! Steward!"

There were some NCOs going on leave who'd also met up with their messmates.

The cabin table is strewn with bottles of wine and jugs of beer.

I've never heard such wild sounds of gaiety and laughter! They're playing cards, setting light to punch, drinking bishops[4]; there's the smell of lemon.

And now they're singing!

A quartermaster sergeant breaks into a barrack-room song—the others all join in the chorus!

I join in too and my shrill treble blends with their men's voices: I've had a drop to drink, I have to admit, out of my father's glass—his cheeks are pink and his eyes are shining.

After the third round of drinks, he plucked up the courage to confess to Chanlaire that his pockets were empty.

The missus is holding the purse strings!

"Would you like twenty francs? You can pay me back in Nantes, we'll be seeing each other again there, I hope; we'll have lots of fun and games. But the little guy can hear what I'm saying . . ."

"No danger from him."

No, father, there's no danger from me. Oh, how young he looks! And I've never seen him laughing as heartily as this!

He's talking to me as if I'm a big guy!

"Come on, old boy, have a drink!"

Then an idea strikes him.

"How about a snack? Those pig's feet look interesting to me, I'd like to have a few words with them . . ."

This really is bold language from the mouth of a teacher at a senior primary school! But the headmaster in Saint Étienne is a long ways away and the headmaster in Nantes isn't there yet and the pigs are offering their fragrant toes . . .

I can still taste the Saint-Menehould sauce with its tangy ravigote . . . and the aroma of the white wine we drank with it!

They give me a knife and fork, just like the rest of them, and I'm allowed to serve myself and pour my own wine. It's the first time that my father's treating me as a *pal* and we're having a drink together like a couple of friends.

I'm using my napkin to wipe my face—who cares?—I'm placing my chair where I want—again, who cares? My table manners are nonexistent, I'm comfortable! Nobody says anything about my elbows or my legs, I'm using them to please myself. It's a quarter of an hour of sheer bliss. It's the first time I've ever known something like that. I'm realizing that I'm young—and I realize that my mother's asleep.

Forget about feeling young—my mother's woken up . . .

She makes her appearance in the cabin like a ghost—she

was in the aft cabin, we're in the forward one. She marches straight over to us and she's going to make a scene . . .

Bad luck! Her voice is drowned by the din. The stewards are dashing around, the cook goes past laden with dishes, the NCOs are prowling around with bottles clasped to their chests, someone's organizing a practical joke, there's a burst of singing—what a racket and hullabaloo! Her rage doesn't last long.

"A woman on her own." She's bound to fail; what's more, she's caught sight of some money in my father's hand as he's paying for the pig's feet.

"Yes, we've got cash," my father admits cheerfully and teasingly as he proceeds to shout: "Another bottle of that sweet white!"

"I'm not thirsty."

"But I am. And Jacques's thirsty as well, aren't you, Jacques?"

It's his joyful comeback for yesterday's exchange, but mischievous, not vicious, since drink has mellowed him.

"And how about you, dear lady?" he inquires, holding out a glass and the bottle.

There's no way she can take offense. My mother recognized the red light and knew that she was on tricky ground. She replied, not too crossly, "I'm going up on deck. You can come and pick me up when you're ready. You come with me, Jacques!"

"No, Jacques's staying with us! We're going to have a game of dominoes and we need him to make a third."

Make up the third, beside these NCOs, at the same table; I push the bottles to one side to put down my pieces, with the stewards apologizing to me when they knock me as they go by! I can't contain my pride . . . and it's me, the boy who's whipped, beaten, and *belted*, sitting down there now, taking off his tie, stretching out his legs, able to laugh out loud . . . and get my sleeves dirty!

The game of dominoes is over.

"Go and tell your mother, Jacques, that we're coming up on deck."

We had forgotten her and now that the first flush of excitement has died down, I feel a bit of remorse.

My mother greets me with a stern, threatening look; remorse evaporates. It seems to me that she should have guessed that at that moment I was thinking of her, that a feeling of affection had emerged above the explosion of high spirits, and I resent the way she's welcomed me.

"When we arrive, I'll make you pay for all this!"

Pay for all what? A moment of happiness? Have I done anything wrong? I've just dipped the tip of my tongue in a few bubbly glasses and where I could see a sunbeam dancing. I'd have to pay for that—oh, that's worth any price and you can beat me when I arrive . . .

It's my lucky day!

A lady came and sat beside us and we fall into conversation. Madame Vingtras is always thrilled to the core whenever a well-dressed woman does her the honor of talking to her.

They're chatting, and now and then the lady's children come over to exchange a joke with their mother. They want me to play with them.

"Stay where you are, Jacques!"

"Oh, let them play together," says the elegant lady, with a friendly look in my direction.

"Aren't you afraid they'll fall into the water and be drowned?"

My mother was unable to think of anything else to say, but she's gratified that her son is being invited to play with

193

children from a well-to-do family, and if I get drowned, that's just bad luck!

I really do think that she's afraid of my being drowned! When we go near a fire, she's afraid I'll get burned. One day, a balloon was taking off in the school yard and she cried out, "It's going to carry you away!"

But doesn't she realize that each time she pours cold water on my curiosity or sneers at it, my desire merely swells up like my skin when I'm whipped?

I just can't help it. I tell myself that I mustn't be more cowardly than the others. I take every opportunity I can to join in the fun with my schoolmates; they don't get drowned or burned or carried away by balloons. And I've never missed an opportunity of *piggybacking*; I'm anxious to play truant as often as possible in order to go boating on the Furens or to see the forge at the big factory where Terrasson's father is the foreman.

I climbed up the tall tree on the Pélissier's garden at Saint-Étienne and went way out to the end of the big branch.

All this is coming back into my mind at the moment; my brain is exhilarated! I can see myself weighing up two alternatives: if I'm prevented from going near the water or the brickworks or balloons, I'll keep quiet—I don't want my mother to be scared—but as soon as I get the chance, I'll walk into the river right up to my waist and I'll hold my foot over the *castings* of molten iron . . .

My mind's made up. Meanwhile, since my mother has left me free to choose, I'll do everything I can to avoid being drowned.

If she'd forbidden me to play, I'd have been unable to stop myself from leaning over the paddlewheel or from trying to catch the froth in the hollow of my hand . . .

We keep running from one end of the ship to the other;

we call out to the engineer, we pester the helmsman, we collide with the rigging, we finger the capstan, we try to lift the anchor . . .

The day goes by in a flash; evening's falling.

Like adults—men—we respond to the melancholy influence of twilight; with cold cheeks and a shiver down the back of our necks, with our flowing hair tossed by the wind, we contemplate the furrow of the ship's wash, we stare at the first stars twinkling in the sky and our eyes trace the trail of moonbeams in the shot-silk of the water.

The engine is going *thud, thud!*

Now it's the bell's turn to say something: we're approaching a bridge.

We've reached Tours, we're spending the night here.

Monsieur Chanlaire knows a cheapish hotel. We can all go there if we like. It's agreed. And ten minutes after landing, we're at the Stag Hotel.

We eat dinner at the table d'hôte.

There are traveling salesmen, an Englishwoman, a priest: everybody's exclaiming about the cooking, which smells good, and a certain Dijon mustard is enjoying a success that is benefiting the cellar: it carries a sting that makes you thirsty.

My eyes are as round as saucers; my nostrils twitch; my ears prick up. What luxury! All those silver chafing dishes! Ten different choices! We're all gabbling and wolfing . . .

"Pass the jugged hare, please! Like some salmon?"

I feel as if I'm having a meal from the *Thousand and One Nights*.

I'm shocked to see how everyone is riding roughshod over the precepts my mother has inculcated into me regarding the proper way to behave in company. Even the priest has his elbows on the table and his chair is as close to it as mine was this morning on the ship with my glass of wine and my pig's feet in front of me.

My mother's sitting beside the lady from Paris who's placed us—her sons and me—on her right.

I'm almost *free* and I'm hurling myself on the various dishes. My mother's not complaining and at one moment seems almost angry because I don't take something.

"As if we were trying to starve him! It's definitely a fixed-price menu, isn't it?" she asks Monsieur Chanlaire.

"Yes, two francs per person."

"Take a bit of everything, Jacques!" she calls out quickly.

She makes it sound like a call to join a Crusade, a battle cry: "A bit of everything!"

Her voice can be heard above the clattering spoons and forks and raises a laugh from one whole corner of our table.

She just can't leave me alone! From where she's sitting she keeps a continual eye on *her child*.

"You don't spread mustard on bread and butter, Jacques! Jacques, you know very well that I don't like you sucking your fingers! Will you please *not* make so much noise blowing your nose! You don't know how to eat the parson's nose, Jacques!"

And now I can see her surreptitiously picking up food left lying on the table and slipping it into her pocket. Other people notice too. I turn red in the face . . .

"Now Jacques, will you please stop blushing like that!"

She's completely ruined my pleasure . . . I can see that our fellow guests are laughing at her and the waiters are watching her out of the corner of their eyes. And I'd been hoping to look like a man, ask the waiters for some more—"Pass me that dish!"—lean back wiping my mouth with my napkin and as I was finishing, say, "That's something the Prussians won't be able to get hold of!"

Monsieur Chanlaire is on his feet.

"Ladies and gentlemen and boys, I'm inviting you to take some champagne."

"You'll drink it out of my glass," my mother observes in the same tone of voice in which she would say: *No one will take my son from me.*

"No, he'll be drinking it out of his own glass and he'll be the first to have a taste from this bottle," Monsieur Chanlaire said, pressing against the cork which shot out like a bullet, "Children first!"

He fills my glass until it overflows and says, "Bottoms up!"

My mother cast a terrible look toward me and raps on the table, meaning: *Look at me, will you!*

I don't dare look or drink.

"For goodness sake, don't just sit there like a stuffed dummy!"

Stuffed dummy! Monsieur Chanlaire says it loudly and it's heartbreaking. My hand is shaking and I spill half my champagne on the dress of my neighbor.

"You fool!" exclaims the soaked woman.

Dummy! Fool! It's all my mother's fault that I've behaved so stupidly.

She continues to lecture me even more afterward.

I'm going off to bed, dejected and pathetic.

"This way to your room," the steward says.

Just as I'm saying good night at the end of the hallway to the lady from Paris and her sons, who've been so kind to me all that evening, my mother's voice booms out: "THE TOILETS ARE ON THE FLOOR BELOW, JACQUES!"

In her voice, there's a commanding tone—solicitous, too. She's taking precautions on behalf of her son—precautions which, with the thoughtlessness of youth, he'll have failed to take into consideration.

My new friends smile, their mothers blush, my mother says good night.

Even today, in my dreams, sometimes in a drawing room among women in low-cut dresses, at a ball, I can hear, like Joan of Arc, a voice which says: "The toilets are on the floor below, Jacques!"

The next morning we catch the boat again.

Once more, the lady from Paris is with my mother and I'm with her sons.

They're more active than I am and don't keep coming to a halt in the middle of the deck with half-opened mouths and twitching nostrils to breathe in, to drink in, the tiny passing puff of morning breeze which is ruffling the leaves in the treetops and the lace around the necks of the female passengers. The sky is clear, the houses are white, the river's blue; on the banks there are gardens full of roses and I catch a glimpse of the lower part of the town tumbling cheerfully down toward them.

Up there, a bridge over which peasant women are scuttling and a beardless, gray-haired old man in a broad-brimmed hat is slowly walking; he's wearing a long coat of the sort worn by priests and he has a Jesuitical look as well.

"It's him! It's him!"

Someone has mentioned the name of the man walking up there and he's been recognized.

"It's the *bard* of *Les Gueux*, Jacques, it's Béranger!"[5]

My father says this in the same tone of voice as he'd said, "It's the Maid!"

I think he's taken off his hat and assumed a solemn look, as though he's praying. My father has enormous respect for our glorious monuments and he's prepared to risk catching a cold to honor them . . . He hasn't yet succeeded in instilling the same veneration in me, and while we watch Béranger on the bridge, I look into the distance at birds circling around a tall tree in a large field, swooping down to plunge into the silvery aspens and golden rushes.

In my geography books I've learned that this region is called the Garden of France.

The Garden of France! Yes, and that's exactly what I, though I'm only a little boy, would have called it! And certainly that's an impression that has remained in my mind—those scents, that stillness, the riverbanks dotted with houses so spick-and-span, all pink and green, fringing the blue ribbon of the Loire.

This ribbon is dotted with black spots; all of a sudden it takes on a tinge of sea green and seems to be churning up dirty sand or mud. It's the ocean approaching and spewing up its tide; the Loire is nearing its end, the Atlantic is beginning.

We're arriving, here are the broad meadows of Les Mauves![6] All day I've been under the spell of that morning stillness, I didn't play with my little friends very much and my silence has puzzled them.

Space has always reduced me to silence.

We're close to the suspension bridge and in the distance I can read "Flower Hotel." It's Nantes!

NANTES

My mother nagged away at Monsieur Chanlaire with such persistence to tell her the best place to stay in Nantes that he told her—under his breath—to go to hell and slipped away as soon as we'd landed, hastily giving his address to my father. He gave his suitcase to a porter and was off like a shot.

The lady from Paris goes in another direction. We shake hands with the children, and now Monsieur Vingtras, the new professor of the junior class of the Nantes *lycée* is left standing in the street with his trunks, his wife, and his son.

Our family has one specialty: we can insure that, quite un-aided, we can disrupt and our luggage can obstruct the life of any city that we are about to enter. For the moment we seem to be intending to linger by the dock; people will be imagin-ing that we're going to light a fire and have a picnic supper. We're hindering commercial activity; unloading is being made difficult. The three of us are occupying more space than we're allowed in a commercial port and people are already starting to gather in groups around our colony.

My mother *tackles* my father.

"Couldn't you have asked Monsieur Chanlaire . . . ?"

"But you were doing that."

"I was doing that?"

Her shrill voice makes the passersby turn their heads. People are beginning to gather.

A porter comes up.

"How much to pick up all this?" my mother asks.

"Three francs."

"Three francs!"

"Not a sou less."

"Well, in that case, don't worry, I'll find someone else who will do it for much less," my mother says, handing over her parcels, her shawls, and a box to my father and heading to-ward a poor wretch in rags standing nearby.

He'd scarcely had time to reply before the porter comes up, pointing to his official badge, and breaks into the group, showering blows on the man in rags and insults on the Vingtras family.

In the scuffle, the boxes get knocked over and roll away toward the river.

"Jacques, Jacques!"

I pursue one package, my mother chases after another; she's shouting, the man in rags is shouting; the police show up and go over to my father; I run back to support him; we're encircled ... And that's how we made our entry into Nantes.

Phew!

We're settled in; it wasn't easy.

We spent a week in an inn kept by a man called Houdebine, I recall ... It's a name I shall *never* forget.

I hardly need to say that we had arguments with him and that my mother managed to turn the whole place upside down: trouble in the halls, squabbles on the staircases, *upsets* with travelers' wives. We argued over the bill; the maid demanded a tip. They kicked us out: once more, by noon, we found ourselves on the street—Monsieur Vingtras, spouse, and offspring.

Luckily Monsieur Chanlaire turned up at the very moment when we were standing guard over our trunks. I myself had gathered all the bags so as to be able to move off like a fully equipped division as soon as we found out in which direction to march.

We were already well known in the district, which had taken note of our quarrels with the porter. This fresh display on the open street of our goods, this pile of boxes once more obstructing people from going about their business, my own appearance, my mother's screams, and my father's embarrassment had all created a sensation and, after whetting people's curiosity, was beginning to arouse their suspicions.

How I longed to be on board a ship, engaging in a naval battle, boarding ax in hand, under a hail of bullets—and far away from our luggage.

We were standing in the street—my mother on one side, me on the other, and my father dismally scouting around—when who should appear out of the blue but Monsieur Chanlaire; he's definitely our guardian angel.

He led us, like a gang of prisoners, to a lodging house that he knew; I think we were tailed by the police: they were wondering what this family was up to . . .

As the inn was unworthy of my father's status, he refused to reveal his identity, and we were shrouded in mystery.

My father started work the day after we moved in and immediately proceeded to put the fear of God into his pupils, thereby guaranteeing permanent peace and quiet in his classroom, as well as private lessons galore. He looks *like a mean bastard*—let's ask for private tutoring!

So all's well! Now let's have a look around the town.

All my illusions about the Atlantic have disappeared into thin air! All my dreams of raging seas have collapsed—into river water. Yes, it's *river water*!

No vessels with gaping cannon mouths or naval officers in their caps; no artillery salvoes or military maneuvers; no faces of corsairs, no powder magazines; no rehearsals of clearing the decks for action; no drill for boarding the enemy ship; no whiff of the salt sea, just the smell of tar. One hope remained: I heard someone mention a pile of *death's heads*[7] on the deck of a three-master—they were Edam cheeses . . .

How stupid a sailor's life seems to be!

On the ground floor of our house, there's a little bar where I go to pick up a small jug of wine for our dinner and there I rub shoulders with sailors. They never mention fighting; they won't dive from the topgallant into the foaming waves—for the simple reason that they can't swim, so they'll never be tempted to struggle against the fury of "the white-maned breakers." If they fell into the sea, they'd drown. There aren't five sailors in ten who'd be capable of swimming across the Loire. Well, thanks very much—for nothing!

It must be admitted that we're living at the top end of town, the big ships are farther down the river, on the Fosse; but I can't see much difference between merchant vessels and any other ship. In the absence of either cannon or uniforms, I regard jolly tars and merchant seamen with equal contempt. In my disillusionment, I don't distinguish between old salts and the shippers of Edam: I view them both with equal disdain.

MY TEACHER

My teacher is a small man with silver-rimmed glasses, a pointed nose, a high-pitched voice, a little fluff on his upper lip, and short rather bandy legs—which won't stop him from making his way in the world—a sycophantic, snooping, sly, ferrety, weasel-faced mole; he's newly arrived from Paris where, like Turfin, he was among the top of the list in the *agrégation*; in Paris he has left behind people to protect him who find this little fellow's wit funny; he's brought with him an amusing, pretty wife who must find all these provincials very stupid.

Monsieur Larbcau—that's his name—doesn't much care about his students: he pampers the sons of anyone who's influential and handles them gently; he's become very popular with them because he treats them like big boys, but he's not very hard on the others, either . . . As long as you laugh at his jokes—he likes punning and sometimes organizes charades; he's known as "The Parisian."

I think he sees me as something of a *ninny*—because I don't find his jokes funny; in addition, he's heard from a schoolmate, who's taking private lessons from him, that I wanted at one time to be a cobbler and that now I'd like to be a blacksmith. He also thinks I'm common; furthermore, my mother seems to him vulgar and my father strikes him as a poor devil. But he doesn't persecute me and seems to believe me even when I say I've *forgotten* my homework or that I've *prepared the wrong lesson*.

At the end of the year, for prize essays, he reads us Walter Scott's novels.

The solemn award ceremonies are due; I haven't won anything. Or perhaps I did win something. I seem to remember picking up one or two prizes and being embraced on the podium by a man with bad breath—as always!

But I wasn't a true believer and I didn't give a damn whether I got a prize or not as long as they left my father in peace.

OUR HOME

We're living in an old house that has been plastered up and repainted but which smells *old* and in hot weather exudes an odor of turpentine and cast-iron that causes a smarting sensation, like the smell of steamed potatoes: airless, hemmed in!

This is where I spend my time, hour after horrible hour—particularly on Sunday. The only sound I hear is of bells, and in fact even during the week I feel more depressed in this region of clear skies than under the smoky sky of Saint-Étienne.

I used to love the noise of the carts, the feeling of being surrounded by ironworkers, the fire of braziers, and the tales of accidents in the mines and the anger of the miners!

Here, at least in our neighborhood, there are no factories shooting sparks, no men with fiery eyes, like almost all the men who work with iron and spend their lives in front of furnaces.

There are peasants with lank, thin hair, sad and ugly; they plod silently along through the town behind their carts, and they look dull and gloomy, like people who are deaf. No lively gestures, no self-confidence, no strength in their voices! They're thin-lipped or sharp-nosed, their eyes are sunken, their temples are like the forehead of a snake—unlike the peasants of the Haute-Loire, they don't look like cattle; they don't smell like grass but like mud; they don't wear roomy cow-colored jackets but dirty-white short-sleeved vests, like grubby surplices. I think they look pious, harsh, and false, these sons of the Vendée, these men of Brittany.

The Avenue Saint-Pierre seems so empty, with its sprinkling of old men who come and sit on benches. A few shadowy figures are creeping like black beetles around the church . . .

I feel like bursting into tears!

Nobody's beating me now. Maybe that's the reason: I'd gotten so used to being hurt or angry—I was always living in a kind of fever.

Nobody's beating me now. The headmaster doesn't belong to that school of thought. He'd learned about one of his teachers who was applying my father's method to his son's rear end and he sent for him.

"If you're so keen on that," he said, "I suggest you go away and thrash your boy somewhere else . . . But if I ever hear that you're continuing that practice here, I shall ask for you to be transferred and *demoted*."

News of this interview reached my father's ears—and saved mine.

My mother got to know a teacher's wife who's a hunchback.

In all weather, we go for a walk every evening.

I look like a prisoner allowed out for a breath of fresh air. I walk in front, under orders not to go too far away, and not to run; I can't even bend down to pick up a branch or a pebble—I could split the seat of my pants.

One day, my pants did in fact split and Madame Boireau took great offense, even though her eyesight isn't too good. I've been forbidden to bend down until I've had a new pair of loose trousers made.

Now they've been made and the danger has been averted—I can stroll around comfortably—but I look like a duck with a tail that's beginning to sprout . . .

Of course, I'm aware that people are giving me strange looks, and the boatmen gather around, although they show respect for a stranger! My schoolmates, who do know me, play tricks on me, pulling at the seat of my pants like a dog's tail as they go by—they sprinkle me with salt, and they call me Circe.[8]

CLOTHES AND POLITICAL BETRAYAL

My anguish over my clothes is beginning again. Lots of people think I'm a Legitimist[9]: I wear a neck band that goes around my neck three times, similar to that worn by the Incroyables[10] and the royalists under the Restoration. However, any hopes that this might have raised among the royalist faction have been quickly dashed. At the bottom of a trunk, next to a dog collar, my mother unearthed a horsehair collar that I'm now wearing, so this time they're shouting Bonapartist! It's the emblem of the Loire brigands,[11] the neckwear sported by the duelists who frequent the Café Lemblin.

Have I come in order to pick a quarrel with the members of the "white club,"[12] which happens to be on the square? Everybody's puzzled but they get another shock when they see me appear in the avenue one Sunday dressed in a very different getup.

I'm wearing a maroon coat with tails, a gray hat, and carrying a green umbrella.

This is my *midyear* outfit. My mother can see that I'm growing up and she's trying to dress me like a member of the *middle classes*, someone of substance, who, while not aspiring to be a young dandy, is nevertheless stylish. I'm certainly stylish, but I'm a modest young man and I'd prefer to live in obscurity, not arouse hopes among various factions only to stifle them overnight—and what's more, to stifle myself too, because this dress coat is so heavy and its sleeves so long that I can't even blow my own nose . . .

A Legitimist today, a Bonapartist tomorrow, a Constitutionalist[13] the day after, that's how people's consciences are perverted and the masses demoralized!

And my schoolmates are never very far away—they nickname me Louis-Philippe, which can be dangerous during these times when regicide is so fashionable.[14] On these *middle-school* days when I'm decked out as a *middle-class citizen*, I come home completely devastated.

OUR MAIDS

We've got a maid—it seems my father's in the money.

He's giving *tons* of private lessons; he has six or seven boys, each worth twenty-five francs, and for an hour he teaches them things that they never pay attention to. At the end of the month, he sends out his bill—and by distributing participles[15] among his two classes, he makes quite a sizeable amount each term.

These private pupils receive fewer punishments and are able to stroll around leisurely even during the rough-and-tumble in the halls. That's when they write or draw on the blackboard facetious (illustrated) remarks directed at members of the staff—someone's nose, someone else's horns, with raunchy comments added in charcoal. They are undoubtedly *over the top* and the wife of the deputy headmaster is embarrassed as she goes by them.

We watch her through various holes and cracks: she's very pretty and fresh and young; she married the deputy headmaster first of all, because he had a penny or two and, second, because one day he'll be headmaster—this was the story I heard someone whisper to my mother who also added that she dresses badly.

"If that's Paris fashion, then I'd sooner have *our'n*."

She says this good-humoredly, country fashion, with a sly little laugh. Well, I don't prefer *our'n*!

I have no interest in the matter, since I amaze even the local tailors, and I'm dressed in a way unknown since classical times up to the present day! As a tailor's dummy unconsciously representing political affiliations that I don't understand, a reluctant chameleon, my evidence must carry some weight!

I definitely prefer the pink scarf that the deputy headmaster's wife drapes around her slender waist to the drab yellow shawl my mother is so proud of. I prefer the Parisian lady's hat and its tiny quivering flowers, with two or three golden-eyed daisies, to the headgear worn by her who gave me—or had me given (I can't remember exactly)—the breast; on her hat there sits a small melon and a bird with a potbelly.

So we're a happy family.

I'm annoyed that we've got a maid. At least I had something to do when I used to fetch water or bring in firewood or move the heavy furniture around. I loved wielding a hammer or a saw—shoving with my shoulder made me feel strong, and I practiced carrying cupboards on my back and buckets with my arms outstretched. Now I'm not allowed to touch anything and I can't even scrape the mud off my shoes if I'm in a hurry.

"They've got mud on them!"

"That's the maid's job!"

"Just with the big brush?"

"We've got a maid and we don't employ her to sit and twiddle her thumbs all day!"

Poor girl! She doesn't have much time to twiddle her thumbs. My mother's got a sharp eye!

But she's not her daughter or her niece! So why show her the same consideration as she does me? She's treating a stranger the way she treated Jacques. She's not making any distinction between her servant and her son. Oh dear, I'm beginning to think that she's never loved me!

The poor girl can't bear it any longer. Yet she gets plenty to eat. My mother gives her all our leftovers.

"I'm not one to keep my maid short of food!"

And she pushes the gristle, the skin, and the fat to the edge of the plate.

"It's good for her constitution, that sort of thing. And cold meatballs are very strengthening!"

Poor Jeanneton! Just think how she'd waste away if she weren't so well looked after! Even on this diet, she's not very healthy—she's not fat, far from it!

I have the feeling that Jeanneton is not too crazy about my mother and that she's trying to get under her skin.

"Would you like a glass of cider, Jeanneton?"

"Well, ma'am . . ."

"Does that mean 'yes please'?"

"No thank you, ma'am."

"Don't you like cider?"

Jeanneton mumbles something.

"Please yourself, girl!" And in an offended voice, she adds, "I'll put a glass for you down there, so you can drink it later if you want to. You can let it go flat, if that's the way you like it."

The cider won't go flat, it's been flat for some time now . . . It's been left in a bottle that my father rejected because it smelled vinegary and they'd forgotten to cork it. A cockroach had fallen in, and my mother had carefully fished it out, just as she would have done for herself. It was after she'd had a sniff of the cider that she'd decided to offer it to the maid.

"New cider, when it's fresh, has acidity which is harmful for women who aren't strong . . . Just remember that, my girl."

I'll remember that. If I ever have weak lungs, I'll drink cider like that, the sort that *hasn't any acidity*, that smells sour and musty. Will I have to put a cockroach in it?

My mother had seen me thinking as I watched the cockroach.

"It's a sign that the cider's good. If it had been bad, the cockroach wouldn't have gone for it. Insects have got their heads screwed on the right way too!"

What cunning little fellows they are! This is another remark that I'll make a note of: when there are insects in something, it's good. And there I was not wanting to eat cheese with maggots and preferring oil which didn't have any flies in it!

Jeanneton has left, once again refusing a glass of wine. My mother offered it to her as a farewell gesture.

"Jacques," she'd said, "will you go and fetch that bottle which we wanted to make vinegar in, you know, the one that's got *flowers* . . ."

Jeanneton turned down the offer . . .

Now Jeanneton has been replaced by Margoton.

However, by now our house is known for handing out pieces of gristle, skin, and fat. When accepting the job, Margoton laid down her conditions.

"I haven't got weak lungs," she says, giving herself a punch in the stomach—a large stomach, swaying to and fro beneath her cotton print dress. "My lungs aren't weak and I'm fond of meat. I want hot meals."

Margoton is playing a risky game.

But Margoton is coming to us under the auspices of the headmaster's wife and so Margoton's stomach is as well protected as young Vingtras's backside. Authority is vested in the maid's bodice just as it is in the seat of the boy's trousers. Monsieur Vingtras wouldn't openly lose his job for having, just by chance, given his offspring a hiding or choking his maid with a hunk of meatball or mutton fat, but he'll be well advised all the same not to arouse the Big White Chief's displeasure with regard to his brat or his maid.

Oh what a mistake that was to turn to the headmaster's wife, as a gesture of respect, in order to be seen to be seeking her guidance!

In the face of such a recommendation, we dare not reject the services of this blatantly fat and pretentious girl. She's got the job.

As a result of this appointment, my mother has one hand permanently planted on her roast leg of lamb . . . and one foot in the grave . . .

She's not a robust woman and carving makes her tired. Carving a slice for her husband and son is her duty as a wife and mother and she will never shirk that!

But as for having to serve Margoton . . .

"Are you still hungry?"

"Yes, ma'am."

"Like that?"

"Just a little bit more, if you don't mind, ma'am."

She'll be the death of my mother, I can see it by the grunts she makes as she picks up the knife, by the expression in her eyes when she adds the gravy, and when it comes to the dessert, she's so tired that she's forced to put the cherries on the maid's plate one by one, as if her heart was breaking.

And Margoton keeps on asking for more . . .

But now my mother has a new lease of life; she looks a different woman! Thank God! Thank God!

In this revival, she has recovered her sense of mischief and the color has returned to her face. One day she went into my father's study, bubbling over with joy.

"Antoine!" And she whispered something into his ear.

"You're sure?" my father said, stupefied, nearly knocking off his smoking cap.

She merely smiled and nodded.

"Now the only thing we need is to catch her at it!"

She whisks off my father's smoking cap and with a mixture of affection and impishness, deposits on the forehead of her husband, my father, Antoine, a furtive kiss.

This morning something unexpected has occurred, I'm not quite certain what, but my mother has put on her yellow shawl and her best hat—the one with the little melon and the obese bird—and gone off to see the headmaster's wife.

She comes back rubbing her hands and swaying her head with glee, threatening to dislodge the melon and the bird.

Ten minutes later I see Margoton packing her bags and receiving her final week's pay. She's left some meat on her plate . . . What's up?

Tears are coming out of her eyes like bubbles on a piece of soap.

"He's got honorable intentions, ma'am!"

"Honorable intentions! In the cellar!"

What can honorable intentions mean? Nobody told me anything but a few days later, chatting with my father, my mother says, "What a piece of luck to get rid of her without offending the headmaster! Supposing she hadn't had that carter as a lover!"

I don't understand.

It's been decided that we won't have a maid anymore: it's too tiring for my mother!

So one morning, in comes a big girl—red, really red!—with freckles; she's short and round, a dumpling. She's got goggle eyes and a gut that bursts through her dress! We're certainly getting a lot of stomach in this house . . .

She'll be coming in to do the dishes, the dirty work, and to go to market with my mother to carry the groceries. My mother even wants her to accompany me whenever I go out, so as to show that we still have a maid, that there is a servant attached to my person. I do what I'm told, walking slightly in front of or slightly behind Pétronille—that's her name. Unfortunately, she's a mad talker and sticks close to me; people can see we're together.

People see us and one morning, on my way to school, I found myself being called Barley Sugar. On the classroom wall, I see a picture of my father with Barley Sugar written underneath and from then on, we're never called anything but Barley Sugar.

Here's the reason.

As a sideline, Pétronille sells barley-sugar sticks on the street and the boys know her very well. Seeing me with her, they wondered what mysterious link we have to each other and the rumor goes around that at night, we make barley sugar—that my father has taken up this line of business to supplement the income he receives from his teaching.

They claim that the quality of the barley-sugar sticks has declined since he joined forces with Pétronille.

———

How bored I am! I think it's wrong they won't let me stay at home, that they make me go out for walks but won't allow me to pick flowers. Sometimes I am told to pick them, but then it's as if I'm a sort of performing dog—like the one that was famous in Paris for a while for playing cards and dominoes. The flowers are dominoes and I'm supposed to pick them up when they make a sign. I have to pick one up like this and then set it out like that . . . Well done! Good doggy!

I get stung by nettles, pricked by thorns, it's a total chore, a real bore! I reach the point of hating gardens, loathing bouquets of flowers. I mix up the *grand* flowers and *comic* ones, the actual roses and the rosehips!

I'm always supposed to take long strides, it's more *manly*; it also saves shoe leather. So I take big strides and it seems like I'm always on the way to relieve a sentry, to rejoin the colors, or to march in a parade. I'm going through life with my back as straight as a ramrod . . . and at the speed of a magic lantern.

And that little tuft of cloth always sticking out of my backside!

I wish I was shut up in a prison cell, chained to a table leg or to a ring in the wall; anything rather than having to go for this evening walk with my parents.

This morning I stepped with bare feet on the bottom of a bottle. (My mother says that as I'm growing up, I must get ready to go into "society," for which purpose she wants me to "watch my language" and from now on I must say the you-know-what[16] of a bottle and when I'm writing, replace the "you-know-what" by a dash!)

So I stepped on the ——— of a bottle and got a splinter of glass in the sole of my foot. And oh, how it hurt! When the doctor saw the cut he was scared.

"That must be causing you a good deal of pain, my boy?"

Yes, it is, but at that moment the wind had swung open my window a little and in the distance I'd caught a glimpse of the outer suburbs, the edge of the miserable strip of country-side where I'm dragged off for a walk every evening . . . And I won't be going for walks there for quite a while because I've cut my foot . . . What luck!

And I look blissfully at my deep, ugly, painful wound . . .

I MAKE MY DEBUT IN SOCIETY

Not content with instructing me to use *proper* language, my mother wants me to combine propriety with elegance.

She has hit on the idea of having me take lessons in "gentlemanly behavior."

There is a Monsieur Soubasson who gives lessons in danc-ing, deportment, and savate.[17]

He's an ex-soldier, a heavy drinker, and a wife beater, but he can swim like a fish and has won a lifesaving medal: he pulled an inspector of schools who was drowning out of the water. He's been given the *chair* of savate and dancing in the school as a reward and a means of livelihood. He has added his course on deportment, which is highly popular because Monsieur Soubasson is shortsighted, hard of hearing, and a drunk, and once you've offered him a few swigs of his favorite rotgut, you're free to do whatever you like for the rest of his lesson.

God alone knows what we got up to!

But I'm taking private lessons, out of school. Monsieur Soubasson comes to the house. He brings his son with him, and my father is giving the boy a smattering of Latin in ex-change for my lessons in deportment.

My mother is always present.

"Now slide your foot out—one and two and three—and now the bow—and smile!"

"Are you paying attention, Jacques? Smile!"

"You're not smiling, Jacques!"

I'm not smiling? But I don't have the slightest desire to smile!

However, I must make an effort, so I pucker up my lips like the you-know-what of a duck.

Meanwhile my mother is simpering in front of a mirror, working on her smile, trying it out, and, finally finding one, offers it to me—as a smirk . . .

"There you are, just like that!"

I'm also required to stick my little finger straight up into the air. It's exhausting!

"Don't forget the auricular finger!" Monsieur Soubasson keeps insisting; he's had the scientific names of the fingers explained to him and considers that Latin is a very good thing, since it's always with his little finger that he picks his ear. He picks it a bit too often for my liking.

It's impossible for me to give an adequate account of all the caustic comments made to me by my mother in the course of these lessons on deportment, the amount of suffering I'm inflicting on this poor woman's elegant tastes, how common I am, how much like a peasant I look . . . I can never succeed in gliding my foot or even holding my little finger straight up!

"I thought you were supposed to be strong," my mother would say, knowing that I like to think of myself as brawny; she wants to wound my pride.

It seems I'm not strong, since at the end of ten minutes my nerveless auricular finger collapses, begging for mercy, shriveling like the tail of a poisoned rat. Even now the mere thought of it makes it feel strained and tense and gives me goose bumps.

At the end of two months I'm still barely able to make a bow—with a triple glide—and in any case I find it impossible to talk while I'm doing it. If I were able to talk, I think it would be like a yokel, because I'm bowing and scraping like the country idiot in some play. When I'm rehearsing with my mother, I feel like calling her Nanette[18]—which isn't true, of course, and even naughty, as I know!

But the time we've spent on all this mustn't be wasted. Sooner or later I have to put my lessons in good behavior into practice and prove myself a credit to Monsieur Soubasson and my mother.

"Saturday night, Jacques, we'll pay a call on the headmaster's wife. Make sure you've got your *deportment* all ready."

I frantically hang on to my auricular finger, make one bow after another; I sweat over it during the day, have nightmares about it at night.

Saturday arrives and we make our way with due ceremony to the house of the headmaster.

Knock, knock!

"Come in!"

My mother leads the way, I can't see how she's faring, I've got a mist in front of my eyes . . .

Now it's my turn!

But I need plenty of room and automatically make a sign for the people present to stand back.

The assembled company draws back in amazement, as if in the presence of someone who's going to perform tricks.

They're puzzled as to what it's going to be: Am I going to produce a wand, am I a magician? Or will I be turning somersaults? They're waiting expectantly.

I advance into the center and begin.

One—I execute a glide . . .

Two—I retreat . . .

Three—I again move forward . . .

But I've cut a deep gash into the carpet . . . there's a nail in the sole of my shoe.

Standing modestly at the back, my mother hasn't seen a thing.

She prompts me in a stage whisper: "And now *smile*!"

I bare my teeth.

"And he's even laughing about it!" the headmaster's wife exclaims indignantly.

Oh yes, I am . . . and I'm continuing to rip the carpet too.

"This is too much!"

People surround me and take me away like a prisoner. My mother is apologizing profusely.

I've lost my head and start calling, "Nanette! Nanette!"

"That's five years' promotions down the drain," my father says that night, as he's going to bed.

Next day Monsieur Soubasson gets fired for being an uncouth oaf and all three of us are greatly upset. I can go back to being bad mannered . . . I'm not sorry as far as my little finger is concerned; it relaxes and returns to its normal shape. It's better to have bad manners than for my auricular finger to look like the tail of a poisoned rat.

My accident's brought me luck.

The wound in my foot hadn't healed properly. Now and again it opens up and I tell a fib or two as well, in order to have the right not to go out, on the pretext that I can't walk. I even scratch it and I'd scratch it harder except that it tickles.

This you-know-what of a bottle (yes, I'll obey you, mother dear!) has done me a really good turn. I can stay at home and don't need to lurk any longer around deserted paths lined with trees that I'm not allowed to climb and fringed with grass that I'm forbidden to roll in and in the dust of which I drag myself along, like a maimed insect in the mud.

I spend my time sitting at a table on which there are books that I can pretend to read while dreaming about things no one suspects . . .

My father works opposite me and doesn't disturb me except when he blows his nose too vigorously. He really takes great care of his nose.

I don't need to study much for school. I'm often at the top of my class, I only have to slam the pages of the dictionary so that my father imagines I'm looking up a word. Meanwhile I'm pursuing memories of Farreyrolles, Le Puy, Saint-Étienne . . .

Looking back on those things fills me with strange joy.

Sometimes we're given a landscape to describe *in the form of a narrative*. I put my memories into my essays.

"Your work this week has been poor," says the teacher, not finding any Virgil or Horace in it, if it's verse; or any scraps of Cicero, if it's Latin, or Marmontel or Thomas,[19] if it's French.

But one of these days, I'm going to end up on the bottom!

I can feel I'm growing up, I'm neglecting the *classics*, I'm thinking more about what I'm going to become rather than what some Roman emperor became. My *ability*, my imagination are vanishing, are dying, they have died (Bossuet,[20] *Funeral Orations*)!!!

A certain Monsieur David, the president of the Poetic Academy of Nantes, holds large evening parties. He invites teachers and their wives to dances at his house.

It's a large, bare drawing room with a bust of Socrates on the mantel. One young wife looks at it and remarks, "So a philosopher is as ugly as that?"

My mother comes with my father, *of course*; at first they even took me with them.

The announcement of our arrival is received with pleasure. We're given a warm welcome.

As always my father looks thin and gaunt; he has a beaky nose and a forehead that juts out over his gray eyes like the eaves of a house, so that they look something like the eyes of a cat under a gutter. He gives an impression of awkwardness.

My mother . . . hmm . . . hmm . . . my mother . . . is wearing a blood-red dress with a yellow belt; in addition, yellow bows on her wrists, slightly puffed, like the straw bows that are tied around a horse's tail. It's her only ornament. Her motto is: simplicity.

On one occasion only, she did add the bird from her hat—as a brooch, attached with the beak downward, the you-know-what upward. It was a flight of fancy, just to experiment, like Metternich's wife wearing a snake as a bracelet.

"What's the bird doing there?" they ask her.

Some people would have preferred the beak to be pointing upward and the you-know-what downward.

My mother simpered, teasing its beak as if it were a real live bird.

"Diddums-den! Pretty little birdy . . . he's my little dicky bird!"

My father managed to persuade her to let the bird stay on her hat . . . the pretty little dicky bird!

But as for the bows, when he tried to allude to them.

"Now, Antoine," my mother replied, "am I or am I not an honest woman? You're hesitating, you're not saying yes or no! Your silence is becoming insulting!"

"My dear . . ."

"You do think I'm an honest woman, don't you? And you've never had any cause to suspect that our child, our Jacques, was of *impure origin*, a tainted, worm-eaten fruit?

"A tainted fruit," she continues. "Well, have faith in me. Your wife may perhaps be a teeny weeny bit flirtatious—after all, we're all daughters of Eve, aren't we? Well, have faith in me, Antoine. If I were to go too far—as you know, I'm not very worldly-wise—you'd have every right to reproach me . . .

But that isn't the case and you mustn't imagine that any small tribute that someone happens to pay to my touch of elegance and good taste is the sign of a guilty passion!"

She taps her skirt and fiddles with one of her yellow bows, then gives my father's hand a tiny slap:

"You naughty, jealous man!"

People are dancing.

"You're not dancing, Madame Vingtras?"

"We're too *old* for dancing," my father says, with a smile and a nod.

"Too *old*?" my mother exclaims. "Is that supposed to include me?"

This scene is taking place in a niche where she has cornered Antoine, behind a curtain . . .

"That can only mean me, because the gentleman concerned happens to be younger than his wife. Now listen to me, Antoine . . ."

"Not so loudly!"

"I'll speak as loudly as I like!"

She raises her voice still more.

"Oh, don't think you can stop me from talking! No! If you want to insult me, I don't intend to let myself be insulted, do you understand? Too *old* indeed!" (Looking him up and down from head to foot.) "Too *old*! Because I'm not as young as that Brignolin woman, is that it?"

I was on tenterhooks and I made a little noise with my feet and with my mouth. To drown their voices, in my corner I imitate the sound of wind instruments—at the risk of being maligned!

Peace finally prevails in the niche behind the curtain.

I don't find the headmaster's parties much fun; people think I'm not cheerful enough—I've got a new outfit. But they've chosen an odd material, I look as if I'm inside a woolen stocking; it's a *ribbed* material but so drab!

And the color runs, so that I leave a stain on other people's clothes . . .

So people steer clear of me. Even my mother speaks to me only at a distance, almost as though I'm a stranger. Oh God!

"*I am going to dance,*" she had said. And dance she does.

She gets the quadrille into a muddle, she treads on people's feet, but who cares? She gets away with it by making little jokes and putting on little airs—really schoolgirlish, I can tell you! In the final galop, she suddenly hits on the idea of involving her son in these terpsichorean delights and, breaking away from the other dancers, she grabs me and whirls me off. When the galop has come to an end, I'm still bobbing up and down, and she's looking like a Savoyard[21] with his marionette—and I'm suffering agonies under my arms!

For some time now, she's looked pensive.

"Your mother's planning something," my father says in the voice of someone conscious of impending disaster.

She's shutting herself up on her own and we can hear noises, little cries; the floor shakes, we've had glimpses of her through the door holding her forehead and preening herself in front of the mirror.

An evening party at Monsieur David's house: the history teacher's wife is of Spanish origin; she dances a few steps of a quite lively fandango—*olé*, *olé*—albeit "revised and corrected" like the select passages in an anthology compiled by an archbishop . . .

The German professor's wife, from Alsace, sings an *umpty-tiddle-i-dee* while dancing an Alsatian waltz.

That's all. She takes a seat on a bench against the wall, leaving the area where they've been dancing empty.

We hear a little yell.

Youpy-you youpy-you oh!

My father, sitting facing me, looks as if he's having a stroke. I rush across and *fling myself into his arms.*

Youpy-you-oh!

Youpy-you!

At the same moment an apparition darts across the drawing room and circles around the floor . . .

The apparition sings:

> *Che la bourra,*[22] *la la!*
> *Yes, la bourra, fouchtra!*

Then the voice suddenly becomes urgent, almost biblical: *Anto, my man!*

This Anto is Antoine who at the very first *youpy-you* had foreseen the danger—and my father is now hauled onto the floor, exactly as I had been the day of the marionettes.

"*Anto*, my man, *Anto!*"

And my mother sets him up in front of her, telling him off for being a *schofty*—to the *schtupefaction* of the assembled company who hadn't been forewarned of this interlude in dialect from the AUVERGNE.

"Now sing, sing, sing!"

I'm terrified that I too may be *schosen* and I vanish as fast as I can into the toilets. For the rest of the evening, I kept calling out, "It's occupied!"

By the time night came, I was exhausted . . . and evacuated . . .

When the last light had been put out, I eventually emerged and went home, where no one was thinking of me.

My mother was alone with my father, whispering into his ear, "Anyway, isn't a *bourra* as good as any fandango?"

And in a voice that trembled a little, she added, "Please say it is!"

It was a combination of impishness and pride, of mischief and happiness!

Everything's going wrong.

My father—Antoine—has refused to attend any more social evenings with my mother.

That party with the *bourra* has gone to my mother's head, she's become intoxicated with her success; following the same line that she's discovered and persisting in it, she now talks Auvergnat patois all the time, calling people *mishter* or *mushter*.

In the end my father forbade her to use dialect.

She replied bitterly, "Well, what a fat lot of good it is to be educated and then to be jealous of your wife whose only advantage is her natural wit. You're a poor thing, for all your Latin and Greek, you're reduced to forbidding your wife, who's only a country girl, to *eclipshe* you!"

The squabbles turn nasty.

"You know, Antoine, I've made sacrifices enough, don't demand too much from me! You wanted me to stop saying *ishtatue* and I did. You wanted me to stop saying *copbard* and I did. But don't push me too far or I'll start doing it again!"

She goes on.

"And first of all, my mother always used to say *ishtatue* and she was as good as yours, don't you ever forget that!"

My father finds himself threatened on all fronts, between *ishtatue* and *moshter*.

He takes a firm stand—too firm!—on both of them.

My mother takes her revenge by insulting him: she tries to find words that will offend him; eshtablishment ... eshpectacle ... eshcalope ... eshkeleton ... Such diphthongs pierce deep into my father's heart. The following Saturday evening, he gets dressed in silence and goes off to the party without her.

And the Saturday after he does the same again, but at midnight my mother comes and wakes me up:

"Get up, you must go and wait for your father outside Monsieur David's and when he comes out, you're to shout: *La la, fouchtra!* Then I'll come along and you must go away."

I did shout: *La la, fouchtra!* It was a mistake.

She made a scene in front of everybody, saying loudly that he was letting his family starve in order to go out gallivanting at all the dances.

"For someone who's supposed to be starving that boy's got quite a sturdy backside," a guest remarks.

"Yes," my mother repeated, "he's letting us all starve."

For dinner, we'd had a big plate of soup, followed by sausages and, finally, rabbit—I'm not starving, and she ate a lot, too.

My mother continues to shout.

"My son hasn't got a shirt to his back. Just look at his clothes!"

I'm not wearing black today but a gray coat and gray trousers—I look like a medical orderly.

People are gathering in large numbers; my father tries to get away by ducking under a carriage and is caught up in the horses' legs. Finally he's pulled out.

When he emerges, his hat has been squashed like an accordion. My mother seizes him by the arm like a policeman.

"Come along, my child," she says with tears in her eyes. "Come and tell him you're his son!"

He knows that perfectly well. Didn't he recognize me? Have I changed since seven o'clock?

All the way home, I look out for a mirror, in the doorway of a milliner's or a tailor's shop. I want to see what I look like now that I'm starving.

STRAINED RELATIONS

Home has become almost as gloomy as it was in the days of Madame Brignolin, which were so dreadful. My father has stopped going out to parties.

I don't know where he goes now.

One evening my mother ordered me to follow him, secretly. But at that moment my father reappeared . . .

I was standing in front of her, very scared, and wondering to myself: *Is it right to spy on your father?*

"Do you want to turn your son into a policeman?" he asked. "I heard what you were telling him to do, *Madame Vingtras*."

The cold formality of his tone made my mother go pale and she never again suggested doing anything like that.

She's struggling to win back, in some way or other, the ground she has lost; you can sense it in her tone of voice and see it in her gestures.

"The truth is, Antoine dear, that it's not very pleasant for me to be woken up every night when you come home."

"I'm not going to be waking you up anymore, Madame Vingtras," my father retorts.

That night he went upstairs to the attic and brought down a folding bed and a mattress.

At home silence reigns. We were each living in our little corner, hardly speaking to one another.

Our cleaning women all left after a week, saying that a house like that gave you the creeps.

What a miserable dump! That's what they all say in the neighborhood.

It's been going on for a long time now. My mother insists on my staying at home with her every evening and I read sacred texts to her in her bedroom by the light of one small candle and beside a fire emitting the faintest glow.

The texts are all concerned with pain and hell—these *church* books are always mournful.

A fight!

Cleaning out an old trunk, my father discovered a heavy object that tinkled.

It's a stocking, ankle-full of five-franc pieces.

He's eyeing it in amazement when my mother rushes in like a fury and flings herself onto the stocking trying to tear it out of his grasp.

"That's my money. I saved it on my clothes."

My father won't let go, my mother is shrieking.

"Come and help me, Jacques!"

But the only thing I can do is to run from one to the other crying, "Father! Mother!"

My father is left in possession of the bag and locks it away in a cupboard.

They've made up.

My mother quite simply went to see my father and said, "I can't go on living like this. I'd rather leave and go back to my sister and take my son with me."

———

But she doesn't want to go away and, finally, says so openly, admitting it to Antoine, and confessing that she was in the wrong—and she asks him to forget.

He's had enough of it, no doubt, and pretends to be reluctant as a pure formality, but he's flattered at being begged for mercy; that's what he's like, at bottom: he wants people to grovel. And now that he's sure of ruling the roost, and she has surrendered, he prefers to avoid the strain of living in a permanent atmosphere of gloomy silence.

"Tell me if I'm to take the folding bed and mattress back upstairs, won't you, Dad?"

I'm sorry I said it: I can see they're both embarrassed.

"Go play with the boy downstairs, Jacques," my father replies.

XIX. LOUISETTE

MONSIEUR BERGOUGNARD was at school with my father, in the same class.

He's bony, deathly pale, and always formally dressed.

In essays, he was first, ahead of my father; but my father always came first in Latin verse. They still have deep admiration for each other, like two statesmen who have been adversaries but respect each other's ability.

Both are convinced that they were born to achieve great things, but that life's demands have kept them away from the battlefield.

They've divided their realm between them.

"You represent Imagination," Bergougnard says, "a fiery imagination . . ."

My father pulls himself up and makes a frantic effort to put a gleam into his eye, casting a slightly bemused look heavenward—and in private, ruffling his hair to appear disheveled . . .

"You are imagination in all its wildness . . ."

My father puts on a distraught look and makes terrible faces.

"As for me," Bergougnard continues, "I represent Reason, icy-cold, implacable reason." And he plants his stick upright between his legs.

At the same time he adjusts on his nose, which is of a yellowish hue flecked with tiny black dots like a dice, a pair of gleaming spectacles that resemble solar lenses and make me fear for the safety of my coat, which seems awfully dry.

You imagine that they might burn a hole. Sometimes I even wonder if they might not have cooked his eyes, which look like large black spots behind . . .

"I am cold, icy-cold, implacable reason . . ."

He's fond of that phrase. When he says it, he almost grinds his teeth, as though crushing a dilemma and chewing up its horns . . .

It's very obvious that he too has been a teacher but he resigned to marry a widow—who thought that she was marrying a great man and brought him a small private income that has allowed him to work on his magnum opus: *Reason and the Civilization of Ancient Greece.*

He's been working on it for the last three years, always to the apparent accompaniment of a grinding of teeth; he twists arguments as if he were wringing out washing, he wants close reasoning, he can't bear loose thinking—this seems to cause him to suffer from bad constipation and nasty headaches.

"It's the brain, you see," he says to my father, tapping his forehead with his finger.

"It's not the brain," the doctor tells him; he thinks it's a disorder of the lower bowel, as a result of which he doesn't quite know whether Monsieur Bergougnard is a philosopher because he's constipated or constipated because he's a philosopher.

People discuss the matter; it's given rise to little arguments, quite sharp, in the local cafés. The brain is not without its supporters.

In the beginning, my mother had expressed her view very vigorously.

One day my father had had the idea of appointing Monsieur Bergougnard as his orator-advocate to go and solemnly plead his cause, armed with his threatening teeth—and Reason—to persuade her that sometimes in her treatment of her husband she had infringed the laws of respect, as understood by both Ancients and Moderns, involving him in scenes that had no counterpart in the great classical authors.

"I've come to put a dilemma to you."

"You'd do better to stick a mustard plaster on yourself—you know where."

He ran off and would never have come back, if my mother hadn't overcome her dislike of him, for my sake.

She blamed her rather sharp retort on her high spirits: she was a countrywoman who liked a bit of a joke. Never one to apologize, she did on this occasion so as to entice Monsieur Bergougnard back—on my behalf, out of love for her son.

Yes, it was for her Jacques that she stooped to saying sorry and induced this living monument to constipation to sit down beside her—insofar as he was capable of sitting down at all.

For my sake! Because Monsieur Bergougnard taught me, offered me textual evidence, proved to me, book in hand, that the ancient Greek and Roman philosophers beat their sons with might and main; he beat his own sons in the name of Sparta and Rome—Sparta was the day for whacking them, Rome the day for tanning their hides . . .

Despite her repugnance, my mother, out of love for me, had thrown herself back into the horribly desiccated arms of Monsieur Bergougnard who, as a man, had obstructed bowels, but not as a philosopher; who would soak his offspring's shirts and get them thoroughly wet in order to engrave his philosophical principles on their you-know-whats—like nailing the colors to the mast or planting the flag.

My mother had guessed that I wasn't a believer in such cutaneous treatment.

"Ask Monsieur Bergougnard! Watch Monsieur Bergougnard! Look at young Bergougnard's back!"

And, after sticking my nose four or five times into the Bergougnard's household, I decided my own situation was positively delightful in comparison to that of the Bergougnard boys: sometimes with their heads held between their father's legs, thereby enabling him to strangle them a bit and beat them in comfort; at other times facing him, picked up by their hair and dusted off with a cane—really thoroughly—until there was no hair and no dust left.

Sometimes you could hear terrible screams coming from their house.

In the neighborhood, men would point out the Villa Bergougnard to people of importance.

"That's where the philosopher lives," they'd say, indicating the house. "That's where Monsieur Bergougnard is writing his *Reason and the Civilization of Ancient Greece.* That's the house of the *sage.*"

All of a sudden, his sons would appear at the window, wriggling like monkeys and howling like jackals.

Yes, the blows I receive are caresses compared to those administered by Monsieur Bergougnard to his family.

He's not content merely to beat his sons for their own good—the good of Bonaventure or Barnabas—and for his own pleasure.

He's not selfish or self-centered—he is devoted to a cause, he's addressing mankind when he pulls up Bonaventure's shirt with one hand and with the other signals to men of learning that he is going to practice his system.

He administers a thrashing the way he'd fire a cannon, and he's pleased when Bonaventure starts uttering piercing screams that would startle a train . . .

He would have taken his son's bleeding buttocks to the rostrum[1]; in Turkey he would have taken them, like a head stuck on a pike, to plant them outside the palace gates.

———

I'm just an isolated case, obsolete, useless—I serve no purpose whatsoever—I get beaten and I don't know why, whereas
Bonaventure is an exemplary case who is moving *backward*,
but deeply, into philosophy...

I feel no sympathy toward Bonaventure.

Bonaventure is very ugly, very stupid, and very cruel. He
beats younger boys in exactly the same way his father beats
him; he makes them cry, and then he laughs. He once cut off
a cat's tail with a razor and you could see it dripping blood
like wax from a candle; he went through the motions of seal-
ing letters with the drops of blood. Another time he plucked
all the feathers off a live bird.

His father was delighted.

"Bonaventure likes to get to the bottom of things, he's got
a scientific mind..."

Ever since he cut off the cat's tail and plucked the bird
alive, I've loathed him. I'd let him be smashed by a stone like
a toad. Am I cruel too? The other day he was twisting the
wrist of one of the little boys, and I kicked him, hard again
and again, and bashed his nose against the wall.

But his little sister! Dear God...!

She'd been staying with her aunt in her native village.
The aunt died and she was sent back home. Poor innocent
little girl; dear, unhappy creature!

My heart has often been hurt, I've shed many tears; more
than once I've thought I would die from sadness; but never
have I felt such pain and anguish in the presence of love, defeat, or death as at the time when I saw Louisette being killed
under my very eyes.

What had this little girl done? They were right to beat
me because when I was beaten I didn't cry—I even laughed

because when my mother was really angry, I thought she looked so funny—I was tough, I was brawny, I was a man.

I never cried out—as long as I didn't risk having any bones broken, because I would need to earn my living . . .

"Don't make me a cripple, Dad, I'm poor!"

But this dear little creature who was being beaten as she begged for forgiveness, falling on her knees, clasping her tiny hands, crouching terrified in front of her father who still kept on hitting her without stopping!

"Hurting me, Daddy, hurting me, Daddy, Daddy!"

Her cries were like the cries I had once heard from an eighty-year-old madwoman, tearing out her hair one day when she saw someone in the sky trying to kill her!

That madwoman's cry had gone on echoing in my ears. The voice of Louisette, mad with terror, was the same!

"Please forgive me, Daddy, please, please do!"

I'd hear one more blow; in the end, all I could hear was a stifled moan, a gasping breath . . .

On one occasion, I thought that her neck had been snapped, that her little chest had burst open, and I went into the house.

She was lying on the floor, her face all white, too weak even to sob, convulsed with terror, in front of the cold, livid face of her father who had stopped only because he was afraid that this time he might have actually finished her off.

All the same, he did eventually kill her . . . At the age of ten, she was killed by pain . . .

By pain! Like someone who dies from grief.

And also from the harm caused by his blows!

They caused her so much pain! And she begged for mercy in vain.

As soon as her father came near her, the tiny spark of reason in this angelic little girl started to tremble . . .

And they didn't send that father to the guillotine! They didn't apply the law of an eye for an eye and a tooth for a tooth to this murderer of his own child; he wasn't tortured, he wasn't buried alive beside the dead girl.

"For God's sake stop whining!" he used to shout at her because he was afraid the neighbors might hear, and he would strike her to make her keep quiet; this made her twice as terrified and she cried even more.

When she arrived, she was so pretty, cheerful, happy, so pink.

After a while she lost all her color, and when she heard her father come home, she would shudder like a beaten dog.

When we'd gone with Monsieur Bergougnard to pick her up, like a bunch of flowers at the coach station, I'd kissed her and stroked her plump warm cheeks.

Lately—(oh, it didn't take long, luckily for her!) she was as white as wax and I could clearly see that she knew she was going to die, young as she was—her smile was like a grimace. But Louisette looked so old when she died at the age of ten—of *pain*, I tell you!

My mother saw how sad I was on the day she was buried.

"If your own mother had died you wouldn't cry so much—would you?"

I didn't say a thing.

"Your mother's speaking to you, Jacques. She expects an answer! Answer my question!"

I'm not listening to what they're saying, I'm thinking of that dead little girl. They'd seen her martyrized just as I had. They'd allowed her to be beaten instead of stopping Monsieur Bergougnard from hitting her. They told her that she mustn't be unkind, that she mustn't make her father unhappy!

Louisette unkind? That little mite of a girl, with that gentle voice, those moist eyes?

And my eyes fill with tears and I kiss something—I'm not

certain exactly what. I think it was a scrap of scarf that I'd taken from around the murdered little girl's neck.

"Will you leave that grubby bit of cloth alone!"

. . . .

My mother hurls herself on me. I clasp the scarf against my chest, she catches hold of my wrists in a fury and won't let go.

"Let me have that!"

It had belonged to Louisette . . .

"So you won't? Antoine, are you going to allow your son to treat me like this?"

My father orders me to let go of the scarf.

"No, I won't let go!"

"Jacques!" shouts my father angrily.

I refuse to budge.

"Jacques!" He's twisting my arm.

They're robbing me of that little bit of silk that I'd gotten from Louisette.

"And there's another dirty bit of stuff in a corner that I'm going to get rid of too," my mother says.

It's the bunch of flowers that my cousin gave me.

She'd found it at the bottom of a drawer when she was rummaging around one day.

She goes off to get it, tears it apart, and *kills* it. Yes, it seemed to me that they were killing something as they tore my faded bunch of flowers to pieces . . .

I went and shut myself up in my little closet so that I could go on cursing them under my breath. I was thinking of Bergougnard and my mother, of Louisette and my cousin.

"Murderers! Murderers!"

I kept sobbing these words and repeating them for a very long time. I was shuddering hysterically.

In the night I woke up, thinking that Louisette was sitting there in her shroud on my bed, with her arm sticking out, thin as a stalk, bearing the marks of blows.

XX. MY CLASSICAL STUDIES

WHAT AN idiot my teacher is this year!

He's just graduated from the *école normale*; he's young, going bald; he wears pants with stirrup straps and is working on a translation of Pindar. He says *acuminate* instead of sharpen, and when I bend down to tie my shoelaces, he calls out: "Do not advance your digital extremities in the direction of your *cothurn!*"[1] And fine *cothurns* they are, too, clotted with dung, and gilded with manure.

On my way to school, I spend a lot of time lurking around a stable near our house—I know some of the grooms there. I get dung on my shoes, and I must have some in my books as well.

He says *cothurns* and *acuminate* with a half smile to prevent people from laughing at him too much, but it's obvious that he basically believes in doing this sort of thing, he enjoys these classical allusions. *I know it* (that's from Bossuet).

He likes me because I can put together good Latin verse.

"What imagination!" he says, "what a gift. His godmother must be Minerva!"

"His godmother is Aunt Agnes," my mother points out . . .

"Auntagnes, auntagnetos, auntagnetiton."[2]

"Just as you like," comments my mother who seems taken aback by one of these conjunctions of sounds; she blushed at the genitive plural!

238

"What imagination!" my teacher repeats, to save the situation.

And I allow him to say that I'm *gifted*.

BUT I'M NOT!

The other day we were given the topic "Themistocles haranguing the Greeks"—I couldn't think of a thing, not one single thing!

"I reckon that makes a wonderful topic, eh?" the teacher said, licking his lips with his tongue—which is yellow and his lips are coated in a crust.

Clearly a wonderful topic and certainly not one that's set in any old school—only in the large royal schools and only when there are worthy pupils like me.

What on earth am I going to say?

Put yourself in Themistocles' place.

They're always telling me to put myself in the place of this person or that—with my nose cut off like Zopyrus or with a roasted wrist like Scaevola.[3]

They're always generals or kings and queens!

But I'm fourteen years old, I've no idea what to make Hannibal or Caracalla say, or Torquatus[4] either!

I JUST DON'T KNOW!

So I just look up adverbs and adjectives in the *Gradus* and merely copy out whatever I can find in *Alexander*.

My father doesn't know this and I wasn't about to tell him.

But what about him, himself? (Oh dear, I'm giving away a family secret!) I've seen some of the essays he did for the *agrégation*—and they're made up of odds and ends too. Are we a family of morons?

Sometimes he composes a speech intended to be spoken by a woman—the lamentations of Agrippina,[5] Aspasia[6] to Socrates, Julia[7] to Ovid.

I can see him scratching his beard in horror—he's an

Agrippinus, an Aspasios, he's not an Agrippina, he's not an Aspasia!—in despair, he tugs bits of his beard out and chews them!

I feel my natural inferiority and it causes me considerable anguish.

I suffer from being covered in praise I don't deserve; people think I'm bright when I'm just a petty thief...I steal left and right, I pick up odd bits of other people's books that they've *thrown together*. Sometimes I'm even dishonest...I need an epithet, why bother about the truth! So I take down the dictionary and find the word that fits, even if it's the opposite of what I originally intended to say. I'm losing any sense of justice: I need my spondee or my dactyl. Never mind—the quality is unimportant, it's the *quantity*[8] that counts...

They never want you to stray far away from the Janiculum.[9]

I can't imagine myself as a citizen of Rome.

When I ask to leave the room at school, I'm not going to the Vitelline latrines[10]; and I haven't been to Greece either! I'm not interested in Miltiades'[11] laurels—it's onions that I can't stomach! In my *narrative* I boast of the wounds I've received *in front, adverso pectore*; I've certainly received more than a few from behind...

"You'll describe life in Rome in this way, in that way..."

But I've no idea how they lived! I do the dishes, I get knocked around, I wear suspenders, I'm pretty bored! But the only consul I know is my father who wears a large tie, shoes that have been resoled, and as far as old women are concerned (*anus*[12]), there's Ma Gratteloux who's the cleaning lady of the people on the second floor...

And people keep on praising my "gifts."

This hypocrisy is becoming too much for me. Remorse is making it hard for me to breathe.

The history teacher is Monsieur Jaluzot; at school, everybody likes him. He's supposed to have a private income and to call a spade a spade. He's nice.

I fling myself at his feet and confess everything.

"M'sieur Jaluzot!"

"What's wrong, my boy?"

"M'sieur Jaluzot!"

I'm covering his hands with my tears.

"What's wrong, sir, is that I'm a thief!"

He thinks I've stolen someone's purse and starts to tuck his watch chain out of sight.

In the end I confess to my borrowings from *Alexander* and even that I've been regurgitating material already swallowed by others. I tell him about the back passages I use for my Latin verse.

"Get up, my boy! So you put all these scraps into your essays? But that's just why you're here, to go on chewing over and over things that have already been chewed by other people!"

"I can never manage to put myself in the place of Themistocles!"

For me this is the most painful confession of all.

Monsieur Jaluzot's reply is to burst out laughing, as if he couldn't give a damn about Themistocles. It's easy to see that he really has got lots of money.

As for my *narrative essays* in French, once again I succeed only by renovating and resoling, by lying and stealing.

In these essays I say there's nothing better than liberty and the fatherland to uplift the soul . . .

I don't know what liberty is myself or for that matter what the fatherland is either. I've always been beaten and had my face slapped—so much for freedom. As for the fatherland, the only thing I know about it is our apartment where I'm bored stiff—and the fields, which I like but where I'm never allowed to go.

I don't give a damn for Greece and Italy, for the Tiber and the Eurotas.[13] I prefer my little brook at Farreyrolles, cowpats, and horse dung, and picking dandelions for a salad.

RECITATION FROM MEMORY

"Louder, Jacques!"

That's my mother speaking; today she's being exceptionally gentle. She says "louder" in the tone of voice of a hospital nurse talking to a patient while holding his burning forehead. "Louder! That's it! Keep going! That's right!"

I fall back completely exhausted into an armchair, my nerveless arms dangling. Like a murdered rabbit, I've even got a drop of blood on the tip of my snout; what's more, all around my skin is reddish and smooth like an onion skin, so smooth! If I did have a few little wayward hairs, they're now gone, drowned in the enormous amounts of water which have flooded through my nostrils since this morning.

Today, in fact, we have a recitation of a classical passage to be learned by heart. My mother is keen for me to win the prize.

To do this, you not only have to know the passage but to *deliver* it properly; and a nose that has been energetically *clarified* gives you a clear voice.

My nose has been *clarified*.

My mother took hold of it and held it under water, where it stayed for a very long time! Minutes felt like centuries. Finally she took it out with great efficiency and said, "Now sniff, my boy, sniff!"

I couldn't sniff.

"Make an effort, Jacques!"

I made an effort.

Like a flabby syringe, my nose drew in and sprayed out water for the next half hour, perhaps longer. I feel like I've been emptied out—as if my head's attached to my neck like a pink balloon to its string: it's swaying to and fro in the breeze. I put my hand up. "Where is it? Ah, there!"

The nose is all-important: it hurts like nothing else and glows like the stopper in a decanter.

I hold on to it myself, grasping it by its tip, and am able to lead myself very gently back to my desk to continue working.

Sometimes I don't achieve my aim, and my nose keeps on dripping little drops of water all over the place, like a washcloth on its hook. Then I say, "Bom."

BOM is how I now address the woman who gave birth to me!

In class when I recite the first song of the *Iliad*, it comes out as: *Benin aeide!*—atchoo!—*thea Beleadeo*—atchoo!

I'm making old *Hober* sound ridiculous!

Atchoo! Atchoo! Zim, mala ya boum, boum!

Sometimes I don't catch a cold. I just sound like a trombone with a hole in it—a hole where my nose is. I give an excellent imitation of the man depicted by a philosopher as a tube with a hole at each end.

There's nothing better for a child's head, the headmaster says, referring to the exercise in nasal purification when my mother mentions it to him. Yes indeed—nothing better designed to turn him into a lump of dough!

Despite—or *despide*—everything—or *eberyding*—and with or without atchoos *I'b bery bery* good at reciting; good at reciting; *by bebory* soaks up *Hober* like my nose soaks up water and I sniff whole cantos of the *Iliad* and whole choruses of Aeschylus, not to mention Virgil and Bossuet—but it all goes out just as easily as it comes in.

I forget Bossuet as easily as one forgets the *salubrious bitter aloes . . .*

MATHEMATICS

"That child has a fiery imagination!"

It's common knowledge: I'm a little volcano (whose vent often gives off a smell of cabbage—we eat so much of it at home).

"A fiery imagination, I tell you! Ah well, he's not likely to be any good at math, then!"

They seem to be establishing the fact that being good at math is all right for those who've got nothing else "up there . . ."

In Rome, Athens, or Sparta, was there at any time any mention of numbers? And in fact it's true that I don't like doing subtraction, or addition problems with lots of zeros in them, and I don't understand division at all, at all!

My father treats it as a joke, my literature teacher too.

I'm always among the last six.

But one fine day, news spread around the school . . .

Great surprise . . . Rumblings in the playground, under the arches . . .

I was first in geometry.

The literature teacher looks at me with suspicion. Am I—or am I not—a volcano?

The result is so unexpected that people wonder whether I haven't been stealing, cribbing, *cheating*, and they call me up to the blackboard to see if I can do it, chalk in hand.

I can—and I can go even further . . . I turn toward the class and explain the problem to them, demonstrating with my hands, producing books, picking up pieces of wood; I roll up cones, I construct figures, and I keep on until the teacher says to me in an offended voice, "How much longer do you intend to continue your little game? Are you teaching this class or am I?"

I return to my seat amid murmurs of admiration.

At the end of the lesson, they question me.

"How on earth did you do it? When did you learn it?"

How did I learn it!

In a little side street, there's a miserable house with a few broken windowpanes papered over; at the second-floor window, hanging above a pot of flowers shivering in the wind, there's a black cage.

A poor man lives here, an Italian refugee.

The first time I saw him, I shivered; I was moved. The background of my translations was about to be revealed to me, in flesh and blood, in the person of a man who had bathed in the waters of the Tiber: Tacitus, Livy, Caesar's horse, Septimus's goat, Nero's torch!

But what a gloomy place it was!

A dismal lamp alight on a table covered in old books, a dog who gazes at me blankly, and a gray-haired man with thick spectacles mending a pair of ragged trousers.

This was the Roman.

"My father, Monsieur Vingtras, sent me."

And I handed over the letter I'd been asked to deliver. He read it; I followed his eyes.

Was he really from Rome? Did he belong to that land of gladiators, this gray-haired old man who looked like an owl in a cobbler's booth and was stitching up the seat of his pants?

Were these trousers his *vexillum*?[14] Was this needle his sword? Where was his shield and helmet? He's wearing a wool sweater.

I looked at him and noticed that he had three fingers missing; the round lumps of bone which are left are ugly. The remaining fingers look like two horns.

As he folded up the letter, he was shaking.

"Please thank your father very much," he said.

I thought I could see a little bright speck, a drop of water in his eyes.

He was crying—but did Romans cry?

I was beginning to think that there must be some mistake— or that he'd lied. He held out a little book.

"I wrote this," he said. "Do you like mathematics?"

He realized from my look that the answer was no.

"No? Well, you might still enjoy reading my book all the same . . . Look, here's the box that goes with it."

He showed me out, still carrying his pants in his hands and holding up his glasses with the blunt tips of his fingers; I heard him talking to his dog.

"It's two francs a lesson: I can find you something to eat and I'll get some bread for myself . . ."

He'd been brought to my father's attention by chance and my father had found him some tutoring. That was the subject of the letter.

"Do you like mathematics?"

Hadn't he seen right off that I was a volcano? Did *he* like mathematics? Had this descendant of Romulus the soul of a *bookkeeper*? With his pants and his glasses he certainly showed no sign of being a *civis* or a *commilito*.[15]

What's in the box?
  Bits of plaster, cut up into slices.
  And in the book?
  Geometry.

The next day was a Sunday and instead of visiting a friend, as my father had given me permission to do, I spent the day with the book and the pieces of plaster.

It was on the following Saturday that I was first in geometry.

In my glee, I went around to tell the man all about it, and he told me his own story.

He'd been beaten almost to death by the Neapolitan police who had come to arrest him on charges of conspiracy and whom he'd resisted in an attempt to save some incriminating papers. That was the occasion when they'd hacked his fingers off. He'd managed to drag himself into a hideaway where he'd been picked up, rescued, and helped across the border into France.

"A conspiracy! You were a conspirator?"

"Luckily I was a stonemason and I was able to use my skills to make geometrical models. Incidentally, it would seem that you were able to understand my system?"

"I only needed to look and to touch. Would you like me to explain it to you?"

Picking up the plaster casts lying around, I repeated my demonstration . . .

"That's right, that's right!" he kept saying, nodding his head. "They try to teach children what a cone is, how to cut it into sections, the volume of a sphere, and then keep showing them just *lines*, nothing but lines! Give them a cone of wood, a figure in plaster and teach them that, the same way you cut up an orange! Their old system is nothing but theology! Always God, the Good Lord!"

"What was that about God?"

"Oh, nothing, nothing!"

He seemed to be recovering from a fit of anger and started talking about geometry again, using pieces of string and plaster.

XXI. MADAME DEVINOL

"WELL, MONSIEUR VINGTRAS, when Jacques is first in his class, I'll take him to the theater.

"Are you agreeable?"

It's Madame Devinol who's asking; she has a son in my father's class; he's a dunce and a troublemaker. If Monsieur Devinol wasn't rich and influential, they'd have expelled the brat long ago.

But his mother is distinguished-looking, maybe her complexion's a little dark, but she has such dark eyes, and such white teeth! When she looks at you, everything seems to light up. When she takes hold of your hands, she squeezes them. It's soft, it's nice.

"Why are you blushing?" she asks me abruptly.

I stammer something and she gives me a tap on the cheek and says, "Just look at that big boy! Yes, every time he's first in his class, I'll take him to the theater."

My father is flattered for me to be seen in the company of such an important person but my mother is taken aback!

"Aren't you afraid he'll embarrass you?"

"Embarrass me! Don't you realize what a fine, well-built boy your son is, a little mulatto and with such a soldierly bearing?"

"He's got a very big belly!" my mother says. "You might not think so but it is big."

Me, a big belly? I make signs of protest.

"No, it's the truth, perhaps not quite so much nowadays

but you certainly used to suffer from distension, my boy."
(Turning to Madame Devinol) "I hide it by the way I dress
him."

Madame Devinol is looking at me and smiling.

"Well, I like him just as he is. Go and get your hat, young
man, and keep me company."

What hat? The gray one? The *middle-class* one that makes
me look like Louis-Philippe?

My mother agrees to let me go out in a cap.

As it happens, I'm wearing a fairly clean coat, won in a
lottery. There had been a charity raffle. A shop selling off-
the-rack clothes was offering a suit; my mother had bought
a ticket in my name.

It won.

"You see, my boy, virtue is always rewarded!"

How about those who didn't win?

"God moves in a mysterious way... Anyway, it's not
pure wool."

Madame Devinol carries me off.

"Give me your arm properly, not just a little bit of it...
That's right, just like that, that's good! I can lean on you,
you're so sturdy."

I can't understand how I manage not to explode in all
directions, because I'm inflating and tightening my muscles
so much to let her know what powerful biceps I've got...

"And now tell me, is there something special about that
gray hat? And you were *distended* as well. You've got all
sorts of interesting secrets, do tell me about them!"

I'm feeling shy and my face is turning alternately red and
pale. Oh well, never mind, I tell her everything...

She laughs, she laughs out loud, she wriggles on my arm
and says, "Really, the polonaise and that roast leg of lamb!"

And she keeps on chuckling loudly, with little oohs and ahs of amusement that tinkle like tiny silver bells.

I tell her about all my troubles.

I threw my gray hat to the winds and revealed all my secrets, with something of a flourish; I think that once I may even have addressed her as *tu*, like a classmate.

"Don't worry," she said, noticing my worried look. "After all, I'm calling you *tu*, aren't I? Are you quite happy to be called *tu*, Monsieur Vingtras? In any case, I'm old enough to be your mother, you know!"

My goodness, wouldn't that have been marvelous!

"I'm an old woman. Tell me, don't you think I'm terribly old?"

She's looking at me; her eyes sparkle like stars . . .

"Oh no!"

"Do you think I'm pretty or ugly? You're afraid to say? That means that you think I'm ugly, too ugly for you to kiss me . . ."

"Oh no, that's not true!"

"Well then, give me a kiss!"

Every time I'm first in the class, she takes me to the theater, as we'd agreed.

We've known each other for a month.

"Do you enjoy going out with me?" she asks me one day.

"Yes, Madame, I like going to the theater, I'm very fond of comedies."

In Saint-Étienne they once took me to see *The Devil's Pills*, a sort of pantomime, and I came out crazy with excitement and for two whole months I could talk of nothing else but Seringuinos and Babylas. Now it was plays, sometimes an opera. There weren't so many scene changes! But how my heart was touched by the miserable life of orphans, the misfortunes of the heroes! And Meyerbeer's *Les Huguenots*, with the consecration of the daggers! And Donizetti's *La Favorite* when Mademoiselle Masson sang, "Oh my Fernando!"

Her hair hung down loose; she was wringing her hands:

> *Oh my Fernando, all earthly good!*

She sang it so soulfully, like one of those Christian martyrs they told us about at school. But she wasn't praying to heaven but to a tall man with brown hair, a black mustache, and Russian leather boots.

So it wasn't just for God that people sighed and rolled their eyes.

> *Oh! Come to another motherland!*
> *Come and hide thy happiness . . .*

My legs were shaking and my collar was all wet down my neck—my dear mother kept complaining that those evening shows were the ruination of my linens . . .

Even before the curtain went up, I felt exhilarated. I was bursting with excitement.

I would open my nostrils as wide as I could to sniff the smell of gas and oranges, of hair oil and flowers, which made the atmosphere so heavy, even oppressive. How I loved that feeling of warmth, those scents, the half silence! That rustle of silk on *first nights*, the sound of clogs *in the gods*! Ladies in low-cut dresses leaning over the front of the boxes; hooligans booing and throwing programs; rich people eating ices, poor people crunching apples; lights glaring everywhere . . .

I was on a magic island watching these women swinging the trains of their gowns, like sirens swinging their tails in myths. I would think of Circe, of Helen of Troy.

When the members of the orchestra came in to take their seats in the pit and started tuning up their instruments, you could hear the moaning of the trombones, the wail of the violins, the *pschh* of the cymbals, muffled like the whispering of thieves . . .

Whenever Mademoiselle Masson was onstage, I'd forget I was with Madame Devinol.

She obviously noticed this.

"You like her better than you like me, don't you?"

"Oh no! Yes . . . I do like her pretty much!"

One day Madame Devinol had come to fetch me earlier than usual to go for a walk, and we were strolling along near the theater.

On the way we passed a woman.

"Did you see who that was?"

"Who do you mean?"

"That woman over there, going past the café, wearing a silk cape."

I look.

"Mademoiselle Masson?"

I'm still not quite sure.

"Yes, *my Fernando*!" said Madame Devinol with a laugh.

What a disappointment! She had an almost masculine face and too many things around her neck: a shawl, bits of lace, a feather boa, and also some unidentified furry stuff—wool, perhaps?—too much of it, hanging from her belt, and she was holding her skirt up so awkwardly!

"Well, well!" said Madame Devinol to me.

At that very moment the manager of the theater went by, and seeing the actress first, he raised his hat to her and then to Madame Devinol.

They acknowledged his greeting: the actress in the normal

way, Madame Devinol with a nod of her head and a flicker of her eyelids, which made her look a bit like a nun—but such a pretty one and such a proud look, really proud!

When the manager had vanished, she leaned on my arm again.

"Well, do you still like her better than me?"

"Oh no!"

"And he says that with such feeling! Get along with you, you big schoolboy! So it's me who's the favorite now, is it?"

When I'm in her box, she makes me sit close to her, very close.

"A bit closer . . . So you're scared of me, are you?"

I am, just a bit.

I'm working so hard on my Latin essays these days!

But sometimes I fall by the wayside, and this time I'm not first in my class.

Just once! Latin verse!

We'd been told to write about the death of a parrot. I'd said everything anyone could say when confronted by such a calamity: that I'd never find consolation; that when he saw the cage—now transformed into a coffin—Charon would drop his oars; that moreover I'd be burying him myself—*triste ministerium*—and that we'd be scattering flowers—*manibus lilia plenis* . . .

In one of my ingenious lines, I'd exclaimed: "Now, alas, you can plant parsley on the tomb!"

The teacher compliments me on this last subtle touch; but I've come second to Bresslair, who showed even deeper emotion and more sincere grief . . . He hit on the idea, borrowed from hymn tunes, of introducing a repeated refrain:

Psittacus interiit! Jam fugit psittacus, eheu![1]

Eheu repeated *four* times! I can't complain about that! That's really good!

So I'm only second and I won't be going to the theater. It's enough to make you tear your hair out—which I do . . . I even save it up. Who knows?

And my goodness, isn't my hair greasy! That's because I've taken to using hair oil. I'm taking care of myself, these days. I'm shaving as well. I'd like to have some stubble on my chin . . .

My father keeps his razors hidden away. I've got hold of a knife which I've stuffed under my mattress because it has a thin blade, very blue. I've worn it down by rubbing it on the grindstone.

In the morning, at daybreak, I take it out of its hiding place and slip away, like a murderer—into a private spot.

No one will disturb me here, it's too early!

I hang a mirror on the wall, I froth up my soap, make all the little preparations, and begin . . .

I scrape away and keep on scraping. I succeed in making a greenish juice exude from my skin, the sort you'd get by beating an old sock.

I'm gashing myself horribly.

The gashes are often horizontal, which my natural sciences teacher finds very perplexing—he lives on the second floor and when he can find time, he takes my head into his hands to examine it.

"Either this boy is holding his head deliberately to one side to let the cat scratch him, which is unnatural . . ."

He breaks off and ponders and then questions me.

"Do you hold your head down sideways to let the cat scratch you?"

"Sometimes." (I'm trying to pull his leg.)

"But not all the time?"

"No, sir."

"Not all the time! So it must be the cats who are changing their habits and customs! After scratching people *vertically* for centuries, now they're scratching them from right to left! What a strange, cosmic mystery! What a peculiar metamorphosis in animal behavior!"

He walks away shaking his head.

We were at the theater. Madame Devinol says to me, "You're looking funny today. What's wrong? Are you annoyed?"

Annoyed! She thinks I could be annoyed with her, I who am fifteen years old, with leather shoelaces—and an extra assignment to finish by tomorrow, I, the hopeless idiot!

No, I'm not annoyed. But yesterday I almost lopped off the tip of my nose while shaving and there's a little red patch there shaped like a ring.

All the same, I'll say, "Yes, I am annoyed."

It's extremely convenient: it makes a good excuse to turn my back and hide my nose . . .

I took care not to be first in the class as long as the scar on my nose continued to look like a ring. I was out whenever she came by. Finally there was just one little white spot left on the side of my nose. I could talk to her in profile.

What wonderful evenings they were!

We used to come back from the theater together, sometimes entirely on our own; her husband doesn't pay too much attention to her. He's always at the Café des Acteurs, where they play cards after the show. He's a gambler. She's the one who takes my arm first and squeezes it. She lolls against me, I can feel her whole body from her shoulders down to her hips. One of her hands is always touching my hand; the tips of her fingers stroke my wrist between my sleeve and my glove.

When we reach her doorway, we retrace our steps and repeat the whole procedure until she herself slowly releases her grip but without letting me go.

"You always take such a long time to let me go home . . ."

Me? I've never tried to stop her from going home, in fact I was amazed the first day when, instead of going home, she wanted to continue walking and sauntering around like a cat, on the footpath where her little boots were going *click-clack* . . . She was holding up the hem of her dress and I could see her kidskin boots fitting tightly over her ankles and wrinkling each time she put down her tiny foot; she was wearing white stockings—a golden white, like wool, and a little slippery, like flesh.

She stopped a couple of times.

"Haven't I lost my medallion?"

She was feeling around her golden-brown neck and she had to unfasten a button.

"Can you see it? Oh, it must have slipped down!"

She was fingering inside her little collar the way I finger my tie when it's too tight.

"Help me."

At that very moment the medallion emerged, glinting in the moonlight.

She looked almost furious.

"Have you also lost something?" she said pretty sharply as she saw me bending down.

"No, I'm just tying my laces."

I'm always having to tie my laces because they're too thick and the eyeholes are too small and there's a split buttonhole too.

———

"If you're first in the class on the second Saturday of this month, Jacques, I'm going to take you to Aigues-la-Jolie . . . I'll tell my husband that I'm going to pay a visit to Jacqueline's foster mother and we'll go off on an excursion, just the two of us. We'll eat green apples in the orchard and then truffles in a restaurant."

Truffles? Oh, I have to tie my laces!

Once a friend of my father's mentioned truffles, and my mother blushed.

So, I'm first!

I produced a Latin poem that was greatly admired.

"One could imagine that one was hearing the gallinacean itself, couldn't one?" the teacher said.

Once again he was referring to a bird—on this occasion, a rooster.

One of my lines began: *Caro, cara, canens* . . .[2] (Alliteration *plus* onomatopoeia!)

As agreed, we'll go to the country.

Here we are in the courtyard of the inn where the stagecoach for Aigues-la-Jolie stands waiting. The driver is just finishing hitching up the horses.

I'd been hiding around a street corner to see *her* arrive. I came out only after she'd arrived. I was afraid of having to wait by myself. Suppose someone had asked me, "Who are you waiting for?"

She's told me that when someone else is present, I'm to call her "aunt." She told me that yesterday, and now, as we're getting into the coach, she reminds me again.

A drop of water falls on the carriage window, like a drop of spit.

The sky turns black—there's a clap of thunder in the distance and the rain comes pouring down.

A passenger on the top deck asks if he can take shelter with us. We didn't like to refuse but we all spread out a little to avoid having him sit near us.

My "aunt" is the only one to move over and indicate that there's room beside her, on her left . . .

She's so kind, always ready to sacrifice her own comfort— she moves over to her right. She's sitting almost on top of me. It's giving me goose bumps.

At each clap of thunder she gives a start and seems dreadfully scared. I'm afraid she'll be able to see my little ring-shaped scar and I don't know where to hide my nose. But this woman, half in my arms, with her breath warm on my back, isn't that nice . . .

We've arrived. It's still raining.

Under the porch, while they're unhitching the horses from the coach—its canvas cover streaming with water—and I'm stretching my legs, she picks up her skirt.

"Is there any chance of getting a carriage?"

"A carriage to go into Aigues-la-Jolie, where the roads are a foot wide and have ruts as deep as canyons? You must be joking, dear lady!"

"Tell me, Jacques, what can we do then?"

She looks at me and laughs. "Is there a room where we can take shelter and watch the storm?"

"We do have a room," said the landlord.

"Ah!"

———

IN THE ROOM

"You know, I feel absolutely drenched . . ."

Drenched? Drenched from walking from the coach to the porch!

"Drenched . . . I've got water running all down my neck. It's dripping down my front too. Oh, it's cold. I'll have to take my bodice off . . . Do you object? Am I making you scared, my dear?"

. . . .

Shouting! An explosion of shouts!

I can hear people calling my name . . .

There must be a dozen people shouting "Vingtras."

It's the gang from the second prep class. They've come on an excursion to the country and have scuttled for shelter in the inn.

I can see it all through the window.

Madame Devinol rushes over to the door and locks it; she then has second thoughts.

"No, better for you to get out; quickly, now, off you go!"

I look around for my hat; it's not there.

"Have you seen my hat?"

"Get going, will you, then I can lock the door again."

"All right, I'm on my way . . . But what am I going to say?"

"Say whatever you like, you IDIOT!"

This is what had happened.

Coming into the inn, they'd noticed a strange overcoat— my overcoat—lying on the table together with my shaggy hat.

I'd been recognized!

———

EPILOGUE

I've got to leave town. My adventure had given rise to gossip.

The headmaster advised my father to send me away.

"If you like, my brother-in-law in Paris will take him in, at a reduced fee, since he's a bright boy," said the fifth-form teacher. "Would you like me to write to him?"

"Oh yes, please, my goodness, yes!" exclaimed my father; he's keen to have a look around Paris himself and this is a golden opportunity.

They agree on a fee. I throw myself into my mother's arms and tear myself away. Off I go!

We're headed to Paris, at full speed!

XXII. BOARDING AT LEGNAGNA'S[1]

I'M IN PARIS.

I arrived with my face swollen. When Legnagna, the headmaster of the school, saw me, he was amazed. "He's not a pupil, he's a bladder!" he said to his wife.

Anyway, that doesn't prevent boys from winning prizes in competitions.

"You're prepared to work hard, aren't you?"

And I reply—my cheeks being largely composed of lip, "Ob gourse."

He found me not quite so bright as he'd expected: I'm putting some of my own ideas into my work . . .

"I keep on telling you, you mustn't put anything of *your own* into your work. You must stick strictly to the classical authors."

He's addressing me in a loud voice and making me aware that I'm being charged less than other boys.

He alludes to this on the second day. They were serving spinach; I don't like spinach, so I didn't take any.

He happened to be passing by.

"You don't like that?"

"No, sir!"

"You're more used to caviar at home, perhaps? And your diet has to include partridge, I presume?"

"No, I prefer fat bacon!"

He shrugged his shoulders, sneered, and walked off muttering "Peasant!" under his breath.

On Sunday evenings he gives parties. I'm invited.

I often use the expression "Gosh!"—it's just a habit of mine which I don't leave behind even in drawing rooms.

"*Mossieu* Vingtras," he calls out from the top of the table for all to hear, "where were you brought up?—Did you have to look after the cows?"

"Yes, sir, with my cousin."

He loses his temper and goes red in the face.

"Can you believe it, Madame!" he says to the woman sitting next to him.

And turning to me, "Go up to your room at once!"

I'm in the senior class. They make fun of me a bit but I don't mind; they seem to think themselves clever but I find them terribly stupid . . . There's one star pupil, an examination freak, who's thin and green, suffers from a sort of Saint Vitus' dance, and is always scratching his ears and trying to catch the end of his nose with the tip of his tongue.

There's also a mini-star—Anatoly.

He believes in good relations between teachers and students; he'd like them to get on well together—why?

I look a bit of a *brute*: when I play prisoner's base, they find me clumsy. I'm teased for being a country bumpkin. Anatoly stands up for me.

"Just leave him alone, he'll be all right! Give him a month and he'll be like us; and two months from now, you'll see!"

Oh, they don't bother me much! I'm pretty tough and I haven't got my parents to make me feel self-conscious or ashamed or awkward. On the whole, I couldn't care less about being teased, I'm not dazzled by my *pals*.

They never, ever, stop talking about the same things—the boy who won a prize, the other one who nearly got one; Gerbidon who'd committed a *barbarism*, some other boy who'd committed a *solecism*.

"At Labadens's place, you know, they had this guy who was going to get the prize for Greek translation, well, he didn't turn up because his father had just died that morning, and Labadens went out to get hold of him and promised him he'd drive him to the funeral afterward. He didn't want to and just kept on blubbering . . ."

They seemed to think that the boy was being stupid.

Our school prepares boys for the Lycée Bonaparte.[2]

On Tuesdays we're allowed to stay late to put the finishing touches on our work, but I only wait until the teacher has vanished around the corner before clearing off myself. Now I have one whole free hour after which I'll go to his place and hand over to the concierge the work that they think I'm busy *polishing up*!

I stroll around the streets full of young women, hatless, and looking so cheerful and pretty in the long smocks they wear at work! I listen to them humming to themselves. I watch them through the windows lunching in the company of silversmiths in white tunics and printers in their white caps. That's all I look at.

I'm not interested in historical buildings, even though there aren't any piles of luggage to prevent me from doing it now. In my view, all stones look just the same. I only like things that walk and are bright!

So I don't know anything about Paris except the area around the Faubourg Saint-Honoré, the way to the Lycée Bonaparte, the Rue Miromesnil, the Rue Verte, the Place Beauvau, where I meet lots of domestic servants in their red waistcoats and ladies' maids wearing their caps with ribbons floating in the air.

On Sunday we go for walks.

More often than not, it's in the Tuileries Gardens, in the Sanglier,[3] an Avenue named after a statue of a boar.

What a bore it is! I loathe him; his stone snout gets up *my* nose!

However, I'm not quite so bored now that the prep assistant, Monsieur Chaillu, has been put in charge of us.

He's an unbeliever. On Sunday, he lets us go off alone, on the condition that we're back by six o'clock.

For our part, we make for Les Hollandais in the Palais-Royal. It's the café frequented by cadets from Saint-Cyr and by the cockerels. The term *cockerel* is used to describe anyone intending to go into one of the official institutions where a uniform must be worn and who already has one—trousers with an orange stripe, salmon-pink collar, hard-peaked kepi, and gold or silver braid.

Although I'm an arts man, I get along with the cockerels. Unfortunately, I get only twenty sous a week for pocket money and have to think twice before I go out for drinks with anyone.

One day I had a terrible fright. We'd been playing for money and I'd lost a franc and a half. I tried to get up and leave the table after the first game but I didn't have the courage.

"Oh, come on, don't go now!"

Sweat down my back, shivers on my scalp . . .

I'm playing badly and tip my dominoes. There you go: I've blown it.

Luckily, a brawl broke out. A quarrel erupted between one of the yellow cockerels and one of the red ones, some junior and senior Saint-Cyr cadets; decanters started to whiz through the air.

There was a free-for-all and I flung myself into the fray.

I was counting on being knocked out. No such luck! I hit a lot of people with my stick, but don't get hit back.

I was saved all the same.

They cleared the room by throwing us all out, and I went off to the Sanglier still owing one and a half francs at Les Hollandais—but I've got until next Sunday to pay.

I sold a Latin speech for the Tuesday test—one franc, cash down.

I did this sort of deal from time to time, thereby providing a good grade for someone expecting a visit from an uncle or who wanted to be able to show off for his birthday, in a word, anyone who had any interest, one way or another, in getting into the *top ten* . . .

I went back to Les Hollandais clutching my thirty sous. They didn't want my money: the breakages and the drinks had been paid off by the bursar of Saint-Cyr or by a subscription from the cockerels.

I'd ended up with money in my pocket and a reputation as someone spoiling for a fight.

All the same, I'm always worried when I leave that rich man's pub! And in my schoolboy's bed at night, I wonder to myself what will become of me, destined to go to a school which I'm scared of going to, and who, unlike the cockerels, won't be doing what I want, not pursuing my own goals—and who won't have any money behind him to back him up.

All of a sudden, my Sundays have been transformed!

At school in Nantes, we'd had a model pupil by the name of Matoussaint.

He's coming to stay in Paris and my father has given him a letter authorizing him to take me out on Sundays.

Matoussaint's not free until two o'clock. Half a day will be more than enough—we don't know what to do before five o'clock anyway: to avoid spending money we don't want to go to the café. He's brought me twenty francs from my mother but I want to hang on to them.

Killing time in the afternoon is difficult—I find it boring to be sauntering around when everyone else is doing exactly the same thing and we all look stupid. If only this was a weekday! We'd see swarms of people. Today everything's dead, people are creeping around like priests.

We ought to go out to Meudon![4] In Meudon people are laughing and having fun . . .

But Paris to Meudon costs ten sous. We'll have to wait until we've made our fortune!

"It's doing us good to be walking around like this when it's cold," says Matoussaint, trying to make believe that he's enjoying himself while he's shivering like a chandelier being dusted.

I'd be happier feeling less healthy and a lot warmer.

When it rains on Sunday, we visit museums.

"You can always learn something," says Matoussaint when we go to art galleries.

"What do you learn?"

"You contemplate the pictures, the sculptures."

"So what?"

Matoussaint calls me a philistine and remarks bitterly, "And to think you write such lovely Latin verse!"

Well, that's true enough!

Matoussaint can see that he's shaken me and pursues his advantage.

"You're rejecting your own gods, you're spitting on your lyre!"

"Now, gentlemen," shouts the park attendant, pointing his stick to a pile of sawdust in a corner, "if you want to do any spitting that's the place to do it!"

Five o'clock at last! I'm not crazy about masterpieces and as for historical monuments, definitely not!

Five o'clock is when we're joined by Lemaître. Lemaître is a counterjumper[5] and Matoussaint has a poor opinion of him; he reserves his high opinions for the "noble" professions.

However, as Lemaître has connections with people who are "stinking rich" and "fond of a lark," Matoussaint welcomes him with open arms.

Lemaître arrives and we all go off for an absinthe at the Rotonde or the Pissote, where we hope to meet Grassot. "Ah, there's Sainville! No! Yes, it is!"

Having sipped our absinthe in the fading light—it's nearly six o'clock—we move off in the direction of the Palais-Royal where we're due to meet friends at Tavernier's. They always sit at the corner table in the main room.

Dinner costs thirty-two sous.

Lemaître's pals, also draper's assistants, have brought their girlfriends along with them; they're wearing pretty shoes, they're charming, laughing their heads off at everything that's said, whether it's funny or not . . .

And the food's good too!

Crécy soup! Cutlets Soubise, with Montmorency sauce! Excellent! That's the best way to learn history![6]

What a prickly, spicy flavor they all have, with their sauces!

Monsieur Radigon, the wit of the party, is not impressed by all this "fancy stuff."

"Grilled pig's foot, waiter . . . And if you can't find it, just take your own feet and scratch!"

They laugh. For my part, I don't say anything, I just sit and listen.

"Is your friend dumb, Monsieur Matoussaint?"

I make a face and give a grunt, to prove that I'm not a disciple of the Abbé de l'Épée.[7] They're talking about me at the corner of the table.

"There's something in his face—and eyes—but he looks a bit of a drip."

To redeem myself, I put on an exhibition of strength: I arm-wrestle, crush fingers, lift soup tureens with my teeth, and hold my breath for eighty seconds, thoroughly scaring the people sitting at adjacent tables who can see my veins swelling while my eyes are popping out of my head.

"I don't like to see anyone doing that near me when I'm eating," one man remarks.

Even Radigon has had enough.

"God, how boring can he get with his breathing exercises!"

After dinner, I have to leave.

The other boys can stay out till midnight. To spite me, Legnagna requires me to be back by eight.

I leave the company and go off in the direction of the Faubourg Saint-Honoré.

There's still a quarter of an hour to kill before going back to school but if I came back early, it would look as if I hadn't been able to find things to do to fill in the time.

I'd prefer to go back now. I'm not afraid of being alone in the dormitory where I can hear my schoolmates come in one by one. I can think, talk to myself, it's the only time when things are really quiet. I'm not distracted by the noise made by all the others in which I feel isolated by my shyness, I'm not disturbed by the sound of dictionaries, by accounts of results in major examinations.

I can remember all sorts of different things: a walk to Vourzac, harvesting on a lovely sunny day! And in the calm of this school which is settling down to sleep, with my head turned toward the window through which I can glimpse the broad field of the sky, I dream not of the future but of the past!

One day I'm summoned to go and see Monsieur Legnagna.

He hands me a parcel sent to me by my mother. He seems infuriated.

"And you can take this away too," he says, handing me a jar as he shows me out.

I'm completely at a loss. I unwrap the parcel, which includes a letter.

My dear son,

I'm sending you this new pair of trousers for your birthday. Your father has cut them out of one of his old pairs and I've sewn it together. We wanted to show how much we love you. In addition, we've included this blue coat with gold buttons. By the same post I'm sending Monsieur Legnagna a jar of good pickles so as to encourage him to treat you nicely.

Keep working hard, son, and don't forget to push your coattails aside when you sit down.

There was a note added by my father.

I'd written telling him that Legnagna was doing everything to humiliate me and that I'd like to be taken away from the school because his constant attacks were making me really miserable.

My father's reply nonplussed me. Is he putting on an act? Is he really a kind man, basically?

Don't lose heart, my dear boy! I don't want to point out that it's your own fault if you're in Paris. Be patient, work hard, reward the school by winning lots of competitions and then you'll be in a position to speak up and tell him a few home truths!

No references to the past, nothing at all? Not a single word of blame, almost a touch of kindness, and of sadness! If he had been there, I would have flung my arms around his neck!

So I'll do as he says: I'll bide my time and try to win prizes . . .

But how boring all this Latin and Greek is! What interest can *barbarisms* and *solecisms* have for me?

And all the time, day in, day out, this Grand Competition![8]

The teacher's name is D——.

He has a small, tight-lipped mouth, he waddles like a duck, when he laughs he sounds as if he's clucking, and his wig has a featherlike sheen. He's won the Grand Competition three times running; last year he was given a decoration; he has a red crest . . . He speaks something like an Incroyable; he says: Cicewo, Howace, and alma pawens.

Being the Latin teacher, he speaks his own variety of French.

When boys cut lessons to visit cafés or to go bathing and he notices their empty desks, he says, "I see a lot of boys who aren't here!"

The French teacher is called N——. He's the brother of an academician who has not just one but two moral principles — one for the ordinary people, the other for princes. Well, you can't have too much of a good thing.

He's thin and lanky and red, wears a sort of clerical frock coat, really weird specs, and speaks in a thin, cracked, wheezy voice.

This is the voice in which he reads the tirades from *Iphigenia* or *Esther*, and when he's finished, clasps his hands together, raises his eye toward the spider-bedecked ceiling, and exclaims, "Kneel! Down on your knees! Pay homage to the divine Racine!"

On one occasion, one of the new boys actually did go down on his knees . . .

And with a gesture of disdain, thrusting aside the book lying in front of him, he continues, "And all that we can do now is to cast aside all your other books!"

For this, he has my unconditional support . . .

"And to admit one's impotence!"

Here, he can speak for himself.

At first I was always near the top of the class for essay work.

I rapidly declined.

From being second, I've gone down to tenth—to fifteenth!

Asked to describe a group of peasants drinking to the health of the king, I wrote: "And they all got together and drank a GOOD glass of wine."

"A GOOD! The boy has absolutely no idea of elegant language, not a glimmer...I shouldn't be surprised if he wasn't being deliberately provocative—GOOD!—when our language is so rich in felicitous turns of phrase to express the operation we accomplish in raising to our lips the juice sacred to Bacchus, the nectar of the gods! And why did he not remember the modest and at the same time bold image of our own Boileau:

Drinking a glass of wine that laughs in the bracken![9]

In point of fact, I've never understood that line! Drinking a glass of wine that's splitting its sides with laughter in some grass, in a little hazel grove!

I'm more lacking in feeling than he suspects because there are a lot of other things that I don't know either.

"Nothing much there," the teacher continues, placing a finger on his heart.

He pauses for a second.

"But nothing much here either, that's for sure," he adds, tapping his forehead and shaking his head with an air of deep compassion. "He succeeded on one occasion because he'd read Pierrot[10]—but there you are, he's a boy who'd always prefer to put 'gun' rather than '*the weapon that spews forth death*'!"

The truth is that that's the way these ideas come into my head! That's the way we'd talk at home and the way they talked in the houses I used to visit—oh, we moved in such poor circles!

I fall back on Latin verse once more; Latin verse is what I'm good at.

It was high time.

I could feel the hour nearing when that miserable man Legnagna, in resentment at my lack of success, would become unendurable. Some fine day, I'd've killed him.

One time I even thought of going away altogether, not in order to go strolling along the Champs-Élysées or to watch the traveling circus performers as I did when I was playing hooky but to get away from school for good and like an escaped convict, go underground in Paris.

What would I have done? I've no idea.

But I've often wondered if it wouldn't have been just as well to have run away. Then the decision that my life would be a constant struggle would have been made once and for all. Yes, it might well have been better.

In fact, I'd almost decided to do it, but my plans were changed by Anatoly the Peacemaker, who felt it would be a good thing to warn Legnagna.

Legnagna sent for me and told me that he knew what I had in mind. He said that he'd warned the authorities, and if I ran away, I'd end up in the hands of the police. That scared me stiff.

It was during all this that I composed a piece in couplets that was, it appears, a revelation. If I could reproduce that sort of performance in the Grand Competition, I'd win the prize.

I'd like to win that prize: I'd pay off my debts and then, on my way out of the Sorbonne, I'd lay hands on Legnagna's ears in the middle of the main courtyard and tie them in knots.

The day of the Grand Competition has come.

We get up very early. We've been given a *net*, one of

the school's trophies, into which they've put some wine and cold chicken. Legnagna offers me his hand; I can't refuse to shake it, but I do so awkwardly. I find this bogus gesture of friendship worse than silent hostility.

"Show them what you can do . . ."

He gives a nervous laugh.

Anatoly and I go off together; the weather's sharp, a bit chilly.

We almost arrive late.

I'd never seen Paris calm and quiet before, in the cool morning sun, and I stopped for five minutes on the bridge looking at the pale sky and listening to the water swirling against the arches of the bridge.

Down at the water's edge there was a man wearing a hat and washing a handkerchief. He was on his knees like a washerwoman. He stood up, wringing out the tiny square of linen and held it for a minute to dry it out. I followed him with my eyes; he carefully folded it, unbuttoned his coat, and furtively slipped the handkerchief inside before rebuttoning his coat.

He picked up something which I'd noticed lying on the ground; it looked like a dictionary.

Anatoly tugged at my coattails—we had to get going; but I had time to see a pale face suddenly appear up the steps.

I can still see that face and it stayed with me all that day—between me and the blank sheet of paper. It would be truer to say that it stayed with me for the rest of my life.

In fact, the face of that man washing his rag—a face whiter than his badly washed handkerchief—had given me an insight into his life!

That he had a book had told me that he too had been a scholar, perhaps a prize scholar. In that single moment, I'd been reminded of my father, of the stupid headmasters, the heartless pupils, the cowardly inspectors, and the teacher himself always humiliated, unhappy, threatened with disgrace!

"I bet that poor guy we've just seen under the bridge has some sort of academic qualification," I said to Anatoly.

I wasn't mistaken.

Just as we were being summoned to go into the Sorbonne, a Charlemagne student pointed to a dark shadowy figure going up the street and shouted, "Look, that's the man who used to be a tutor at Jauffret's!"

It was the pale face, the handkerchief man, the poor chap with the book!

They're dictating the essay subject.

Shall I bother? What's the point?

To get a dreary job as a tutor like that man and become a washer of handkerchiefs under bridges? What's the life story of that poor creature whom I can't get out of my mind?

I don't know. He may have slapped the face of some deputy headmaster, perhaps not even slapped, merely laughed in his face!

Or he could have written an article in the *Argus de Dijon* or Issingeaux's *Petit homme gris* and been dismissed as a result.[11]

Not a profession for me, thanks very much!

All the same, I have to do the decent thing: I've got to do my best.

But I can't think of a thing to say, not a thing! I feel queasy, just as I felt once when I ate too much treacle as a little boy.

Well, finally I've managed to *craft* forty alexandrines.[12] Here's my *fair copy*.

"Finished?" my neighbor inquires.

"Yes."

"Me too. Want to grill some sausages with me?"

He produces a little spirit-stove and hides it away among his dictionaries, then brings out a small frying pan.

"It's going to sizzle, look out!"

The monitor was a man called Deschanel, an intelligent guy—he could hear the sausages sizzling . . . During this long session, we were allowed to eat cold food—so he reckoned that we could eat cooked food too. If the examinee was holding a pan handle instead of a dictionary, that was his bad luck, in this battle.

"Now for some coffee. I like coffee, don't you?"

The Charlemagne boy made the coffee.

We needed a little swig of something or other, so we sold a few parts of our essays, a slice or two of our work, to some candidates from Stanislas and Rollin[13]—obvious lightweights, wearing stiff collars and sitting on elegant cushions, with money in their pockets. So we took a good swig and then a bit more, for luck. To end the meal, I personally take charge of setting light to the brandy . . .

"Got your rough draft?" asked Anatoly the Peacemaker as soon as I got back to the school.

Legnagna came in and they went through it together in detail.

I'm aware that my work is no good and now that my memory of the pale face is fading and the fumes of our feast have evaporated, I feel upset and even remorseful.

Legnagna doesn't say a single word. He's looking at me with hatred.

The results are out—I haven't won a single prize.

But neither has Anatoly or anyone in our class, and the school itself hasn't won much. It's a disaster.

The grinds and the eggheads haven't done any better than I have: my conscience is clear.

Prize day comes. I attend unhonored and unsung! *Fractis occumbam inglorius armis!*[14]

And we all go our separate ways.

But I stay on.

I'm waiting for a letter from my father to tell me what to do. Nothing comes. I'm here at the mercy of Legnagna, who hates me.

There are four of us left.

One hasn't any parents and his guardian is paying for his upkeep; there's a Creole from the Caribbean who goes out only intermittently, and a Japanese boy who never goes out.

They're all paying high fees. I was let in at a reduced rate and was supposed to win prizes. I didn't win any prizes and I eat a lot.

I've written home. If my parents don't come tomorrow, if I don't get any reply, I'm going to leave this place and go away.

To save money, Legnagna won't stop me. This time there won't be any question of calling in the police.

Oh, these long-awaited letters! All the time my eyes were peeled looking for the mailman! All those urgent requests and my father and mother are treating it like a joke . . .

I was almost in tears as I wrote, begging for someone to

come and take me away because Legnagna is constantly re-proaching me. He's always on my case.

It was bad enough having to feed me during the year—and now he has to put me up for the vacation!

Then one day there's an explosion: it's about my father. Legnagna comes in, disheveled, foaming with rage.

"It's monstrous!" he shouts.

"I've just heard that your father is *coining* money, that he's made *eight thousand francs* this year. He's cheated me and made a fool of me. I charged you a beggarly fee when you could have paid the full rate, the rate of a rich man. That's sheer dishonesty, young man, do you realize that?"

He stamps his foot and makes for me . . .

Oh no, Legnagna, that's close enough! Steady as she goes, Legnagna!

He takes my warning . . . and goes off raging, venting his fury on the door as he slams it hard against the wall.

As soon as he's left and the sounds of his imprecations have died down, I start reflecting on what he's just said . . . and I come to the conclusion that he was right.

Father, you could have spared me all these humiliations!

"Is it really true that you're not poor?"

It's true—the man who's informed Legnagna is his brother-in-law, who arrived from Nantes yesterday.

After this scene, Legnagna came and spoke to me in the courtyard.

"I wouldn't have said anything," he said, "if your father had taken you away at the end of term, but you've been left here a whole week without any news; it looks as if they're making a fool of me, don't you see?"

I stammer and can't think of anything to say; I agree with what he's saying.

"My father will pay you for that extra week."

"He can do that . . . This year your father earned more than I did and he had no need at all to come and ask for a reduction of three hundred francs on your fees."

So I've had to put up with all this suffering and worry for a mere three hundred francs!

XXIII. MADAME VINGTRAS IN PARIS

"JACQUES!"

It's my mother! She comes toward me and, mechanically, grabs my head. The Japanese boy laughs, the Creole yawns—he yawns all the time.

My head's been grabbed sideways and my mother's having trouble finding a suitable spot to place her kiss!

We've been shown into a room where it's difficult to see; it's evening. The candle brought by the housekeeper is very dim.

"What a big boy you've become! How strong you are!"

These are the first words she speaks. She doesn't give me time to say anything, she keeps turning me around and around, moving herself around on her short legs.

"Now give me a proper kiss, don't be unkind to your mother!"

She says this quite cheerfully. She's still exclaiming. "You're so sturdy! I've brought you a French-style coat. I'll get some boots made for you. But let me have a good look at you: a mustache, you've grown a mustache!"

She can't contain her pride and joy: she raises her hands to heaven. She's ready to fall on her knees.

"The truth is that you're a splendid young man, you know!"

She still can't take her eyes off me.

"The spitting image of your mother!"

I don't believe her. My face is rugged, my jaw sticks out. I've got bony cheeks and sharp fangs like a dog's. In fact, I'm a bit of a dog—and I'm also like a whipping top, with a complexion as yellow as a piece of boxwood.

And as for my eyes, the sewing maid Madame Allard—who once asked me if I thought she was plump—claimed that I could never hide the fact that I was from the Auvergne because my eyes looked like two freshly mined lumps of coal . . .

"And you look like you're a serious young man too, you know?"

Well, maybe. This past year was the hardest until now—utterly humiliated with nothing to make up for it.

I'm also sick at heart; I've become completely disillusioned with Paris.

Wherever I look, I can see nothing but stupidity, a dreary life, the prospect of an ugly future. I'm living in Babylon—yes, that's the word, a modern Babylon.

Everybody's so petty! The people around me only talk Latin!

Day in, day out, even on Sunday, I've been at Legnagna's mercy—Legnagna, a weakling to the core, envious, a sneak, and even more embittered by his lack of success.

These last ten days in particular have been one long horrible nightmare!

"Why didn't you write?"

"I was expecting to come any day."

It was to save the price of a stamp!

I told her how my poverty had been flung in my face, the humiliations I'd been forced to swallow.

"So he calls us poor! When he's made as much as your father has this year, then he'll have a right to say something!"

"But in that case, if my father has been making all that

money, why didn't he pay the same fees as the others when I wrote to tell you how he was insulting me and making my life so miserable?"

"Insulting you? Insulting you? So what? Are you any the worse off for that? We've still saved three hundred francs and you'll find them very handy when we're dead! Look, there are three hundred francs and more in there . . . He's certainly not going to be getting hold of those!"

She laughs as she taps her pocket.

"That's what you have to do in life, don't you see? Now that you're all grown up, you have to understand what's what. Do you imagine that he took you on because he liked your looks or out of sheer kindness of heart? No, he took you on like you buy a good cow, you haven't produced the calf he was hoping for because you didn't win any prizes in the competition . . . he should have made a better choice—he ought to have checked up on you before he took you on. And I'll be telling him what's what, you'll see!"

It hurts me to see her angry like that. I find myself feeling sorry for the man I thought I hated!

At the same time as she announces her intention of telling him *what's what*, my mother says, "Pack your bags!"

We were already in the hall—the concierge was there too.

"Nothing is to be removed from the house, Madam."

"All this stuff of my son's? I'm not to be allowed to take his linen with us? My child's socks? Is it your *Gnagnagna* who's ordered that?"

"No, Madame, it's the landlord who's owed money by Monsieur Legnagna and has issued those instructions."

And there's also the baker who has an overdue bill . . . and the butcher too . . .

What a pathetic man he is, really pathetic! He bullied anyone who's poor—I wasn't the only one he treated badly. He taunted anybody who'd been left defenseless or was paying reduced fees. He even used to strike the little boys.

He's stupid—with the other crammers his name is a by-word for pedant—a bit thick, something of a humbug.

I'm impressed by my mother's arguments and the parallel with a cow: she's calmed my scruples.

What she says about that cow is true! They certainly didn't take me on for my pretty face, that's for sure!

"No, there's no reason for you to worry at all," my mother continued, reading my thoughts in my eyes and in my silence.

All the same, I feel pity for the poor man. I persuade my mother not to create a scene, and we succeed in getting the landlord to allow us to leave with my things.

We're leaving, I'm not quite sure how. We take a cab to the coach office where my mother has deposited her trunks.

She's still muttering insults against Legnagna, with various exclamations and sneers, making fun of him and attacking him with word and gesture as if he were still there . . .

"Will you please shut up? Oh, if you'd spoken to me like you spoke to him!" (Turning toward me.) "It was feeble of you to let him treat you like that! You're no son of mine!"

Am I a foundling, then? Have I been beaten for the last thirteen years purely *by mistake*? Please tell me, you who till now have always been for me *genetrix*, my mother, for whom I was always the *cara soboles*, the beloved offspring! Do tell me!

"And now where are we going?"

My mother asks me this question after we've piled into the carriage and the driver is already waiting.

"We don't intend to sleep in the cab, do we? You've spent a

whole year in Paris and you don't know where to take your mother, you don't know where we can find a room?"

I know the Sorbonne, the Sanglier. Would they make up a bed for her at Les Hollandais?

"Ah well, I suppose I'll have to take charge . . . Oh, you children!"

She pushes me in the direction of the carriage door.

"Call the driver!"

"Driver!"

He comes to a halt and bends down.

"Do you know the Écu-de-France?"

"The Écu's in Dijon, lady."

"There's an Écu-de-France in every town!"

"I don't know one here!"

Gathering her shawl up around her shoulders, she picks up her travel bag in one hand and grasping the door handle with the other, she springs out of the cab.

"I don't intend to stay one instant longer in this vehicle!"

"Please yourself, lady! I don't like carting people around who get so het up. Just pay the time you've had me for and here's your baggage!"

We pay up, and the story of Orléans and the mail, of Nantes and its quayside, begins all over again. We're standing here beside a stack of packages and hat boxes that's about to topple over . . . My mother finds it impossible to enter any town without causing a traffic obstruction!

She prods me with her umbrella.

"Get a move on!"

I get a move on as best I can. I need to keep an eye on the boxes—there's not a great deal of me that's actually free, everything's occupied, though I do have one last finger.

"Get another cab!"

I make a sign to another cabdriver but the laws of equilibrium are strict and can't be violated with impunity! The mountain of luggage tips over—my mother yells—carriages come to a halt—the police come running—as always, unfailingly! It's their specialty . . .

What would've become of us if there hadn't been some philanthropists passing by?

They didn't ask us anything embarrassing about our politics or religious convictions. Nothing at all! They gave us advice, without demanding we compromise our consciences or become recreants: Jesuits wouldn't have acted like that!

Their advice was to cross the street, "Where there's a little sign." They told us that the furnished rooms were meant for those who hadn't any . . .

"So you didn't know that, Jacques?" said my mother. "It must be the Latin verse that's made you like that. Or perhaps you've been hit by something? You haven't by any chance fallen on your head, have you?"

"No, only on my rear end."

My mother seems to have calmed down a bit.

We've moved in: a bedroom and a closet.

Calls from my mother's room.

"Jacques, Jacques!"

I barely have time to slip on my pants. I have great difficulty in keeping them on.

She's seized me by the seat and drags me backward toward her.

"Are you my son?"

I'm beginning to get really worried. She's already asked me that once.

Spread out on the table are the two pairs of trousers and two jackets that I've been wearing all year.

She suddenly swings me around and stares at me as if she still suspects that I'm masquerading as someone else.

In the end, almost persuaded that there's no deception, and reminded moreover of her blood ties, she gives vent to her pain.

"Jacques," she says, "Jacques, are those the trousers, the jackets, the blue coat—cornflower blue!—that I sent you? I know the way any sort of coat that you put on gets grubby right away, naturally, but I can't imagine that you simply bleached out all the color for fun, and in any case, the things that I sent you were much, much roomier. There was room to spare in the seat, spaciousness, airiness, everything you'd ever need! And here there's nothing, nothing at all!

"Jacques, your father and I sewed it together! I wrote to you about it, you knew all about it! Oh, what have they done to my son!"

That's the third time that she's gotten worried about that! I feel myself to see if I'm there.

"Explain yourself, you idiot!"

So she recognizes me at last.

I explain the story of my clothes.

I'd worn out the ones I'd come to Paris in. The ones they'd sent me, which my father had tailored for me and my mother had sewn, were much too big, there was room inside for two. I didn't know anyone to invite . . .

Then I happened to meet Rajoux who was twice my size and whose clothes were too small for him.

He asked me if I'd like to swap—I looked pretty funny with that incredibly baggy bottom. A lot of people were worried seeing what a hard time I was having walking. All sorts of things were being said!

One day in the dormitory we clinched the deal; he gave me his old clothes, took mine, and once again I was able to play prisoner's base.

———

My mother said nothing; I waited in dread. Finally she broke her silence.

"Well, the cloth's not too bad ... But your Rajoux can't have known much about it, you could have asked for something in addition, a flannel waistcoat, some underpants. Oh dear, if only I'd been there ... Anyway, it's a good cloth but we haven't got anything to patch it with." (Examining a striped trouser seat.) "For this seat, the only thing I can think of is my bedroom rug ... The lining I might manage with some old curtains."

Oh Christ!

"You're not going to be making any conquests in these, that's for sure. For my part, I like a man who's a bit stylish in his clothes: green tails, check trousers. Oh, not that I like them to be outrageous: pleasing, not plunging into vice; being well-dressed doesn't mean being a dandy, not in the least, but say what you like, there's nothing wrong with a touch of originality, and I would never have held it against you if people had turned around to look at you walking arm in arm with me in the street ... But who's going to turn around to look at you? Not a soul! You'll pass and no one will ever notice. Well, if you're of a modest nature ..." (There's a touch of irony and disappointment in her tone.) "But that's just fine, I'm not saying that it's bad at all."

"Where are you taking me for dinner?"

She says this in an almost coaxing voice, a childish tone that touches me. Immediately I mention Tavernier's and its menu at thirty-two sous.

"I'd like to go just once to a really nice restaurant—Frères-Provençaux or Véfour. There can't be anything really wrong in that, can there? And your father did so well last year!"

I had the greatest difficulty in dissuading her from Véfour. She was in a mood to "make a splash." If we had to spend ten francs, we'd find them somewhere! So what! It'll be a party!

Ten francs! I could see the bill going up and up to twenty, my mother calling them bandits. "I know the cost of meat! You can't teach me anything about kidneys! Twenty sous for a bit of cheese!"

I told a fib: I said that friends of mine who'd eaten there had sworn they'd been charged thirty sous for chops.

"They were pulling your leg, my boy...Oh, you're still as innocent as ever despite this Paris of yours! You can't tell me that they wanted thirty sous for a chop. At home, you can buy a whole suckling pig for that amount!"

"And it's not as good as people think," I ventured timidly.

"If it's bad, I'll tell them what's what, for their ten francs, don't worry!"

But I am worried. I insist: "Let's try Tavernier first. Trust me..."

We go to Tavernier.

The first thing she said as we went in was, "It's too fancy for it to be a good deal. It's all la-de-da, can't you see?"

She spoke in a loud voice, as she does at home. I saw that the lady at the dessert counter could hear her, and I was ashamed.

To find a seat we went three times around the room.

People start commenting at the number of times we were circulating! Finally, my mother makes a decision.

"We'll be all right here—no, the other side. Just go over and see if we can sit there, in back, by the window."

I walk through the restaurant blushing to the roots of my hair.

We're blocking the waiters' way. They can't do their job. A couple of times I come to a standstill in front of a sole and a fried egg...The waiter veers left—so do I. He veers right—there I am again! He tries going straight on—not a chance!

In the back of the room, they're starting to place bets.

"He's going to get by! He'll be stopped!"

My mother announces, "That's my son!"

"Congratulations, Madame!"

Finally I manage to get back to her.

Greeted with warm applause, the waiter ducks beneath my arm. The people who lost their bets cast angry sidelong glances at me and pay up.

We're stronger when we can present a united front; my mother doesn't want to get separated.

"Let's stick together," she says.

So we make our way to a strategic spot where we seem safest and hold a council of war.

A lot of people are watching.

"Are you hungry? You poor child!"

Why on earth is she calling me her "poor child" in front of all these people?

Some of them are organizing a sort of chant:

> Give a drink to the poor . . .
> Some relief to the poor . . .
> Some food to the poor . . . poor child!

But someone has gone to get the manager who was bottling wine. He comes up with his napkin dangling over his arm.

"You do intend to eat here?"

I speak out boldly: "No."

Amazement on his face. Murmurs among the guests.

I said "no" because he seemed so infuriated.

"You haven't come to dine? Why have you come here then?"

"My name is Madame Vingtras. I've just arrived from Nantes. His name is Jacques!"

Cheers from around the room. "Give her an ear. Listen to what the lady has to say!"

My ears are ringing. I can't hear anyone properly. But I do manage to hear the owner saying, "This has gone on long enough!"

They're winning: we're cornered at one end of the room.

Finally I have to admit that we *have* come to dine.

Now they're serving us: the waiters are cautious.

"I know their sort," said an elderly waiter. "They're cheats, they pretend to be donkeys so as to get some free hay. Later, they'll slip out."

"I'd just as soon go on to another restaurant," says my mother. "How about you?"

"Me too. I can't stand that bit about *Give a drink to the poor... Get rid of the poor...* We'll go to Bessay's, it's around the corner in fact and it's only twenty-two sous."

My mother settles in at Bessay's.

"Well, what have you got for us, mister?"

"You don't say 'mister' to a waiter, mother."

"So you've now lost your manners, have you? You mustn't be so snooty with people. You never know what might happen one day, my boy!"

The waiter hasn't made any response to my mother's polite question; he's busy with a customer. She asks, "You do have calf's head, don't you?"

The man indicates she's right: he has a calf's head for sure.[1]

The waiter comes back to our table.

"Well now, what do you recommend?" my mother asks.

"I recommend the braised veal."

"Oh, I haven't come to Paris just to eat what I can get

back home—certainly not—tell us what you'd order for yourself."

She's hoping he'll be able to give her some *friendly* advice.

"Well, what's good? Where are you from?

He suggests something that she seems to accept. No, not exactly! She's had another idea.

"Call him back, Jacques!"

"Waiter?"

I call out tentatively, the way you do at a dentist's door . . . I'm hoping he won't hear.

"Can't you see he's leaving? Run after him quickly!"

I catch up with the waiter; he has one foot suspended in the air, he's bending over, and shouting downstairs in a stentorian voice, "What about my tripe?"

He swings around.

"What's the matter?"

"We don't want the roast."

"What do you want, then?"

My mother shouts from the other end of the room, "A nice chop, with not too much fat! If it's got fat, we don't want it! And a very hot plate, please . . ."

"Here we are: one chop!"

"I said *without fat!*"

"There isn't any fat, madam."

"Oh, come on now, my dear sir, let's be honest!"

The waiter has vanished.

My mother turns the chop over and over with her fork; finally she comes up with a suggestion.

"You go down to the kitchen, Jacques, and ask them if they'll let you have another one . . ."

"Oh Ma!"

"As if we're not allowed to eat what we want when we've

paid for it! You'd think we were asking for charity!" Then, in a tender voice: "So you want me to eat something that will be bad for me, do you? Please go and ask them to change it, dear..."

I don't know where to hide: all eyes are on me and every ear is listening to us. I think of a way out: with an arch, rather sulky look (am I even biting the tip of my little finger?), I say, "And I'm so fond of fat too..."

"So you're fond of fat now, are you? What did I say to you when I used to have to whip you to get you to eat it? That one day you'd be crazy for it! Well, my boy, enjoy yourself now!"

I still can't stand fat but I don't see any other way of avoiding taking the chop back and maybe I'll be able to get rid of some of it—in fact, I do succeed in stuffing a bit into my waistcoat and another bit in my pocket.

But one evening my mother takes me aside: she wants to have a serious talk.

"Enough's enough, my boy: we must work out what we're going to do. We've been spending our time in the theater and stuffing ourselves in restaurants for the last week and we still haven't decided anything about your future."

Every time my mother talks to me in that solemn tone of voice, cold shivers run down my spine. For the last seven days, she's been extremely amiable; and now, on the eighth day, she points out that while I've been relaxing and enjoying myself, she's been pinching and scraping.

"It's easy to see it's not your money we've been spending. The restaurant may cost only twenty-two sous for one person but for two, it's forty-four—not including the waiter... And you wanted to tip him three sous! All right, I did give them to him, but two would have been quite enough. If it had been me, I wouldn't have given anything at all, not even two!"

She has a way of emphasizing the entertainments she's given me that somehow spoils them.

When we went to the Palais-Royal, for example, and I had to go about looking incredibly cheerful for the next two days, to prove the money had been well spent. If I'm not bursting with delight, she says: "Well, that certainly was a waste of two francs!"

I keep laughing as much as possible. I can relax a bit when she's looking the other way, but it's hard work all the same.

She took me to the Hippodrome—we returned on foot. She's fond of walking—not me. I have a melancholy air.

"So we're sad now, are we? You weren't looking sad when you were playing the dandy in your nice balcony seat or were ogling the lady horse riders!"

The dandy???

"Well, what are we going to do with you!"

"I don't know."

"Don't you have any ideas?"

"No."

"You must finish your schooling."

I can't see any need for that.

My mother reads my thoughts.

"I bet—yes, I bet—that he wouldn't mind if all the sacrifices we've made on his behalf simply vanished into thin air. He'd be perfectly ready to leave school, in fact. He'd be willing to abandon his studies!"

Well, for all the fun I get out of them and for all the good they'll do me (I'm making all these observations to myself).

"Are you going to give me an answer?" my mother shouts! "Will you answer me?"

"What's the question?"

"What are you thinking of doing? Have you got any ideas, anything in mind?"

I make no reply but in a voice that she can't hear, I say to myself: Yes, I do have some ideas, I do have something in mind... My idea is that the hours I spend on Latin verse, on all this Greek—all this nonsense—are a sheer waste of time. And I have in mind that I was right when I was a little boy, to want to learn some trade! I want to start earning my living as soon as possible and become independent!

I'm tired of all the things I've had to suffer and tired of all the entertainments I'm being offered too. I'd prefer not to be educated and not to be insulted. I don't want to go to the theater on Monday only to be blamed on Tuesday for having been taken there. I can feel that I'm never going to be happy as long as you're in a position to tell me that I cost you even a sou.

That's what I think, Mother.

And there's something else I want to tell you as well—in spite of myself, I still recall the days when, as a little boy, I suffered from your bad temper. Sometimes I'm overcome by bursts of anger and let me tell you one thing, I will never be happy until I've gotten away from you!

And then there came a moment when all these thoughts burst out into the open!

My mother went pale as a sheet.

"Yes, I'd like to go into a factory, I want to be in a workshop, I'll be a porter carrying cases, I'll mend the shutters, I'll sweep the floors, but I'll learn a trade. Once I've learned it, I'll be earning five francs a day and I'll pay you back every sou you've spent at the Palais-Royal—and that tip you gave the waiter..."

"So you want to break your father's heart?"

"I've heard just about enough about broken hearts. I don't want to follow in his footsteps. I don't want to become a performing dog! I don't want to become stupid like N—— or

D——, I'd prefer to wear a leather apron like Uncle Joseph, pick up my pay on Saturday, and have the right to go wherever I like on Sunday!!"

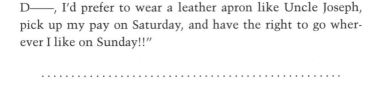

"And so you're saying that you never want to see us again?"

She's forgotten all my other angry remarks, the remarks that hurt her pride, ruin her plans, upset her life. She remembers only the one sentence when I yelled at her that I didn't love them and that I never wanted to see them again, ever!

Her look of misery shocked me. I grasped her hands.

"Are you crying?"

She was unable to choke back a sob and in a gesture of grief which I've seen depicted in churches, she sinks her head into her hands ...

When she looked up again, I could no longer recognize her: this peasant woman was the image of the poetry of suffering, her face as white as the face of some grand lady, the tears in her eyes like glittering pearls.

"Forgive me, Mother!"

She took my hand. Once again, I asked her forgiveness.

"It's not for me to forgive you, my boy ... you see, all I ask is for you not to go on saying those cruel things to me."

She lowers her voice to a whisper, "Particularly if I deserve them, my son."

"Oh no, no, you don't deserve them!" I said. Now I was crying too.

"Maybe," she replied. "I'd like to be alone this evening. You can go out. Just leave me ... leave me ..."

She arranged for me to have the key—"so that he can stay out till midnight," she said to the landlord, Monsieur Malou.

I went off, haphazardly, taking the first street I saw, and wandered around, not knowing where; and that whole evening, my mind was filled with those touching words which had canceled out so many harsh ones—and so many cruel acts.

"Jacques, will you stay on at school, as a favor to us?"

"Yes, Mother, I will."

From that day on, until she died, I never called her anything but Mother.

"Oh, that makes me so glad! Thank you, son . . . You see, I'd've been so sorry if, after going all the way through school, you'd have stopped before you finished. It was your father I was sorry for. You'll make him a happy man, you'll pass your matriculation and afterward . . . Well, afterward you'll do whatever you like, since you wouldn't be happy doing what we'd like."

After that tearful evening, it had been decided that we wouldn't discuss the question of going on to the university and that I'd simply prepare for my baccalaureate.

I had agreed, glad that my promise would dry the poor woman's tears, and that they'd be wiped away by this sacrifice!

She no longer speaks to me in the way she used to in the past.

She talks so solemnly and she's so scared of offending me!

"I've hurt you a great deal because of my silly ideas, haven't I?"

And she adds with emotion, "Now it'll be up to you to rebuke me! In the first place, from now on it'll be you who'll be in charge of the spending. Don't protest, I'm anxious for you to do that, I really want you to. I'm an old woman, and you must be bored being with me the whole time. I can very easily stay here and chat with Madame Malou. She can take me around with her and show me all the lovely things as well as you can. I want you to feel free in the evenings at least. Call on your friends again, your classmates. Go and see Matoussaint."

I went to see Matoussaint again, in a room in the Latin Quarter where he's living with a man ten years older than he is; the man's a Jacobin and writes for a Republican newspaper. He's working on a history of the *Convention*, which he's dictating to Matoussaint.

I arrived in the middle of a serious discussion. They made me welcome but continued their conversation.

Their words sounded to me like the jingling of spurs.

"A journalist must be like a soldier—the sword must never be far from the pen. And be ready to let blood drip on your desk—there are times in the life of nations . . ."

Matoussaint and his friend—we call him the *journalist*—loaned me some books. I took them home on a Thursday . . . By the following Sunday, I was a changed man.

I'd been delving into the history of the French Revolution.

My eyes had been opened by a book which spoke of destitution and hunger, which dealt with people who reminded me of Uncle Joseph or Uncle Chadenas, joiners armed with calipers that opened like weapons, peasants whose pitchforks had blood on their prongs.

There were women marching on Versailles shouting that Madame Veto[2] was starving the people, and the pikes on which they'd stuck their chunk of black bread—their flag, indeed—burst out of the pages and leaped into my sight . . .

I saw that they were simple people like my grandparents, that their hands bore scars like my uncles', that the women were like the poor beggar women we used to give a sou to in the street, noticing that they had children they were dragging along by the wrist; it was hearing them speak like the rest of us, like old Fabre, old Ma Vincent, like me . . . and I was moved from the soles of my feet to the roots of my hair.

This time there wasn't any Latin. They were saying: We're hungry! We want to be free!

I'd eaten too much bitter bread at home. I'd been too brutalized by my family for my heart not to have been seized by these cries.

In my imagination I tore to shreds all those botched up clothes I'd had to wear that had turned me into a figure of fun. I replaced them with the uniform of the French Republican Armies. I slipped into the ragged gear of the *Sambre-et Meuse*.[3]

You weren't being beaten by your mother or father, you were being fired on by the enemy and dying like Bara.[4] *Long live the People!*

And the people in this book that I'd just been loaned were wearing leather aprons, workers' jackets, patched breeches. These were the only people I loved because the only people who'd been kind to me when I was young had been the poor.

I found myself remembering words heard at wakes, songs I'd heard sung in the fields, the names of Robespierre or Bonaparte at the end of refrains sung in dialect, and a really old man with white hair who lived at the far end of the village and who was called the Madman. Sometimes he'd put a red cap on his white head and sit staring at the ashes of his fire.

I recalled the man the police called the *sans-culotte*[5] and who couldn't bear priests. On the day his wife, on her deathbed, had asked to receive the last sacraments, he'd walked out of the house.

I remembered too the gestures that I'd seen people making, angrily slapping the butts of their rifles or pointing their barrels toward the château of the local lord of the manor.

And my blood—the blood of the son of a peasant mother, the nephew of working men—boiled in my veins, the veins of a reluctant scholar!

I felt an urge to write to Uncle Joseph, to Uncle Chadenas: "You can rest assured that I haven't forgotten you, that I would be happier with you at the plow or in the cowshed than in this house full of Latin, but if you ever march against the aristocrats, call on me to join with you!"

"You've been looking all worked up recently," my mother observes.

It's true: I've made a leap from a dead world into a living one. The history I'm devouring isn't the story of gods or kings or saints—it's the story of Peter and John, of Mathurine and Florimond, the story of my country, of my village. In these annals, written in an ink still barely dry, there are poor men's tears, the blood of rebels, the sufferings of my own folk.

The freedom granted by my mother has filled me with a passion that is boundless. Every day I turn up at Rue Jacob and plunge wildly into their books or listen to the journalist talk about the Republican flag they set up on the bridge and defended to the cry of "Long live the nation! Down with the monarchy! Liberty or death!"

Freedom? I didn't know what it was but, young though I am, I *do* know what it is to be a victim!

Sometimes with Matoussaint, we imagine that we're campaigning and each of us has his own dreams.

He'd like to be in the army wearing a Saint-Just hat, gold epaulettes, and the wide tricolor belt.

I see myself as a sergeant and I call, "Off we go, men!" We're all from the same district, sitting around the same campfire, talking about the Haute-Loire.

In *my* dream, my epaulettes are wool, my belt is a piece of cord.

I'd like to be in the Moselle battalion, with peasants and workers. Our captain would be Uncle Joseph, with Uncle Chadenas as his lieutenant.

We'd come back to be carpenters or to bring in the harvest, "after the victory!"

RUE COQ-HÉRON

One evening the journalist takes us to see the press, on the dark ground floor where the paper is printed; he's a friend of one of the workers.

The machine spins around swallowing up the sheets it then spits out, the belts are humming, there's a smell of resin and fresh printer's ink . . .

It smells good, like dung, and it's as warm as inside a cowshed. The workers are in shirtsleeves, wearing paper hats. Orders are being rapped out, as if on a ship in distress. Like a cabin boy, the feeder is watching the machine operator who's like the skipper keeping an eye on everything.

One of the rollers has broken. Hey! Look out!

They stop the machine—and five minutes later the iron-and-wooden beast starts puffing again.

I've discovered my vocation.

I'm going to wear the blue jacket and brown paper hat too. I'll press down on that wheel, I'll speed up those rollers, I'll breathe that scent as intoxicating as rough wine . . .

Compositor? No—printer, that's the idea!

What a wonderful trade, where you can listen to a machine living and whining, where at some moment everyone is gripped by emotion, as in battle.

You need to be strong, stretch your arms wide . . . There's iron and noise, I like that. You're earning your living and you're the first to read the newspaper.

I'm not saying anything about it. I'll keep my plan to myself. I feel that when you want to do something that other people don't want, keeping quiet gives you strength. So I'm not going to say a word—but what bliss it is!

There's also a touch of vanity and cruelty in that sort of bliss.

I feel that I'm going to be so superior to my pals who are leading a bohemian sort of life—there's no doubt about it—because they're never certain of having a job, while I'll be making my five francs a day no matter what, and only my arms will be tired.

I won't be dependent on anyone. At night, I'll read, on Sundays I'll write—I'll join a secret society if I want to, and when I go there, I'll have a full stomach and I'll still be able to give something for the political prisoners or for buying weapons . . .

To live by my work and to die in the fight!

"I've had a letter from your father, Jacques, and he's decided that we'll go back to Nantes so that you can study for your baccalaureate with him."

I'd stopped thinking about such things, I was up to my neck in the revolution, I'd come to love Paris. That printing press! And we'd been going for cheap meals in small restaurants frequented by workers who'd been members of the secret society of Les Saisons and taken part in riots.

Smocks and tails would be sitting at the same table, drinking to each other's health.

On Sundays we'd go to the riverside cafés, the *Lyre Chansonnière* or *Les Enfants du Luth*—I can't exactly remember now which one it was.

I found it a bit boring when they sang dirty songs, but suddenly someone would say, "There's Festeau, there's Gille," and I seemed to hear the muffled *rat-a-tat-tat* of a distant Republican drum and then it would grow louder and Gille would sing the opening chords and the music would send volleys of sound through my heart.

Yet in some ways, perhaps I prefer the songs about threshers of wheat or blacksmiths—sung by a tall mechanic at the top of his lungs, gentle as a lamb and strong as an ox—to all those songs about going off to fight and die . . .

He's talking about the poetry of workshops—the roaring of the fire, of the brazier—of the housewife who exhorts him, "Keep going, my love! Work on—it's for our little boy . . ."

At one point the singer lowers his voice, someone says, "Close the window." And when the refrain comes, they give a salute:

And the flag that the people flew at Saint-Merry![6]

There's hidden revolt tucked away inside that song—at least, I can put a bit into it myself, because yesterday I started reading the *Histoire de Dix Ans*[7] and I've gone beyond 1793. I'm in Lyons[8] with the black flag, the weavers are angry and they're shouting, "Bread or lead!"

"We'll be leaving for Nantes on Monday, Jacques."

Being stabbed with a dagger couldn't have hurt more.

A month ago I would have been glad to leave and might even have spat as we went through the gates of Paris, because

I'd felt so stifled, so disillusioned by my schoolmates and my teachers.

But during that month I'd seen my mother's tears, and the next day had achieved my freedom. I'd even had the odd couple of francs with which to enjoy a bite of pork with my friends and on Sundays, braised beef at Ramponneau's.

I've joined the crowd, I've heard people laughing heartily even if they did speak bad French . . . I've listened to talk of "the People," of citizens; they've been talking about "Liberty," not "Libertas!"

And all around me, I've heard people talk about being poor. My father had been humiliated because he was poor. So had I. But lo and behold, instead of Cato and Cicero, instead of people with names ending in *-o,-onis,-us,-i,-orum*, I've seen people meeting in public and discussing true destitution, asking for work or for death, saying, "Hey, Jean-Marie, there's not even a crust of bread left in the house. Why not throw in our hand once and for all?"

Go back there?

Who will I talk to about the Republic? Who will I revolt with?

Have they ever had any revolts like that in Nantes? Lyons is another story!

If only I hadn't given my word to my mother! If only she hadn't cried!

If only she hadn't cried, I'd have said, "I don't want to leave." The journalist, the *puritan*, would have found me a job, as an office boy, as some sort of gofer, on one of the newspapers.

As it happens—what a stroke of luck—there's a job open at the *National*, offering thirty francs a month for someone to read out the text to the proofreader. I could survive on those thirty francs. And once my job was finished, I'd go down to the printing room and sniff the ink and the paper and ask the workers to teach me their trade.

Why not mention it to my mother?

I do mention it to my mother.

"But you told me . . ."

"Yes, I know I did."

I go and say good-bye to the journalist and Matoussaint.

The journalist tries to cheer me up.

"You'll be back, old man!"

"But write me!"

"I'll write. Even," he added with a grin, "if it's to ask you to come and join in the attack on the Elysée!"[9]

"In that case, citizen, for sure!"

XXIV. BACK HOME

WHAT A sad homecoming!

My mother can tell how miserable I am, and she tries to console me. That irritates me and I have to make an enormous effort not to be rude. I'm annoyed that I'm so depressed: I lack guts!

I do. They call out the name of each station as we go through, and I feel a stab in my chest as if I was being gored by a bull.

Beaugency! Amboise! Anceny!

They draw our attention to a château, a ruin; that means that we're closer to Nantes.

"Well, young man, we're only twelve miles away from Nantes now."

Oh God!

"Here we are."

How empty the streets are! On the quayside where we live, there are two or three passersby—no more. I recognize a former ship's captain sitting on the bench where I used to see him in the old days on my way to school; then a black man dressed in rags, who had children living on charity.

Everything's so quiet! You'd think you were in the country.

I look up at the window of our apartment.

There's my father, gaunt, looking morose, now moving.

When I was a little boy, when I was thrust into his arms for a kiss, he used to push me away.

Now, each time there's a solemn occasion, a leave-taking or a reunion, we're both embarrassed.

This time, his face pale and stony-eyed, he does offer to embrace me.

I don't dare.

My mother gives me a gentle shove, I stick out my neck, he does the same—my hair gets into his eyes and his beard pricks me. Looking resentful, we both scratch at each other.

Without a word, we go upstairs.

My mother follows behind; you'd think it was an execution in the Tower of London.

If only the execution could take place right now; no chance of that—my father's taking his time to *strike a solemn note*.

It's a result of all this Latin—it's the memory of those fathers who murder their children in Roman history: Cato, Brutus. My father's not actually thinking of murdering me, but at bottom I'm sure he feels that's just cowardice. He'd like his son, his little Brutus, to feel grateful to him for allowing him to survive, and each time I make some gesture, or a caustic comment, he frowns, bites his lips (that must be tiring for such a very dignified man), and seems on the verge of saying, "Aren't you forgetting that you're living here on my sufferance, that I could cut you down with an ax or hand you over to the *lictor*?"[1]

He maintains this antique posture—until he feels a sneeze coming on, until he can't keep it up any longer.

Eventually the effort to appear indignant leaves him exhausted. From time to time, he even finds himself obliged to relax his jaw.

He's never been more Brutus-like than today.

He tosses back the tassel of his smoking cap, as if it typified weakness. He sits bolt upright in his armchair as if he were a magistrate in Rome.

"You are my son, I am your father."

"Oh yes indeed, Antoine, you can be sure of that," my mother seems to be saying.

"In Rome there was a law" (are you paying attention, my boy?) "a law which gave a father disgraced by one of his family the right to have that . . . that kinsm . . . kins . . . kinsman . . . *suum* . . . put to death . . ."

He's lost the thread. He's getting confused.

PHILOSOPHY

"You'll be working in the philosophy class until Easter. At Easter you'll sit for the baccalaureate."

That's what's been decided.

I get a lot of looks when I make my reappearance in the school yard. People gather around and stare. A boy who's come back from a stay in Paris . . . Something must have happened . . .

The teacher in charge is a young man who was at the top of the list at the *école normale*, then first in the *agrégation*; he's always the first into the classroom and the first at the bursar's office to collect his salary. He lives on the first floor in a house tucked away in a drab little street. He goes to first nights at the theater and sits in the first row . . .

It's his mother who's responsible for all this.

"I insist that wherever you go and whatever you do, you're always the *first*."

This teacher treats me quite well. He's relying on me to provide the *peripatetic*[2] element for him in his garden.

In the past, he's had people who would draw water for him and irrigate his vegetable patch; now he doesn't have anyone.

He thinks that as the son of a colleague—also initiated into the Eleusian mysteries[3]—I'm excellent raw material to become his disciple and water his garden . . .

I've no idea how he got his appointment.

In Paris, I thought the teachers in the rhetoric class were boring, but I was assured that among the philosophy teachers there were people capable of arguing and thinking, people with something in their heads.

There was even one who came around to shake hands with the journalist, in spite of his being a Republican.

I had a high opinion of these seekers of virtue.

But this one is such a clown!

IN CLASS

"Monsieur Vingtras, what are the proofs of the existence of God?"

I scratch my ear.

"You don't know?"

He appears greatly surprised. He seems to be saying, "You don't know and yet you've only recently come back from Paris!"

"Gineston, proofs of the existence of God?"

"I don't know, sir, there are some pages missing from my book."

"Badigeot?"

"There's the *consensus omnium*, sir."

"And that means?" (The teacher assumes the posture of Socrates about to let his genius speak.)

"Which means . . ." (Badigeot whispers to his neighbor, "Come on, help me out, can't you?")

"Which means," the teacher continues, putting the poor

boy out of his misery, "that everybody is agreed in thinking that there is a God?"

"Yes, sir!"

"Do you not feel that there is a being above us?"

Badigeot eyes the ceiling closely!

That morning Rafoin had thrown up to the ceiling a little paper figure of a man suspended from a thread and held there by a pellet of wet bread.

"Yes, sir, there's someone up there."

"Someone? Someone?" the teacher says (he's shortsighted and hasn't seen the little paper figure hanging from the ceiling), "But He is also the God of the Bible. His right hand is terrible . . ."

Nevertheless, he didn't object to the word.

"I rather like that unceremonious tone," he said to himself as he left the classroom. "There's someone up there . . . The voice of a child expressing his idea of the divinity!"

He mentioned it in more exalted circles.

"What do you think, headmaster? Isn't it rather like the voice of innocence speaking with the voice of experience? 'Yes, there is *someone* up there . . .'"

Next time he gave the class, he spoke to Badigeot again, reminding him of the word he'd used.

"So there's *someone* up there, is there, Badigeot?"

"No, sir, he's not there now."

The piece of bread had come unstuck. He'd fallen off the ceiling . . .

MY SOUL

Now the teacher tackled the question of *the properties of the soul* with me.

The others haven't reached that stage yet: he's doing it specially for me.

In this school you're not taught the composition of the soul until after Easter.

There are seven *properties of the soul*.

"Count them off on your fingers, that makes it easier," the teacher said.

The visit to Nantes of a celebrated university professor, Monsieur Chalmat, is announced. Chalmat himself is within our walls, in person!

He knew my father in Paris, when he was working for the *agrégation*.

They had been dining together, side by side, in a fixed-price restaurant. Monsieur Chalmat finished his meal first and departed, leaving behind a manuscript which was picked up by my father. It had an address on it and my father returned it to its owner, who was in despair.

"Should you ever need help," the philosopher said, "please count on me."

And now here he was, in the flesh, quite by chance, and also quite by chance he was occupying a furnished apartment in our building. He was our neighbor.

Monsieur Chalmat was sleeping on *our very own floor*!

He slept rather badly and during the night he talked out loud. I could hear him saying, "There are *eight*, there are *eight*, yes, there are *EIGHT*!"

He wanted to give me a present.

He took my father and me aside; he opened his heart to us . . .

"Dear friends," he said (he did me the honor of including me in this category), "I want to give you something in return for the service you rendered in the past by rescuing my manuscript. I'm not a wealthy man but I shall give you what I can—the result of twenty years of reflection and research."

My father seems to be saying, "This is too kind of you!"

"No, not at all! Listen carefully!"

We're holding our breath, you could have heard a pin drop . . .

"You've always been told that the soul has seven properties . . . IT HAS EIGHT!"

So I was being misled! I was being robbed of one? How come? What was the meaning of that?

"Yes indeed. It's like this." And Monsieur Chalmat held up the five fingers of his right hand and three others lying tucked away in the left.

He was even kind enough to add, "I give you permission to take advantage of this discovery; people don't yet know about it; it won't be in my book for another two months."

I arrived this morning. Tomorrow we have translation. My father would have liked to come along to Rennes with me but he's had to stay behind to look after the boarders.

I've come second in translation.

Not a bad performance, but I stuck too close to the text. Otherwise I'd have been first.

The oral's this afternoon.

I go over the handbook again and again, as if I could swallow it all in three mouthfuls.

"Monsieur Vingtras!"

My turn!

They pick the passages at random.

"Translate this passage first and then that one."

I translate like an angel.

"One cannot fail to see," says the chairman of the examiners, addressing everybody, "that not only have you been cradled in the lap of an academic mind but also that you have passed through the splendid school of Paris and drunk deep at those noble springs which we have all imbibed!" (Thinks again . . .) "No, not all of us, of course—we have here today our colleague Monsieur Gendrel . . ."

Monsieur Gendrel is the teacher of the local philosophy class. He has his degree from a *provincial* university and a *provincial* doctorate. Unlike them—and unlike me—he hasn't drunk at all these enriching springs, and as, according to reports, he's a sanctimonious humbug, the chairman of the examiners takes a dig at him whenever he has a chance. Now I'm his pretext.

Monsieur Gendrel is yellow, yellow as a quince, with glasses like Bergougnard's.

Before moving on to him, I have to face the mathematics examiner.

I don't understand very much about what they're asking me but the public praise that I've just received induces the examiner to be indulgent.

"What is a compensation pendulum?"

"It's a pendulum which compensates, sir."

"Excellent. Well done!"

Leaning toward the senior examiner, he whispers, "An intelligent young man!"

Turning toward me: "And what is the air pump?"

"The air pump?"

"Oh, I'm not asking for the exact technical details. It's to create a vacuum, isn't it? And if you put birds into it, they will die, will they not? Good, excellent!"

He resumes: "In geometry you have conic sections?"

Oh yes, but to give a proper demonstration, I'd need a hat, such as I used with the old Italian's plaster casts—but I go ahead as best I can . . .

Picking up a hat that happens to be lying there and removing an old handkerchief from it, I proceed to cut my conic section.

In the examination hall, people are laughing because the lining of the hat is very greasy and the handkerchief extremely grubby; the examiners are watching me and smiling good-humoredly.

It's the turn of the mathematics examiner to speak; he's definitely eager to butter up the senior examiner (he's engaged to his daughter). He says, "Young man, it's plain that you prefer Virgil to Pythagoras, but as our chairman expressed so excellently before, you have drunk at those rich springs by the banks of the Sequana[4] and Pythagoras himself has benefited thereby . . ."

Murmurs of approval.

Another dig at Gendrel!

He's the man I now face.

He inspects me closely: his glasses glint like freshly minted one-franc coins.

He needs to blow his nose.

He looks for his handkerchief. It's the one I took out of and then put back into the hat with the extremely greasy lining.

That was Gendrel's hat . . .

I'm sunk!

He's got a grudge against me because of the slighting references that the chairman of the examiners has been directing at him, using me for an excuse; he also has a grudge against me because of the hat and the handkerchief.

He allows me no time to gather my thoughts.

"Young man, we are asking you to discuss the *properties of the soul*."

Speaking in a firm voice: "How many are there?"

He has the look of a prosecuting magistrate intent on making a murderer confess or a horseman hurtle the breastplate of his charger against a phalanx.

"I asked you, young man, how many properties of the soul there are?"

I'm bewildered.

"There are EIGHT, sir."

. . . .

Stupefaction in the audience . . . Commotion on the bench of examiners . . .

There's a sudden reversal of feeling as sometimes occurs in crowds and whispers of *"Eight, eight, eight . . ."*

Whew! Eight . . .

I'm waiting to hear Gendrel's views. He's staring me squarely in the face.

"You are stating that there are eight properties of the soul? You are reflecting no credit on those *high academic springs* which our chairman was earlier so generously congratulating you on imbibing. In the school of Paris where you were studying there may perhaps, young man, have been eight. In the *provinces* we know only of seven."

While the examiners may resent Gendrel, they cannot publicly accept my theory of eight properties of the soul and I am about to be penalized for openly, in an examination, putting forward a view which required many tomes and a famous name to make it respectable . . .

The senior examiner comes back and announces curtly, "Monsieur Vingtras is referred to present himself for examination at later date."

The crowd goes off wondering who I can be, what it is I want, and what would happen to everyone if people played fast and loose with the soul like that. I'm undermining the foundation of the human conscience.

For my part, I haven't the least desire to do any such thing: it's Monsieur Chalmat's fault, he was the one who told me there were eight. I'm not being manipulated by any sect or faction.

I just said what he told me!

So there are only seven properties of the soul: I've been deprived of one—and I couldn't care less. But I'll still have to take the exam again under the auspices of Rennes University— and that I do care about. I'm very sad.

My father meets me, tight-lipped, frowning, hollow-eyed. He's not only suffering for my sake. His pride is suffering!

A pupil who bears him a grudge is twisting the knife in the wound.

On the evening of the same day that the news of my failure became known, a notice appeared on our door:

AT THE SIGN OF THE BLACK BALL
FAILURES ESPECIALLY WELCOME
(both *agrégation and baccalaureate*)
(*local deliveries of participles can still be arranged*)

Local deliveries of participles can still be arranged! Meaning that private tutoring will still be available and that it'll cost twenty-five francs a month, just as though one had passed the baccalaureate the first time up and received one's *agrégation* on the first try—as though the son of the house had been able to juggle with white and not black balls!

———

"It'd be better if you don't take your meals with us, Jacques."

My poor mother has given up. Every day she has to stand by and witness dreadful scenes.

My father begrudges me the bread I eat.

Food is brought to me in my bedroom as if I were someone in hiding.

"I can't stand this sort of life any longer! I want to go back to Paris!"

"In those clothes?" says my mother, looking at the rags I'm dressed in.

So I'm going to be humiliated and crushed forever by my clothes!

But, in spite of everything, I have to get away.

My father got wind of my intention.

"If he does try to leave, tell him I'll set the police on him."

Legnagna had already once threatened to do that. "So you want to turn me into a criminal, do you, Father?"

But he has the right to have me picked up as a criminal, he has the right to treat me as a thief, he *owns* me like a dog!

"Until you're twenty-one, my boy!"

He flung this angry statement at me, tapping a copy of the Civil Code with his finger; that evening I discover it lying in a corner and read it in secret by the light of the streetlamp that shines into my bedroom: *May be locked up by order of his parents, etc.*

Have me arrested? On what grounds?

Because I refuse to let him go on telling me that I don't earn the miserable rations he doles out! Because I won't let him spend his time hitting me—me, who could demolish him with one finger. Because I want to learn a trade and he feels humiliated at the thought that he, who has struggled so hard to acquire his rusty brown *academic dress* should have a son who'll be wearing a leather apron or overalls.

Perhaps he'll have me handcuffed and order the police to fasten them tighter if I resist. And all this because I'm refusing to become a schoolteacher like him. The fact is I'm impugning his whole existence by declaring that I want to go back to the sort of trade my grandparents followed. Saying that I wish to work in a workshop is telling him that he was wrong to leave the plow or the cowshed.

So he'll have me hounded by one police force or another, and if it's not tonight, it'll be tomorrow or next month. Until I'm twenty-one, if he can manage it.

Someone had the idea of asking me to do some tutoring.

My success at school has won me a reputation; and a few people, perhaps suspecting the silent drama being played out at home, are trying to help me.

One of these persons approaches my mother; it's a lady who'd like me to teach her son a little Latin. My mother replied, "I'd be delighted if he could earn some money because then he wouldn't be quarreling with his father all the time. They both mean well but they're always at each other's throats. You'd need to have a word with Monsieur Vingtras, of course, to ask him to buy a pair of trousers for Jacques, unless you want him—forgive the expression—to come buck naked to your house. I'm talking bluntly, like the country woman I am. The fact is I've come from nothing—in my time, I've had to look after the cows, you see!"

I can hear what she's saying from my room. Poor mother!

The lady who came to ask about private lessons goes off scared of being hit by a decanter or seeing a bottle heading in the wrong direction if my father happens to come in and we get into a brawl. And she doesn't feel quite up to the task of negotiating about a pair of trousers for me. In a word, members of our family have looked after animals in the past and she wants a teacher, not a shepherd.

My mother is waiting for a reply (I'm supposed to let her know by letter).

"But I only told her what she needed to know," she says, folding her arms. "Oh—those people with money, those rich people!"

Oh—that peasant!

Even so my scholarly reputation does succeed in getting me a job as a tutor, but to humiliate me, my father won't even let me have a fresh pair of trousers from his wardrobe. My own clothes are in tatters.

So I'm forced to sit sideways.

One day, I was terrified when they said to me, "Why don't you go out and give your lesson in the garden, Monsieur Vingtras, and take your overcoat off. It's so hot in here, you're sweating!"

"Oh no, thank you, really I'm quite all right!"

The sweat's pouring off me.

"He seems shy and rather anxious," they told my mother when she arrived unexpectedly one day to inquire if they were satisfied with me and to speak on my behalf.

"Oh, don't be too sure of that!" my mother said, "And if you have any attractive young ladies, don't let 'em run around too freely when he's here. We've already had a bit of trouble! In that respect, he's very Parisian, you know, and even before he went there, he'd already . . ." (She puts her fingers on her forehead to make horns.) "Oh yes, it's God's truth I'm telling you!"

The next day, I'm fired.

Still, I'd been working for a month and they pay me the full amount. Fifty francs!

———

With that money I intend to order some clothes. My mother intervenes.

"I'll make them for you myself, we'll buy the cloth."

"Oh no, not that, definitely not!"

"My son doesn't love me anymore," she informs her neighbor that evening, who's in her confidence. "If only he'd just let me choose the material."

I buy a ready-made suit.

My mother follows me around furtively, and while I'm completing my purchase, she asks to have a private word with the owner of the shop and tells him the whole story.

"Make sure it's really durable cloth," she whispers, tears in her eyes!

Now that I'm no longer shabby, I meet a few people. My mother asks me to come with her to visit some of her acquaintances.

She's so proud and happy!

But in the middle of the conversation she'll suddenly exclaim, "But it creases so easily! And anyone with half an eye can see that it's only half-lined! If only you'd stand like this, it wouldn't be so noticeable." And she gives my waistcoat a tug to make it hang better and fiddles around with my tie.

She adds sadly, clicking her tongue, "I bet you're satisfied with having bought something that picks up dust so easily! And he didn't even ask for some extra cloth!"

My father can tell how eaten up with despair I am. One day he sees the color drain from my face, and he takes fright.

"Your son has been trying to poison himself," he tells my mother.

He's reached the point of believing that!

The poor woman stands there frozen and speechless.

But he himself is weary of the life we're leading under the same roof. The house seems cursed.

"Tell him to write and let me know what he intends to do."

These are the last words he addresses to my mother after the shock of my suicidal appearance.

It's frightening to take this large blank sheet of paper to write to your father. For the first time in my life, I'll have to address him formally, like a stranger.

I can't see very well by the light of a tallow candle.

"Can you let me have a wax candle, Mother?"

"That won't give a better light, you know, it's a bit cleaner, but it isn't so bright and it's much more expensive, you see."

I'm writing to my father. I keep on scratching out my words!

As I write, I start to feel some sympathy. I'm afraid of appearing weak.

I start again: it's difficult and painful.

No, no, no good! I tear it up yet again.

I'm going to restrict myself to just two lines. No, not two lines—six words. That means I won't have to address my father directly but I'll still be able to say what I want to say. I simply write:

I WANT TO BE A WORKER.

"Your father's furious," my mother whispers in my ear. She'd just handed over my scrap of paper.

He meets me in the hall.

"So you want to screw with me!"

He raises his hand. I think he's about to destroy me.

The breach can never be bridged. Something terrible is going to happen.

XXV. DELIVERANCE

THE DISASTER has occurred!

Sometimes—very rarely—I go out in the evening. What would I say to anyone I met? I don't have a sou to go to the café where the people from our school go. I don't want anyone to buy me a drink when I'm too poor to pay for a round myself. So I only accept a drink when I've got some money in my pocket. I don't feel like a charity case when I can treat someone in return.

But for ages I haven't had any money at all—not even a sou.

I made a little money from selling off my prizes: Sainte-Beuve's anthology of sixteenth-century poetry, a Bossuet, the works of Monsieur Victor Cousin.[1]

My mother found five francs while going through my pockets and asked me where they came from. She seemed to think I'd stolen them or acquired them by murdering someone. "He's been led astray by bad advice. Bad advice is the ruination of young men . . ."

Where could I have gotten any advice? From my schoolmates? Even though they're my age, I'm older. They haven't been beaten like me. They don't know Legnagna. They haven't experienced the wordlessness of this silent house. Advice from older people? My father's colleagues? They have more than enough to do making ends meet, and anyway they only know things that happened long ago in antiquity, and because of all the tutoring they have to do, they never have time to work out what's happening all around them.

I told my mother how I'd gotten my five francs.

She flung her hands into the air.

"You sold your prizes, Jacques!"

Why not? If there's anything I own, it seems to me it's got to be those books! If I'd found out the cost of bread from them or how to earn it, I'd have kept them. But the only things I found belonged to another world! And with the money I'd been able to buy a tie that didn't look ridiculous and go and have a cup of coffee and brandy at the Mille-Colonnes. I get to read the Paris papers when the postman delivers them still smelling of printer's ink.

But one evening I came face-to-face with my father going by. He made an insulting remark and gesture: "So there you are, you lazy bum!"

And went on his way.

"Lazy bum?" I wanted to run after him and ask him how, without even looking at me, he could throw these words right in my face—words which cut me to the quick!

"Lazy bum!" Because in the glacial silence at home, where I am always studying for the baccalaureate, always struggling with people who are long dead, I am bored to death; because the battles of Rome are less hard than my own. I feel a lot sadder than Coriolanus! Don't call me a lazy bum!

If my father were a different person, I'd go up to him and say, "I give you my word that I'm going to work and work hard. But stop treating me so cruelly!"

He'd call me a liar and send me away. I saw that plainly when I was younger.

Two or three times when he was going to mortify me or beat me, I promised that if he didn't do it, I'd do anything he wanted. He brushed my promises aside with contempt. I was young, but still I resented him for having so little trust.

Even today he'd laugh in my face and think I was just a coward!

Never mind! I'll go on living with him the way I would with a prison warden. I'll go on working in spite of everything! That's settled.

But the following evening my mother came to me, very frightened. She told me that my father didn't want his son hanging around in cafés like a tramp, that in the future I must be home by eight o'clock or else sleep in the streets.

I slept on the street.

It's a long job, killing time all night, and around two o'clock, it rained. I was soaked to the bone, my feet were frozen, and I took shelter in doorways. I was also scared of the police. I kept walking around and around near our house. Just as he'd threatened, the door had been locked at eight o'clock: locked and bolted.

And if he's as determined as I am, it'll be bolted again tomorrow.

I don't like prowling the streets. I'd be happier in my bedroom. But I'm not going to be intimidated. I'm shivering. My teeth are chattering.

How cold it is when the sun comes up!

I didn't go back home until after my father should have already left for school, at eight-thirty in the morning.

He hadn't left. This is the first time he's missed school since that terrible fight with my mother.

Had he seen me? Was he waiting for me? Was he sick with rage?

The door had barely closed when he flung himself on me. He was as pale as death.

"You filthy no-good!" he screamed. "I'm going to break every bone in your body!"

AT HOME, ONE HOUR LATER

"What's happening?"

"It's the Vingtras boy—he tried to kill his father!"

I didn't try to kill my father. He would have liked to cripple me. He kept screaming, "I'll break every bone in your body!"

Oh no, you won't! You're not going to break anybody's bones. I'm not going to hit you but you aren't going to lay a single finger on me! It's too late, I'm too big now and too grown up.

JUST KEEP YOUR HANDS TO YOURSELF OR...
WATCH OUT!

MIDNIGHT

My father is going to have me arrested, that's for sure.

Tomorrow, I'm going to jail—like a criminal!

My life is going to be a battle. That's the fate of anyone whose life begins like mine, I can tell.

Even if I stay in jail for only a week, no more—still, in a provincial dump like Nantes, people will be pointing their fingers at me for years to come.

I almost thought of making an end of it all.

If I committed suicide tonight, it would be my father who'd murdered me!

And what crimes have I committed? Mistakes of grammar, false *quantities*, that's about it . . . And then, because I'd been given wrong information about the *properties of the soul*—I said that there were eight instead of seven!—is that a reason to hang myself from the window?

I've done nothing to blame myself for.

I haven't even been guilty of *sneaking off* with some other kid's marble! Once my father gave me thirty sous to buy an exercise book that cost only twenty-nine . . . I kept the spare sou . . . That's the only thing I've ever stolen. I've never been a snitch, definitely not, and when I had to fight, I never turned tail and ran.

If only this was Paris! When I came out of jail, there'd still be people ready to shake hands with me. Not here!

Well, I'll *serve my time* and then go to Paris. And once I'm there I'm not going to hide the fact that I've been to prison, I'll proclaim it . . . I'll defend the RIGHTS OF CHILDREN in the same way others defend the RIGHTS OF MAN.

I'll be asking whether fathers have the right to do whatever they please with their sons; if Monsieur Vingtras has the right to *make a martyr* of me because I've been afraid to accept a life of drudgery and if Monsieur Bergougnard can still batter a Louisette to death . . .

Paris! How I love her!

In my mind's eye I can see the printing press and the newspaper, freedom to defend yourself, sympathy for rebels.

On that day, it was the thought of Paris that saved my neck from the noose. I was already fingering my tie . . .

Once again there's the sound of lots of shouting! Two days have passed.

My mother rushes into my room, terribly upset.

"Come with me, Jacques!"

People are insulting my father.

Some days ago, he'd struck one of his pupils. Now, in the same house where yesterday he'd almost killed me, the parents of the boy he'd cuffed are demanding redress; they want Monsieur Vingtras to express regret, to say he's sorry. Monsieur Vingtras was mumbling excuses, someone was shaking a fist under his nose.

There are two of them, the father and the pupil's older brother, an old man and a young one.

"What's going on?"

"What's going on is that your father had the impudence to slap my brother's face. If he wasn't so worn out I'd slap his face!"

"Who do you think you are?"

And I've caught hold of him around the waist. What a lightweight! The old man too. Out you go—there's the door . . . If they hadn't gone quietly, they'd have been in pieces.

Down in the street, they're rallying a crowd.

The older brother is fuming.

"Come on down!" he yells.

"Alright! I'm on my way!"

They found it hard to tear us apart. He's eighteen, a cadet from Saint-Cyr, gutsy, but I can handle him. I'm holding him the way I've seen Uncle Chadenas hold pigs. I've got him on the ground, I don't want to hurt him . . . But he's still struggling. Someone's yanking my hair.

They've barely dragged him free when he taunts me over the heads of the crowd.

"You wouldn't be so cocky if you were facing someone with a sword in his hand. That's the way I fight."

He's waving his arms and babbling on!

What an imbecile!

"Hey, Massion, go and tell him that if he doesn't shut up, I'll work him over again, but if he stops yapping, I'll be glad to fight with swords!"

MEADOW, AT MAUVES, 7 A.M.

Everything's been arranged without anyone at home knowing about it. Of course, the whole school is talking about it, but my father's in bed with a high fever and the doctor has forbidden anyone to disturb him, so I'm free to act.

I've got some seconds: former classmates who have a bit of fuzz on their upper lips and want to get into Saint-Cyr or the Naval Academy offer to act on my behalf.

"You're very young," said one person involved in the preliminaries.

"I'm eighteen."

I'm sixteen; it's only two years' difference. People are asking themselves whether, facing up to Saint-Cyr, I won't *beat it* at the last minute.

They don't realize how bored to death I am, that this duel is like a new overcoat *not chosen by my mother*, that it's the first time I'll actually be behaving like a man. The truth is that I *want* this duel, for Christ's sake! If the other man tried to get out of it, I'd force him to fight!

All the same, I'm tense: maybe I'll look awkward? If people start laughing, I'll let myself be killed on the spot!

We're facing each other.

"Step forward, gentlemen."

The seconds are more nervous than we are. What's more, they're scared of getting the formalities wrong.

Isn't my opponent going to attack? We crossed swords and then he sprang back, leaving me standing there.

I look like a dog who's lost his master.

He's not coming at me, so I advance.

The doctor utters a shout!

"What's the matter?"

"You're wounded!"

"Me?"

"Your thigh's covered in blood."

I don't feel anything.

"Come on then, let's have another go."

Thinking that it's the thing to do, since the other man had leaped backward, I leap too.

"What a clown," the doctor remarks.

Eventually, they lead me over to him, I still can't understand why.

"A flesh wound in the thigh!"

"You think so?"

"And two week's rest in bed—no walking!"

Well, I don't have a wide choice of where to go.

So it seems I'm wounded. I am, in fact, bleeding.

My opponent shakes hands with me and says, "I'm sorry."

I'm not sorry at all. I've been put to the test and it was like water off a duck's back.

I'd left a note for my mother this morning: "I'm staying with a friend."

And she commented: "That's not a nice thing to do when his father's ill!"

I came home in a cab and needed money to pay for it. I didn't have any, so I had to ask my mother for thirty sous. She thought I was crazy.

"So he's taking cab rides now!"

The staircase is in darkness.

I went upstairs, holding my leg, and without a word, I went off to bed, saying I had a headache—they thought I'd been drinking.

But I was barely between the sheets when a neighbor came and told the whole story. My mother leaves her husband's bedside and comes to mine.

"You've *been in a duel*, Jacques?"

"And how's father this morning?"

———

Since this morning he's been moved into the bedroom next to mine—the doctor said he'd get more air there. My mother goes back to him.

I can't quite understand what they're saying but they're talking about me. She's telling him the whole story. I manage to pick up snatches of it.

There had been a noise on the staircase. Now it stops, and I can hear every word.

My father is speaking in an emotional voice.

"Yes, when he's recovered, he can leave."

"And go to Paris?"

"Yes, to Paris. But he's not badly hurt, is he? It's not serious, at least?"

"Didn't I tell you it wasn't!"

A pause.

"He fought on my behalf . . . After that fight we had the day before!"

There seems to be a tremor in his voice.

"Yes, it'll be better for us to go our separate ways, it really will be! When we're apart we won't fight anymore. If we're together, he'll learn to hate me! Maybe he hates me already! But I can't help it. Teaching has turned me into a savage old beast who needs to *appear* nasty and who's *turned* nasty from having to behave like a bogeyman, a sunken-eyed monster . . . It turns your heart to stone. You become cruel . . . I have been cruel . . ."

"Me too," my mother replied, "but I told him so one day in Paris. I almost asked him to forgive me, you should have seen how he cried!"

"*You* were able to tell him," my father said, "but I won't be able to, I'd be afraid of *undermining good order and discipline*. I'd be afraid that my pupils—I mean my son—would laugh at me. I was once a prep-class supervisor and the memory still gives me nightmares. I'll always address him as if he's a schoolboy and think of him as one of those little pests I have to punish to put the fear of God in them, to make sure that they'll not tie any rats to my coat collar. It's better for him to leave . . ."

"But you'll kiss him good-bye before he goes?"

"No, you kiss him good-bye for me. I'm sure I'd still look like a *bastard* without meaning to. I tell you, it's because I'm a teacher. No, you hug him for me and tell him, you can whisper to him, that I'm really fond of him. I'm afraid to do it myself."

"Madame Vingtras, Madame Vingtras!"

"What is it?"

"There's some policemen downstairs!"

"Police!"

And there are in fact some strangers on the staircase. I can hear people talking.

"We've come for your son."

"Because of that fight?"

She comes back upstairs to my father.

"Not so loud, not so loud, my dear! I wrote to them last week to be ready to arrest him! I'm so ashamed . . . At least he can't hear through the wall, can he?"

. . . .

I can hear.

What a good thing it is that I've been hurt and I'm lying in this bed! I'd never have suspected that he loves me!

All the same, wouldn't it have been better to have loved me openly? It seems to me that my heart will always remain scarred by my childhood—fits of melancholy, depression, oversensitiveness . . .

But I'm also about to become a man. I'm ready for the struggle, vigorous, honest. My blood's pure, my eyes are bright and capable of seeing deep into people's souls. And I've read somewhere that having to shed a few tears produces people like that!

And now it's not a question of weeping but of *living*!

With no money and no profession, it won't be easy, but we'll see about that . . . From now on, I'm my own master. My father had the right to hit me; but if anyone lays a hand on me now, he'd better look out! Yes, really look out!

This is what I'm saying to myself as I'm lying stretched out in bed, with a wound in my thigh.

A week later, the surgeon calls, removes the bandages, and says, "Thanks to my dressing—it's a new method—you're cured; you can get up today and tomorrow you'll be able to go out."

My mother offers her thanks to God.

"Oh, I've been so scared! Supposing you'd had to have your leg off! And now I've got some good news for you . . ."

She tells me all the things I already know, that I'd heard through the wall.

"You're going to leave us!" she sobbed.

I'm eager to get up at once to collect my books and get my little trunk ready. I ask her for my clothes.

They're the ones I wore for the duel.

My mother goes and fetches them. She notices that my trousers have a hole and bloodstains.

"I don't know if we can get rid of the stain," she said. "The color's sure to bleach out."

She brushes them again and wipes them down with a damp cloth—she's always taken such great care of my clothes. Finally, shaking her head, she says, "Well, it's still there, as you can see . . . Next time, Jacques, can you at least put on an older pair!"

NOTES

I. MY MOTHER

1 *two sous*: a sou is five centimes, the twentieth part of a franc.

2 *Breuil*: the main square in Le Puy.

3 *southern accent*: often considered comic by those from other parts of France.

II. MY FAMILY

1 *blessed*: a woman wearing nunlike clothes but who has not taken vows.

2 *masterworks*: a work required to become a full guild member.

3 *prefect*: the administrative head of a department, who wields considerable power.

III. SCHOOL

1 *school*: this school was a *collège*. *Collèges* were usually locally funded provincial secondary schools (junior high schools in the United States), generally considered as offering a lower standard of education than the state-funded *lycées* (grammar schools/senior high schools), which took their pupils up to the level of the graduation certificate (baccalaureate) essential for entry into a university.

2 *my father*: not yet a fully trained teacher, he was a supervisor of prep classes; often referred to as *pions* (pawns in the game of chess), these teachers were an underclass. However, Jacques's father clearly enjoys some consideration since he is *pion* to pupils of math, rhetoric, and philosophy, the top classes of the school.

335

3   *agrégation*: an extremely stiff competitive examination; successful candidates would have access to appointments not only in *lycées* but also in universities.

IV. THE SMALL TOWN

1   *Teachers Training College*: such colleges (*écoles normales*) had been established in 1833—for men only; women had to wait until 1879.

V. MY CLOTHES

1   *pickles*: *cornichon*, which means "pickle" in English, in French also means "greenhorn schoolboy."

VI. HOLIDAYS

1   *Christmas clogs*: used to put presents in.

VII. THE JOYS OF FAMILY LIFE

1   *Gracchi*: famous for their attempts, encouraged by their mother, Cornelia, to reform Roman society in the second century B.C.

IX. SAINT-ÉTIENNE

1   *Saint-Étienne*: an important industrial and mining town.

X. GOOD PEOPLE

1   *Arbela*: site of a battle between Alexander the Great and King Darius of Persia. *Mazagram*: an Algerian town in which Captain Lelièvre fought off an attack by greatly superior native forces.

2   *diachylum*: a sort of plaster or salve.

XI. THE SCHOOL

1   *Chalice . . . kiss!*: a parody of the Litany.

2   Tales *by Canon Schmidt*: adventure tales first published in 1826.

3   *Cartouche*: a famous bandit and convict, the subject of many tales.

XII. POLISHING—GUZZLING—CLEANLINESS

1   *pelican*: in a poem by the Romantic poet Alfred de Musset, a mother pelican allows her young to feed by pecking her breast, then she bleeds to death.

2   *Galatea*: in classical myth, a Sicilian nymph pursued by the lustful one-eyed giant Polyphemus.

XIII. MONEY

1   *buy you a man*: to avoid military service it was possible to pay for a substitute.

2   *André Chénier*: a French poet killed during the Terror.

XIV. BACK HOME

1   *going up hills*: passengers had to leave the coach while it went up hills.

2   *François-Xavier de Feller*: (1735–1802) author of a twenty-volume historical dictionary published in the 1830s.

3   *Hudson Lowe*: (1769–1844) the British officer in charge of Napoleon during his exile on Sainte-Hélène.

4   *red crosses*: during the massacre of Huguenots in 1572, the Roman Catholics wore red crosses to identify each other.

XV. PLANS TO ESCAPE

1   *third form*: Jacques is now in the *lycée* section (third year in junior high school in the United States).

2   *Saint-Cyr*: a prestigious military school for future officers.

3   *Quicherat*: a well-known bilingual French-Latin dictionary.

4   *Canada*: the name of a famous circus dog.

5   *rabbit*: hunters squeeze the rabbit's bladder to extract the urine.

6   *The Secrets of Young Albert*: a popular work on magic.

XVI. DRAMA

1   *Digue d'Janette ... Laya!*: Auvergne dialect, roughly translated: "I say, Janette, they want you to marry! You must take a man who knows how to work!"

2   *fouchtra*: an interjection expressing surprise, admiration, or annoyance; the French equivalent is *fichtre*, a polite form of *foutre*, meaning "to fuck."

3   *Capuan luxury*: in classical times, the southern Italian town of Capua was notorious for decadence and luxury.

4   *Gradus ad Parnassum*: a dictionary used particularly by pupils learning to write Latin verse.

5   *Alexander*: a standard bilingual French-Greek dictionary.

XVII. MEMORIES

1   *grammar teacher*: Vingtras senior will henceforth be able to use the grander title of *professeur*; the grammar classes were the three lower classes of a *lycée*.

XVIII. THE DEPARTURE

1   *France Maritime*: four volumes of tales of maritime adventures.

2   *Fulgence Girard*: (1810–1873) author of ancient maritime tales.

3   *boat*: the Vingtras family will now complete their journey to Nantes by passenger steamer down the Loire.

4   *drinking bishops*: spiced mulled port wine.

5   *Béranger*: (1788–1857) a writer who was something of an icon at the time, of patriotic, frequently sentimental songs with a largely Republican tinge. *Gueux* has an archaic flavor and means beggar or underdog.

6   *Les Mauves*: a village near Nantes; it will figure more dramatically in Chapter XXV.

7   *death's heads*: a sort of round incendiary shell, pierced with holes.

8   *Circe*: a sorceress in the *Odyssey* who turned Ulysses's companions into swine.

9   *Legitimist*: a die-hard royalist supporter of the Bourbon dynasty ended by the French Revolution but revived during the period known as the Restoration (from 1815 until finally removed by the Revolution of 1830).

10   *Incroyables*: dandies under the *Directoire* (1795–1799) that had succeeded the *Convention* (1792–1795), the most bloodthirsty of the French revolutionary governments, which created the Reign of Terror under Robespierre and Saint Just. The *Incroyables* were so called because their favorite catchphrase was *"C'est incroyable"* ("I can't believe it!"). They also spoke in an affected drawl in which they seemed to find difficulty in pronouncing their R's.

11   *Loire brigands*: remnants of Napoleon's army which withdrew beyond the Loire after their defeat at the battle of Waterloo.

12   *white club*: the royalist flag was white.

13   *Constitutionalist*: a supporter of the "citizen" king Louis-Philippe, installed after the Revolution of 1830.

14   *fashionable*: in 1846 there were two assassination attempts against Louis-Philippe.

15   *participles*: the grammatical rules governing present and past participles in French are notoriously tricky.

16   *you-know-what*: the French call the bottom of a bottle *le cul*, whose normal meaning "butt" offends Madame Vingtras's sensibilities.

17   *savate*: a form of boxing in which either the hands or the feet are used to deliver blows.

18   *Nanette*: traditional name, especially for a maid, in country plays.

19   *Jean-François Marmontel*: (1723–1799) a main contributor to the *Encyclopédie*, the central vehicle of the eighteenth-century French Enlightenment. *Antoine-Léonard Thomas*: (1732–1785) a long-forgotten academic poet, a specialist in eulogies.

20   *Bossuet*: (1622–1704) a bishop celebrated for grand and pompous sermons and funeral orations.

21 *Savoyard*: people from Savoy (not yet French territory) were traditionally miscellaneous workers, messenger boys, street performers, and the like.

22 *bourra*: bourrée.

XIX. LOUISETTE

1 *rostrum*: in ancient Rome, a public platform in the Forum used by orators.

XX. MY CLASSICAL STUDIES

1 *cothurn*: the thick-soled boot worn by tragic actors.

2 *Auntagnes, auntagnetos, auntagnetiton*: the teacher is pretending to decline Aunt Agnes as a Greek noun. The final syllables of the last form sounds like *teton*, which means "tit"; hence Madame Vingtras's blush.

3 *Zopyrus*: to gain entrance into the enemy city of Babylon, this Persian cut off his nose, claiming that it had been cut off by the Persian king Darius. *Scaevola*: tried to assassinate the Etruscan king Porsena and as self-punishment for failure and to show contempt for any possible torture, thrust his own hand into the flames.

4 *Torquatus*: a Roman who resisted invasion by the Gauls by defeating a giant Gaul in single combat.

5 *Agrippina*: the mother of Nero, who had her assassinated.

6 *Aspasia*: the concubine and inspirer of the great Athenian statesman Pericles.

7 *Julia*: granddaughter of the Emperor Augustus; she was the cause of Ovid's exile from Rome.

8 *quantity*: Greek and Latin verse was divided into the quantity of "feet," either short or long; for example, a spondee was two long syllables (— —), a dactyl one long and two short (— - -).

9 *Janiculum*: on this hill on the bank of the Tiber, a flag was flown in times of peace and removed if danger threatened.

10 *Vitelline latrines*: the deposed emperor Vitellius tried to escape by hiding in the Roman underground latrines.

11 *Miltiades*: an Athenian general who fought in the battle of Marathon.

12 *anus*: this does mean an old woman, but the excretory associations of the word will not have escaped Vallès's notice.

13 *Eurotas*: a river near Sparta.

14 *vexillum*: a flag.

15 *civis*: citizen. *commilito*: comrade-in-arms.

XXI. MADAME DEVINOL

1 *Psittacus...eheu!*: The parrot has died! It has already passed away, alas!

2 *Caro, cara, canens*: flesh, dear, singing.

XXII. BOARDING AT LEGNAGNA'S

1 *Boarding at Legnagna's*: these private schools were coaching schools with associations with various Paris *lycées*.

2 *Bonaparte*: a famous *lycée*, now Lycée Condorcet.

3 *Sanglier*: French for "boar."

4 *Meudon*: a suburb of Paris.

5 *counterjumper*: store clerk

6 *Crécy*: in northern France, was the scene of the defeat in 1346 of the French forces under Philippe IV by the English forces led by Edward III; Crécy soup is carrot soup. *Soubise*: (family name Rohan) a member of the family was one of Louis XV's chief advisers, an earlier one was leader of the Huguenots under Louis XIII; Soubise involves the use of onions. *Montmorency*: one of the most ancient and illustrious noble families of France; their culinary connections seem more obscure, but montmorency is the name of a variety of cherry.

7 *Abbé de l'Épée*: (1713–1789) founder of a school that taught sign language to the deaf and mute.

8 *Grand Competition*: a competition at baccalaureate level between all French schools, which gave immense prestige to the successful schools and candidates.

9 *laughs in the braken*: Boileau's line refers to a kind of glass that was manufactured using ash from braken.

10 *Jules-Amable Pierrot*: (1792–1846) called Pierrot de Selligny, author of school manuals on French and Latin.

11 *Argus de Dijon* and *Petit homme gris*: These made-up names of newspapers echo ones that were typical in the provincial liberal press of the period.

12 *alexandrine*: the standard twelve-syllable line of French classical verse.

13 *Stanislas and Rollin*: somewhat looked down on as *collèges* rather than full-fledged *lycées*.

14 *Fractis...armis*: "May I fall ingloriously with my weapons broken."

XXIII. MADAME VINGTRAS IN PARIS

1 *calf's head*: also used colloquially to mean "bald head."

2 *Madame Veto*: Queen Marie-Antoinette, suspected of vetoing reforms.

3 *Sambre-et-Meuse*: The French revolutionary force on this front defeated the invading Austrian troops in 1794 in a critical battle.

4 *Bara*: (sometimes Barra) a boy hero of the revolutionary army killed in action at the age of thirteen.

5 *sans-culotte*: revolutionaries, so called because, unlike the middle classes and aristocrats, they wore trousers and not knee breeches.

6 *Saint-Merry*: a district in the east of Paris, site of a failed Republican insurrection in 1832.

7 *Histoire de Dix Ans*: memoirs of the Republican Louis Blanc (1811–1882).

8 *Lyons*: site of another failed insurrection in 1831.

9 *Elysée*: a royal palace, now the French president's residence.

XXIV. BACK HOME

1 *lictor*: the agent of a Roman magistrate.

2 *peripatetic*: Aristotle's philosophical school was called peripatetic because its discussions took place while the students walked in a garden.

3 *Eleusian mysteries*: the most sacred and secret of the ancient Greek religious festivals.

4 *Sequana*: Latin name for the Seine.

XXV. DELIVERANCE

1 *Victor Cousin*: (1792–1862) French philosopher and Minister of Education under Louis-Philippe.

TITLES IN SERIES